ROSELAND'S SECRET

ROSELAND'S SECRET

a novel

JOHN SHEFFIELD

I hope you enjoy this mystery,
John Sheffield. Roswell, GA. 2015.

Published by Deeds Publishing in Athens, GA
www.deedspublishing.com

Printed in The United States of America

Library of Congress Cataloging-in-Publications Data is available upon request.

ISBN 978-1-941165-76-8

Books are available in quantity for promotional or premium use. For information, email info@deedspublishing.com.

Cover by Mark Babcock and Matt King
Book design by Mark Babcock

First Edition, 2015

10 9 8 7 6 5 4 3 2 1

ACKNOWLEDGEMENTS

I dedicate *Roseland's Secrets* to my late wife, Dace, without whose encouragement, support and advice it would not have been either started or completed.

I am grateful to Valerie Connors, Vicki Kestranek, Carolyn Robbins, Rosemary Perry, Sid Versaci, and George Weinstein who have read this novel and patiently helped me to refine it. I am fortunate to be a member of the Atlanta Writers Club and appreciate the advice of Lynn Wesch and her literary critique group. I have benefited enormously from the advice of Buzz Bernard and the North Point Barnes & Noble critique group. Finally, I am deeply indebted to my literary editor, Anne Kempner Fisher, for her thoughtful advice, which led to massive and positive improvements.

Thanks to Mark Babcock and Matt King for devising the imaginative cover.

1.

THE SEA AT THE BASE OF THE CLIFFS TOOK ON A SULLEN look, and dark clouds approaching from the west presaged rain. I went from feeling good to feeling insecure on that summer evening, December in Roseland. Following an initial euphoria, I now had mixed emotions about my decision to come to this remote island in the South Atlantic, with nearly 2000 miles of hostile seas, east to Cape Town, west to Buenos Aires, and south to the Antarctic icepack. Even Tristan da Cunha, synonymous with isolation, was hundreds of miles away.

Having the rare opportunity to study the Roseland auk for my PhD in ornithology didn't compensate for my loneliness. I scanned the clumps of gorse on the cliff top for my assistant, Frankie. *Typical.* He'd disappeared.

After two months on the island, I knew now that Roseland was not the calm, slow moving place it had seemed at first sight. For one thing, as far as I could tell there were more men than women, and I suspected that the islanders had strange sexual habits mimicking those of the auks in the rookery, where males also outnumbered females. My mentor in the

States, Professor Gareth Llewellyn Jones, had explained that he wanted me to pursue the reason for this strange arrangement for my dissertation. I soon found out that each of the female auks—"my good time girls"—had a main man and up to three gentlemen friends who assisted in feeding the chicks. My favorite female was Nellie. She and her entourage had been among the early arrivals in October. I studied Nellie closely and, when there was time, I watched the others who occupied neighboring burrows: Beatrice, a prim name, fitting for a prim auk; Dottie; Lola; Virginia; and Prudence—who interrupted attempts at copulation by the gentlemen friends earlier than the others.

I took a last look at the rookery and started up the path through the gorse. The auks who had been out fishing were returning. The gulls and skuas hovered above them, ready to dive bomb and steal the catch. I had a name for the most vicious of the great skuas, Dracula. He went for the throat first.

Skirting low clumps of weather-beaten bushes, I started my descent to the village of Veryan.

"Auk! Auk! Auk!" Frankie shouted, jumping over a low part of the gorse behind me; a game Frankie had played repeatedly since he began "helping" in my research.

"For God's sake, why do you do that?" I muttered.

Frankie turned his ageless face toward me—it was tanned but not weather beaten like the other men—gave a sly grin, and ran away flapping his arms before slowing to his normal ambling gait. After a while, he did a little jig, which was a part of his style of walking, and came back close to me, chanting, "*Rum tum ti tumpti*," a common catch phrase for the islanders.

Somewhere in my research on the island, I had read about pagan rituals. If I increased my pace, I could catch up and ask him if the phrase referred to some ancient ceremony on Midsummer's Day. He'd mentioned the day a number of times. But Frankie loped away like a hunting dog—typical dimwitted behavior. Was it an act?

My mind backtracked to the first dinner with the Prof. He had uttered the same doggerel when he warned me to watch my step on the island, "They led Pavlov, an appropriate name, on a merry dance, *rum tum ti tumpti*." I hadn't paid much attention at the time to learning that the islanders had played games with this Pavlov. Yet I had the uneasy feeling that Frankie wasn't the only one putting on an act for my benefit. Then I came back to the matter of the apparent preponderance of men. Were the islanders hiding their women or.... I had formulated some unpleasant ideas about the excess of male auks—still to be proved. Were the islanders copying the birds? I didn't like to think about the possibilities. I also worried about whether I would get to finish my PhD.

How did I, Andrew Ferguson, get this assignment, studying a pompous little bird with an unusual family life?

* * *

I grew up on a farm near Burnsville in the mountains of North Carolina. Our family's livelihood came from selling chickens, corn, and soybeans, and from the salary my mother earned as the local librarian.

My father's parents had emigrated from Scotland to Appalachia in the 1920s, and my father viewed himself as Scottish-American. Every year, when we went to the Grandfather Mountain Highland Games, he faithfully wore a kilt to prove it. Dad rarely cracked a smile and with few exceptions his life revolved around the farm, his passion for the environment, and being an elder at the Presbyterian Church. If I were to describe our relationship, I guess I would call it distant.

Mom was about ten years younger and liked socializing. She belonged to women's clubs, baking, sewing, bridge, and so on. I got along better with her and even took her advice— sometimes.

Nevertheless, my father was the reason I ended up on Roseland. He had taken me on long walks when I was a kid. They were some of the few occasions, other than my helping out on the farm, during which we communicated. I still remembered what he said one time as we walked into the hills behind our farm.

"Andy, look over there in the bushes. See the American goldfinch? People call them wild canaries."

I was hooked by the brilliantly colored little yellow birds. Later, when I was ten, I wrote a short description of all the birds that visited our farm during the year. It won a prize at school, and for a couple of years I was labeled "Birdman." The year before I left home and went to Epsom College, I took a trip to the Audubon sanctuary on the southern tip of New Jersey and watched the herons and hawks migrating, a stunning sight.

I had no interest in farming, but like all farmers' kids, I had no choice in doing my fair share of the chores. Our mutual interest in ornithology was the only way in which I felt close to Dad. I first understood the reason for this disconnect when I brought my girlfriend at Epsom home for a visit.

"Terrific view," Annie said, looking at the mountain backdrop to our modest farm.

My father came out of the house as we drove in, took An-

4

nie's suitcase, and ushered us into the living room. "I'll put this in the guestroom," he said firmly. "Andrew, you know where you'll be."

As he disappeared, Annie pinched my butt. "Sleeping arrangements clear enough, Andrew?" she said grinning.

My mother appeared moments later with coffee and the chocolate cake she always made for company that she wanted to impress. My father returned and listened with polite disinterest while I told him about progress and problems in my course work. Unlike my mother, he asked few questions until I mentioned that I was thinking about graduate work in ornithology. To my chagrin, he showed greater interest when Annie talked about her plans for pursuing a PhD in materials science at the University of California-Santa Barbara, quizzing her about all the details. For the first time, I could picture my father as the charming young man who had courted my mother.

They would not let us clean up. I waited until they went into the kitchen to ask my question. "What do you think of them?"

"Your father's jealous of you," Annie said raising her eyebrows.

"What? Why?"

"He has to share your mother with you."

"No way!"

"Your mother's a smart and attractive lady…and sexy."

"What?"

"You heard me."

Sexy? My mother? It made me look at her differently. She *was* smart and—I admitted reluctantly—she was sexy. For the first time, I understood why my parents touched a lot, any

5

time they passed each other, a hand on the shoulder, a pat on the bottom.

Annie was right about my father, although I found it hard to accept that he was jealous of the time my mother gave to me, the time that could have been his. Clearly, my presence irritated him, which was why he had always been more affable when I left home than when I returned, had always extolled the virtues of summer camps, and had been supportive of my attending a university that was a good distance from home, rather than Appalachian State, only forty miles away.

As for me, I had gone to college with all the self-assurance of a teen, not accustomed to failure. My time at Epsom followed a similar pattern to that in high school: studies, band, sports, and social activities, though I dabbled less in sports. I ran a little track as a member of the four-by-four-hundred-yard relay team. My social life compensated for any academic struggles. Women still fell for the dark looks I had inherited from my mother that contrasted with the pale blue eyes coming from my father—women now, not like the girls who'd relieved me in the back seat of my father's car at the drive-in movie. That is, until Annie brought stability.

* * *

The image of the apartments near the college that led to the Roseland phase of my life is etched in my brain—called Friar Tuck, and appropriately known to the student body as Triar Fuck.

August through October of 1974 had dragged on remorselessly after Annie left to start her PhD at Santa Barbara. We talked on the phone weekly and commiserated on our frustrations, finding some relief in "disembodied, orgasmic conversation"—her description. The temporary relief only brought home my need for sex that was not disembodied. With Annie out of the way, I was fair game.

On a misty Saturday night in November I was partying. The two bedrooms in a friend's apartment were full. Mindy had me pinned against a wall of the small living room with other partially clothed people. Later I couldn't recall her face. The uncoupled students were still drinking, talking, and singing in the kitchen/dining area. I was in a boozed, giggly state, euphoric but not yet incapacitated, in which any small inhibitions about betraying Annie were way back in my consciousness. Mindy was working hard to remove my pants, while I was working feverishly to arouse her. My pants hit my ankles to the sound of the Beach Boys' "Good Vibrations."

"Let's get back to my place," I said, trying to move away from the wall. I lost my balance and a loafer and came out of one pant leg.

"Later," she snapped.

I pushed feebly at Mindy, but she succeeded in pulling my shorts down, trapping me in place. She buried her head into my neck and bit hard.

"Ouch!" I opened my eyes.

Over her shoulder a hazy figure appeared, silhouetted in the light from the hall—a woman. She worked her way around the other couples until she was standing behind Mindy. The combination of the alcohol and the hall light made it difficult to focus on her.

"How're you doing?" I said. No answer.

"Who the fuck are you talking to?" Mindy shouted.

"Why've you stopped?" She pushed harder against me. The tape moved on to "Fun, Fun, Fun."

"You bastard! I waited for you."

It had to be Annie, but in my drunken state that made no sense. "You shouldn't be here." I giggled.

"Tell the bitch to bug off," Mindy muttered in my ear.

Annie grabbed Mindy's hair and pulled. "You get off, bitch!"

Someone turned the lights on. Annie continued to pull on Mindy, who clung to me. Annie won, jerking Mindy backwards. A curious audience watched my manhood deflate.

"Annie? What are you doing here?" I tried to cover myself.

"I saved all my money so I could fly in and surprise you."

"In the middle of the night?"

"The planes were delayed by bad weather. I didn't think you'd care when I got here."

"How did you find me?"

"Easy. When you weren't at home, I looked for a party. I should have known you'd…oh, fuck it!" Her fists were clenched and I could see that she was fighting back tears.

"It's the first time," I said feebly, trying to pull up my shorts.

"Why couldn't you wait? I did."

"Just keeping the old pecker in shape."

Annie hung her head. "That's it then—the only reason you wanted me was sex?"

"Annie, I'm sorry." I was sobering rapidly. "I screwed up."

"You said it, you shit!" She went toward the door, turning at the last moment to say, "I hoped you'd grow up, Andy. But you still act like a spoiled teenager."

I raised my shorts beyond half-mast. The Beach Boys continued with another hit song. Holding the pants with one hand, I managed to reach the street without falling. Annie had disappeared. I hobbled down the road. Headlights caught me, highlighting my rear end.

"Hold it, sonny!" the police officer said. "You can explain this at the station."

I stopped. "Please, sir. I'm looking for my girlfriend. I've got speak to her."

The cop finished cuffing me and then looked around pointedly. "It don't look like she wants to speak to you, buddy," he said, emphasizing the absence of a woman. "Get your sorry butt in the back of the car."

* * *

The morning of November 16, 1975 came, and after sleeping off the booze and paying my fine I was released from jail. My first phone calls to Santa Barbara went unanswered. When Annie did respond, all she said was, "I've had enough. You need to grow up."

I brooded about Annie's parting words for a long time, realizing that I should have paid more attention to some of the comments in my high school yearbook: some hinted I was self-centered and in a way uncaring.

2.

WITHOUT A STABLE RELATIONSHIP, I STRUGGLED WITH THE course work through my final year at Epsom. Nevertheless, I did well enough to obtain a decent GPA and a degree. I hadn't exactly won my argument with my father about what career to pursue but, for me, the key question then was where to pursue graduate work in ornithology. I wrestled with asking my favorite professor, James MacDonald, for help. He taught biology, helped me with physics, and had mentored me from my freshman year to graduation at Epsom. Like me, he was a birder—amateur ornithologist.

Annie, clearly a favorite student of his, had introduced us. Since the break-up, I had been avoiding him. After brooding for a few hours, I chickened out on going to see him and phoned his office. "Professor MacDonald, I've found two graduate schools." I explained which ones. "Would you write letters of recommendation?"

"Yes. I'm pleased you're ready to move on now, Andy."

"I really want to do a PhD in ornithology." I replied, glad he couldn't see me fidgeting. I could hear his fingers drumming on a desk. Silence. "Now, where were we? Yes, I'll write the letters. Let me know how it goes." He hung up.

Thank God. But it was clear from his tone of voice that he hadn't forgotten about how I'd lost Annie. *Things get around.*

After I returned home, I received letters accepting my applications, but the school in Saskatchewan was expensive, and the other couldn't guarantee me a teaching assistantship for the first year. In truth, I realized that I couldn't afford either.

I explained my situation to my parents.

Son, I love ornithology," my father said. "But a career in agriculture would be a more useful avenue for you. As I see it, the future's in organic farming, making far better use of the manure for both energy and fertilizer."

"I don't know, Dad. I love birds…and I want to move on."

"I'm not saying this because I'm looking for cheap labor." Dad sounded testy. "You know I can easily find casual help."

We didn't seem to be communicating. "I wasn't suggest—"

"North Carolina State's agricultural college has some good programs."

"I'll think about it." But his suggestion didn't appeal to me. I phoned MacDonald again and left a message explaining my problem.

A few days later, I was lying in the backyard hammock, half-asleep, pretending to read.

"Andy! You've got a phone call." My mother shook me so hard that I nearly fell on my butt. "It's Professor McDonald."

I raced into the house and fumbled the telephone to my ear.

"Andy, I was at a meeting in Raleigh last week and talked to an old friend from Harrison University in Virginia about your situation," MacDonald said. "He's looking for a student for a project. Have you come across the work of Professor Gareth Llewellyn Jones?"

"I guess so. I think I saw a paper of his once. What does he have for me?"

"I don't know much about the project or how long it will take, but he will pay your expenses and a small stipend. Llewellyn Jones has a reputation for being a little secretive. I suppose he thinks he's on to something. Strange behavior in birds is all he would say."

"Is he good?" *A dumb question.* "I mean, what do you think?"

"He's an odd bird, too, but he's got a stellar record in ornithology. Because much of his work was done in the British Isles and protectorates, I can understand that you haven't heard how well regarded he is. You should go for it." MacDonald paused. "One thing he told me makes me think you shouldn't go unless you're prepared to start immediately. I understand that the student he was expecting didn't work out."

Not a difficult decision in my situation. "I'd be happy to start tomorrow, sir. I need to get away."

"I thought that might be the case. One other thing: be prepared to travel. I think I know what he's thinking about, but best for him to tell you. He mentioned something about a boat."

I was too excited to consider then what travel might mean. He gave me the professor's address and wished me luck. He seemed to mean it. I wrote a letter to Professor Jones about my interest in bird watching, starting with the goldfinches. In a strange way—like a sudden vision—I knew then that my fate was to study odd behavior in birds.

A week later, the professor's letter arrived.

The Manse
6 Grosvenor Drive
Elkton, Virginia 22827

September 8, 1976

Dear Mr. Ferguson,

It appears from your letter that you share my abiding interest in ornithology and have the background to proceed further in this area. I am therefore prepared to offer you a position as a technical assistant while you pursue a further degree at Harrison. As my assistant, you will be required to travel for extended periods to undertake research. You will need a passport. Please bring one. I should caution you that while your research will be invaluable to your obtaining a doctorate, the travel and the complexity of the project might extend the time to your graduation.

If this is acceptable, I would like to see you as soon as possible at my house to discuss the arrangements. Because time is pressing, you may stay with me. There are a number of ways to reach Elkton by bus and train. I enclose some pertinent information on schedules.

Bring raingear and sturdy shoes.

Yours truly,
Gareth Llewellyn Jones
Professor

I went into the kitchen. "I've got an offer," I said, holding out Llewellyn Jones's reply.

My mother looked up from emptying the dishwasher. "Wonderful. What does it say?"

"It looks like I'll have to travel abroad."

A flicker of concern crossed her face. She put the clean plates down and hugged me. "Does he say where you'll be going?"

"No, but he asked me to bring raingear and sturdy shoes."

"Could be up north." She started on the cutlery. "You sure this is the right thing for you?"

No question. I needed to get away from home. A PhD was my passport. "Yes, Mom, this is important to me."

She opened a drawer and sorted the knives and forks into their plastic trays.

I reread the letter. As MacDonald had said, the professor was an odd bird, too. Bus and train! Hadn't he heard of cars? My old Toyota was no masterpiece, but at least it was capable of making the trip from Burnsville to Elkton. I took all my savings out of the bank, crammed my belongings into a backpack and a small bag, and put my hiking boots in the trunk. On a whim, I tied my trumpet to the backpack.

3.

A HAND-PAINTED WOODEN SIGN ANNOUNCED THE MANSE. A rutted gravel drive bordered by unkempt shrubs, weeds, and grass led to the professor's house. The drive ended next to a veranda that continued around one side of the house. I parked by an old Ford and got out. The stillness of the place was broken by faint clicking sounds. I followed the sounds. A vegetable garden occupied the place where, otherwise, there might have been a garage. A small man wearing a large Panama hat was hoeing vigorously between the neat rows of vegetables, an oasis in an otherwise derelict yard.

The man looked up. "Welcome, my boy," he said. "I see you have alternative transport of your own. Good. Good. It will be of great help in our local endeavors."

"Yes, sir, I drove up. I'm Andrew Ferguson."

"James MacDonald has told me all about you. I, of course, am Llewellyn Jones. As you have surmised, no doubt, I am not originally from this country." The professor had a sing-song voice that betrayed his Welsh ancestry. "You catch me working on my leeks, *boyo*, a fine plant, the national treasure of my homeland. You, I suppose from your name, must derive from Scotland?"

"Yes, sir. My father's parents emigrated here when he was young."

"It's a common bond, my boy, same background and a different manner of speech. I detect something of northwestern Carolina and a mistrust of the English."

"Sir?"

"England—perfidious Albion—the cause of all our troubles!" His bushy white eyebrows wiggled to emphasize the point. "I warrant that's why your ancestors ventured to the New World. Do you like leek soup?"

"I'm not sure I've had it."

"We will have such a soup for dinner. We will eat at seven. Come on in."

The furniture in the house was from the turn of the century. Paintings and lithographs of birds covered the walls that led upstairs. He took me to a spacious bedroom with windows overlooking the backyard, a jungle of trees and ivy.

I came down to the dining room promptly at seven. The Victorian sideboard and gleaming wooden table and chairs reminded me of my Scottish grandparents' home. The professor ushered me to the seat opposite him and rang a silver bell. A moment later, a stern-faced woman wearing a high-necked blue dress strode in carrying a soup tureen. Her brown hair projected in random directions from her head, apparently having a will of its own.

The professor's voice jolted me out of my idle thought that she was a daughter of the Medusa. "Andrew, may I introduce Mabel." His eyebrows lifted. "The arbiter of all things related to the running of my household."

Mabel put down the tureen and nodded in my direction.

"Pleased to meet you, Mr. Andrew." Her voice was surprisingly soft for someone with such a commanding presence.

I stood and held out my hand, which she shook with a firm grip.

As soon as Mabel left, the professor said, "When I was up at Oxford, it was bad form to talk about work or the opposite sex at dinner." His eyebrows indicated support for this system. "So we will delay a discussion of what I have in mind for you until we have finished."

"I hear that Oxford is a beautiful city, sir," I replied, hiding my disappointment that I would have to wait to learn about my fate. I tried the soup. Delicious.

My comment triggered a wealth of entertaining stories about the British Isles, bird watching, the weather, and anything that seemed to come into the professor's head as he rambled on describing his past. In between the stories, as we ate steak and kidney pie, peas and boiled potatoes, he threw in an occasional question. At first, I was mesmerized by the flow of words and the bright black eyes peeping out from below his mobile eyebrows. Later, I realized that he had me talking about quite personal things: my relationship with my parents, views on high school, the university, and life in general. After we had demolished Mabel's incredible sherry trifle and she brought in the coffee, he was ready to talk about my future.

"You're wondering what I have for you to do? Right?"

"Yes, sir."

"Let me see. First, would you fancy a little brandy?"

"Yes please, sir."

"The Roseland auk. That's what it's about." The professor fetched a decanter and two glasses from the sideboard. His eyebrows rose as he added, "An amazing bird, amazing."

"I haven't heard of it."

He poured brandy into the glasses and handed me one. "Not surprising. Few people know of its existence. As to habitat, it is found only on Roseland, an island in the South Atlantic. Then, have you heard of Roseland?"

Vague memories of pictures in an old *National Geographic* magazine flickered in my head.

"I think it's a peninsula in England, the western part that sticks out into the Atlantic … Cornwall."

The professor smiled. "Not quite. Though the people who settled this isolated island did come from that area, hence the name.

This Roseland is in the southern Atlantic and situated a few hundred miles west and slightly north of Tristan da Cunha; more or less on a line from Cape Town to Buenos Aires."

I tried to assimilate the information. *Isolated* took on a new meaning now that I understood where he wanted me to go. I felt my face tighten.

The professor continued, seemingly oblivious to my reaction. "I would like you to continue my studies on the birds of Roseland, specifically their remarkable auk. It has been an on-and-off hobby of mine for many years. No time to pursue it properly once I realized how unusual it was. Er…." He looked at the ceiling, apparently deciding what else he should say. "I'm getting too old and stiff to be clambering around the cliff tops, and…well…that's another matter."

Keep to the subject, I thought; time to discuss traveling later. "What's so remarkable?"

"Oddest thing, there seem to be far more males than females. Makes sex tricky, don't you see? Keeping all those frustrated males happy. I think I know how the females handle it, but I need more data. Obviously, there are also many questions. For example, why are there more males? I thought I was onto something, but then I had to leave before I...."

I wondered what he had been about to say, but ill-formed questions about the auks were circling in my head. Instead of asking them, I gave a typical student response. "I guess I need to take some graduate courses first."

"Oh, no, don't you worry about that. You can do your coursework in parallel with the study. Some reading, my lecture notes, a book or two, some small essays should do it."

"Sounds fine to me," I said, a spur-of-the-moment response driven by a need to get away from home and memories of my ex-girlfriend.

"Now, where was I?" The professor paused. "Yes. I would like you to fly to Cape Town in one week. You need to be in Roseland in the late spring and summer. A fishing boat from Roseland goes to Cape Town a few times a year, when some of the islanders need to travel and there are goods to be shipped or picked up. The next one will be there in about ten days."

My heart rate increased. I had prepared myself for going to Roseland, eventually. But he expected me to go to South Africa and then to this small island, lost in the southern Atlantic, so soon. Earlier imaginings about local travel had not prepared me for such a precipitous dive into graduate work—a scary prospect for a guy whose most adventurous travel had been to stay with relatives in Scotland and spend spring break in Mexico. My stomach clenched, I raised my hands under the table to steady myself, hoping that he would not notice.

"I'd like to do it." It must have been the brandy that gave me the courage to say yes.

I realized then that I was already expected in this remote island. "I'll need to call my parents," I said to buy time to decide if I should really commit to going.

"So you should. Please feel free to use the telephone in the kitchen. I expect you have a young lady friend who needs to hear from you, too, eh!"

"It....No, sir. No one." I shook my head to expel the faint image of Annie catching me with my pants down.

The professor looked closely at me. "Time to join the Foreign Legion, I suspect. Don't worry. Roseland is much more attractive than the Sahara." The professor smiled, and the mobile eyebrows showed concern. "Now, let me tell you something about the island. It's a fascinating place with fascinating people. Cornish origin, you know. They named it after the part of Cornwall that many of them had left—the Roseland Peninsula."

I had mentioned my vague recollection that Cornwall was where the west of England jutted into the Atlantic. "Why did these Cornish people settle on this island?" I asked, having realized that each of my brief questions would unleash a torrent of information, and keep away from topics I didn't want to discuss.

"A strange stroke of fate, Andrew," he replied. "In the autumn of 1864, a sailing ship, the *St. Mawes* out of Falmouth, left England for Cape Town and Buenos Aires. The ship was carrying Cornish families looking for a better life. Some of the families disembarked in Cape Town. Those remaining carried on toward Argentina. Many of the men were unemployed tin miners who had been recruited to work in the southern Argentinean coalmines. Some of the passengers were relatives, including two families who were farm workers with no prospects of owning a farm in Cornwall. They took some livestock with them in the hope of being able to farm in Patagonia. There were also a couple of fishermen and their families. The *St. Mawes* was blown off course by a violent storm and damaged. Fortunately, the skipper knew about Roseland, called Bird Island back then."

"Why wasn't it inhabited before?"

"Good question. Obviously people knew it existed because their skipper knew where to go. It puzzled me, you know. Roseland is more habitable than Tristan or Gough Island, though like Tristan and Gough, it's a long way off the beaten track. Why wasn't it well known? I have read that some trick of the winds kept sailing boats away. In fact, the island was misplaced on maps until well into the nineteenth century. On rare occasions, whalers would come across the island; however, and this may be the key, before the Cornish came, there was no good port. A rocky ledge offshore blocked most of the very narrow entrance to what is now the harbor at Portloe. The sea there is rough, even on the north side, and landing elsewhere would be very hazardous. Some years ago, I came across an older sketch of the island. On it there are comments that there is fresh water but no useable port. The vessel carrying the Cornish needed to be beached for repair. They were fortunate. The *St. Mawes* was carrying explosives for use in the mines. They didn't waste any time using their explosives to widen the harbor entrance, so they could work on the ship."

"Did they fix it?'

"Apparently, yes."

"But they stayed?"

"It took them a long time, into late summer, to repair the ship. By then they had built cabins and explored the island.

They found it to be quite fertile, with a variety of edible native plants and berries. The fishing, except near the rookery, was good enough, and they had the sheep, goats, and pigs they had brought with them. I gather from talking to their descendants that staying on their own island seemed more attractive than going to an unknown future in Argentina."

"It makes sense, but who owned the island back then?"

"I read somewhere that Portugal claimed it. After a year or two, when at last the islanders made contact with the outside world, they turned to Britain, so it became British. No country, least of all Portugal, was going to argue with that mighty sea power in the middle of the nineteenth century about some uninhabited island that wasn't on most maps of the Atlantic. British it remains, and having become British, it has benefited or suffered from all the advantages of being administratively connected to *them*." Professor Jones emphasized the word as if it were an unpleasant concept.

"Have the British done anything with the island?"

"Yes, and that is precisely why you have not heard about it. Doesn't it strike you as curious that you are among many educated people who do not know of its existence?"

"Why is that?"

"I'll be back in a minute." He darted out.

When the professor returned, he was carrying an atlas and a large, folded piece of paper. "Look here!" He pointed to the southern Atlantic. "Along with Ascension Island and the Falklands, Roseland has strategic importance for operations in the southern Atlantic. There's a weather station on the island. For many years, the station served as a major radio relay post for the British Navy, very important, up through the second world war and into the Cold War. Not so important now with satellites being used to watch and relay information."

The professor cleared the center of the table of cruets and empty glasses and unfolded the paper. "This map I drew will give you the lay of the land. The map showed key features: elevation contours, roads, paths, and what I assumed were buildings. The land rose steadily from north to south, where steep, scalloped cliffs faced the Antarctic. A scale at the top allowed me to quickly assess that the island was about ten miles from east to west and roughly six miles from south to north.

"The main part of Roseland is a caldera, created maybe a hundred thousand years ago when the original huge volcanic mount blew out its northern side. The contours show how the land drops from the southern hills."

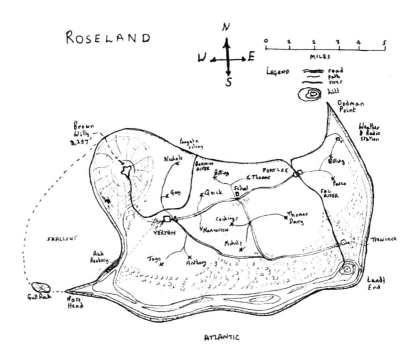

"Where are the auks?" I asked, missing the spidery annotation.

"Here." The professor pointed at the west side of the island. "Later, there was a second eruption that created this arc of cliffs and left shallow water in the bay between the extinct volcano, Brown Willy, and the Nare Head and Gull Rock. There's seaweed there and quite a lot of fish. Everywhere else around the island, the seabed drops off precipitously. The auk colony is here, on the cliffs." He pointed. Along with hordes of other seabirds…including skuas." His eyebrows implied a refined dislike of the bird. "Competition for fish is fierce."

"Do the islanders fish near the rookery?"

"Interestingly no, *boyo*. The seabed is jagged and the heavy swell coming in from the west makes it dangerous for boats."

"I guess I'll be staying near the rookery."

"Yes. In Veryan, I hope. Still working on arrangements, see. There's a path to the auks from the village." He indicated a faint dotted line on the map.

"It looks like about a couple of miles." I noticed the names printed close to path. "What's the significance of the names Thomas, Anthony, Gay, and so on?"

"Those are the families that own the farms. I'll get to them in a minute." The professor's eyebrows adopted a professorial slant. "A farm is a status symbol. Typically, each one consists of a cluster of fields surrounding the farmhouse, a barn or two, and a number of cottages for close relatives. They're more like a hamlet for each clan…over here is the Jago farm, where I stayed. Mabel is one of the Jagos, you know."

That explained Mabel's accent, not quite the same lilt as the professor's. I studied the map noting that two roads met near Veryan. The main road went east, and a little north, to

Portloe. The other road headed toward the southeastern tip of the island.

"What's here?" I asked, indicating Land's End.

"The stream…River Fal." The eyebrows waggled again. "It created a gorge that has isolated the upper end of the valley from Portloe, which is why the road toward Land's End comes from the direction of Veryan."

I had become mesmerized by his eyebrows. The sight of them reminded me of an article my mother had shown me, with its great description of her favorite English character actress, Margaret Rutherford, and the acting powers of her chin: indomitable, triumphant, formidable, regretful, furious, threatening, reluctant, and insouciant.

The professor's eyebrows played a similar role: curious, questioning, surprised, waggish, encouraging, sad, and elated. I managed to free myself from their spell long enough to ask another question. "On the map, the Land's End road finishes in an area in the middle of what appears to be dense woods. It says Trewince."

"A grand house." The eyebrows indicated awe. "Jane Trevenna lives there. She's a most interesting woman and the current Penseythan."

"The what?"

"Penseythan is a Cornish word. It means head of the Seythan—The Seven-Member Council—or governing body of the island. You will certainly meet Mrs. Trevenna."

"Why seven?"

"I understand that it is a way of ensuring that a number of the families have a say in running the island."

"So the island rules itself?"

"Basically, yes. Of course, not foreign policy, you know. The

Motherland takes care of that." As he chuckled, his eyebrows moved in harmony with the sound. "Sometime in the early 1950s, I don't remember exactly when, the Russians tried to establish a presence. They even attempted to buy some land. A Mr. Pavlov was their agent."

I drained the remaining brandy. "What happened?"

"Ostensibly, the reason for Pavlov's presence was to set up a place for rest and relaxation for Russian sailors working in the Antarctic—whaling and harvesting krill. The British government responded rapidly to that ploy and sent a stiff note to the Kremlin, reminding them that Roseland was a British dependency. I understand that the islanders had a field day with Mr. Pavlov." He turned away from me and looked up at the ceiling, smiling at some secret joke. "Before he fled."

My curious nature kicked in. "What did they do?"

"Oh, nothing much, you know. Life can get somewhat boring on Roseland. A little fun wiles the time away. Opportunity for the islanders to play a game, teach him a lesson. They led Pavlov, an appropriate name, on a merry dance, *rum tum ti tumpti*." He chuckled and his eyebrows arched as if this were a risqué subject.

After a pause to close the atlas, he looked hard at me with his brow clenched. "While we are on the subject, let me offer a word of warning. The islanders have their own way of doing things. Do not be too inquisitive, and don't abuse their hospitality. The women are off-limits. As the English would say, 'Don't mess with the birds.' Stick with the avian variety and do not get tricked into doing something foolish. It could be the end of your PhD, or worse."

That explained why he had mentioned Pavlov. "I'll be careful." I fiddled with my glass as I thought about what he had said. "What do you mean by tricked?" I put the glass down.

"Just remembering Pavlov and other events that occurred some years ago." His eyebrows relaxed. "Enough of gloomy matters. All this talk and I had not noticed your glass is again empty. Let me refill it."

"I think that's as much as I can handle, Professor, for the moment."

That night, I fell asleep wondering what Pavlov had done and what the islanders had done to him. It couldn't have been too bad, I guessed. The professor didn't seem like someone who would put me in real danger.

The few days with the professor passed rapidly, extracting equipment from the curio shop he called his laboratory.

"Now, a little reading would be in order," he said. "There are some books in the library you'll find useful. Too heavy to take to Roseland, I think. You should scan them before you leave. Take notes."

Shelves stuffed with books rose up to the library's ceiling. A rickety ladder allowed access to the upper shelves. Books were stacked in piles on the floor with a narrow aisle for the ladder and a space for a desk and chair. It seemed that the professor had a book filing system in his head, for with unerring accuracy, he selected half a dozen examples for me.

"*Auks and I*, there's a useful reference. Of course, it discusses the northern auks, but Henley does a good job describing their habits. *Did*, I suppose is a better description. He's been gone these twelve years." His eyebrows expressed sadness. "*Isles of the Southern Atlantic*, not much about Roseland, although it gives you a feel for the isolation of these places.

You might scan *Seabirds of the South Atlantic*—mainly about penguins, gulls, frigate birds, skuas, and the like."

He opened a drawer in the desk and pulled out a thin dog-eared book, holding it reverently. "This book you should take with you. Guard it carefully. It is the only copy, written in the late forties by an Englishman, Henry Throgmorton, one of those types who built the empire. He traveled the world in a small yacht, coming upon Roseland by chance when he was blown off course as he tried to get from Tristan to the Buenos Aires. I borrowed it some years ago. It should be returned to the library in Veryan." The professor hesitated before handing the book to me.

"I'll look after it."

"Good. Good. I'm sure you will." The professor's eyebrows expressed hope. "Now, you need to show me what clothes you have."

I brought in the backpack and small bag and spread my stuff on the floor. My belongings looked meager when put in the context of a year or more on an island far away in the South Atlantic.

"Good, good, rain gear, and how about boots?"

"The hiking boots are in the trunk of my car."

"Boots in the boot as we say where I come from. Good, good. A trumpet, I see. Might be useful." He eyed it thoughtfully. "Excellent for your social life. More important is warmth. I suggest another sweater and thermal underwear. We will get them tomorrow." He paused, scratching his head. "One other thing, best take some presents for Christmas and the like."

"You mean, like a scarf or ornament for the ladies and some small tools for the men?"

"Yes, a couple of each, I suggest. Very good, very good."

"Where will I put everything?"

"Indeed. I will find you a bigger bag."

"Thanks." I just realized something. "What should I do with my car?"

"It can stay in the drive." He studied me thoughtfully. "Do you mind leaving the keys? My car is acting up. Your vehicle could come in handy. "

"Sure. Remind me to give you the keys before I leave," I replied.

"I will indeed." The eyebrows indicated the intent. "Now, have you called your parents?"

"I tried. They must have been out. Thanks for reminding me."

When I called home later, my mother answered. She was happy when I told her about starting graduate work. There was silence for a moment when I said where I would be going.

"Be careful, Andy." She sounded upset. "I'll get your father."

I told him about the auks. My father had many questions and did not seem overly concerned about my destination. His parting comments were, "Take warm underwear, son. It can be bitter in the South Atlantic. Look after yourself." There was a long pause. "Remember to write. Your mother…we love you."

After making the call, I returned to the library. Among the interesting finds was a photo album. The first page contained black and white photos apparently taken on Roseland. One showed a small house with a tin roof with the caption "Jago Farm." Another was a group photo of a man, woman, boy and girl, captioned "George, Emily, Jacob and Miriam Jago." At the bottom of the page I found a photograph of a young professor and a stern looking woman standing in front of a peculiar looking round house with a cross on top. *Curious*. It was labeled "Me and the Penseythan." The second page, apparently taken in the garden of the Manse, had the professor with a woman and a young girl with erratic hair. The woman looked like Emily Jago. The young girl appeared to be Mabel. I was about to turn to the third page when Mabel came in.

"Is that you with your mother?" I pointed at the photo.

"Yes, Mr. Andrew, that's my mother," Mabel replied.

I turned back to page one. "What's this weird-looking house?"

"You'll find out," Mabel said, taking the album from me. "You're very inquisitive. On the island it could get you into trouble. Watch out."

First the professor and now Mabel had warned me of danger. What the hell, I really wanted to do my PhD and it was too late to turn back.

4.

I HARDLY REMEMBER THE FLIGHTS THAT TOOK ME TO LONdon, Johannesburg, and Cape Town, despite being awake much of the time. I was still in a daze from the speed of my transformation from would-be graduate student to world traveler. The enormity of my situation hit me only after I lay down and tried to sleep. The professor had booked me into a cheap hotel near the Cape Town docks. Its threadbare curtains allowed the light from a flickering neon sign to provide an irritating illumination. Sleep came fitfully through a night marred by brief inconclusive nightmares: I was marooned on a rock in dark seas being attacked by small birds with large teeth, and trying to avoid Mabel who was chasing me with a bowl of hot leek soup, swinging her ladle ominously.

The next day, I inquired about the boat. The most anyone knew about Roseland was that fishing boats from there stopped to pick up supplies and passengers, sometimes. A man in the harbormaster's office pointed out the quay where I would find my ride, if and when it came. While waiting, I changed some dollars into South African rand, which the prof had told me would work on Roseland.

Two days later, when I made one of my hopeful trips to the quay, the *St. Just* out of Roseland—a scruffy boat of uncertain age—had arrived. It looked uncomfortably small. Men were unloading its cargo. I decided to keep out of their way and sat on a bollard on the quay, with my head down to avoid the gusting wind. After a while, a slim woman, escorted by a tall man with a beard and moustache carrying two bags, came off the boat and started toward me. The man nodded as he passed by, unsmiling. The young woman smiled briefly. I glimpsed an enchantingly beautiful face and a fringe of black curly hair shadowed by the hood of her anorak.

I watched the crew finish unloading the cargo and went up and introduced myself.

"I'm Andy Ferguson," I said to the young man who appeared to be in charge. "I'll be going with you to Roseland."

He wiped his hand on his pants and held it out. "Pleased to meet you, Mr. Ferguson. I'm Artley Billing. Best come back tomorrow mornin', by ten. We'll be busy until then."

"Okay." As I started to leave, he joined me.

"Got to go to the Harbor Master's office," he said.

As we passed the bollard, I remembered the woman. "Just curious, but who were those two people who got off the boat?"

"Cap'n Billing and Rose Pascoe." He smiled and we parted ways.

When I returned on the twentieth, Cap'n Billing, the hard-faced, dark-haired man, whom I had seen the day before, took me to a crowded area below decks with six small bunks. These were available for three crew members and up to three passengers. The captain and the mate had separate quarters. My bunk was an upper one, and as I would soon find out, right next to the engine room. He told me to put my backpack and equipment in with the supplies. These, he informed me, were diesel fuel, petrol, kitchen appliances, and some clothes ordered by the islanders.

The boat started pitching soon after we left the harbor and continued lurching for the week we were at sea. I tried to overcome my nausea by lying on my bunk, but the smell of fish mixed with fumes from the engine room forced me topside to hang over the bulwarks where the air was fresh. The crew was kind in its rough way. Crew members had a theory that I needed to get rid of everything in my stomach and start afresh with proper seafaring food, which I supposedly would be able to hold down. Their remedy satisfied the first part of the goal but not the second. Fried fish and chips were the last thing I needed, and I survived on oatmeal, apples, and tea. They served the oatmeal and tea very hot with evaporated milk and too much sugar. This diet was comforting in the cold, biting September wind that scoured the deck.

In between throwing up and when the winds were favorable, allowing the use of the sails, I scanned Throgmorton's book. His words added to the impression the professor had given that Roseland was an odd place. In one curious comment in the book, Throgmorton stopped cataloguing facts and opened up a little. He made an offhand remark about a strange lack of women on the island, observing that families appeared to have more boys than girls. He seemed more concerned about the consequences of the situation than how it might have occurred. The professor had the same question about the Roseland auks.

The crew came mainly from two families whose names Throgmorton had mentioned. In contrast to the unapproachable Cap'n Billing was his nephew, Artley Billing, also dark haired, but with a friendly face and soft blue eyes. Later, I realized that Artley was spelled with an H, a letter dropped in the Cornish dialect. The nephew was known as Young Artley, to distinguish him from Cap'n Billing, whose first name was also Hartley. Sandy Nancarrow made up the rest of the hardworking part of the crew. A temporary measure, Artley told me, so he could shop for his family in Cape Town. Unlike Artley, they kept their distance. I sensed he didn't want me around.

Then there was the inaptly named Frankie Quick. I never worked out Frankie's role. While the weather-beaten faces of the rest of the crew were a testament to their many years at sea, Frankie's tanned face was as soft and unwrinkled as a child's. I wondered if he was aboard to do odd jobs to help the crew, for I rarely saw him do anything useful. His favorite pastime seemed to be pissing over the stern of the boat. I noticed he drank an inordinate amount of water, presumably to increase his opportunities to pee.

"Why does Frankie do it? You know, the pissing over the side."

Artley grinned. "That's Frankie! Don't you worry, it could be worse. Think about it."

I tried not to consider Frankie's other options. When he was not pissing, he hovered around me, chatting randomly with an occasional question about why I was going to Roseland. I told him about the auks, and he seemed to know about them. I asked Young Artley about him.

"Don't you mind Frankie," Artley said. "He likes boats, so we let him come along for the ride. It keeps him out of trouble. It's a favor to his mum, Clara."

The topic came up again a day before we reached Roseland,

when Young Artley approached me. He seemed hesitant. "I was wondering about how you planned to study the birds. Professor Jones used to need help carrying his equipment."

"I hadn't thought about it."

"Frankie could help. He knows his way around the island."

Apparently, we all had to help Clara Quick with Frankie. "Let me think about it."

Artley smiled and went below deck.

Shortly afterward, Frankie appeared on deck. He did not come straight up to me, but circled in gradually, looking at me sideways as he did. I waited until he was close before speaking. "Frankie, do you know where the auk colony is?"

"Up by Nare." He was looking slyly at me, his head slanted away.

For a moment, his answer puzzled me. Then I remembered the professor's map. "Oh, you mean on the Nare Headland?"

"Yes, sir. Up by Nare."

"Could you show me?"

He looked at me sideways. "Maybe could."

I waited for him to continue.

"If *me* mum says I can."

"You'll ask your mom then?"

"Mum," he answered. "I'll ask *me* mum."

"Should I speak to her, too?"

"Why?" he asked suspiciously.

"Oh, just to help."

Frankie looked sideways at me again, until he appeared satisfied with the answer. "I expects you'll want to know about the *rum tum ti rum tum tum*, too." He giggled and nudged me in the ribs. "They all want the *rum*…"

"What is this *rum tum* stuff?"

35

Frankie giggled again. If he had an answer, I didn't hear it.

"Frankie!" The wind had muffled Cap'n Billing's approach. "Sandy needs a hand below." Frankie scuttled away.

"Maybe you can tell me," I said. "What is this *rum tum ti, tum tum* business?"

"What did Frankie say?" Cap'n Billing's blue eyes glared at me.

"Just *rum ti tum tum*, as if it meant something. The professor said something similar."

"God knows what Frankie talks about. As to Professor Jones, you must have misunderstood him. *Rum ti tum tum*, what will Frankie think of next?" He turned and walked to the wheelhouse muttering, "*rum ti tum tum*." Had it not been for the boat lurching, I could have sworn he skipped in what looked like a couple of dance steps.

Frankie stayed away from me until the late morning of the next day, when he found me in my regular place on deck, leaning over the bulwark looking at the water. "*Thar tis,*" he whispered in my ear. I stood up to look to where he was pointing. He had good eyesight or maybe just knew where to look, because it took another five minutes before I could make out the patch of clouds above Brown Willy and the faint blur of distant land, and it took an eternity before the island filled the horizon.

So this is my home for at least the next year, I thought. It looked bigger and higher than the impression given by the map. The professor had not done justice to the ruggedness of the coast, and this was the gentler northern side of the island, I realized. Even at a distance, I could see the waves crashing on the rocks of the Dodman Point, which formed the northeastern end of the island.

We passed the Dodman, and Portloe came into view. The

weather and radio station—an array of aerials and low buildings—were to the left of the village, tucked into the backside of the headland. I remembered that radio messages allowed Mabel and the prof to stay in touch with the island. To the west of Portloe, the land rose gently from a low, rocky shoreline to a backdrop of hills in the south. The shore facing the boat presented an unbroken wall of foam.

Cap'n Billing turned the *St. Just* toward the southeast, and I could make out a break in the white water leading into the cove of the village of Portloe. Soon, the swell of the open ocean was behind us, and we were gliding between the flat layers of rock that surrounded the harbor. Along one side of the channel were the pens used to store the lobsters that the islanders caught around the island. The professor had told me that lobsters, wool sweaters—knitted during the winter—and scrimshaw carved in whalebone were the island's main exports. Looking ahead, I saw wooden houses with corrugated iron roofs nestled alongside a road and a stream tumbling down the valley that led up from the harbor.

When we approached the jetty, children ran across the rocks shouting excitedly, while adults crowded the small jetty and slipway. I should not have been surprised. Sandy Nancarrow, in a rare conversation, had told me that the *St. Just*, the largest of the island's fishing boats, made the journey to the Cape only a few times a year. Its return was a major event, like Christmas, with goods and presents from the mainland. It looked as if all four hundred and fifty of the islanders had come. The number in residence varied, because of extended fishing trips and absences to work in South Africa—the main way they raised funds for major purchases, like building materials, appliances, and engines.

I had asked the professor if I would have to walk everywhere.

"Oh, no." Professor Jones had said. "They have two old buses, a few cars, and a number of farm vehicles. The garage on the road to Veryan maintains them. Bicycling and, for some of the farms, horseback riding are other ways of getting around. "You see, boyo, petrol—gasoline to you—is very expensive. Can't afford to waste it."

Sandy Nancarrow jumped onto the dock and caught a rope from his brother and secured it around a bollard. After he repeated the process at the stern, a pretty woman rushed ahead of the crowd and embraced him.

"Go for it, Jenny," Sandy shouted, elbowing me in the ribs. "My brother Sam's wife. Wants to find out what I got for her."

At the front of the crowd on the jetty was a tall, untidy-looking woman in a long floral dress and tennis shoes. Her worried look changed to a radiant smile when Frankie popped up from behind the bulwark and, not waiting for the boat to stop, leaped onto the jetty. He was carrying a parcel, which he thrust into her hands.

"Frankie's mum," said Artley as he passed, carrying a packing case.

"I guessed as much."

His mum tried to embrace him, but Frankie was impatient to show his present and started tearing at his package. The crowd pulled away briefly, watching in amusement as pieces of paper flew in all directions. When Frankie and his *mum* left, she was clutching his present—a teddy bear—and scraps of paper in one arm and Frankie in the other. The crew started to unload the cargo. I received a few curious looks, and for a while, no one spoke to me. The various families were too en-grossed in picking up their new possessions.

I was taking in the sounds of the breaking waves, the faint slurp of the boat as it rocked against the key, and the salty, fishy smell of the harbor when a hand on my shoulder caused me to turn.

"Mister Ferguson, you need to go ashore now," said Cap'n Billing. "We have to wash down the boat."

I looked at the remaining crowd on the jetty. "Who do I talk to?"

"Mary Pascoe will look after you." He sounded displeased. He pointed to the back of a woman who was talking to one of the departing families, and then he turned away.

Young Artley was still chuckling as he helped me put my collection of bags and equipment on the jetty. "Don't mind my uncle. You'll understand soon enough why he's unhappy about you staying with Mary."

The woman in front of Mary Pascoe signaled my approach. I was not prepared for the sight of the face that turned to greet me—jet black hair, black eyes, pink cheeks, and such a smile that I nearly forgot how to move one leg in front of the other. But I had seen the look before on the dock in Cape Town—Rose Pascoe.

Later, I came across an article discounting the theory that these looks originated from the few sailors who managed to swim ashore from the sinking boats of the Spanish Armada; instead, the author assigned the looks to a natural Celtic vari-ation. More fancifully, they derived from the ancient Phoeni-cians who had traded for tin with the Cornish.

"M-ma-am," I stammered, "I'm Andy Ferguson."

"Welcome to Roseland, Andy Ferguson. I expect Cap'n

Billing told you I'm Mary Pascoe. You'll be staying with me. By the way, except for a few of us islanders, we don't stand on formality." She nodded in the direction of the boat and Cap'n Billing. "So, Andy, you should call me Mary."

"What should I do with my gear, Mary?"

"I'll get the driver to put it in the back of the bus. The professor did tell you about the island, didn't he?"

I nodded.

"My house is in Veryan."

I met the busload of people in a welter of introductions, including Frankie's mum, Clara Quick, who sat in the front seat clutching her son's arm. She shook my hand. Her pale green eyes scanned me intently, as if to discern something about Frankie's trip. Clara had the ageless complexion that she had passed on to Frankie. When Clara stopped looking worried, her face had an ethereal beauty.

Above the low cliffs at Portloe, the land was flat and filled with fields outlined by stone walls. Some of them had been plowed in preparation for summer crops. On Roseland, coming out of winter at the end of September, grass and evergreen trees and bushes gave most of the color to the drab, early spring landscape. The road wound around fields on the seven-mile drive to Veryan. I concentrated on the scenery in a vain attempt to distract myself from the softness of Mary's full body pressed against my side on the narrow seat. To the left of the bus, the south side of the island rose abruptly through a line of trees. In front of us, the slopes of Brown Willy soared into low clouds.

Mary pointed to the mountain. "Over there is where you'll be working, Andy, on the cliffs between Brown Willy and the Nare. Our auks are curious birds. Strange habits they have." She elbowed me and grinned.

"A bit of the *rum ti tum tum*, is it?" I don't know why I made the connection.

She smiled, as if the words meant nothing, nevertheless I could feel her body tense. "How do….I'm sure I don't know what you mean."

I smiled back, acting as if I did know. She seemed to be on the point of saying something, but at that moment we stopped at a fork in the road to unload people. The signpost pointed ahead to Veryan and back to Portloe. On the other branch of the road, which returned to the southeastern end of the island, there was one word—Trewince. Two miles on, the bus passed between two oddly shaped, small houses signaling the beginning of the village.

"Andy, those round houses, did the professor mention them?"

"No, he didn't," I said. "I saw a photo and asked Mabel. She said I'd find out."

Mary chuckled. "That Mabel. They're placed on each side of the road to keep the devil out of the village. Some of our families came from Veryan in Cornwall, where the original ones are. We copied them."

"Does the shape have some significance?"

"Yes, the devil likes to lurk in corners. That's why they're round."

"Did I see a cross on top of the thatched roof?"

"Yes. That helps, too."

"Have they worked well?"

"I think so…most of the time."

The bus passed scattered cottages before turning left and parking in front of a long building with a sign—Nancarrow General Store. From there, the road curled around the south side of a grassy square and exited to the west toward Brown Willy. When we had unloaded my gear, Mary pointed out the main buildings.

"The prof said I could charge things at Nancarrow's," I said.

"How about in the pub?" Mary said, pointing to a smaller sign on the south end of the store, Roseland Arms.

"I'm on my own. I reached in my pocket and showed her some of my South African rand notes."

Mary chuckled.

"Where do you live?"

She indicated a terrace of four two-story townhouses on the north side of the square, with painted white wood siding and corrugated iron roofs. "I'm in the third house over. Clara and Frankie live in the last one next to me." She took my arm and pointed to the other buildings. "That larger building across the green, beyond Clara's, is the village hall. Carrying on around, you come to the chapel."

The chapel was built sideways to the square. Of course, I thought, so that it can face north, toward Jerusalem. "That looks like another round house across the road. Only one?"

"Don't need two. We've got chapel on t'other side of the road."

"That round house is bigger than the other two. Any reason?"

Mary looked aside, smiling. "It comes in handy on Midsummer's."

"How so?"

Mary did not answer but said, "This next building's important. It's the Seythan House."

I looked at the single-story building that faced Mary's

house across the square. "I read about it. There's a meeting room for the Seythan, your governing body, a library, and the island's records."

"Very good, Andy. One other thing, the meeting room can also be used as a courtroom."

"Is that often?"

"Rarely, and don't you go giving it a reason to meet."

"You're joking."

"Sorry, Andy. I was thinking of something that happened a few years ago." Mary squeezed my arm and gave a gentle pull in the direction of her house.

"There's a school, isn't there? I saw it on the professor's map."

"It's where we stopped, halfway between Portloe and Veryan on the right side of the road." Mary rattled off the names of the families who lived in the twelve houses that completed the center of the village. I couldn't focus on the information because I had just noticed a strange contraption between the Seythan House and the Round House.

Mary laughed. "You've noticed the stocks. That's what I meant when I said you don't want to end up in court. Like the round houses, they're inherited from the old country. The stocks were on the boat, you see."

"The original boat?"

Mary nodded.

"Why would anyone have brought them?"

"Nobody knows, exactly. Clara says they took them as a keepsake from the old country, as a reminder of why they were leaving."

"They sure look old. Are they ever used?"

Her lips pursed. "Like the court, not often."

5.

"IT'S A SMALL HOUSE, ANDY. WE'LL NEED TO STORE SOME OF your stuff in the shed," Mary said, as she led me through the living room into the kitchen and dining area at the back of the house. The kitchen contained a black stove, which also provided hot water for the sink, and a small bathtub that was in a corner of the room behind a curtain. The kitchen door opened into a small garden, at the end of which were two sheds. We stored most of my ornithological gear in the larger of two wooden sheds behind her house. The smaller shed was a one-hole outhouse.

I took the cameras and my backpack upstairs to my bedroom—one of three small rooms. Mary's bedroom was at the back of the house. My home for the next year or more was at the front, sharing a wall with Mary's room. It had a window with a view of the square, the Seythan House, and the stocks. The furniture consisted of a narrow bed, a chest of drawers, a wooden chair, and a rickety bamboo table. I put my notebooks and pencils and a couple of bird books on the table, along with Throgmorton's book to remind me to return it to the library. Upstairs, the bathroom—more or less a large cupboard—contained only a mirror, a small table, two large bowls, a water jug, and mugs for toothpaste and toothbrushes. Mary's make-up and toiletries were on a shelf.

"Would you like some tea?" Mary shouted up the stairs.

"Sure, thanks." I went to the kitchen, assuming we would sit at the table. Mary shooed me out. Apparently tea, which also meant bread and butter and strawberry preserves—she used the English word, jam—was a living-room affair. Mary placed the tray on a low table between the worn, old-fashioned sofa and armchair. A fireplace with a hearth at floor level and brick seats on each side took up most of the wall that was shared with Clara's house at the chapel end of the row. On the walls were an old hand-drawn map of Roseland, with annotations in spidery writing; a painting of a seaside village, somewhat like Portloe; and faded sepia photographs of groups of people.

"Islanders?" I asked, pointing at the photos.

"Yes. When you've been here a while, we'll do a test to see who you can recognize. I'll give you a clue. You've already met some of them."

"Like your daughter, Rose," I said grinning.

"How did you….Oh, on the dock in Cape Town, wasn't it?"

"I didn't meet her, exactly. A glimpse as she walked by with Cap'n Billing. And she's in this photo." I pointed at a face in a group picture. "She looks very pretty. Takes after you."

Mary grinned and wagged her finger. "Andy Ferguson, I'm going to have to watch you."

"Where was Rose going?"

"Back to Manchester University in England."

"Studying?"

"You'll find out in good time." Mary smiled mischievously.

"You've got to allow us our little secrets. There's not a lot to do here, you know. Cinema once a month in the hall's about it. Old films, mostly. Then there's the dances. Do you want milk in your tea?"

"Which one is your husband?" I should have asked about the dances and regretted my tactlessness immediately.

"My husband's gone, Andy."

"Sorry, I shouldn't—"

"You couldn't have known."

"It can't be easy for Rose leaving an isolated place like this and going to England."

"Not easy for me, either. Fortunately, I've got a boyfriend and so, I guess, has she, a boy from Roseland."

"He's here and she's there?" I asked.

"No. He's at university in England, too."

"You sound unsure whether he's her boyfriend."

"There's a sort of understanding."

"How long is Rose going to be away?"

"Too long. She's still got three years to do. I've been lonely without her. I am glad you're here, Andy. Somebody to look after."

We sat in silence for a while and then chatted about the island. I asked her what she thought of Young Artley's suggestion that Frankie could help me with my studies of the auks.

"Artley said that, did he?" She looked concerned. "You've seen what Frankie's like. Certainly, he knows his way around the island. I remember when he was younger, instead of coming straight home from school, he'd crawl behind the walls and hide. We'd all be out looking for him. It drove poor Clara all frantic-like."

"So you think it's a bad idea?"

"Not exactly, he knows the ways around the cliffs. You should talk to Clara."

"Should I go to her house?"

"Better to catch her in the Seythan House tomorrow morning. She looks after the library."

"I'll do that. I have a book the Prof asked me to return." I wanted to ask her more about why she and Artley felt the need to look after Frankie, but guessed she wouldn't answer. I assumed it was typical behavior of a closed community looking after its own.

After tea, I strolled around the square. Nancarrow's store was a two-story, stone-walled building with the corrugated iron roof that seemed to be the standard for the island. The veranda in front held tables with fruit and vegetables on one side and gardening equipment and other non-perishable goods displayed on the other. The store appeared to fill the entire ground floor, and I guessed that the owners lived upstairs. Inside and to the left, steps led down to a stone floor with shelves and one small refrigerated cabinet. This was a food section, containing mainly shelves packed with cans and bottles. It smelled of the cheese and dried fish in a counter display. The stocky, gray-haired man behind the counter eyed me curiously. "You must be Mr. Ferguson," he said, with an accent I could now recognize as Cornish. "My son, Sandy, talked about you."

"Yes, I met him on the boat. You have an interesting store."

"Thank you, *sorr*. I'm Isaac Nancarrow, butcher." He wiped his hands on the slightly stained white apron that protected his suit and tie and held out his hand. I shook it.

"I expect you're wondering why you can only see dried stuff and cans," he said. "The fresh is out back." He pointed to an open door.

"I haven't seen any cows, but I guess the cheese is local?"

"Yes, Morley Thomas has a dairy. He supplies all our milk and makes the cheese." He apparently saw me looking at the loaves of bread behind the counter. "Bakery's in Portloe. I get a delivery twice a week. Fishmonger's there, too. Easier to keep fish fresh in the pens."

He glanced over my shoulder. "My brother, Arthur, looks after the other part of the store. Arthur, come and meet Mr. Ferguson!"

I turned to see a small man with thinning hair and a pinched face. He also wore a suit and tie. When we shook hands, I could smell the faint aroma of mothballs.

"Pleased to meet you, Mr. Ferguson." Arthur smiled as he said it, but his expression did not show any great pleasure. In fact, he seemed to be assessing me.

I remembered Mary's comment about informality. "Mr. Nancarrow, I'm Andy."

Isaac Nancarrow nodded, curtly. "Arthur will show you the rest of the store."

The rest of the store was a continuation of the floor at the level of the veranda and was built from old wooden planks that were worn and uneven. They looked as if they might have come from the deck of a boat. Mr. Nancarrow—I did not know whether I should call him Arthur—showed me around the neat shelves of hardware and pharmaceuticals. Prescription drugs were in a cabinet behind a glass-covered counter. The counter had a modest display of jewelry. Farther into the store was the clothing. Most of the clothes were made of practical, durable materials. In contrast was a prominent display of a woman's dress and a man's suit. I had the impression they might have been there a long time, because the fashion was a decade or so out of date.

"Not much by American standards, I suppose," muttered Arthur.

I was surprised by his negativism and thought hard before responding. "Mr. Nancarrow, I come from a small town in rural America." I smiled. "We have a store just like yours, but it doesn't carry such a wonderful variety of goods, and it isn't a thousand miles from a big city."

He looked surprised and, I sensed, a little pleased. He changed the subject. "On t'other side of that wall is the pub. The door's outside." It sounded like he might not approve of it. I thanked him for the tour and shook his hand. As I went back on the veranda, he called after me. "Andy, they call me Arthur." I turned. He smiled, and this time the smile was genuine.

I continued around to the south side of the square, passing a row of houses similar to Mary's terrace. At the southwest end was the Seythan House. Unlike the store, it was a single-story building. I stepped onto the veranda and opened the front door and could see the shelves of the library to the left.

"Anyone here?" After hearing no response, I felt like I was trespassing. I closed the door and continued around the square. I came first to the stocks: four horizontal wooden pieces mounted in pairs between heavy posts that were set into thick wooden boards that squashed the grass—an uncomfortable seat for any prisoner who would have to sit with legs and arms extended. Grass grew out from under the baseboard. A rectangle of bare earth nearby indicated that the stocks had been moved recently.

Just beyond the stocks was the Round House. It had white

walls and a conical thatched roof with a cross on top. Small windows were set high in the wall. The thick wooden door was locked. I wondered how they expected the devil to get in and be trapped. Maybe he had a key. I grinned inanely at the thought. Across the road was the chapel. It looked more like a glorified shed. A corrugated iron roof down its length led to a tiny wooden steeple and a cross that was identical to the one on the Round House. Plain glass windows, nothing fancy, I noted. Veryan Baptist Chapel was printed on a sign by the road. Beyond the chapel was the village hall. Behind and two plus miles away to the left, the peak of Brown Willy loomed massively, 2,000 feet above the village. Stretches of the stream that started in the lake at its summit were visible as the water tumbled down toward the sea north of Veryan. I passed Clara Quick's house at the end of our terrace. The sun was setting fast, and a light was on. I did not stop; talking to Clara could wait.

Mary served dinner in the kitchen: battered fish and chips (fries), assorted fruit from a tin (can) in jelly (Jell-O) for pudding (dessert). I was learning a new language.

I commented on meeting the Nancarrows, remarking that Arthur Nancarrow had asked me to call him Arthur.

Mary looked amazed. "What about Isaac?"

"Mr. Nancarrow," I replied.

She chuckled. "The butcher's an important man, member of the Seythan, too."

"How will I know who to be formal with?"

"You'll not find it difficult. It's not a question of airs. There are people who have important positions on the island, like Captain Artley Billing, Mr. Isaac Nancarrow, and Mrs. Trevenna. And, of course, the professor was…well regarded."

Why the pause? I wondered, but said.,"The prof said that Jane Trevenna is the Penseythan."

"She is, Andy. The Penseythan wields a lot of power on Roseland. You need to remember that."

"That's what I heard, and someone on the boat said that the governor only comes from St. Helena once a year."

"Comes in second week of September. You just missed him." Mary sniffed dismissively.

"You don't sound impressed."

"He's all right, with his entourage and his airs. Stays up at Trewince. We get to see him in the hall when he gives his little speech. 'Fine island, Roseland. Keep up the good work. Remember you're British. I have told the Penseythan to let me know if I can do anything to help. Is it time for a beer yet?' Then he goes to the pub, downs a pint, and plays darts to show he's one of the lads…harmless really."

"He sounds like the mayor in my hometown, Colonel Hamish McIntyre. Nobody seems to know what he was colonel of, and nobody calls him Hamish except his mother."

"What about your family?"

"My dad's parents emigrated from Scotland in the 1920s, and we think of ourselves as Scots-American."

"I thought I could hear a trace of Scottish," Mary said. "But that black hair, dark complexion, you don't look like my image of a Scotsman."

"My mother's Italian-American."

"And you got those pale blue eyes from your dad."

"Sexy," I said, attempting to bat my eyelashes.

"Not when you look like that." Mary laughed. "Did you bring your kilt?"

"Not…likely. My dad used to make me wear one on special

occasions. The girls liked it but the guys made fun of me. I stopped in high school."

Mary pointed her finger and said, "You remember to write to your parents. The Veryan post office is in Nancarrow's."

"I will. And to the prof, too. How often does the boat go to the Cape?"

"It depends on the weather. Every two months or so in the summer and never, maybe I should say rarely, in the winter."

After dinner, I helped wash the dishes.

"Your parents did a good job. I'm glad you're here." Mary gave me a radiant smile and a hug.

Her body was soft and her breasts pushed against my chest. It was not a sexual hug, but it reminded me of Throgmorton's comment on a lack of women. Despite the professor's warning, I wondered if there would be anyone for me.

"Here, take this torch," Mary said, handing me a flashlight as I went to my room. "The electricity is only on for a few hours in the early morning, lunchtime, and again in the evening, more in the winter after dark."

"Where do you get the electricity from?"

"Hydro off stream up Brown Willy. When you go to rookery, you'll see the dam."

"So that dam does the whole island?"

"My, your inquisitive." Mary laughed. "Not a good habit around here."

"Sorry, just curious."

"Just for Veryan," she said. Portloe and Trewince use hydro on the Fal."

You'll need this torch for reading and to get to the toilet. I can't have you tripping over in my garden. Oh, and when the batteries run out, you can get new ones from Nancarrow's." She smiled; apparently, charity only went so far.

I read Throgmorton for a bit before falling asleep. I had not realized how tired I was. I was woken in the early morning by a rhythmic creaking sound. It seemed to come from Mary's room. I tried to ignore it, but it went on for an interminable time, until I could hear small moans of pleasure and the creaking became more urgent. Muffled talking followed. Much later, I thought I heard the sound of footsteps on the stairs and the back door being opened and closed. I felt lonely and frustrated enough to hand myself some quick relief. It would have to be like that until I got back to the States, I thought ruefully.

6.

THE NEXT MORNING, A KNOCK ON MY DOOR WOKE ME EARLY
for breakfast. I dressed quickly, reckoning to clean up later,
and went downstairs. Mary wore a robe over a long flannel
nightgown. She was frying bacon. "Mornin', Andy. Sleep
well?"

I smiled uncertainly. Her hair was tousled and her face
slightly puffy. She looked tired, happy, and sexy.

"More eggs?" Mary asked, leaning forward as she ladled
scrambled eggs onto my plate. Her robe had loosened, and I
could see her breasts swinging in her nightgown right in front
of me.

I laughed. "No more, please, I'll burst." I was not referring
only to the food.

Mary could see where I was looking. She grinned, unself-
consciously. "A growing lad like you needs to keep his strength
up."

"That's not all a growing lad needs," I said quietly, without
thinking.

"Andy, I'm surprised at you." She shook her finger at me,
smiling. "I have to go to work. Could you finish the washing
up? Clara won't be at the library till around nine."

"Sure." In our brief discussions, we had talked only about Veryan and my work. "What do you do?"

"I'm a teacher."

"Interesting. What do you teach?"

"A bit of everything, really, reading, writing, arithmetic, English, French, geography, history…for the up-to-eleven-year-olds. Mr. Cocking does upper classes, stuff like algebra, geometry, and science. Mrs.…." Her voice trailed off as she walked out the door.

Upstairs, I brushed my teeth and dressed before grabbing Throgmorton's book. I went to the toilet and sat on the two planks that formed the seat. The smell emanating from the one-holer brought back memories of a crummy summer camp from my childhood. Throgmorton confirmed and added to what the prof had told me. As of the 1940s, the main families on Roseland remained the descendants of the folk that had been stranded there—Jago, Pascoe, Nichols, Nancarrow, Trevenna, Anthony, Cocking, Gay, Quick, Billing, and Thomas.

The island was an overseas territory of the United Kingdom, coming under the Governor of St. Helena. The leadership of the Seythan passed from one family to another in some prescribed yet unexplained manner. The legal system was based on British law and had no death penalty. In the rare event of a crime, the members of the Seythan acted as constables. The Penseythan acted as a magistrate, dealing with all minor matters. The Seythan, under the leadership of the Penseythan, were the jury in major cases.

A tax system, based on a tithe of ten percent, was used to pay for common needs such as the upkeep of the harbor, roads, and the school. The islanders could pay the tithe in cash, goods, or work on community projects. It seemed to be an enlightened society. The British government provided a grant every year, in return for which the islanders maintained and operated the weather station and the radio station and stored supplies for the navy near Portloe. As part of the grant, the navy provided fuel for the island: gasoline and diesel fuel for buses and for an electrical generator that supported the needs of the radio station and some of the farms and businesses. In total, it was a few hundred tons of fuel each year.

As to health care, about all I could find in Throgmorton's book was a mention of a midwife. I guessed that Throgmorton never became ill.

On my second visit into the Seythan House, I could hear voices coming through the door to my right, which I guessed led to the council chamber. The library, to the left, seemed to be empty. I started a circuitous route among the bookshelves and nearly tripped over Clara Quick. She was on her hands and knees, peering at old books on the lowest shelf.

"Oh, Mr. Andy, you startled me." I helped her to her feet. "Mary said you have a book for me from the professor." She appeared flustered.

I handed her Throgmorton's book.

"My word, it's a long time since I saw this. What was it about?" She scanned it quickly. "Oh, yes. I remember about poor Mr. Throgmorton." A secretive smile glimmered briefly. "Now where should we put you?" She scanned the binding. "There's no number. Where do you go?" She seemed to forget I was there as she paced the aisles looking for a suitable resting place for Throgmorton's book.

"Mrs. Quick, could we talk about Frankie? Did he say anything to you?"

She stopped pacing. "What about Frankie?"

"I'm sure Mary told you, I'm here to study the auks."

Her face with its pale green eyes was uncomprehending.

"I'm doing my doctorate under the professor. He wants me to research the auks. He has a theory about them."

Clara stared at me blankly.

"He believes they are unusual."

Silence.

"He thinks there are more males than females, leading to strange sexual behavior."

A slow smile appeared. "*Rum tum ti*…." Clara turned away and made a pretense of looking for a slot for Throgmorton. She was unsuccessful and turned back to peer at me. Her face was expressionless again.

"You're working for the professor?"

I nodded.

"Frankie doesn't work for the professor."

"I know, but I would like him to help me. I could pay a little. The prof says Nancarrow's will handle it. I need someone to show me where the auk colony is and help me with equipment. It would only be part-time."

"You'll keep an eye him? He's all I've got."

"Yes, and I'm sure he'll look after me." I was not sure, but it sounded like the right thing to say. "I don't know the island. Young Artley said Frankie knows all the places."

This time Clara appeared to like the idea. "Frankie knows too many places, but he could help, I suppose. I'll talk to him."

"Would today be possible? I'd like to get up there and start work."

"Today?" She shook her head. "I don't know about today." She turned away and went back to trying to place the book.

When I went outside Frankie was sitting on the rail of the veranda.

"What did *me* Mum say? What did she say? I can do it, right?"

"You need to ask her, Frankie, just to be sure."

"Can't go in Seythan."

I did not try to find out why and went back into the library. "Frankie's outside, he wants to speak to you," I said.

This time the loop was closed, and Clara agreed to let Frankie help me, starting then. Arthur Nancarrow had advised me to pay him five shillings an hour, which I worked out to be about forty or fifty cents.

I noticed that Clara was still carrying Throgmorton's book.

"Can I ask you something about this?" I said, reaching for the book.

"Certainly, m'dear," Clara replied, handing it to me.

I found the page that had a postscript, written in a different color ink, and read it to her.

Unfortunately, I was right to be worried about what was happening. Just before
    Midsummer's Day, my friend John committed suicide. The events following his death are too strange to write down. It seems the hints I have been given about pagan rituals were correct. Who are the "maskers" and what do the masks signify? I shall soon be back in Cape Town. Thank God!

"Oh, my!" Clara looked away in the direction of Brown Willy.

58

"What does it mean?"

"Can't say." Clara grabbed the book and scurried back into the Seythan House.

She'd left me with another puzzle—what had happened to Throgmorton? Was he a dancing fool, like Pavlov the Russian? Had he made a pass at a married woman and been rebuffed? Why had Throgmorton's friend killed himself? What were the rituals?

7.

FOR SOME REASON, WHEN FRANKIE TOOK ME TO THE ROOK-
ery he did not want to go straight there. We started in the
right direction, to the west out of Veryan, but then we veered
north, following a stream. After half a mile or so, we came to
the dam that Mary had mentioned. Frankie continued moving rapidly up the path toward the summit of Brown Willy.
Unlike the area around Veryan, where the islanders had planted European trees, the mountain was covered with native veg-
etation; tussock grass and small trees I did not recognize were
near the base. Higher up, dwarf tree ferns clustered in a wide
band, and above them mats of crowberry and moss covered
the ground.

"Frankie, what are those trees?"

"Dunno, really. Roseland trees, I calls 'em." He increased
his pace.

"Why are we going up Brown Willy?"

"You'll see." He moved faster.

I had little choice but to follow. Fortunately, I was not carrying much equipment. We were about halfway to the top
when he sat down by the edge of the stream that tumbled by

the side of the path. He had kept up a fast pace, and I was happy to join him.

"Birds," Frankie said, grabbing my arm and pointing to the south.

Thousands of sea birds spiraled and swooped over the cliffs that stretched down to the Nare Head and out over the water to the Gull Rock. An occasional gust of wind from that direction carried their cries. The sight of my new workplace was sobering too, for the cliffs plunged dramatically into the broken waves of the sea.

"Auks." Frankie pointed at a bright green patch on the cliff top hemmed in by a fuzz of green and yellow bushes.

"It's fantastic, beautiful, Frankie. Thanks for bringing me here."

Frankie smiled a deep, contented smile and grabbed my arm again, turning me to face the other end of the island. I could make out parts of the Veryan to Portloe road, the schoolhouse midway between them, and the houses at the edge of Portloe, eight miles away.

Frankie pointed at something else, to the south of Portloe, where the dense woods climbed into the southeastern hills. "Trewince," he said.

"Remember, Frankie, my eyesight isn't as keen as yours." I grabbed my binoculars and then could see the face of a large house in a clearing. In front of the house a stream tumbled in over rocks in a gorge. Trewince and the River Fal had been marked on the professor's map. "Is that where Mrs. Trevenna lives?"

"Big house," was his answer, and he was gone back down the hill toward the auk rookery.

I followed. The action of the wind had bent over the small

trees that grew on the Veryan side of the path. On the seaward side, the path followed a spectacular route through low, prickly bushes with small yellow flowers, just feet from where the ground dropped away. The bushes were gorse, imported from England to control erosion. They were successful at erosion control, and at attacking my legs with their dry thorny branches. In between showing me books on birds, the prof had mentioned gorse. I recalled the occasion...

"Here are a couple more on birds," the professor said. "Glance at them if you have time."

While I glanced at them, he rummaged in a pile of books on the floor.

"Ah, yes, I think you'll find this interesting, *Flora and Fauna of Southern Atlantic Islands*. These pictures will give you a feel for what these islands look like. Fortunately, Roseland is somewhat less barren. The islanders planted a variety of trees and shrubs, and some have done quite well—rhododendra, larch, firs, elms, beech trees, and the evil gorse." He paused, appearing to be trying to find something else for me to read.

"What's the evil gorse?"

"You'll find out, boyo, soon enough. With apologies to The Jabberwocky, 'Beware of gorse. The bush that grabs, the thorns that cut.'"

The noise of the birds grew louder as we approached the rookery. Suddenly, Frankie, who was about twenty yards ahead of me, disappeared. The path he had taken was hard to see, simply a descending line of stepping points between the gorse. I followed, trying not to look down to where the waves pounded the base of the cliff a hundred feet below me.

After a descent of about thirty feet, the path leveled out, and then a few hundred yards farther on I came upon Frankie who was sitting behind a boulder and grinning. When I joined him he motioned for me to keep low, pointing over the boulder.

"Auk, auk, auk, auk!" He had to shout, because the noise of the wind was deafening.

I looked out from our hiding place and saw that we were above the rookery, a broad field of green that was thickly covered with tussocks of grass. From a distance, it had looked flat and smooth compared to the gorse that grew along the top and down the sides to the cliff. I guessed it ran for a couple of hundred yards along the cliff and was maybe fifty yards deep. When we moved farther down, I could see that the rookery consisted of a series of ledges that dropped some ten to fifteen feet from the top to the cliff edge. The auk burrows were tunneled between the mounds of grass. A few auks scuttled between the tussocks. They must have known we were there, because some of them flew above us on their landing path; however, they paid us little attention.

"Can I go closer?"

Frankie looked at me craftily. "Takes time, like when you gets eggs."

"You take auks' eggs?" I snapped, in surprise.

"Not auks' eggs. Not allowed to. Gulls' eggs good." He smacked his lips.

"Why not allowed?"

"Seythan says so."

It seemed that the islanders respected the auk—interesting. I knew that in the northern hemisphere people ate the eggs of the northern Atlantic auks. They had also killed the birds for food, which had driven the great auk and some colonies of lesser auks to extinction.

"Where do the gulls nest?"

"On cliffs below auks and over to Brown Willy," Frankie answered as he sidled around the boulder and crawled slowly onto the ledge.

I followed.

Frankie stopped at the edge of the grass, which was covered in bird droppings and looked slippery. The fishy smell was overpowering. We were getting too close to the rookery, and the nearby auks fussed at us. After the dull photographs at the professor's, I enjoyed seeing the birds in color. The auks were about twelve to fifteen inches tall, and comparing them to the Atlantic Puffin, tubbier than they appeared in the pictures the professor had shown to me. Again, I recalled his comments...

"As you can see, Andrew, their wings and backs are black and their chests and cheeks are white. See how their legs and the orbital rings around their eyes are a yellow-orange? These pictures don't do justice to the coloring." He paused. "The beak has multicolored stripes from yellow-orange at the tip through slate gray and white to yellow at the base. It's gaudier than shown here."

"Plus, the beaks look the same as the puffins' beaks, curved triangular shape and the full height of the head at their base," I said.

"Yes, and see the same rosette of loose skin at the corner of the mouth, which allows the beak to open wide for catching fish. Note that it's orange, an interesting example of evolution. The Atlantic puffin has a yellow rosette."

Now that I was close, I could see the other black markings

in the feathers on the cheeks and small, black, leathery patches above and below the auks' eyes.

When the auks were agitated, a few feathers on the backs of their heads would rise, looking like ears. The overall impression they gave was of a pompous clown. I studied them for a while and then signaled that we should return to the boulder.

"There aren't very many of them yet."

"You just wait," Frankie snickered. "You just wait!" He pointed to the sea.

About half a mile out, a large patch on the sea was dark. Using the binoculars, I could make out thousands of auks bobbing on the surface. I remembered that auks normally rendezvoused offshore before returning to land.

"I'll need to build a blind so that I can study them without causing problems."

Frankie's face looked blank.

"A blind is a little covered area where I can see the birds, but they can't see me."

"You mean a hide," Frankie said, laughing at my ignorance of the English term.

He moved away, staying low on a barely discernable path through the bushes that had grown back over the worn trail. They scratched me as I scuttled after him. Frankie had moved near the rookery and an open area where sparse clumps of grass dotted the earth. Twenty feet down the slope, the ground dropped off precipitously. A thin line of gorse separated the dip from the rookery and provided cover. While the gorse was encroaching on the dip, the lack of gorse suggested that it had been used before, by the professor, I assumed. The third line of burrows above the bottom ledge was close to the dip.

"This is great. Did you come here with the professor?"

"Long time ago. I were a kid." He looked shifty. "I saw him up here."

"Thanks," I said and patted him on the back. He flinched and looked worried. I smiled reassuringly, but his expression did not change. Had he been beaten as a child? Surely not by his mother. What about his father? Where was he?

I took my pad and a pencil from my backpack and sketched a layout for the blind. It would need poles to support the plastic sheet the professor had given me. I decided to ask Arthur Nancarrow about the poles and a seat.

Frankie had returned to my side of the dip and peered over my shoulder. "Little house," he said, "hide, hideaway, hide, auks no see. Auk, auk, auk, auk!"

"*Rum, tum, ti, tumpty,*" I replied, and he looked at me slyly. It seemed that he had been warned against saying anything—by Cap'n Billing, I guessed.

"Frankie hungry," he said, making it obvious he was changing the subject. Fortunately, Mary had persuaded me to go to Nancarrow's and make up some cheese and ham sandwiches. Frankie chose cheese. I had a flask of water and reluctantly shared it. Frankie dribbled and left wet crumbs around the rim. I decided to bring two bottles next time.

Frankie wiped his mouth. "Good food."

"Glad you liked it. Come on, Frankie; please tell me about the *rum tum....*" I did not finish the request. All I saw was Frankie's retreating backside.

I stayed a little longer, studying the auks, keeping low to avoid disturbing them.

The coloring was interesting, and I was beginning to distinguish between males and females. Building a blind was a priority, because without it my view was limited.

Frankie was waiting for me at the top of the cliff. He grinned and started away the minute I approached him. All I could see on the way back to Veryan was an occasional glimpse of him in the distance. I had needed Frankie to find the auk rookery, and he could help me carry equipment, but I wondered how useful he would be from then on.

Nancarrow's was open when I returned to the village. "Can I help you, m'dear?" Arthur asked, greeting me at the door. On the boat, I had found out about this Cornish way of greeting, or I would have been concerned about Arthur's orientation—and not just because he wore an ornate ring with a carved red stone on his right pinkie finger. I explained about building the blind, showing my sketch. He took the sketch and led me to the back of the store and into a large shed. On the way we passed a tall cabinet with a hand-lettered sign that read, WOMEN.

"What's that, Arthur?"

"Women's personal things, m'dear. Easier for Isaac and me if they get what they need themselves. Less embarrassing, you know." As I followed him outside, I had the idle thought that the personal things might include contraceptive pills besides sanitary supplies. Two buildings stood behind the store: a wooden shed and, farther back, a long building fronted by a concrete pad with a drain in the middle. Faint red stains marked the concrete.

"Abattoir," Arthur said, wrinkling his nose. "I leave that to Isaac and the boys."

An image of Sam and Sandy wearing blood-stained overalls flashed through my mind. "Dad never liked that part of raising pigs," I said. "That's why he raised piglets and sold them for fattening."

Arthur opened the door to the shed and ushered me in. An amazing assortment of goods faced me—furniture, barrels, tools, lamps, nets strung from the rafters, bales of plastic and kapok, various pieces of wood, and even a tent.

"You'll need to set posts in ground." Arthur pointed at my sketch. "A box frame like yours won't handle wind. It can get right fierce up on the cliff. You'll need some'at to dig holes for these posts," he said. "Frankie could get somethin'."

Arthur reacted quickly to my look of surprise. "Don't be put off by his antics. He's smarter than he acts." Arthur turned away quickly, as if he had been speaking out of turn, and changed the subject. "You plan to use your piece of plastic for the cover?"

I nodded.

"It'll not be strong enough. Wind'll tear it up. Use it for the floor. This is what you need." He dragged an old piece of tarpaulin from behind a barrel.

It smelled of fish. I wrinkled my nose.

"Auks'll like the smell." He laughed. "Anything else you need, like some cord?"

"Yes, please. How do I pay?"

"I'll put it on the professor's account. Best to rent. It makes no sense to buy them, you being temporary-like. You don't plan to take it back to the States, do you?"

I laughed. "Can you imagine Mabel's face if I put this tarpaulin in her living room?"

"I wouldn't hear the end of it, either." Arthur chuckled. "You can leave it all here until you're ready. Let's see if Frankie's around. We can get him started on finding you tools."

We went outside. There was no sign of Frankie.

"He's here all right," Arthur said, shaking his head in mock despair. "That's Frankie for you. I wonder what he and Clara are up to now."

"What do—"

Arthur walked away, answering over his shoulder, "Don't you worry none. I'll talk to him."

8.

IT TOOK ANOTHER DAY FOR FRANKIE TO ROUND UP THE tools. Strangely, he wouldn't help me get the tarpaulin from Nancarrow's shed. Instead, he waited in the square for me to fetch it. We managed to tote everything to the rookery in two trips. As it turned out to be usual, the wind gusted strongly, and I could not have assembled the blind without Frankie to help me put the frame together and maneuver the tarpaulin on top. Worse still, the damn gorse snagged everything and scratched my hands. Somehow, as we fought the gorse and the wind, Frankie managed to emerge unscathed. Obviously he had a much better sense of where his body was than I. When we had finished, I offered silent thanks to Arthur who had given me such good advice on setting the posts in the ground and using a tarpaulin as the roof. The plastic covering on the ground protected me from broken gorse thorns trapped in the grass.

I spent most of the daylight hours over the next weeks at the rookery. I did not need Frankie's help anymore; nevertheless he turned up. He loved to sneak up and then watch from some hidden hollow in the gorse. On a couple of occasions he waved a branch in front of the observing slot in the tarpaulin. I shouted at him to go away, more in surprise than anger. I worried the auks would desert the part of the middle ledges that was my study area. For some reason, the auks fussed if they saw me. In contrast, they did not mind when Frankie stood on the cliff top and pissed over the edge. At other times he came by to announce his presence and then disappeared, going over the cliff edge at the near side of the rookery and returning later with gull eggs. The gulls nested on the rocky, steep parts of the cliff below and to the north of the rookery. Frankie's route was scary looking, with crumbling ledges and the sharp, foam-covered rocks at the base of the cliff. In addition to the auks and gulls, skuas from the Northern Hemisphere wintered on Roseland in the southern summer. No eggs from them; they bred only when they were in the North.

When I paid close attention, I could distinguish one auk from another by the small pattern variations of their beaks and faces. Like Atlantic puffins, the auks had no grooves in their beaks until age four, when two grooves formed. During the mating season, through some miracle, their beaks exhibited stripes in orange, yellow, and slate-gray. I had read that the female auks found the coloration sexy.

The professor's color Polaroid camera was a great help, and after a few weeks I had photographs of most of the adult auks in my little part of the colony. The photos, coupled with notes from studying each bird through binoculars, allowed me to establish a beak color code. With other features, such as injuries to their bodies or patterns in the feathers, I could identify nearly every male and female in my area—paired and unpaired.

Although the males were slightly bigger, when I found it difficult to distinguish the gender, I used their sexual behavior as a final determinant. The professor's thesis was correct; the number of males far exceeded the number of females. Only about twenty to twenty-five percent of the birds were female, leading to some very interesting behavior. I studied, checking on the professor's hypothesis, whether he was right about how the female auks handled the situation in which two-thirds to three-quarters of the males were randy and unpaired during the mating season. At the time, I had commented that, if I remember correctly, some kinds of auk mate at sea. I remembered the professor's reply...

"Yes, very good point, and that is true for what I believe to be the Roseland auks' closest relative, the Atlantic puffin," he had replied. "Fortunately for us, the Roseland auk copulates mainly on land. Why the difference, I do not know. It would be a good topic for another dissertation, eh!"

Fortunate for me indeed. If, like many birds, the Roseland auks paired for life, what was the role for the spare males? Did they help in caring for the chicks?

I called the females auks "the good-time girls." My favorite was Nellie. She and her entourage were among the early arrivals. I watched Nellie closely, and when there was time, I watched the others who occupied neighboring burrows: Beatrice, Dottie, Lola, Virginia, and Prudence.

Most interesting to me was how they handled copulation. The islanders had theories, and I had received a number of hints on the boat about the female auk's behavior. In fact, the islanders seemed to have a private joke, like the *rum-ti-tum*-whatever crap. One of their theories was borne out when I watched as one of Nellie's boyfriends attempted copulation, a clumsy affair made more difficult by the fact that she would not move her tail out of the way for him. Nevertheless, he seemed to get satisfaction and left her to nestle in the thick grass, contentedly capturing the warmth of the sun. Nellie scuttled away to reassure Fred, her mate. Through all of the sexual hijinks with the gentlemen friends, she kept letting him know he was her main man. I suspected that Fred was an older auk. He rested a great deal between fishing expeditions. But this was not a time to rest, though; Nellie had not finished with sex. After a moment of gentle nuzzling, she let him know she expected action. Fred did not need much encouragement and quickly mounted her. She moved her tail out of the way and stayed with him until he climaxed.

* * *

Curiously, the island's human population was also lacking in the female of the species, as suggested by Throgmorton, who had written...

> The excess of men is a puzzle. It is more than is obvious in a casual census of observed islanders, because a number of the men are absent, fishing or working in southern Africa. Some odd comments overheard in the pub and in casual conversations make me wonder just how the islanders handle the problem. Can many of the men be celibate? There do not seem to be any "foreign" women here. Florence Billing, Clara Trevenna, Patricia Jago, Jane Cocking,

Prudence Nancarrow, and the formidable Penseythan, Agnes Nichols, are all local women. Are some of the ladies of uncertain virtue? For a time I thought so, but it did me no good. I even took part in a play to help press my case for female attention. She, I will not say which one, made me look like a fool, a dancing fool. Agnes Nichols had strong words with me about behaving myself and not being involved with the "chosen one." There have been hints about what "chosen" means, except the implications seem too absurd to believe. If they are correct, I have a fear it will end up badly. In the future, I will keep to myself, even if a woman makes advances. It has been nearly a year that I've been here without the pleasure of true female companionship. I will be leaving soon, so I may never know how they cope, a further point of frustration. I need to get away from this remote island and its strange people.

Confirmation of this strange situation came when Mary Pascoe took me to the dance in the village hall in Portloe. The dance was an every-other-week event, alternating between the village halls in Portloe and Veryan. Fewer than half of the riders on the bus to Portloe were women, and most wore wedding rings. The women sat together at the front of the bus, and I could not tell which men were their husbands. Mary and I also sat near the front, so that she could introduce me to other riders as they boarded.

When Sam and Sandy Nancarrow got on, they brushed past us without a word.

"Wonder what's got into them," Mary said, adding in a whisper. "They're rough those two. Take after their father. Watch out."

I wanted to find out more, but Mary had turned to chat to Clara who was sitting across the aisle.

The night was warm and humid, and when we reached the hall, Mary indicated I should leave my jacket with the others hanging from pegs in the entry hall. A moment of silence greeted Mary and me as we entered the hall. I could not decide if it was because of my presence or because the arrival of Mary had doubled the number of attractive women. Men of a variety of ages sat on chairs around half the dance floor looking hopeful. Unlike me, they were wearing white shirts and ties. I was wearing my best T-shirt and jeans. When we entered the hall, Mary motioned me to join the men, and I was pleased to see Artley Billing, who grinned and indicated the chair next to him. The women sat together, filling one side of the hall. Most of the older women wore dresses with floral patterns. The younger girls generally wore blouses and skirts, some quite short. I could see that the number of young women was less than the number of young men. A trio of musicians with a piano, bass, and drums occupied a low stage at the end of the hall.

Young Artley tapped me on the shoulder. "How's it going with the auks, Andy?"

"Very well, thanks. Frankie's been helpful. He really knows his way around, doesn't he? He's a bit scary around the cliffs, though."

"Going after gulls' eggs, is he?"

"Yes."

Artley shook his head. "I'll get Cap'n Artley to speak to him. You know, about not taking chances. If Frankie got 'urt, it would break Clara's 'art."

"Arthur Nancarrow helped too, with material for a blind.

It's built now, and I can watch the birds without bothering them. They're fascinating."

"Is it true what they say?" He paused. "You know, about there being too many males?"

"It looks like it, Artley. I'm trying to understand how the auks handle it."

"You has to make do with what you've got," he said, indicating the lack of young women in the hall with a wave of his hand. He checked to see if anyone was listening. "Of course, the lads aren't happy about you bein' here. Not a lot of opportunity for them, you see."

"How does the dancing work? I mean, do I ask a girl?" I did not feel comfortable asking Artley, right out, how the islanders handled the more general problem of having few women.

"Oh no, Andy!" Artley grinned. "We have a simple system. The women will ask you." He laughed. "Don't you worry about it none. Everybody's curious about what you're doing."

He was right. The women were careful to ensure that every man had his opportunity to dance, though it became obvious that some men were favored, including me. Dancing was tricky because the trio played old-time music, with some Beatles and Elvis songs to show they were only twenty years or so behind the times. Mary guided me through the first dance—a foxtrot, she told me. Jane Billing, Clara Quick, and Susan Anthony—how did they pick that combination of names?—then wheeled me around the floor in half-remembered gyrations. Clara was a good dancer and not as frail as the impression she gave with her ill-fitting dresses and dowdy appearance.

"How's my Frankie doing?"

"He's a big help, Clara," I gasped as we whirled around in

an old-fashioned waltz. A little smile appeared, and on the next twirl, I felt a gentle hug. "Frankie isn't dancing much."

"The girls ask him, but Frankie's not keen on it. He'll dance with Esther, though."

"Which one's Esther?"

Clara maneuvered me expertly toward a large girl, who was energetically twirling with her partner. "Esther," she whispered and surprised me by abruptly adding, "It can't be easy for a healthy young man like you being alone on this island."

"It is different."

"Did you leave a girlfriend back in the States?"

"No one in particular." I hoped she didn't feel my arms tense.

"How are you doing with the girls here at the dance, Andy?"

"They have lots of questions. You know, like why am I studying the auks? What are women wearing in the States?"

I did not add that I received numerous comments on the strange behavior of auks. One woman, looking embarrassed as if she had spoken out of turn, said, "They're a lot like us."

Patsy Jago, a plump, toothy teenager, grabbed me early on. I found out later that she lived on a farm near the rookery. She wore a short skirt and spun a lot to show off her legs and panties. Patsy made eyes at me, asked me to dance twice, and squeezed my hand suggestively during some ancient dance— the Gay Gordons, for God's sake. I vaguely remembered dancing it at a Scottish Festival at home. Why the Gordons were gay I had no idea. If any male group had the need to be gay, it would be the Roseland men; the female situation was pitiful.

By the end of the evening, I could sense that Artley was right; the local lads did not appreciate my competing for the limited amount of talent available. Sandy Nancarrow had barged into me in one dance, and another man had managed to kick my shin. Looking at the slim pickings, how could I blame them?

Patsy looked as if she wanted to grab me for the last waltz, but Mary intercepted me before I could go on the floor with her. Esther was with Frankie. Toward the end of the dance, the lights went off, and Mary hugged me. It felt good when her soft lips brushed mine. Then the lights came on. Patsy's face appeared to the side of her partner's head, Young Artley. She gave me a toothy grin in the middle of smeared lipstick.

Mary saw me looking and brushed the lipstick off my mouth. She whispered in my ear, "You weren't expecting that, Andy Ferguson, were you? We have our quaint customs here. Just imagine what Patsy Jago would have done to you, and you so innocent."

"I don't want to think about it," I replied. Untrue, I did think about it. I could still see Patsy, who was now with Esther. She was looking at me again and ran her tongue over her lips, suggestively. Mary noticed and wagged her finger at Patsy.

"I suppose I'd better explain something to you, but not here," Mary said.

On the return trip, the bus seating arrangements were different. Married women sat with their husbands. Mary and I sat together in silence. She seemed distracted.

Patsy and her girlfriend, Esther, were among those who got off the bus at the schoolhouse. Patsy managed to brush against me as she passed. Mary glared at her, and Patsy pouted mischievously. When we left the bus, I asked Mary what she wanted to explain to me.

"I'll tell you inside." We walked across the green. "There's another thing. Clara wanted to know if you've ever done any acting."

"I tried once. I wasn't very good. Why did she ask?"

"Clara puts on plays." She opened the front door. "She's always looking for people."

"You're kidding! I thought Clara…."

"You thought what?"

"Well. That she was kind of out of it."

Mary pursed her lips. "Sometimes she is, sometimes not. She's led a hard life."

"What kind of plays?"

"Mostly British, you know…Shakespeare, Bernard Shaw, Noel Coward. This time it's Shakespeare's *Tempest*. We'll go, if you like."

"Sure."

Mary closed the front door and turned to face me. "Patsy has been chosen, and you will get into bad trouble if you go after that little virgin."

"Chosen for what?"

"Midsummer's Day. Can't say more."

"One of your quaint customs?"

"I've said enough."

"*Rum tum ti*…."

Mary ignored me and went straight upstairs to her room.

Apparently it would not be smart to make a move on Patsy or for that matter any of the girls—chosen or not—whatever that meant. I would have to be on my best behavior for the next year.

I wondered about Mary Pascoe, not a little girl or a virgin, a very attractive woman, but she had a man. I had certainly heard his effect on Mary. There seemed to be no set time when this phantom lover came. I had tried sneaking out to the toilet late at night, waiting to see him come in or leave. It never worked out. Mary was evasive when I dropped hints about her visitor. When he visited, they made love for what seemed like hours, keeping me awake. It got me thinking about women I'd been with. I began to fantasize about Patsy Jago while dreading the thought of having to play up to her girlish interests—she loved romance novels. Like most men, I had never indulged any girlfriends by pretending to be interested in fashion and teenage stars, but now I had started doing it to indulge the island's women.

In a strange coincidence, a few days after the dance, when Frankie and I were making our way along the top of the cliff, he stopped and pointed at two farmhouses in the valley to the south of the Veryan-Trewince road. "Anthony's and Jago's," he said. The Jago farm was a couple of miles to the east of us and the southernmost of the two.

"Relatives of Patsy?" I asked, remembering where she had gotten off the bus.

"You know Patsy?" He seemed not to have noticed that we had both been at the dance.

"Met her at the dance."

"*Rum tumty ti tum*," he replied.

"What the hell does that mean, Frankie?"

"For me to know, you to find out. That's Patsy's house."

"But she got off the bus at the school."

"You notice a lot, don't you?" He grinned, slyly. "She was staying with Esther Cocking."

"It's hard not to notice the younger women, Frankie. There aren't very many of them."

"Like auks." A sneaky smile crossed his face. "Got to find eggs."

I went on to the rookery alone to find Nellie servicing one of her boyfriends, Dick this time. I hoped that my pictures would do justice to the moment. During six weeks of watching, this was the first time I had caught one of the girls at it when I had my camera handy. Murphy's Law, the wind, rain, incompetence, and Frankie had screwed up my previous attempts. The pictures were going to contribute to a great doctoral dissertation, "The Sexual Habits of Aukus Roselandis." Aukus Interruptus was a better description, I thought. Nellie was amazingly skillful at organizing coitus interruptus. One second, the male mounted her, humping away. The next second, she executed something like a lateral arabesque, and he was on his own, shuddering to a climax. The sight made me think erotic thoughts of Patsy.

9.

AT BREAKFAST ONE MORNING MARY SURPRISED ME WITH A question. "When I was cleaning your room yesterday I noticed a trumpet. Did you play in a band?"

"Yeah, in a marching band in high school and a little bit in college."

"What did you play?"

"All kinds...marches, pop, show tunes. Why do you ask?"

"Andy, we have a local band. Not the one you heard at the dance. This one plays at fetes and so on. Their trumpet player's been ill. Would you be able to play in his place?"

"Sure, I could give it a try, if it doesn't interfere with my studies too much."

"Good, I'll tell Charlie Gay. He's the band master."

My comment about not interfering with my work was a fake. Secretly, I looked forward to having something else to do. I took my trumpet to the rookery and practiced with a mute, watching the burrows through the observation slot. The noise of the birds and the wind must have drowned out my playing, for it didn't disturb the auks.

Charlie Gay, the bandmaster, came to the house early the next

Saturday. He asked about my experience, and I played a few short pieces on my trumpet; thank God I'd practiced.

"Ernie Anthony's laid up, and the band don't sound right without him," he said. "We'd be right pleased if you'd join us."

I didn't need any persuading. If women were off limits, I needed more than the occasional dance as recreation. "Thanks for asking. I'd like to do it."

"We'll practice this Monday in chapel hall here, starting at six thirty. Every other Monday we use the hall in Portloe. You can come with me." He paused. "Oh. You'll need a uniform. I'll have to see what we've got."

I worried for a moment about whether I'd have enough time to practice. "When do we perform next?"

"On Guy Fawkes Day, November fifth. There'll be a big bonfire in a field near the school."

"Not much time to practice, but—"

"You'll be fine. I suppose you Yanks don't celebrate Guy Fawkes. You should. He tried to blow up Parliament." He laughed. "When the governor visits, some of us wish Fawkes had succeeded."

"I heard about Guy Fawkes when I stayed with my relatives in Scotland," I said.

"Scottish, eh? I thought I heard a trace of a burr."

"Any other events?"

"There'll also be Midsummer's Day, the Summer Solstice…December twenty-first, here in Veryan. I think you'll find it interesting."

"Any particular reason?"

"You'll see," he grinned. "I reckon you won't know most of the pieces we play, so I brought you some sheet music. Oh dear, I'm getting late for the bus. The missus will be upset.

We're visiting her brother this afternoon." He shook my hand and rushed away.

I sat on the sofa and scanned the music. I knew a few pieces, like the "Wedding March," the "Londonderry Air," and some marches by Sousa. But some titles I'd never heard before—"Lamorna," "The Oggy Man," "The Floral Dance," "Poor Bugger Janner," and "Starry Gazy Pie." I went to my room and picked out the melody of each of them in turn on my trumpet. They were simple enough. The one that caught my attention was "The Floral Dance." The refrain had a rhythm that could be hummed as *rum tumti ti tum / ti ti rum tum tum* in 4/4 time. It sounded like something was going to happen on either Guy Fawkes Day or Midsummer's Day. From what Throgmorton had written, one or both might involve pagan festivities. I wondered what Patsy Jago would do, since she had been chosen.

I joined the seven men and two women in the hall that Monday night for practice. Charlie introduced me. "I expect you all know that Andy Ferguson here is visiting us from America. He has kindly agreed to take Ernie's place on the trumpet."

I had seen a number of them at the dance. I was surprised to find Patsy Jago in the group, carrying a flute. She grinned at me. "Nice to see you again, Patsy," I said, smiling.

The burly man standing next to her looked at me closely. He was Patsy's father, Jacob Jago, and the big bass drum player. Arthur Nancarrow was a violin player. Edgar Cocking played the euphonium, George Anthony the bassoon, Jim Nichols the trombone, and Roddy Gay—Charlie's son—the clarinet.

Petunia Gay, Charlie's wife, was another violin player. She had a flower-like face befitting her name. Short brown curly hair with a touch of gray framed a light tan, flashing white teeth, and twinkling bright blue eyes. It was an interesting face with one peculiarity: it appeared that at some time her nose had been broken. She reminded me of somebody.

We practiced hard, tough going for me even though I read music fairly well. There was the sheet music, which had a few annotations to explain what each player had to do, and then there was the way they were used to hearing the music. By the end of the evening, I had the rudiments in their versions, of "The Oggy Man," "Lamorna," "Starry Gazy Pie," "Anchors Aweigh," and the British national anthem. We also had a go at a few tunes I had played before: "The Saints Go Marching In," "the Tennessee Waltz," and surprisingly, the Elvis hit "Heartbreak Hotel." After two hours, we decided to go to the pub—except the Jagos. I could hear Jacob Jago and his daughter arguing.

Petunia took my arm. "Poor Jacob, that Patsy's quite a handful. Thank the Lord it will be over soon."

"You mean, because she's been chosen?"

Petunia let go of my arm quickly.

"I'm sorry. Did I say something wrong?"

"Never you mind." She headed toward the door.

Then I remembered where I'd seen an image of Petunia—on the dock in Portloe. I held the door for her. "Jenny Nacarrow looks—"

"My daughter," Petunia said smiling.

The inside of the pub looked better than it appeared from the outside. An old Victorian bar, with mirrors behind it, took up most of the wall that abutted the store. Mary was behind the bar. Her hair was up, and she was wearing a blouse that showed a lot of cleavage. Two men I'd seen at the dance were sitting on bar stools chatting with her. She waved to me.

Bench seats stood against the back wall and the side facing the bar. Wooden chairs were clustered around the tables in front of wall-mounted bench seats. The walls and ceiling were paneled and dark brown from years of smoking. A dartboard was on the front wall to the side of the entrance. The front door opened toward it, protecting new arrivals from errant darts. Old lithographs of English hunting scenes were scattered over the remaining wall area. The air was hazy with tobacco smoke.

As we went to our seats, an older woman came over and took Petunia's arm. Petunia motioned to me. "This is Andy Ferguson," she said.

"I've heard about you," the woman said, grinning. I'm Martha Nancarrow. Nice to meet you."

Isaac's wife, I'd heard, but not a bit like him. "It's a pleasure," I said.

"Please excuse us, Andy," Martha said. "Pet and I have a lot to talk about."

Charlie motioned for me to sit between him and Roddy.

Mary came over and bent to talk to Charlie. "What'll you have?"

"We'll all have the usual, Mary." He turned to me. "Beer okay with you?"

"Sure, beer will be great," I replied distractedly, as I tried not to look down Mary's blouse. I could see that it was also an effort for Charlie and Roddy. To hide my embarrassment I decided I had to say something else. "What's Starry Gazy Pie?" I blurted out.

Now they were both grinning. "So that's what you were thinking about, Andy? You seemed very absorbed. You tell him, Mary!"

"I've got customers to serve," she said, chuckling. "I'll tell you later, Andy. In fact, better still, I'll ask Clara to make it for you. She's a good cook."

"Stargazy Pie," muttered Roddy, shaking his head. "It's not what I were thinking about." We sat in silence until the drinks came, foaming pint mugs of Cornish beer— the sign above the bar said St. Austell Brewery's best. Imported? I guessed not.

"You did right well, young Andy," said Charlie.

"I think I'm getting the hang of it. I've got most of the notes okay, but I'm still learning the phrasing."

"You're doing fine, isn't he, Roddy?" Roddy nodded. "It'll take a little longer to get used to our way of doing things, Andy. Now, we don't have to have a trumpet in every piece, so I think it would be best if you concentrated on a few of the tunes for Guy Fawkes. I'll give you a list."

"Thanks," I replied. "That sheet music you gave me was very helpful. I noticed we didn't play all of the music today."

"That's right. Some of the music is for special occasions. Like the 'Wedding March.'"

"'The Floral Dance' too, I suppose?"

A moment of silence before Charlie said, "We'll take that up after Guy Fawkes."

"For Midsummer's Day?" When would somebody let me know what was going to happen? Why the secrecy?

"Yes."

I hummed a few notes, "*rum tumty titum.*"

Charlie looked at me quizzically. "I don't know what you've heard, Andy, but some things are best left alone. Enough said. Tell us about America."

The rest of the evening passed quietly. I talked about where

I came from, about my family, and how I had met the professor. They also wanted to hear about the auks. I explained the professor's theory and said he seemed to be right. They did not appear surprised.

"Got to play with the hand you're dealt," Roddy said ruefully, in an apparent allusion to the lack of girls on Roseland.

At the end of the evening, I watched my friends walk and bicycle away, appearing more sober than I felt. I wove my way home across the grass, picking up my feet to avoid tripping on the clumps of grass, in the exaggerated manner of a typical drunk. As I approached Mary's house, I sensed that something about the square was different. I turned to see if my eyesight had let me down. It had not. The oil lamp, permanently burning by the door of the Seythan House, illuminated a strange figure wearing a top hat, slumped in the stocks.

"Are you okay," I asked on reaching him.

No answer. I put my hands down and lifted the drooping head. A garish papier-mâché bearded face gaped at me from under the top hat. I jumped back in surprise, tripped, and fell. Were islanders watching me and laughing? No. The square was dark. I was alone with the dummy, which dropped to its original position. I scuttled home and went to bed. Later that night I had to pee. When I returned to my room, I looked out of my window. The dummy was sitting up.

When I went down to breakfast, the dummy was gone. I told Mary what I had seen.

She raised her eyebrows. "Too much beer, Andy. I should have warned you about the band. Drunken lot."

"But I did see it."

Mary shook her head and ladled scrambled eggs onto my plate. After breakfast, she picked up her school bag and headed for the door. I started on the eggs and was surprised when a she returned a moment later, carrying a paper.

"Newsletter," she said, dropping it on the kitchen table before heading out again. "You're famous."

I finished the dishes and picked it up. A grainy photograph of me arriving in Portloe filled half the front page. The headline read, "Yank comes her to study auks." The accompanying article mentioned how I had been sent by Professor Gareth Llewellyn Jones and was staying with Mary Pascoe. More space was devoted to telling how Frankie Quick and Arthur Nancarrow had helped me get started. I turned to the back page and found—surprise, surprise—that Clara was the editor and main reporter. Other articles described a soccer match between Portloe and Veryan—score 3-2 to Portloe—a women's sewing class at the Portloe hall, a summary of the month's fishing catch, and an advertisement for an upcoming performance of *The Tempest* by William Shakespeare, arranged by Clara Quick. Arranged? What did that mean? There were no entries under births and deaths.

* * *

During the following period, Nellie prepared her nest in the burrow at the end of the ledge nearest my blind. Fred brought her presents of dried grass and feathers to line the nest. I continued to practice the trumpet at the rookery using a mute. It helped to fill the time until Nellie would lay her egg in the last week of October. Her burrow, obviously an old one, was about two or three feet deep. Like all auk's nests it had a bend where the young auks did their business so as not to soil the nest area at the back. Using a mirror on a long stick, I found out later that there were two eggs, very unusual. From then on, either Nellie or Fred remained in the burrow incubating them. Usually they would stay for a couple of hours. Fred spent more time at the job than Nellie. I could picture him napping contentedly.

The egg-laying increased as we approached Guy Fawkes Day, and I saw a similar scene playing out all over the rookery. This was a difficult time for the spare males. They didn't have a role. Nellie's men friends—Tom, Dick, and Harry—hung around and occasionally left food at the entrance to the burrow, usually small thin silvery fish called *snaveling* by the islanders. All the other extras seemed confused and spent a lot of time pacing on the ledge. I didn't have time to pace. I had only a short time left to practice for Guy Fawkes Day. I was looking forward to the experience.

* * *

One interesting fact emerged at the next band practice; Patsy would not be playing in the band after Guy Fawkes Day. Patsy's brother, Paul, a toothy male version of Patsy, showed up with her. Paul had plenty of musical talent. It seemed to confirm that Patsy had some other role to play at the festival. She had been "chosen," whatever that meant.

Other than the auks, I did not have a lot to think about on the island and not knowing this secret bugged me. Again, I came back to the professor's story about Pavlov. What was it? Something about life on Roseland being boring....

"Having fun whiles the time away," he'd said. "Mind games to teach him a lesson. Pavlov was his name, you see. Very appropriate! They led him on a merry dance, *rum tum ti tum.*"

Was this how the islanders had fun in this isolated spot? Could I be a candidate for their games? Far-fetched, I thought, and I soon forgot about it.

10.

FRANKIE WAS STRANGELY EXCITED WHEN GUY FAWKES DAY came, and he pestered me at the rookery with questions and comments about why we did not have it in the States, how I felt, and how great the bonfire was going to be. He was talking to himself, never listening to my answers, and never accepting that we did not celebrate the occasion. Over the previous weeks, on my trips to Portloe for band practice, I'd seen the huge pile of wood growing in a field near the school. Frankie was right—it was going to be a hell of a blaze, and I was excited, too. I left the rookery in the early afternoon to join the band for one last practice session in Veryan.

Our practice was not marked by any of the complicated marching that I had been used to at football games. We stayed together in a group as we paraded from the small Round Houses along the road to the square and around it once. Charlie Gay, sometimes walking backwards, led us and conducted with his hands. Jim Nichols was next, playing the trombone with abandon; he was in front so that he would not hit anyone with his instrument. The fiddle players came after him. Roddy Gay on the clarinet and Patsy's brother, Paul, on the flute were next in line. I followed with Patsy. Charlie explained that Patsy and I would both sit out the pieces that I did not play, as he could easily drop out a row. It did not make a lot of sense to me. I had mixed emotions about being alone with Patsy but what the hell. Behind us were the bassoon and euphonium. Patsy's father brought up the rear with his drum.

The practice went well. During our off time in Veryan, Patsy and I sat on the stocks and chatted. I had hoped to be asking the questions. Not so, Patsy wanted to know everything about the States. She sat very close to me, making sure we were touching. I hoped her father was not paying attention. She asked what American girls wore, about the latest fad in music, about television, and if it was true that everybody owned a car. She listened raptly to my answers.

"Ooh, I'd so love to go to the States."

"Maybe you will some day."

"I dunno when I could. My dad wouldn't like it, what with me being...."

"Chosen?"

"How did you...." She stood up. "Anyway, I want to go. I'll write to my Auntie Mabel. That's what I'll do. I've got lots more questions. They can wait until tonight"

How come they could ask questions, but they deflected mine? "About being ch—"

"Look. Charlie wants us back." Patsy interrupted my question.

"Is that the Mabel Thomas who works for the professor?"

"You've met her? Of course you have. The professor sent you here, didn't he?" She rolled her eyes and poked me in the ribs.

What did she imply? Was there more to their relationship?

* * *

When Mary came downstairs on Guy Fawkes Day, she was wearing a long white dress—like a priestess—a purple belt, a strange, ancient-looking necklace and—unusual for her—a ton of makeup. I must have shown my surprise.

"We women like to dress up for Guy Fawkes."

"You look—"

"Tarty? That's the idea."

"I was going to say sexy. Boy, I wish you were with me."

"I am."

"You know what I mean."

Mary shook her head and smiled. "If I was younger, Andy."

"I don't care."

"The Cap'n would. Now, you behave yourself."

I remembered Artley's comment on the boat about his uncle being unhappy that I would be staying with Mary. Now I was sure that the Cap'n was the lover I had heard but not seen.

We did not speak on the way to the field by the school. As she left me to join the Cap'n, she kissed me quickly on the cheek. "Have a good time. Be careful!"

Careful about what? Patsy, probably. I scanned the crowd but couldn't see her. It looked like the entire population had come to the field. Large open-fronted tents contained tables covered with food, and small tents at the bottom of the field acted as temporary toilets. In the center of the field was a ten-foot-high pile of wood. A bulkier version of the figure that I had seen in the stocks was tied to a post that rose out of the stack of wood.

Our band assembled. Charlie waved his hands and we

marched once around the woodpile playing, "Lamorna." When we stopped marching, Cap'n Billing emerged from the crowd, leading six members of the Seythan, including one woman, Petunia Gay, who also wore a long white dress, purple belt, heavy metal jewelry, and too much makeup. The men, including Isaac Nancarrow and Jacob Jago, were wearing naval looking hats and chains of office. Frankie was close behind them. Cap'n Billing raised his hands and we stopped playing.

"Mrs. Trevenna is unable to be here, and she has asked me to speak for her. We are gathered to celebrate the foiling of Guy Fawkes's attempt to disrupt the rule of Britain. In doing so we remind ourselves of the need to be ever vigilant in our efforts to maintain order on our own island. God save the Queen!"

"God save the Queen!" the crowd chanted in unison.

This was our cue to play the British national anthem. The islanders sang with emotion. While this was happening, someone prepared a torch. Cap'n Billing took it, saluted the crowd, and plunged it into the pile of wood. With a tremendous swooshing sound, flames enveloped its base. Our band celebrated by playing "Anchors Aweigh" and then "The Oggy Man." When he heard the music, Frankie jumped up and down with excitement and ran around the fire, whooping. He was joined immediately by a weird-looking figure wearing a long black cloak, black trousers, and boots. As the figure came toward me, the fire flared and lit up the devil's mask that covered its face; lurid eyes stared at the crowd, and bright red horns thrust ominously in the air. Other outlandish figures followed. They wore witches masks above flowing white dresses and belts and jewelry like Mary's and Petunia's as they pranced around the fire, taunting the burning figure strapped to its summit. The crowd cheered. We finished the march, and the beer and cider started to flow.

"Best take a break now, lads," said Charlie. "Mustn't miss the beer."

"What the hell are they, Charlie?" I asked, pointing at the strange figures.

"Maskers. We don't forget the old times, Andy."

So this was what Throgmorton had meant. "Like Carnival?"

"I guess so."

Patsy grabbed my arm before I could ask more questions. "Come on, Andy. I'll show you where the good stuff is."

"Tell me about those maskers!"

"Can't!"

"Why not?"

"Don't know, really."

She didn't *know* or she didn't know whether she could *tell* me? Before I could ask, she steered me to a keg at the side of the field. We joined the line in front of it. Esther and a small, rotund man were handing out plastic cups.

Patsy introduced me. "Andy, you've met my friend Esther. This is her dad, Edgar Cocking."

"I've heard about you, Mr. Ferguson." He grinned. "Having fun with the auks?"

"Yes, thank you, sir. It's going very well. Frankie's been a great help."

"Good." Mr. Cocking smiled. "Now, young Patsy, if you're going to look after Mr. Ferguson, you be careful! These Yanks have quite a reputation." His face was stern and he was not grinning anymore.

Patsy made a face. "I can't imagine what you're thinking, Mr. Cocking."

I paid for our beers.

"Come on, Andy, everyone wants to meet you." "Everyone" included Patsy's girlfriends, whose interests were mainly about clothes, music, teen idols, and dating in the States. I did my best to answer their questions.

Back in the band, we played our full repertoire over the next hour or so, with useful breaks for more beer and food. In between playing, I managed to escape Patsy's attentions for a while, and Arthur Nancarrow introduced me to more of the islanders. Every one of them wanted to hear about the auks. They seemed to be very proud of the Roseland auk, and they were amused by my research.

By the last break, I was beginning to feel lightheaded from the beer and cider. I found a stand offering that wonderful meat, potato, and rutabaga (swede to them) turnover—the Cornish pasty. I ate it quickly and recovered my equilibrium enough for my final stint with the band.

The bonfire had eliminated Guy Fawkes up to his top hat, which was by now a smoldering shape on top of the huge pile of embers. Except that the remains of the hat were perched on what looked like a charred skull with fragments of skin and white hair still attached to it.

"What the hell?" I said turning to see if anyone else had noticed, and finding a masker standing behind me.

A muffled man's voice said, "Someone's idea of a practical joke. Forget about it."

"But, I saw…."

The masker disappeared into the crowd of islanders who were moving to the east side of the field, where the fireworks

97

had been set up for viewing against the darkest part of the sky. I looked at the skull again—sheep's head—the Nancarrow boys' idea of a joke. I returned to the band. We stood to the side of the crowd, ready to play a special set of music to accompany the display. But Patsy and I were not included. I needed to pee, so I headed toward the toilets.

"Where you going, Andy?" she said.

I motioned at the toilets.

"I'll come with you." Patsy did not give me a chance to argue and grabbed my arm. The area at the bottom of the field was deserted. Before I could go into the toilet, Patsy pulled me behind the tent.

"Patsy, what—?"

Her arms were around my neck and her mouth was covering mine, her tongue forcing my lips open. To be honest, I didn't think of resisting for more than a millisecond. God, I needed the feel of a woman even more than I had needed a pee. My hands were against her breasts. I gave them a squeeze and then slid my hands down to grasp her soft round bottom. She held me tighter and ground her body against me. Her right hand came down to between my legs and she started caressing me. She knew what she was doing. When I started to move my hands around the top of her legs, she suddenly let go and backed away.

"Kissing's okay, and I can touch you, but you mustn't touch me like that. It's the rule. I shouldn't have." Looking frightened, she took a mirror, lipstick, and a handkerchief out of her bag and repaired her makeup. "Best get back. I'll go first."

I wiped the lipstick off my face while I stood in agony waiting for my erection to go down so I could relieve myself. Despite the discomfort, I managed to wonder what she meant by "The rule." Whose rule, the Seythan's? I watched the fireworks as I walked back, a surprising display for this isolated island. The crowd was engrossed in watching, and I concluded that no one had seen Patsy and me. I stood at the back and watched the end of the show. People started to disperse. I felt a hand on my shoulder.

"Where were you? I was looking everywhere," asked Mary.

"Toilets. I had too much beer."

"We need to get the bus. I heard you in the band. You play well."

"Thanks."

"Have a good time?"

"Sure did. Except, I've learned not to mix beer and cider. Boy, that cider's something else. Where I come from it's not alcoholic."

"Really? How strange. Are you okay now?"

"I think so. Thank God for Cornish pasties. I reckon they absorb booze."

Mary laughed. "I'll make them for dinner some time. Oh, by the way, Clara's invited us to her house on Wednesday. She's going to make stargazy pie. Now, you'd better like that, too. It's Frankie's favorite."

Patsy wasn't on the bus. Staying with her friend Esther, I guessed. She would not be coming to band practice until after Midsummer's Day and I probably wouldn't see her again for a while.

I followed Mary upstairs. As she went into her room, she turned. "You can wipe lipstick off your face, Andy, but it's harder to get it off your collar. I warned you before about Patsy. Please don't do anything stupid."

I took my shirt off. She was right. Damn it. I wondered who else had noticed.

11.

I HAVE HEARD STORIES ABOUT TRIBES IN THE MIDDLE EAST offering a sheep's eye to foreigners. Supposedly it is an honor to eat this delicacy. Another side of the story is that the Bedouin hosts smirk behind their beards as they watch the discomfort of their polite guests, who do not want to cause offense by refusing the honor. I reckon that the Cornish invented that fish concoction, stargazy pie, for the same reason. Mary showed me the recipe later. After the fish are cooked in milk, the meat is removed from the bones and put in the pie with potatoes and other vegetables. Fine, but the little fish heads are retained to stick out of the crust, and their glazed, dead eyes stare up at the cosmos—hence the name.

I could see Mary watching me covertly as Clara brought the pie from the oven to the table. Clara's face showed only the concentration of not wanting to drop the hot dish. Frankie's bright eyes were focused on the pie. He was holding his knife and fork and jiggling on his chair in anticipation. Mary looked hard in my direction, her eyes warning me not to say anything. Unlike a Bedouin, she did not have a beard to hide her expression. Clara served the pie with extra potatoes and carrots. Each of us received a piece of the crust with a head in it. Frankie stuck his fork through the head and raised it to his mouth. *Oh shit*, I thought, *I am not going to do that.*

Clara's solemn face changed to one of childish delight as she suppressed a giggle. "You should see your face, Andy. Frankie's been waiting for this for days."

I joined in the laughter, "Very funny." In that strange way that the brain makes connections, I suddenly realized I no longer had anyone to share in the joke. My face must have shown my mood change.

"Are you all right?"

"I'm fine, Clara. I just thought of…oh, nothing."

"The one you left behind?" Clara's voice sounded wistful. "Nothing should come between true lovers—not time, nor distance, nor cruel people." She seemed to be talking to a painting of Brown Willy on the wall. Later, I wondered if it was a line from a play.

"Let's eat before it gets cold," said Mary.

Despite its strange look, the pie tasted good. We continued in silence until the plates were clean. After we had cleared the dishes, Clara shooed us into her living room. Frankie stayed with her in the kitchen, and I could hear laughter.

I glanced at some watercolors of seascapes. To my untutored eye, the paintings looked very professional. They were signed "Clara Trevenna."

"Did Clara do these paintings?" I asked Mary.

"Yes, Andy. She's always been very artistic. It's a pity…."

"Something happened to her?"

Mary shook her head. "Can't say…pudding's coming."

Clara appeared, carrying a tray with a plum pie and cream. Frankie followed with bowls and spoons.

"Who should I serve first?" Clara muttered to herself. She looked distracted.

"Ladies first," I said, indicating Mary.

"Yes, ladies first." She dithered.

"Mary says you're putting on a play," I said after she had ladled pie into Mary's bowl.

Clara stopped dithering. "*The Tempest*. It's one of my favorites."

"Who's in it?" I held out my bowl.

"Frankie plays Caliban and James Thomas is Antonio. Esther will be Miranda. Jane will play Prospera if she's feeling better."

"I thought it was Prospero!"

"No dear. It's Prospera." Clara smiled sweetly. Mary and Frankie had their heads down, but I could see that they were grinning.

I shrugged. "What about you?"

"I'll be Ariel. It's a good part," she answered mischievously.

"When's opening night?"

"Weekend after next in the hall."

Seeing the expectant look on Clara's face, I said, "I'll be there."

"Would you like to be in the play?" Clara asked, looking at me sideways. "You could be the governor's aide de camp."

"I tried acting once. I wasn't very good."

Clara cajoled me. "I could teach you." She paused and looked at the painting again. I decided to wait and see what her plays involved before taking it on. "Maybe next time," I said.

"I'll remember that, Andy. I don't give up easy." Clara smiled, but her eyes were cold.

As we ate the plum pie—which was delicious—Clara, prompted by Frankie, asked me about the auks. I explained what had happened so far, being careful to emphasize Frankie's role in helping me. Clara nodded. However, I could not tell whether she understood what I was saying, except for the bits about Frankie. I wondered if she had suffered a nervous breakdown when she was young, another puzzle on this curious island. On the short walk home I tried to find out more, but Mary was uncommunicative. The only fact I learned was that Jane Trevenna was Clara's sister-in-law. It was hard for Mary to be coy about it because the name "Clara Trevenna" was on the paintings.

* * *

The final weeks in November crept by. At the rookery, most of the auk pairs had finished their nests and laid eggs. Nellie and Fred took turns at incubation, although Fred continued to spend more time in the burrow than Nellie. She spent most of the time between fishing trips on the ledge fussing around her territory and chatting to her friends. Fred used the time to rest. I imagined him sitting happily on the nest thinking profound auk thoughts. I tried unsuccessfully to identify marks that would distinguish Fred from the gentlemen friends. During this peaceful time, I wrote notes and sketched the birds and the scenery to supplement my photographs. Frankie must have had some other job to do, because he rarely appeared.

We had now started rehearsing "The Floral Dance" and I practiced with a muted trumpet. The days continued to be peaceful until the morning when I heard Patsy calling to me from the top of the cliff. "Andy, I know you're there. I heard you playing the trumpet."

I briefly considered taking Frankie's route down the cliff and hiding, rationalizing that it would encourage Patsy to follow and put her in danger. In fact, we were on the edge of her family's farm, and she probably knew the cliffs well. I peered out of the blind.

"I'll come up to you."

Patsy ignored me and came to the blind, picking her way through the gorse with ease. She was wearing jeans and a shirt that was unbuttoned at the top to show the bulge of her breasts.

"So this is your little hidey hole, Andy." She brushed by me to get inside. "It's real good," she said, kneeling to look through the slot at the rookery. "You can see everything. Which one's Nellie?"

I pointed. "That's Nellie, the one fussing at those other auks. They are her gentlemen friends."

"Oh, you mean the ones that don't get the real thing?"

"You were listening when your friends were asking all those questions, weren't you?"

"I always listen to you, Andy."

We were wedged together, looking through the slot. Her body was soft against my side. "Oh, shit," I muttered under my breath, "Here we go again."

Patsy turned quickly, grabbed me, and pulled us down onto the plastic floor. She was on top, her mouth open against mine, her tongue working feverishly. I tried half-heartedly to move away, then gave up and held her round backside. After a while, she lifted up and rolled beside me. She slid her hand down and stroked expertly. "Remember, Andy, you can't touch me like this."

"You're kidding."

"No I'm not. I'll make it nice for you. I've been trained."

"You've been what?" I laughed.

"Can't say no more. Do you want me to do it?"

"You mean give me a hand job? Are you good at it?"

"I don't know. You'd be the first real one."

"You mean like you practiced on dummies?"

"You might say that."

"Can I touch up here? I ran my hand across the top of her shirt."

"Suppose it would be okay."

I unbuttoned the rest of her shirt and pulled it up. She took it off and let me remove her bra, releasing firm, hefty breasts. Patsy knelt over me, swinging them across my face. Oh God, being with a woman again gave me a warm and sexy feeling. She turned, unzipped my pants, and then pulled everything down. She studied my erection with interest. "Are they all, like, this size?

"It's not a subject I've studied, Patsy." I wasn't convinced she didn't know the answer, but I looked again. Sitting in a hide on a remote island in the southern Atlantic answering questions about my penis was not what I'd anticipated doing as part of my PhD. "Some bigger, some smaller I guess."

"Well, I'll soon find out."

"Midsummer's Day?"

"Maybe." She started to stroke me. Whoever had taught her had done a good job. She now had her back to me and I reached around to hold her breasts. I was so aroused that I came quickly.

"Watch out!"

She continued to watch intently, until I had finished, then

turned, showing me her wet hand. Her face was excited. "Did I do right?"

"Oh yes, Patsy. You did fine."

"I so want you to do it in the proper place, Andy." She motioned between her legs.

"You'll have to tell me when. I don't understand what your being chosen and 'hands off your stuff' means."

Patsy looked worried. "I can't tell you." She wiped her hands on the plastic floor and leant over me, her face close to mine. "I really love you, Andy. I had to do that business with you first. My dad'll kill me if he finds out. I told him I was going to pick blackberries."

"Did you?"

Her face took on a crafty look. "I picked some yesterday and more today. They're in my basket back there."

"You're a clever girl. What did you mean when you said you wanted me to be the first?"

She did not answer for a while. "You mustn't tell anybody. Cross your heart and hope to die."

I looked at her incredulously.

"I mean it."

"Okay, I swear I will not tell anybody." I crossed my heart. It felt silly, like I was back in elementary school, but it satisfied Patsy.

"I'm to do it for the men."

"You mean all the men?"

"No silly! The Seythan picks seven unmarried men."

"You mean like Frankie."

"Ooh God, Frankie! I hope not. Now you've got me worried."

"Is that all, then? You give them a hand job?"

"Yes, but not exactly all."

"There's more?"

"You see, I'll be the Queen."

"Like a Midsummer's Day Queen?"

"Yes, and there's a King. He gets to have me." She giggled. "You should see your face."

"You've got to be kidding. Does the Seythan choose this King from the seven?"

"Yes."

"Do you know who it will be? Or who the seven will be?"

"The Seythan announces it the week before."

"Has this been going on a long time? Does every girl do it?"

"Not every girl. I know my mother did it. That's how she got Dad."

"Mary, Clara, Petunia, did they all do it?"

"Might have. Of course, poor Clara." She stopped and buried her head on my shoulder. "Don't like to think of that."

"Did something go wrong? Is that why everyone is so concerned about Frankie?"

I heard a muffled, "Can't say."

"How do you feel about doing it?"

"I'm scared, but it's an honor. I will think of you all the time." Her mouth closed on mine, and we lay for a long time gently kissing.

When she had gone, I picked up my trumpet and played "The Floral Dance." I did not use the mute. Patsy had explained the reason for the *rum ti tumpties* and the hints that had started with the professor, Throgmorton's book, and the stuff about the Russian, Pavlov. It was hard to believe, although Patsy and her efficient, trained hand job gave it credibility. In a few weeks, the big day would arrive and I would see for myself. Well, what would I see? Presumably, the Queen and her gentlemen friends didn't do it in public. Where did the islanders get the system? Was it because of a permanent lack of women? Why not bring in more women from the outside? What about relief for the single men who were not chosen, and what did they do the rest of the year, for God's sake? It was frustrating having so many unanswered questions.

12.

ON THE FIRST SATURDAY IN DECEMBER, I WENT WITH MARY to the dance in the chapel hall. Patsy did not come, but her friend Esther was there, wearing a very short skirt and dangly earrings. Cap'n Billing came and Mary did the last waltz with him, adding to my belief that he was her mysterious lover. Esther grabbed me, and when the lights went out her arms were around my neck and her mouth was working passionately against mine. *What the hell,* I thought and responded. She disengaged quickly before the end of the dance and whispered, "Wipe your mouth. I don't want to upset Frankie." When the lights came on, she was looking at me coyly. Her lipstick was smudged and she had lost an earring. As we looked for it on the floor, I whispered. "You need to fix your lipstick." Esther did so while I found the missing earring.

"Thanks, Andy." Esther smiled, showing lipstick-covered teeth.

"Say hi to Patsy, will you?"

"Can't say I'll see her before you know what." She winked and left. Mary had disappeared, so I went back to the house alone. I heard her come in a few hours later, also alone it seemed.

The auk eggs hatched during the next week. I had been curious about how old Fred would cope with the demands of providing food. I had not anticipated the help provided by Nellie's regular customers from the mating season, Tom, Dick, and Harry. When the two eggs hatched, men-friends all brought fish for Nellie and her youngsters. Was this another reason for the strange arrangements of the auks: to handle the short supply of fish in the sea below the rookery? Frankie had told me that the islanders did not go there because of the jagged rocks and dangerous currents. I wondered if the stock was marginal for feeding the huge number of sea birds. I made a note to ask young Artley.

Another problem might be the skuas. I had seen them stealing fish the auks had caught. As an auk came up from the sea, a skua would dive-bomb it, causing the auk to tumble in the air. Often, the poor auk would panic and release its fish. Quickly, the skua would scoop them up. Bastards! Unfortunately for the auks, three types of this bird inhabited the island: the great skua, the long-tailed jaeger and, a surprise so far from the mainland, the parasitic jaeger.

I was thinking about these problems when, in mid-afternoon, Patsy came into the blind. She looked at me angrily. "I heard what you did with Esther at the dance. I'm never going to speak to her again. How could you?"

How did she know? Her brother, of course! "She caught me by surprise, Patsy. I wasn't expecting it."

"Says you." She was close to me now and I put my arms around her.

"Are we okay then?"

"Guess so," she pouted. I kissed her and she responded passionately. I removed her shirt and bra. She pulled my pants down. This time when I moved my hands down she did not resist. She stroked me, I stroked her, and she was moaning. I kissed down her body and removed her shoes and socks. I buried my face into the warm denim between her legs. "Take them off," she whispered. I undid her belt and pulled her jeans and panties off. "Andy, promise me, you can do anything but you mustn't try the real thing."

I smiled and lowered my hand towards the mound of dark hair.

She grabbed my head and pulled me back up to her. "I mean it."

I nodded.

She kept her mouth glued to mine as we helped each other to a frantic climax. A fleeting image of another woman appeared at the last moment. Like Annie's face but confused by the images of other women I had known.

"I won't be seeing you again until after Midsummer's. You stay away from Esther! I've got to go."

"I have a question, Patsy. Where do you do it?"

"In Round House in square."

Some time after Patsy had left, when I was outside the blind above the rookery, Frankie appeared. "I saw you. Mustn't touch Patsy! She's been chosen."

"I don't know what that means, Frankie," I lied. "So I don't know what I can't do."

"Can't say." Frankie looked uncertain. I had presented him with a problem—if I didn't know, how could I be doing wrong? Apparently, he had not heard the saying that feigned ignorance of the law is no excuse. "I won't tell. You keep away from Patsy!"

"Okay, Frankie. You're a big help. Thanks for being my friend."

"Friend, am I?" He seemed to like the idea. "There'll be dancing, Midsummer's. Do you like 'The Floral Dance'?"

"Oh, yes."

"So do I." Frankie loped away toward the cliff edge and the gulls' nests.

Patsy had done more for me than give me temporary relief. She had made me relaxed, and I now found it easier to concentrate on the auks. I worked hard for the next hour or so observing their behavior and taking copious notes. The early afternoon had been sunny with the sea appearing in a multitude of blues and greens, the white caps small and orderly as the waves rolled in. As the afternoon progressed, clouds grew out to sea and over Brown Willy, the wind picked up, and the temperature dropped. The sea became blacker and the white caps reared violently.

I took a last look at the colony of auks before heading back for dinner. A spattering of wind-blown rain from the towering band of thunderclouds moving in over the sea to the west caused me to pull my parka's hood over my head.

By the time I reached the outskirts of the village, the rain pelted down and the wind tugged at my parka. The branches of the trees bordering the track whipped about. The sight of the Round House looming ahead made me think of the devil. I was glad that the villagers had built the strange house and the chapel across the road. I quickened my pace and ran between them as if the devil were behind me. The rain became more violent and I took shelter on the veranda of the Seythan House. A flash of lightning illuminated the Round House and the stocks, casting eerie shadows of tree branches on the walls. I felt isolated and scared—scared that something would happen to me because of Patsy. The rain abated briefly, and I ran to my house. A note on the kitchen table said that Mary would not be back until late and that I should fix my own supper. I changed my clothes and made tea and sandwiches.

The next day, Mary seemed distracted when she returned from school. Eventually, she spoke. "Andy, the Penseythan called the school. She wants to see you tomorrow afternoon. Mr. Thomas will pick you up in the Lagonda."

"Any particular reason she wants to see me?"

"I don't know exactly. She hasn't met you, and nothing happens on this island without her finding out about it." Mary's tone of voice showed concern.

I wondered whether she had heard about Patsy and me. Could Frankie have said something to Clara, who passed it on to Jane Trevenna? She probably wanted to ask about the auks. The happy thought escaped quickly as the professor's words rang in my head, "...*don't abuse their hospitality. The women are off-limits. Do not get tricked into doing something foolish. It could be the end of your PhD, or worse.*" Oh shit. "I guess it'll be my turn to find out."

"Be careful!" Mary looked worried.

13.

AN ANCIENT SEDAN PULLED INTO THE SQUARE, A 1930's
British Lagonda I found out later, a relic of a strange time
when an eccentric and independently wealthy Englishman
had been assigned to help run the island. He had insisted on
having the vehicle delivered, along with spare parts. It was a
condition of his contract. When he died—I never found out
how he dies—the car remained, one of only three cars on the
island. The other two were old Austins used as taxis.

The driver got out and motioned me to come to the car.

"Mr. Ferguson, I'm James Thomas. Mrs. Trevenna sent me
to fetch you." He ushered me into the back of the car quickly.
A sliding glass partition separated the driver from the rear
seats. It remained closed as we drove to Trewince. Shortly
after leaving Veryan, we passed a track on the right that I
remembered led to the Anthony and Jago farms. I wondered
how Patsy was doing. From then on, for the eight or so miles
to Trewince, there was only the turning on the left that led to
the school. The road traversed two hills that descended from
the southern cliffs, then it followed a gentle slope through
dense woods and crossed the river Fal before winding around

an extensive lawn to reach the house. The house was grand by the island's standards—two stories with a tiled roof, a substantial front door, and two large windows, downstairs and upstairs. Neat flowerbeds with roses graced the ground under the windows.

Mr. Thomas ushered me into the living room. Two straight-backed chairs were set in front of a large window that faced west and gave a spectacular view of the island spread out below Trewince. I could see the gorge and woods that descended to Portloe and a view of the farmland all the way to Brown Willy and even to the top of the cliff near the rookery. Large naval binoculars were mounted on a tripod in front of the left part of the window.

"Mrs. Trevenna, Mr. Ferguson is here to see you."

I turned. A tall woman entered stiffly, balancing with the aid of a silver-handled cane. A large hound padded next to her. Its ears were alert and it looked ready to lunge.

"Down, Winston!" The dog's head dropped. Its still eyes watched me warily. "I am Jane Trevenna. Please excuse me not shaking your hand. I need to use this silly stick until my leg gets better." She motioned at the other chair. "Sit with me and don't mind Winston. He can be protective, but he won't harm you while I'm here."

"He looks ready for action. I won't make any quick moves." My attempt at a joke fell flat. It sounded weak, like my knees felt.

"That would be wise, Mr. Ferguson. Mr. Thomas, would you be so good as to ask Miriam to make us some tea?"

Mrs. Trevenna wore a high-necked pleated blouse and a long gray skirt. Her iron-gray hair was in a bun, secured by a tortoiseshell clasp. Her sharply defined blue eyes looked at me out of a stern face. After some pleasantries about how I was settling in, she came to the point. If her intent was to intimidate me, she was successful. I felt like I was in the principal's office in elementary school.

"I would like to hear about the auks," she said.

Thank God for that.

"But first, Mr. Ferguson, let me be very clear about one thing. Patsy Jago is a silly young girl; nevertheless, she has an important role to play. I do not want to know what she has told you. Anyway, you are observant and it is possible that you might have discerned it on your own. Let me just say that we live on an isolated island. We have had to deal with the fact that there has been a...dearth of young women." She paused.

Dearth of young women. My mind wandered as I tried to imagine a young Jane Trevenna servicing seven men. These mind-boggling thoughts must have shown in my expression.

"It seems you are amused by this."

"Oh, no, ma'am. I don't understand it." *What the hell,* I thought. I might as well ask one of the questions that bothered me. "For whatever reason, if there are fewer young women, why don't you do what they did in the American West when there was a large surplus of men? Advertise for women who want a husband."

"Mr. Ferguson, it is not a simple matter. We are a very isolated community. This island can support only so many people. Many years ago, a wise predecessor of mine made a careful analysis of all aspects of living here, taking into account not only the obvious issue of food production, but also the need to maintain the essential skills. That Penseythan wrote a very well-reasoned paper that defined an appropriate population range and the—how would you say it—breakdown of jobs for the islanders. We have maintained such a stable population since then."

I glanced down at Winston. He seemed to be snoozing. Time to ask the other questions. "Why is there a dearth of—"

"A peculiarity…like the auks." She looked at me hard. "I understand that ours are the only ones outside the Northern Hemisphere?"

"That's what the professor told me. The furthermost south Atlantic puffins breed is Morocco. He thinks that a long time ago some of them must have migrated south and established a fresh colony. Possibly, a storm disoriented them when they were at sea."

"A plausible theory." Jane Trevenna looked thoughtful before returning to my question. "It is important to us that all of our population should have a similar ethnic background, by which I mean British. As to your first question: originally, the island's population was very small, and before the Penseythan's analysis we did advertise; too great a number of the applicants were unsuitable."

"So nobody leaves and nobody comes to stay permanently?"

"Of course not. A few do leave. Unfortunately, they are usually the ones who go away to improve their education. Then again a few have returned with a spouse, which is one reason we do not encourage the young people to travel."

I wanted to ask who these people were, but I could see she was becoming impatient with the subject.

"Back to Patsy Jago. You may not consort with her. She must fulfill her role on Midsummer's Day. If she is foolish enough to try to contact you in the meantime, you will ignore her. Am I clear?"

"Yes, ma'am."

"I understand that Jacob Jago does not know. This is fortunate. If he found out, I could not guarantee your safety."

"If he doesn't know, how do you?"

"That is my business. I see many things, Mr. Ferguson. We'll leave it at that. Again, do I have your assurance that you will not have any dealings with Patsy?"

"Yes, ma'am. I didn't understand how serious her role was."

"Good. As Penseythan, and on behalf of the Seythan, I make judgments on this island on how to handle bad behavior. In turn, you as a student of Professor Llewellyn Jones have been accepted here as a member of our island family. I have heard good reports from the many people with whom you have been involved. Mr. Gay says you are a good musician and an asset to our band. I appreciate the way you have worked with my nephew, Frankie, but you have abused our hospitality. If it happens again, I will be obliged to deal harshly with you...very harshly."

"I'm sorry, ma'am." Time to change the subject. "On the way to the rookery, I noticed some trees I've not seen before. They're native, I guess."

Before she could answer, Miriam came in carrying a large tray, which she placed on a low table to the side of the Penseythan's chair.

"Thank you, Miriam. My favorite, a Victoria sponge. Oh, and there's a little something for Winston." She put a plate on the floor.

The large piece of red meat disappeared in a flash. Winston licked his lips. I had the uncomfortable feeling that up till then he had been eyeing my ankles.

Jane Trevenna poured the tea and served each of us a generous slice of the cake. To take my mind off Winston, I concentrated on eating the cake; it was round and yellow with a ring of raspberry jelly oozing from the middle, and mouthwateringly delicious.

"Back to your question," she said. "Probably you're referring to the *Phylica arborea*, a kind of buckthorn. Now, let's get back to the auks. It seems that Gareth Jones is correct in his thesis about their behavior."

What a relief to get to a topic I enjoyed talking about. "I think so. As far as I can tell, there are three to four males for each female. She chooses one as a mate. I don't know how that choice is made."

"How does the female handle the advances of the spare males?"

"My favorite, Nellie, keeps her tail down. At the critical moment for the male, she does a kind of lateral arabesque and he's on his own."

Jane Trevenna chuckled. "How very clever of Nellie."

For a moment she looked very different and I could picture her in the Round House on Midsummer's Day.

"What do you plan to do to find out why the male to female ratio is so skewed?"

I started to give a very simplified answer.

She interrupted me. "Keep the children's answer for children, Mr. Ferguson. I am asking about genetics, chromosome anomalies, and so on."

"I'm sorry, I wasn't expecting you—"

"Mr. Ferguson, we may live in an isolated situation, but we are not uneducated. Our brightest children go on to university, generally in England, sometimes in the Americas. I attended Cambridge and then went on to take medical training."

She continued before I could ask whether she had qualified as a doctor. "So, what do you plan?"

"I'm going to try and get blood samples and look for features that might show some difference between the two types of male."

"I hope you don't plan to kill any of the auks."

"No, ma'am. Sometimes, the skuas kill or severely injure them. That's how I'll get samples."

Jane Trevenna nodded her head in approval.

"Earlier you commented on the study of island population done by one of the Penseythans," I said. "You said that he had done a jobs-analysis and implied you followed his recommendations. How do you do that?" I understood my error quickly.

"*She* did this analysis, Mr. Ferguson. Incidentally, she was an amateur ornithologist and wrote about our island's birds. I believe that she had a theory about the gender unbalance in the auk colony. But I have no record of it. Anyway, s*he* realized we would need medical expertise, teachers, farmers, fishermen, mechanics, and so on. Later, we added an electrical engineer and electricians for our telephone system, the radio and weather stations, and our power plant. We are very fortunate that the British government sends us our fuel as partial payment for operating the two stations and performing other…services."

I was about to ask what other service she meant, but she continued.

"My predecessor also set up our present educational system. It is based on the British system. Generally, we have about seventy children in the five-to-fifteen age groups. They all study the basics—reading, writing, mathematics, science, another language, history, geography, and art. The most capable, usually two each year, take further courses to prepare them for the possibility of attending a university or technological college abroad. Only a few of the brighter ones get the opportunity. I'm sure you can understand that it is hard for us to fund even such a small number of young women and men. Fortunately, we have done well in receiving grants, and kind friends have helped...such as Professor Llewellyn Jones. Recently, Mary's daughter, Rose, has been one of them, and also my son, John."

I wondered if John Trevenna was Rose's "understood" boyfriend. "You must be proud of him."

Her face softened and she turned to look at a photograph of a young man on a side table. "I am. He's doing well. Takes after his father."

"What is he studying?"

"Electrical and mechanical engineering, so that he can take responsibility for the island's power station, workshops, and weather station. John and Rose will handle some of the most important jobs for the island. They make a fine couple." She looked fondly at the photograph.

I decided to change the subject in case I asked the wrong question. "What about the rest of the children?"

"They are assigned as apprentices to learn the various trades we need."

"That's impressive, Mrs. Trevenna, I...." I stopped, wondering whether I should ask my next question. *What the hell*, I thought. I had nothing to lose. "I'm curious how you manage to maintain the population so tightly. Is there a restriction on the number of children, and—?"

"Maybe we could discuss that another time, Mr. Ferguson. Of course nowadays, contraceptives are readily available.

Now, please excuse me. I have various matters that require my attention. James Thomas will be here in a minute to take you back to Veryan. We must have tea again when you have learned more about the auks. There may be important lessons for the island." She left the room without elaborating. Winston went with her. *Phew.*

During tea, I had been eyeing the binoculars, wondering how much could be seen through them. Mr. Thomas had not appeared, so I went to take a look. I turned the binoculars toward the rookery and was amazed to find I had a clear view of the path running across the fields from Jago's farm. Jane Trevenna could have seen Patsy coming to visit me. I then took a quick look at the photograph of John Trevenna, seeing a pleasant enough face with dark eyes looking into the distance. I wondered if he had sported the fledgling moustache and beard to make him appear older.

A discreet cough alerted me to Mr. Thomas's arrival. "You get an amazing view, Mr. Thomas," I said, pointing to the binoculars.

He grunted noncommittally and indicated the door. We returned to Veryan as we had come, in silence. I found it hard to imagine this taciturn man as an actor. *The Tempest* would be on next week and I would find out whether he had hidden talents. I smiled at the thought.

* * *

On the following Friday afternoon, I went with Mary to see the play. I had a vague recollection of Shakespeare's plot from a high school performance in Burnsville. I know it did not take place on Tristan da Cunha, and the sets looked more like

Roseland than my image of an island in the Mediterranean. Prospero, the deposed Duke of Milan, was now the deposed Penseythan of Roseland, called Prospera and played by Martha Nancarrow, Arthur's wife. Jane Trevenna, who was helped in by Mr. Thomas, sat in the front row by the aisle. The usurper to the position of Penseythan was still his/her brother, Antonio. Alonso, the King of Naples had become her Majesty's governor on the island of St. Helena. Basically, the plot was like the original, however the dialogue had been adjusted to fit these new realities. The actors made comments about the importance of the Penseythan being a woman with midwifery skills. The actors made fun of Tristan da Cunha and the acting was fairly good.

To my surprise, James Thomas was quite professional, and Esther was suitably sweet. Clara was a totally different person than the one I had seen before. She was completely absorbed in the part, and her acting was brilliant. Frankie started off well, but as the play progressed he acted as if he had forgotten his lines, and he made many comments about Roseland. The rest of the cast went along with whatever Frankie did, ad-libbing magnificently to cover for him. At the end of the play, when the cast came out, Frankie received the most applause.

"What did you think?" Mary asked as we returned to the house.

"Clara can really act. As for the play, it's different."

"That's Clara for you. She loves to adjust the plays."

"Apparently so. Does Frankie really not know his lines?"

"Hard to tell. He likes to fool around. Of course, Clara might have scripted it for him. Did you notice the smart remarks about Edgar Cocking?"

"I didn't understand what Frankie was getting at."

"Edgar is Esther's dad. He doesn't like Frankie."

"You mean, because of Esther?"

Mary raised her eyebrows. "What do you think?" She put her coat over a chair and turned toward the kitchen. "I'll make some tea."

Mary returned and started to pour the tea.

"Mary, one thing bothered me when I went to see Jane Trevenna. She used the phrase 'dearth of women.' I asked her about it. Is there a restriction on the number of children?"

Mary's hand shook and tea slopped onto the tray. She put the teapot down. "I forgot. I have to work pub tonight. Wash up when you're finished." She grabbed her coat and ran out of the door.

I had been foiled again, but that made me more determined to understand how they controlled their population.

14.

I SPENT MUCH OF THE FOLLOWING WEEK AT THE ROOKERY.
By now, the young, fluffy-feathered auks could be seen squatting just inside their burrows, looking anxiously for their parents. Like typical teenagers, they were ravenously hungry. Somehow, instinct told them to stay hidden and not venture out to where they would be prey for the circling gulls and skuas, which would dive threateningly at their parents in an attempt to get them to drop their fish. I could recognize the auk's nemesis, Dracula, by a strange broken white flash near his left wing tip—lost a feather, I guessed. To gain the fish, he usually went for an auk's throat.

Despite the danger, Nellie's chicks started to come out when they were hungry. Their occasional squawks added to the general din of bird cries and pounding surf. Whoever of Nellie's entourage was around would quickly shoo them back. Nevertheless, I managed to snap some pictures of the youngsters. The adult auks barreled in periodically carrying small fish, which they fed rapidly to their offspring before returning to the sea.

I was curious about the chicks' genders. I could distinguish between the adult males and females, and I wondered whether the chicks would show similar differences. The adult male was a bit bigger than the female, similar to the situation for Atlantic puffins. The coloring of the male beak and the ring of color around their eyes were brighter, at least during the breeding season.

It seemed to me that Nellie's chicks—one male and one female—were different. I also decided that the more aggressive and slightly smaller cute bundle of fluffy feathers was the female. I noticed that when Nellie was out fishing, other females fussed at the gentleman friends when they tried to feed this female chick. At the time I did not pay much attention, I had named the male Artley and was trying to come up with a good name for the female.

Frankie surprised me a couple of days later as I neared the blind.

"Auk, auk," he shouted rising from behind a clump of gorse.

"For God's sake, Frankie, grow up."

He ignored my comment and said, "What are you going to call 'em?"

"Who?"

Nellie's chicks."

On the spur of the moment, I replied, "Artley and Patsy."

"*Rum tumti titum*," he said, and this time there seemed to be notes to the gibberish.

"It's 'The Floral Dance,' isn't it?"

His face took on a sly look, and he skipped away from the blind toward the cliff top without answering. The sudden movement surprised the auks and a number took off and headed out to sea, just clearing Frankie's head.

"Watch it," I shouted.

He waved without turning and disappeared.

Tuesday on the week before Midsummer's Day was balmy, and the wind was unusually quiet. I left the blind and went down the side of the rookery to the point where Frankie had gone over the edge to find gulls' eggs. To my left, the cliffs of the Nare Head plunged into tumbled boulders by the water. Half a mile out from the Nare, clouds of birds circled Gull Rock, the last bit of land going west until you came to Argentina. To my right, Brown Willy soared into its halo of cloud.

I had a memory of a visit, years before, to the Air Museum in Dayton, Ohio, and seeing World War II planes. I remembered vaguely that there was a German dive-bomber with a name that sounded similar to "skua." In front of me, there was a scene straight out of a movie about that war. Those bandits, the skuas, were dive-bombing the auks, frightening them into dropping their catch. The sound of screeching birds replaced the terrifying sound of a diving…that was it, *Stuka*. I watched as Fred fluttered back to the rookery. He went fishing rarely now, but his sense of duty kept him trying. When he returned, Nellie would make a big fuss over him; to my eyes, he looked pleased as he went back to his resting place. This time, Fred had nearly made it home when he was assaulted by Dracula. I watched in horror as Fred tumbled down through the air, just in front of the cliff. Dracula attacked again when Fred started to turn away from the cliff to gain altitude. I could see that Fred was hurt, but he would not release the fish.

"Come on, Fred," I shouted, "it's not worth it." Fred was determined, and though Dracula harassed him repeatedly, he didn't reach Nellie but managed to fall onto the lower level of the rookery. I could see he was in trouble. He tried to stand, then sank down among the tussocks and remained motionless. I waited for a while in the hope that he would be all right, but he was dead. He never released the fish.

I fetched my trumpet from the blind, returned to the cliff top, and played "Taps." I was crying. That was the moment Frankie appeared. I tried to hide my tears.

"Why you cryin'?"

"It's the wind."

"Ain't the wind."

"Fred's dead. Dracula got him."

Frankie's face crumpled. "Damn skuas," he shouted to the air, "I'll get you buggers!" He tried, ineffectually, to hit one of the skuas with a stone then turned away. He was crying, too. I joined him in pissing at the skuas. We stopped quickly when the wind from the west picked up. We trudged to the blind in silence.

I lifted the flap and looked out of the opening to watch Nellie. It took a while for her to realize something was wrong. She found Fred and nuzzled him. When he did not respond, she circled him, emitting a strange sound. Tom, Dick, and Harry appeared and she fussed at them. Can a bird appear to be distraught? Who knows, but the description fit her behavior. By now, some gulls had spotted Fred's body and were flying closer and closer, preparing to feast on him. Nellie went to his defense, but the gulls became too intimidating. After a short mourning period, Nellie gave up guarding Fred and flew out to sea to fish. Immediately after she had delivered her catch she flew out again. A gull landed near Fred. I could not bear to watch anymore.

"Come on, Frankie. I've had enough for today. I'm going to take Fred's body for study. Maybe I can persuade Isaac

Nancarrow to let me have some ice to pack him in while I work out what to do." I ignored the angry gulls and clambered down to the lower ledge. I moved quickly as the stench of decaying fish, dead auks, and bird droppings caused me to gag. I collected Fred and returned to the blind, where I bound his legs to my backpack with cord.

"Nellie'll have to choose," said Frankie, as we walked to Veryan.

"You mean between Tom, Dick, and Harry?"

"Yes."

"We're well into the summer season. Then they'll all go out to sea. Maybe she'll do it next year. It'll be interesting to see which one she picks. They're so different."

"She'll pick Harry."

"Why so sure?"

"Most like Fred."

"I think you're right. Tom's a bit crafty, sneaking up on her trying to get the real thing. Nellie has a problem shaking him off."

"Dick's too aggressive and all, too. Just like some people," said Frankie.

Surprise. He sounded serious and out of character. Only for a moment, then he grinned inanely and loped off as if to reestablish his flakiness.

When he returned, he muttered, "They didn't pick me. They never do."

"For what?"

"Didn't Patsy tell you?"

"Oh, I see. You mean for the seven?"

"Yes."

"You didn't mention about Patsy and me, did you?"

"No, you're Frankie's friend."

"Thanks." So, I was right; Jane Trevenna must have seen Patsy coming to or from the rookery. "Who's going to be King?"

"Artley Billing."

"You mean Cap'n Billing?"

"No silly, he's been married."

"Who to?"

"Somebody." Frankie moved ahead of me, indicating that he was not going to tell me.

"So Young Artley will be King?" I shouted after him.

"Yes."

"I wish him well."

Frankie circled back. "You don't care?"

I realized then that I had not given it any thought. Did I care? Not really. Patsy was a sexy girl, but she meant nothing to me.

Frankie looked at me thoughtfully then ran off. Patsy had been a welcome distraction, but that was all. I felt lonely and aggravated, and I turned to fretting about what to do with Fred. I decided to ask Arthur, rather than Isaac, for help.

"Auks on ice." Arthur scratched his head with his ring finger and said, "I'll talk to Isaac. It's his area you see, the ice I mean." I could hear them arguing. Arthur was quiet and persistent. He won. "I'll get it, best you stay outside."

"I'll need ice every day until I've had a chance to study Fred and get my samples."

"Fred is it?" He laughed. "I suppose you've names for all of 'em."

"The ones I'm studying, yes."

He returned with a large cardboard box that had been lined with straw and packed with ice. "Straw will help insulate."

"Thanks, Arthur. It'd be tough doing my work without you."

He smiled. "I'll see you at practice tonight."

"Oh yes, I'd forgotten, what with Fred and everything."

I sent a package to my parents on the last boat before Christmas, to be mailed in Cape Town. The package included a scrimshaw for my mother—she'd like it, I knew—a commentary on the auks with photographs for my father—all I could think of—and a letter describing my life on the island. I also sent another package on the auks to the professor. When the boat returned, it brought a letter from my mother, sent earlier and saying that they missed me. A parcel from the professor contained a monograph on the Atlantic Puffin, with a note saying he hoped it would be useful.

During the last week before Midsummer's Day, the islanders completed what looked like a maypole and added the multi-colored ribbons, which dangled to within a foot of the ground. They set up stalls around the edges of the square, and a group of men erected a platform in front of the Seythan House.

Mary and I put Fred in the shed at the end of the garden.

"I hope you won't have too many of these corpses, Andy. This isn't the cemetery."

"It'll only be for a few days. When I've got my samples, I'll bury him at the rookery."

"Good." Mary snorted. "I worried you were going to put him in my vegetable garden."

"Will it be okay to keep the samples in your icebox? It won't be much."

She grimaced. "Make sure it's well marked. I don't want to be cooking it by mistake like."

I spent the next two days studying Fred, taking photographs and collecting blood and organ samples, which I put in a small bottle in the icebox. On the day before the festival, I buried the remains of Fred at the edge of Nellie's patch. The auks fussed at me while keeping their distance. I decided that I would spend more time studying the other families. Then, if one of the other gentlemen friends suffered Fred's fate, I could get samples for comparison.

I also noticed a few more auk corpses among the tussocks of grass, the work of the skuas and gulls I guessed, but there were also quite a large number of dead chicks—some fluffy but also some emaciated ones. I collected a few and did a cursory examination. Most of the emaciated chicks were female. I made a note to try to find out why.

Band practice that afternoon went well. A few odd remarks were made to Jacob Jago about the big day coming up—nudge nudge, wink wink. He took it well, though he was obviously nervous from worrying about Patsy. He was cordial to me. Thank God that he did not seem to know what I'd done. We practiced in the hall before going to the edge of town near the two small Round Houses. From there, we marched while playing to the square and then circled around three times before going up to the Big Round House and then returning to the center of the square. This would be our route for the main dance to be played later in the evening of the big day. When we marched, we played only "The Floral Dance."

15.

THE ISLANDERS STARTED ARRIVING EARLY ON THE MORNING of Midsummer's Day. Most of the women wore sleeveless, floral-patterned dresses. The men wore white shirts with white or khaki-colored pants. I had not realized until then what a fine-looking people they were, lean and weather-beaten by American standards. The women benefited from using little makeup and the men looked rugged. The sensible diet with plenty of fish, vegetables, and fruit obviously helped. Their flashing smiles showed good teeth and made me wonder who their dentist was. I remembered what Jane Trevenna had said about sending the brighter kids to be educated in England. I guessed the Penseythan was both doctor and dentist; it seemed unlikely that the islanders could afford to send two people for medical training.

By nine o'clock, the stalls in the square were all open for business, selling food and crafts. Carnival games—ring toss, a shooting gallery, and darts—were scattered among the stalls. An old wooden swing and merry-go-round for the children were in the field on the north side of the village hall. Next to it were tethered ponies and horses and a sign announcing rides for sixpence.

The morning passed slowly. I spent the time chatting to islanders. They asked the standard questions—what was the States like, and had I learned anything about the auks.

Frankie showed up and I treated him to each of the games. He was much more skillful than I, and he came away with an armful of presents for his mum. I won a tiny, strange-looking doll, carved out of wood.

Just before lunch, I put on my uniform and joined the band. We started with the national anthem then played requests for an hour. Afterward, sweating uncomfortably, we went in the pub for beer, bread, cheese, and pickles on the house. Mary was behind the bar again, looking desirable.

At two o'clock, we walked down the road to the small round houses. All the children came with us, accompanied by their mothers and some of the older girls. The girls were wearing their party dresses and had flowers in their hair. Cute. The boys were neatly dressed—no floral decorations—and looked self-conscious. We lined up facing the square and Charlie signaled the beginning of the first "Floral Dance." I could not see the dancers because they were all behind us; nevertheless, I could visualize what they were doing. Earlier, Mary had demonstrated the dance to me: each boy and girl stepping forward, side by side, then the girl twirling, with the steps repeated as they followed the band. She had sung *"rum tum ti tumpti"* as we did it.

The rest of the islanders were packed along the road and around the outside encouraging the dancers. Some were singing. When we circled the square, I could glimpse the dancers behind us through gaps between the stalls. After one circuit, we went to the middle of the square and continued playing. By now, many of the islanders were dancing. Mary appeared and signaled to Charlie for me to join her in the dance. Charlie smiled and nodded. I left my trumpet on the ground and Mary and I whirled around the square. The locals clapped appreciatively when they saw us. Even Jane Trevenna, standing on the veranda of the Seythan House with Cap'n Billing holding her arm, smiled at me. During this happy time I felt like one of them, more so when the dance finished and I had downed a couple of beers. During the rest of the afternoon, I toured the stalls again and then went to the pub for more beer and food.

"Best eat now, Andy," Charlie advised. "Next time'll be after the main dance."

I could feel the sense of anticipation rising throughout the afternoon. At six, the parents took the fifty or so young children from the square into the field for rides. Soon afterward, the very youngest were taken home.

"Right," said Charlie, finishing his beer, "It's time to go. Let's get rid of the beer first, lads. Jacob, can you handle it?"

Jacob Jago rose, unsteadily. "Have to, won't I?" He held onto my arm as we followed Charlie behind the pub to relieve ourselves. "You're all right, Andy, for a foreigner." He turned to face me. "Patsy will do fine with Young Artley. You understand, don't you?"

I was not sure what to understand. I nodded. "Artley's a good guy, Mr. Jago."

He appeared satisfied with my answer. We walked in silence back down the road to the edge of town. Married couples and a few unmarried women, with their escorts, were waiting for us. Charlie lined us up facing the two small round houses.

"Anthem," he said.

When we started playing, the door of one round house

opened and seven men emerged; they were smartly dressed in white shirts, pants, and shoes, and they had flower-bedecked floppy white hats. They all wore masks. Nevertheless from their build and the way they walked I worked out that I'd seen some of them at the dances in the village halls. Artley, obviously him, was the last to come out. He was more ornately dressed in a white suit and white top hat with flowers around the rim. Each man carried a garland of flowers. They all fidgeted as they lined up in front of the second round house. Artley knocked on the door. At the seventh knock the door opened and seven young women came out, including Patsy and Esther. I had expected them all to be unmarried, but some wore wedding rings. It seemed that, other than Patsy, they were more like matrons of honor than candidates for the next year's festivities. In sequence, each went to her partner, who placed the floral garland around her neck. They were all wearing low cut white dresses, purple sashes, and white pumps and had flowers intricately woven in their hair. Patsy was the last of them. She looked terrific. Artley placed the flowers around her neck. He led Patsy and the other six couples into the middle of the road. Patsy did not look at me as she passed. The rest of the islanders lined up behind them.

In the first dance, the islanders had been wearing conventional clothes. This time, many of them had costumes and were carrying masks. Some of those without masks wore garish makeup, giving a lewd impression. Jane Trevenna was wearing an elegant red gown. Makeup exaggerated her strong features. Mr. Thomas sported a long black coat and top hat. I wondered what significance the clothes had and if it had been Mr. Thomas in a devil's mask on Guy Fawkes Day, but that was hard to imagine. To that point, I had not seen that Mary was with Cap'n Billing. She smiled as she passed me. Cap'n Billing saw it and nodded in my direction. As always, he appeared stern. Mary wore her incredibly low-cut blouse and a long red skirt. The Cap'n wore a black cloak. Both of them were carrying masks.

We went to the front of the procession and started playing. The difference from the first time we had performed was stark. As we led the procession into Veryan and around the square, the sides of the road and the square were empty. All of the islanders who remained joined in the dance. We circled the square three times and led the dancers up to the Round House and back to the square. When we stopped, the dancers circled around us. Charlie raised the tempo of the music. The dancing was no longer sedate. It had morphed into a pagan ritual, a fertility rite. After one circuit, the dancers continued their cavorting except for the chosen men and women. Through the dancers, I could see the seven men and women standing in front of the veranda of the Seythan House. Jane Trevenna spoke to them at length. Then the six matrons of honor and the seven men went to the Maypole and started to dance around it. I wondered where they had practiced, because the way they intertwined and unraveled the long ribbons was intricate. Meanwhile, Jane took Patsy by the hand, and when Mr. Thomas opened the door to the Round House, she led Patsy inside. Some time later, Jane Trevenna came out and pointed at the Maypole. Mr. Thomas escorted the first of the young men to the Round House. Jane Trevenna spoke to him and he went in. The crowd was still dancing, but spending more time between the Round House and the band so that they would not miss anything. My view was blocked; nevertheless, I could tell when the first young man emerged by the great cheer. We stopped playing. He returned to the Maypole, looking rumpled. The other chosen men and women surrounded him immediately.

"They're asking what it was like," Arthur Nancarrow whispered.

"I guess Patsy gave him a good time."

Arthur nudged me in the ribs. "You'd know, wouldn't you?"

"Not anymore," I replied.

Arthur chuckled.

So my affair with Patsy was known widely, and Arthur's laughter suggested that it was not as big a deal as Jane Trevenna had implied.

Mr. Thomas escorted the second man, and we started playing again. By the fourth time, Jacob Jago had seen all he could stand and went into the pub. Charlie picked up his drum. We didn't need a conductor with him banging out the rhythm. Eventually, only Artley remained. He looked excited and nervous. The sun was below the horizon when Mr. Thomas led him to the Round House. The music and the dancing stopped and we went to the edge of the square to watch him enter. The silence was broken by a roar of appreciation as the door opened and Artley tossed his white hat in the air. Charlie signaled that we had to play.

"National anthem, lads, 'elp Artley be upstanding. Least we can do."

"'Ardly necessary. Young Patsy will see to that," Petunia snickered.

We followed the anthem with a number of dances and finished with the last waltz. I went to the pub with Charlie, Petunia, and Arthur. Jacob Jago was asleep in the corner. "Poor Jacob," said Petunia.

"Will he be okay?"

"Yes, it's not just Patsy, you see. That's how he met his late wife, Patricia."

"Oh!" I took a swig of the scotch that Charlie had bought me. "You and Charlie, too?"

She giggled and elbowed me, "Andy Ferguson, you mind your own business!"

"What's with the white and red dresses and the makeup?"

Petunia's witch's face grinned, evilly. "We likes to have a little fun, Andy. If Charlie don't drink too much, he should have a good time later."

"That's it...sex?"

Petunia smiled, broadly. Her teeth were stained red like a vampire's. "Of course, and remembering the old days."

"How old?"

"Before Christianity, I've heard."

"It looks a bit funny."

Petunia grabbed my arm. "It's not all fun, Andy. Don't get on the wrong side of the devil. You won't like it."

"What?"

"I'll say no more. You heard me."

It seemed that she wasn't joking. The dark side of the island's culture had shown its face again. I stayed for a while and tried to buy drinks. No one would let me. A number of them plied me with more scotch and congratulated me on my trumpet playing. When, finally, I was able to get away and met the cold air, I felt too dizzy to go to bed. I walked around the square to clear my head, finding it hard not to look at the Round House and imagine Patsy and Artley. A faint light showed from the slit windows, set high in the walls. The square was very quiet away from the pub. After a number of circuits, I went to my room.

I tossed fitfully until the creaking bed and moans from the next room woke me. I could not sleep and paced around my little room. I had not drawn the curtains, and as I passed the window, I saw that the Lagonda was parked by the Round House. I stopped and watched. After a short time, the door opened and Patsy and Artley emerged, his arm was around her waist and her head was on his shoulder. Mr. Thomas ushered them into the back of the car and they drove away. I stood by the window for a while thinking about what had been happening in that strange house. I still had a nagging feeling that it could not be true, but the notion in the back of my mind that the whole thing was a charade for the amusement of the islanders did not seem credible. How could the organizer get so many people to play along?

I made a decision to find out more. I dressed and crept down the stairs holding my shoes and the flashlight. From the backyard, I saw that the curtains of Mary's bedroom were closed. Just in case she had heard me leave, I went into the outside toilet. After a few minutes, I climbed the back wall and circled around the village hall and chapel towards the Round House. The horses and ponies, now running free in the field, kept their distance. I crossed the road quickly and walked around the back of the Round House to reach the door.

My flashlight illuminated the one circular room. I had thought about what I might see: a sign saying 'gotcha!' A boudoir fit for a brothel. Instead, I saw a small iron-framed bed with a single bottom sheet and a pillow. Beside the bed were a wooden chair, a table holding a china basin and large matching water jug, some towels, a wastepaper basket, and a number of candleholders with the remains of their candles. There was water in the basin and the towels were wet. The basket contained used condoms, and a damp patch stained the middle of the sheet; Patsy's juices had flowed as they had done with me. It seemed clear now that this was one way the islanders dealt with the strange unbalance in the sexes, but it was still hard for me to believe. I wondered what else the islanders did to deal with their strange situation.

I left quickly and circled back to my house. As a precaution, I used the toilet again. I was glad I had, for when I left the toilet, there was a flickering light on in the kitchen—oil lamp time, no electricity this late. Mary, looking fetchingly tousled in a robe, was making tea.

"Too much booze, my stomach doesn't feel so good."

"That's why you went over the wall then?" Mary looked at me knowingly.

"In between using the potty," I replied quickly. "A good walk helps clear the head."

Mary raised her eyebrows. "I thought you might like some tea."

"You were making it for me?"

"Who else?"

I looked at the ceiling. "Whoever's upstairs…"

"Andy, what are you suggesting?"

I did not believe it. In the short time I had been away from the house, her visitor had magically gone. My disbelief showed.

"If you don't believe me, you go and look, Andy!" Mary snapped and turned away.

I could not resist the offer and went upstairs. Her room was empty. What the hell did the noises mean? Had I been dreaming? No way! I paused to study the room. The top sheet was pulled back. The bottom sheet was dry. It looked like Mary was telling the truth. A photograph on her bedside table showed a man—not Cap'n Hartley Billing—could it be Mr. Pascoe? A second photograph was of a young girl, very pretty with curly black hair like Mary's. I passed Mary on the stairs. "Satisfied? Your tea's on the table."

"Sorry, I don't know what I was thinking. The noises though. They woke me up."

Mary did not answer immediately and when she did her speech was measured as if she was being careful in what she said. "Andy, these old row houses carry sound in strange ways. You could have heard something from next door."

"I suppose that must be it," I agreed, not sure whether to believe the answer.

Although the house was quiet, I couldn't sleep. Up until this point it had been fun on the island. The excitement of learning about the auks and the titillation of illicit meetings with Patsy had kept me amused, but I dreaded the thought of staying through winter. The auks would be leaving within a couple of months and opportunities for a woman to relieve my frustration were small.

Unfortunately, I had agreed with the professor, who was paying my expenses, to stay and write some essays on the birds of Roseland to meet course work requirements. Certainly there would be enough material for a PhD, and I needed to sketch out my dissertation. God, I needed to get off the island.

16.

THE BRIEF TIME BETWEEN MIDSUMMER'S DAY AND CHRIST-
mas was a continual party, during which the islanders gave
me many Christmas presents. Thank God, the professor had
prepared me for this situation. I gave a hand-dyed scarf to
Mary, a small pot from a local potter at home to Clara, a
new-fangled universal wrench to Arthur, and the biggest suc-
cess, a Swiss Army knife to Frankie. He must have shown it
to everyone in the village. Clara seemed more excited about
his present than hers. I had something that I could have given
to Patsy, but when I suggested it to Mary she rolled her eyes
and shook her head.

On Christmas Day, I saw Patsy and Artley at the chapel.
Patsy gave me her toothy grin, raising her left hand so that I
could see the engagement ring. I made a clapping motion and
went over to congratulate them. While Artley was distracted
by another well-wisher, Patsy whispered, "Esther wants to see
you." Apparently, she had forgiven Esther for kissing me.

"Is Esther going to be chosen next?"

"Dunno."

I thought of my meeting with Jane Trevenna and decided

to avoid the dances for the time being and concentrate on my work.

* * *

Nellie didn't wait until the next season to find her main man, and she didn't pick Tom, Dick, or Harry. She had already become friendly with a natty younger male. I called him Daniel—Dapper Dan. No sex, you understand, although he played up to her and she coyly encouraged him. Egged him on, I chuckled to myself. I wondered if a gene led to some external difference that allowed a female to detect the difference between her main man and the gentlemen friends. Then, as a corollary question, did the sperm of the chosen males favor production of males? I managed to collect a couple of corpses of gentlemen friends before the gulls shredded them.

Poor Mary now had three small boxes of body parts and fluids in her icebox. I spent many hours studying the remains, my photographs of chosen males, like Fred, and those of a number of gentlemen friends. I also collected more of the dead chicks for analysis. Again they were predominantly female and these looked thin and dehydrated, the reason the predators hadn't eaten them, I guessed. I was relieved that Nellie's chick, Patsy, was not among them. I had kept a close watch on her and found out that Nellie always fed Patsy first and let her gentlemen friends deal with the male chick, Artley. The beginning of a theory was forming in my mind.

I had been slow in understanding the significance of one part of the courtship ritual. Prospective mates brought the females presents of fish—apparently a demonstration of a necessary competence to be a mate or at least a gentleman friend, for the females rarely ate the offerings. Dan was particularly accomplished, often arriving with four of the little fish that Nellie and the other females liked. Finally, I realized that this feature might explain how their whole system had grown as the auk colony multiplied. In the excitement of finding this important part of the foundation for my dissertation, I even forgot about women for a while.

When I finally got around to doing autopsies on the dead chicks, my fledgling—I giggled nervously—theory was confirmed. More than seventy percent were female, and they had essentially no food in them. Starved to death! This was how the females obtained a surplus of males. This was why other females had fussed at Nellie's men when they tried to feed Patsy. A corollary to this result was that tough females like Nellie prevented the starvation by preferentially feeding their female chicks, or at least some of them. Unnatural selection for the fittest, I wrote.

When the auks began to leave in February, I removed my note pads, pencils, and the binoculars from the blind and brought them back to the house. Seeing the auks flying out to sea made me wonder if anyone knew where they survived the winter in the open South Atlantic. In an effort to find out, I asked Clara whether there were any books on birds. She took me to a large shed behind the Seythan House. Stacks of books were piled against the walls and in the middle of the room— many more than on display in the library. Bundles of papers and notebooks tied with string littered the floor.

"What are these, Clara?"

Clara prodded the bundles with her foot. "Sheet music and parts for plays, m'dear, I think." She sounded uncertain and added, "Might be copies of our weekly newsletter, too."

A quick glance suggested she was correct. The plays were heavily annotated and brought back memories of Clara's production of *The Tempest*. They were not likely to have anything to do with the birds so I stacked them in a corner.

"I enjoyed your play. You were great…really professional."

Clara scuffled one foot. "I try my best."

"Why did you change the script?"

She looked away, a small smile hovering on her lips. "I like my little bit of fun, m'dear. People expect it, makes the play more personal for them. Some island in the Mediterranean doesn't mean a lot to us, you see. That governor on St. Helena who hardly ever comes here and thinks he runs the island, now he's fair game." She did not sound vague anymore.

"What about Mr. Cocking?"

"You noticed, did you?"

"It was hard not to, the way Frankie carried on."

"Frankie likes his bit of fun, too, you know."

"Did you and he work it out in advance?"

Clara looked vacant again. "Have you found your books yet?"

"They're not in any kind of order." I shook my head. "I'm going to have to sort them."

Clara looked bemused. "I could help, I guess," she said.

I had a hard time getting Clara to concentrate. She would keep finding something interesting and would stand reading it. After two days we, or rather I, had the books alphabetized under broad topics, including seventeen bird books.

I finished the organizing and took the bird material to the library. Most of the books gave general information on the birds of the world. Five were devoted to the Southern Hemisphere and looked useful. I started taking notes.

Clara appeared after more than an hour, picked up a pile of returned books, and busily started to slot them into their homes on the shelves. I checked later, most were in the wrong place. Poor Clara. What went through her mind, except the library, the plays, and worrying about Frankie? On the other hand, watching *The Tempest* had shown me what a good actress she could be. Was she acting all the time?

* * *

That evening, when Mary returned from school, her face was flushed and her eyes sparkled. "Rose is coming home on the next boat," she said.

"I thought she had like two and a half years to go at university."

"Yes, but it's taking longer than expected for Jane Trevenna's leg to heal. Rose'll help out." She put a bunch of school exercise books on the living room table.

"So Rose is studying to be a doctor?"

"Yes."

I wondered why Mary had not told me before. "I look forward to meeting her."

"Doesn't the Penseythan have anyone else to help her?"

"Yes, Martha Nancarrow." Mary paused. "But Jane insisted on having Rose."

"You don't sound particularly happy."

"It'll be wonderful to see Rose, but...she needs to finish her training."

Strange that the Penseythan had chosen to delay it, I thought, but Mary went to the kitchen before I could ask her why.

* * *

I sank into a routine of going to the pub as often as I could afford. The locals would ask me how my work was going. They never seemed bored in hearing about the auks. The islanders had a kind of pride in that pompous little bird—their version of our bald eagle. By the first week in March, I finished both an outline of my dissertation and part of an essay on island birds and their relationship to other birds of the South Atlantic.

I posted the finished essay and the outline to the professor, also a letter to my parents, in time to catch the last boat going to Cape Town before winter closed in.

Band practice provided a welcome break, although no engagements were scheduled before the spring. Now that the cold season was setting in, Arthur Nancarrow showed movies weekly in the village hall. I read the schedule. The movies consisted mainly of old westerns and ancient British comedies, with one more modern favorite—the Bond movie, *From Russia With Love*. Despite the foul weather, I took long walks to clear my head and work off my frustration. I could not stop thinking about the way the auks dealt with the female chicks. I remembered comments Jane Trevenna had made about the dearth of young women, and that the Penseythan who had set up Roseland's system had studied the island's birds.

I climbed Brown Willy and sat for a long time looking into the cold hard waters of the lake in its crater: a permanent reminder of the darker side of the island. A darker side in which female auks controlled the auk population by starving about three quarters of the female chicks, and—I had a hard time coming to grips with the concept—it was possible that the islanders practiced, or had practiced female infanticide for the same reason. I went to the end of the Nare Head and watched the sea birds circling the Gull Rock. One full day, I walked to Portloe and back. On another day, I found a path through the woods along the foot of the southern hills that took me within a mile of Trewince. If I was correct, it would be Jane Trevenna who adjusted the male/female balance if it became necessary. Winter was approaching and the green island and the sea that had sparkled in the summer sun had become a forbidding place with a murdering doctor. It was an island surrounded by dark, violent seas, the landscape becoming browner with each passing week, and now scary as hell.

17.

ON A DULL RAINY DAY AT THE BEGINNING OF APRIL, MARY asked if I would like to come with her to Portloe to meet the boat and Rose. I was happy for a distraction from brooding about infanticide, although I took comfort in the thought that with modern contraception—the WOMEN's cupboard at Nancarrow's—maybe it wasn't practiced anymore. Despite the rain, I agreed to go with her. By now, I was conscious of the fact that I had not paid sufficient attention to the prof's comments on weather and the misery of the fall season…

"While Roseland is spared the worst of the Roaring Forties, nevertheless it is windy there and rains quite often," he had warned me.

"How much rain?" I asked.

"Oh, not as much as a hundred inches a year, more like seventy."

That did not sound too bad; in Burnsville it rained well over fifty inches a year. "How about the temperature?"

"Eighty would be a hot summer day. Fortunately, in

the winter it rarely drops below forty, but in the damp air the wind chill can be brutal."

Frankie came with us. He appeared irrationally excited by the trip. Mary explained that Rose found his antics funny and that they had been friends since she was a little girl. My face must have shown my curiosity to hear more.

"Frankie dotes on her, and I'll bet she's got a present for him."

We waited for the boat in the shelter of the fisherman's hut on the rise above the harbor. The sea was a cold gray color and whitecaps dotted the deep swell out to the horizon. The rocks were wet with spray and harsh looking. When the St. Just appeared around the point, bouncing on the rough water, Frankie ran down to the end of the jetty. Mary and I waited out of the rain until the boat entered the narrow channel.

The minute the boat was tied up, Artley and the crew started to unload the boxes of goods stashed on the deck. Frankie jumped aboard. He did not offer to help the crew, but rushed into the living quarters. He emerged minutes later carrying a suitcase and a tote bag. The girl following him was dressed in jeans, sneakers, and an anorak, with the hood covering her head. Mary rushed forward to help Rose clamber onto the jetty.

When Rose's hood fell back and she smiled at her mother, time stopped for me. I did not feel the wind and rain anymore. The black and white photographs of Rose that I'd seen did not capture her beauty. She was not wearing any makeup and she didn't need it. Rose Pascoe had the same coloring as her mother, but she was softer looking. Fortunately, she and Mary hugged long enough for me to recover my composure.

So when she smiled as Mary introduced us, I had stopped feeling like a gawky teenager on his first date.

"Nice to meet you, Andy. I've heard a lot about you." Her handshake was firm.

"Good, I hope?"

"Generally, yes."

"Some bad, then?"

Her black eyes twinkled, her pearly teeth flashed between soft red lips. "Not exactly...Patsy's a friend of mine."

"Oh! I see."

Frankie, holding her bags, stomped impatiently.

"Let's get under cover," said Mary, walking toward the fisherman's shelter.

"Andy, please can you take my bags? I haven't seen Frankie in such a long time." Rose took Frankie's hand and they ran to the hut like a couple of kids. I picked up the bags and followed.

On the bus, Rose sat with Frankie. They were giggling like teenagers. I sat with Mary, envying him. Back in Veryan, Frankie followed us into the house. I must have shown my surprise because Mary noticed and whispered, "Frankie knows Rose has a present for him. Look!"

Sure enough, Frankie was eyeing Rose like a dog waiting for a treat. Rose opened her suitcase and handed a wrapped box to Frankie. He tore it open, strewing the paper and cardboard on the living room floor. Inside, two more nested boxes received the same fate. Rose's present was a multi-function knife. From the way Frankie reacted, you would not have known I had given him one for Christmas. He insisted on showing each of us every function before running to the library to show his mum.

"Thanks for not saying anything," said Mary, when Rose had gone upstairs.

"What will he do with two knives?"

Mary laughed. "Carry Rose's to show to people and use yours for dirty jobs, I reckon."

"Rose really likes him, doesn't she?"

"Yes. When Rose was little, she was quite timid. Frankie, who is a few years older, sort of looked after her, like an older brother. They've been close ever since."

"How old is Frankie then?"

"Coming up on twenty-nine. Rose is twenty-two."

"She doesn't look it." Rose was twenty-two. I had another question I would like to have asked, "Had she ever been chosen?" Even though I hardly knew her, in some nutty way the thought of it made me feel jealous.

Throughout the rest of the day, I tried to talk to Rose, but it never seemed to be the right time. She was either helping her mother with the cooking or in her room. I had the feeling she was avoiding me. When I managed to get a question in, she found a polite way not to answer it completely—a verbal version of an old-fashioned striptease.

A day later, I received my mail, two letters. My mother's note thanked me for the scrimshaw I had sent for Christmas. Amazingly, a long note from my father commented on the material I had sent him on the auks. It included some thoughtful suggestions on ways to spot differences between the males. He also said that he had taken a very useful course at North Carolina State on raising pigs and using the manure to make methane to power the operation. At last, we were communicating.

In a brief letter, the professor said that he was pleased

with my essay and my work on the dissertation. He said that if my next essay was as good as the first one, it would satisfy all preliminary requirements for entering the final phase of my PhD. He asked if I would mind if he modified the essay and submitted it as a paper. I showed the letter to Mary.

"There won't be a boat until spring, Mary. How do I let him know it'll be okay?"

"I'm going into Portloe to see Auntie Flo. I'll get the message radioed to Mabel."

"Thanks."

* * *

During the following weeks, I found it hard to concentrate on my work. The glimpses of Rose passing me on the way to the bathroom were tantalizing—slim, pale legs and the hint of a nightie when her robe was loose. She was not voluptuous and overtly sexy like her mother. Hers was a delicate beauty; the way she smiled and moved hinted at potential passion.

In the library, the words on the page in front of me blurred continually. The black ink became Rose's hair and the lines and words morphed into her face.

"What are you thinking about, Andy? You've been staring at that writing of yours for half an hour, at least." Clara's question broke the spell.

"Oh, I...I can't think of anything to write."

"Is that it? You looked moonstruck to me." Clara snorted. "It's Rose, isn't it? She has that affect on men."

I peered at her sharply, but her pale eyes looked at me innocently. I decided to be brazen. "You're right, Clara. I can't get her out of my mind. I plan to ask her to elope with me. Problem is I don't have a boat."

"Mister Andy, you're making fun of me. What will you say next?"

Again, I had many questions. Who was her father? Had she been "chosen"? I tried the safer one, first. "Clara, I'm curious. Who is Rose's father? As long as I've been here, Mary has been alone."

"It's not for me to say. You should ask Mary, but she may not want to talk about what happened."

"Well then, here is the sixty-four-thousand-dollar question. Has Rose ever been chosen?"

Clara stared at me. "What kind of a question is that to ask me? Rose never had that kind of money."

"Clara, it's just an expression. Come on! It can't hurt to tell me."

"Not yet." Clara smiled sweetly and went back to pretending to restore books to their rightful places. The answer did not help me a bit. Then she made a comment that got my attention. "I should warn you, Rose has an understanding." She did not sound vague anymore.

"Understanding about what?"

"John Trevenna. When they've both finished their education, we all expect them to get married." Her face showed no emotion, but the way she said it sounded a little malicious.

"Does Rose expect that?"

"Why don't you ask her?" As she turned away, I thought I heard her mutter, "Doesn't really matter what Rose wants."

My happy daydreaming about Rose had been shot down. It seemed that everybody expected her to marry John Trevenna, whether she wanted to or not. I needed to go for a long walk. I waited for a while so my discomfort would not be too obvious, then packed up my books and took them back to my room. As I left the library, I turned to find Clara watching me and looking pleased with herself—the bitch.

To calm down, I trudged up to the rookery. A light drizzle continued its annual task of washing away the fishy smell. Now that the auks were gone, the skuas ignored the rookery and circled around their own areas of the cliff. The sea below looked bitter and ominous as the waves rolled in against the rocks. I wiped raindrops off my face and studied the blind. Part of its cover had blown loose. I needed to take it back to Veryan before it deteriorated even more. Frankie had not been around for a while, but hopefully, he would help me.

Rose had not been around either, only at breakfast and supper. She was gone all day, helping Jane Trevenna and assisting at the school, she told me. But what if some of the time Rose was not at school but with Frankie? My stomach felt so hollow that I wanted to throw up.

A gull, offended at my presence, dive-bombed my head, jolting me out of my miserable fantasy. Boy! How could I, the college stud, be acting like such a wimp? I waved to the gull in thanks and ran all the way back to the library.

"Clara, I haven't seen Frankie recently. Do you think he could help me carry stuff from the rookery back to Nancarrow's?"

"Frankie's working out on Jago's farm. I don't know when he could do it." She was back in her normal role, appearing flustered.

"Please would you ask him?"

She nodded. "I didn't think to ask you before, how are you

getting on with Rose?" She looked at me innocently. "Living in a house with two beautiful women can't be easy."

Not with the noises at night, I thought, for the first time wondering if Clara had something to do with them. "I don't get to see her much. She's working at the school."

"Is she?" Clara made it sound like it might not be the case.

"So, what's she going to do?"

"Job few people could do. Nor want to."

"What's that?"

Clara did not answer. She had returned to aimlessly shuffling books.

Unfortunately, I knew the answer. When Rose became the doctor and Penseythan, she would be responsible for controlling the population.

18.

FRANKIE APPEARED AT BREAKFAST THREE DAYS LATER. "MUM says you want me to move stuff?"

"The blind's coming apart. Arthur says I can store the pieces in his shed."

"Jacob says I can do it this mornin'." He was talking to me but looking at Rose. He had shaved and combed his hair. They smiled at each other conspiratorially.

"Thanks."

"Patsy told me to say Esther will be looking for you at the dance, Saturday."

Mary and Rose worked intently on their eggs and bacon. Both were trying to hide smiles.

"I think Esther's got a boyfriend." I looked hard at Frankie. "I don't want to get in trouble. Say hi to Patsy. When's she getting married?" Frankie looked blank.

"Two weeks come Saturday," said Mary. "What with Rose coming back an' all, I forgot to tell you. You're invited."

"I'll need to get a present for them."

"You could tell Young Artley where it's at," Mary giggled.

"Mum!" Although Rose acted shocked, her eyes were twinkling.

"Sorry, Precious, but worth it to see Andy's face."

I shook my finger at her. Patsy had not needed any help in that area.

Frankie seemed oblivious to the exchange. "Are we going then? Got to be back at farm by lunchtime." He left.

I gulped down the rest of my breakfast and followed. Frankie was setting such a pace that it took me half a mile to catch up with him.

"Slow down a bit, Frankie! Save your energy. We've got a lot to carry to the shed."

He slowed down. "Shed behind Nancarrow's?"

I remembered his unwillingness to pick up the tarpaulin the day we'd built the blind. Time to find out why. "Yes. Not a problem is it?"

"Abattoir." Frankie made a face. "Bad place."

"For animals," I said.

"That's what you think." Frankie started away before I could ask him what he meant. "Mr. Jago said I mustn't be late," he shouted over his shoulder.

"I'll make sure you're okay. If we're running late, you can leave the stuff you're carrying by the side of the path and you can go on to Jago's farm. I can come back and get it. I didn't want to make two trips all the way to the rookery."

Frankie pondered my suggestion. "Could do that."

"Thanks, you're a big help. I owe you one."

"Owe me one what?"

"A favor, Frankie."

"Oh." He slowed down.

"How long have you known Rose?"

"Me mum took me to see her the day she were born."

"I bet she was cute."

159

"She was a baby."

"Yes. Was her dad there?"

Frankie looked puzzled. "She don't have no dad."

Clara had hinted about some problem. "He's dead?"

"Yes."

"How long has Rose been away? Studying, I mean."

"A long time. I missed her. She's my friend." His face took on a sullen look. "Johnny Trevenna's been away too...in England. I don't like him."

"Any reason?"

"Don't like him." Frankie studied the ground.

I tried another tack. "Rose seems to be a very nice person." Frankie nodded. *This is it,* I thought, *time for the big question.* "Frankie, has Rose ever been chosen?" I tried to sound very casual.

Frankie shook his head violently from side to side. "What are you saying? Rose can't be chosen. She's my friend." I stopped him and held his shoulders. His face was distraught.

"I'm sorry, Frankie. A dumb question, I didn't mean to upset you. Race you to the rookery." I ran up the path not turning around. After a while, I could hear Frankie behind me. I let him win the race, I think. At least I had the answer. Rose had not been chosen—so far.

"You're a better runner than I, Frankie Quick," I said as I caught up with him at the rookery.

Frankie beamed. He seemed to have forgotten about my question. "Auks gone," he said.

"No gulls' eggs, either?"

"Wrong time of year."

We dismantled the blind into two manageable bundles and took a celebratory piss from the cliff top. Frankie, un-self-consciously, sprayed with abandon, reminding me that he was well endowed.

He took me up on my offer to leave his bundle by the side of the path. I went back for it later and finished storing the parts of the blind at Nancarrow's store.

On the first Saturday in May, the dance was in Portloe. I asked Mary if she was going. She looked amused, obviously knowing that I was really asking about Rose.

"Yes, of course. How about you?"

"I think I may. I need to get out."

"Esther will be happy."

"Will you protect me from Esther and her friends?"

"That's your problem. You could always hide in the men's room during the last dance."

"Thanks a lot. I'm afraid Esther would come in and get me."

"I'd like to see that." Mary chuckled. "Rose will be coming. You could ask her for help."

"Would she?"

"You'll need to be quick. You won't be the only one wanting the last dance with her."

"Ain't that the truth."

On Saturday evening, Rose came downstairs a few minutes before the bus left. She was wearing a white dress with faint blue flowers, gathered in above her slim waist so that with the V-shaped neckline it showed the swell of her breasts. Her hair was piled on her head and held by a blue enameled clasp, emphasizing the Grecian look. She was wearing matching small blue earrings and a thin gold necklace. Rose twirled at the bottom of the stairs, showing her slim legs. Mary and I applauded.

"You look beautiful, luv," said Mary, hugging her.

"As they say here, *bloody gorgeous*," I added.

I held the door for them as we left. With her high heels on, Rose was nearly my height.

A surprise waited for me at the bus. Frankie was standing by the door, looking uncomfortable in a suit that might have been made for someone else. Clara was sitting alone in the front seat. Frankie helped Mary in, and she and Clara moved to a seat farther back. Frankie and Rose then sat in the front seat. Frankie looked pleased with himself. I found a seat by myself. A big mistake, I soon realized. When we stopped near the school to take on more people, Esther came and sat next to me. During the ride to Portloe, Esther rubbed up against me suggestively and whispered that she would save me the last dance. Mary's suggestion of hiding in the men's room suddenly sounded like a great idea.

Nevertheless, the dance was fun. I was deluged with partners, Esther being the first. Frankie took as many of the dances with Rose as she would let him, to the obvious disgust of most of the men. He acted as if he were unaware of the system. His dancing was as uncoordinated as his mind. Rose handled it without showing how difficult it must have been. Toward the end of the evening, Mary took Frankie, and Rose asked me to dance. She was light on her feet. As we finished she whispered, "Save the last dance for me. Wait until it starts. I'll meet you by the loos."

"Great! Why?"

"Frankie's my friend. That's all. You understand?"

"Sure, and you can save me from Esther."

"Mutual protection," she snorted.

Just before the last dance I went to the men's room. When the music started, I came out. Rose grabbed my arm and we went into the hall. Esther was dancing with Frankie. She stuck her tongue out at me; her dangly earrings, even longer than normal, jiggled. Clara was dancing with Arthur Nancarrow, and Mary, as usual, was with Cap'n Artley. I wondered if they were in on Rose's scheme. When I tried to hold Rose close to me, she whispered, sharply, "Behave yourself, I don't want to make Frankie unhappy. He's watching us."

I turned to face her. "I'm doomed to dance with the most beautiful woman in the world *and* behave myself. It's not fair." At that point, the lights went out. Rose surprised me. Her body pressed against me. Her soft mouth closed, for a moment, against mine.

"Wipe the lipstick off!" She was gone. I was left standing on the dance floor alone, wiping my mouth. I managed to find a seat before the lights came on. The dance ended. Frankie was standing alone, looking bemused. A smear of Esther's lipstick outlined his mouth. Esther was crawling on the floor, looking for an earring, I guessed. Clara was walking out of the door with Rose. Mary was holding Cap'n Billing's hand. They were looking intently at each other. Her face was radiant. Frankie wandered over to me.

"Frankie, you've got lipstick on your face."

He brushed his lips on the sleeve of his jacket. "You did the last dance with Rose."

"Only a bit of it. She had to go."

"Where?"

I looked around, Mary and the Cap'n had gone, too. "I don't know, Frankie. Rose left with your mum."

We went outside. Only Clara was there. "Come on Frankie...you too, Andy. Bus is leaving."

"Clara, do you know where Mary and Rose went?"

"With Cap'n Artley, I expect."

* * *

That night was the first I had spent alone in the house since
Rose returned, a time to look for clues to my unanswered
questions. My flashlight provided enough illumination for
me to check out Rose's room. The furnishings were simple: a
bed, a chest of drawers, a small dressing table and mirror, and
bookshelves. A clothes rod was mounted across a corner of
the room. Hanging from it were two pairs of jeans, a variety of
tops, a pants suit, two skirts, and two dresses—one with a red
floral pattern and one white and low-cut. Sneakers, pumps,
and a pair of smart black leather boots were on the floor.

Two watercolor paintings of the Roseland coastline were
signed "Clara Trevenna." On top of the chest, a faded photograph showed a dark-haired, clean-shaven man, a woman, a
young boy, and a young girl. The woman was Mary and this
very pretty girl looked like Rose. Was the man her father? The
boy looked a lot like Frankie.

Feeling a little guilty, I opened the top drawer. It held flannel pajamas and plain white underwear. Under the pajamas,
I found a baby doll nightie and a lacy, black bra and panty
set. Had she bought them to wear for a lover? A label on
the pajamas caught my attention, Made in U.S.A. I quickly
scanned the rest of the clothes, the shirts and sweaters in the
other drawers, and the hanging clothes. Half came from the
U.S. and Latin American countries, and half from Britain. It

looked like she had spent time in the States as well as in Britain.

I turned to the books. They were an odd mixture of serious fiction—John Fowles's *The French Lieutenant's Woman* among them—and girlish romances. The non-fiction books covered psychology, religion, art, and medicine, including a worn copy of *Gray's Anatomy*.

Mary's room was bigger, allowing for a larger, more comfortable bed than either mine or Rose's. A heavy wooden wardrobe contained skirts, pants, dresses—including the long white one she had worn on Guy Fawkes Day—with room for Mary's shoes under them. The top drawer in a chest contained not only standard, white underwear, but also push-up bras and lacy panties, in a variety of colors, garter belts and black stockings, and a black and red corset with lace trim. A partially used package of birth control pills was at the back of the drawer—proof that Mary had an active sex life. There was also a pink and red frilly nightie. I scanned the labels. Again, about half were from Britain and half from the States. I wondered if Rose had bought some of them for her mother. They did not look like they came from Nancarrow's. A flannel nightgown hung on the back of the door. There was good reason for the girls to wear flannel during the winter. The nights were so cold and damp that I had taken to wearing thermal underwear.

Photos on a bedside table showed the face of the dark-haired man, Mary's husband for sure. A second photograph showed the dark-haired man and Rose now a few years older.

I was about to leave when I noticed some boxes on top of the wardrobe. I pulled the chair from in front of the vanity and climbed on it to find three shoeboxes. The first contained love letters from a man named David. They had come from many parts of the world, Naples, Gibraltar, Southampton, New York, New Orleans, and Rio. Was he a sailor? The letters were all more than fifteen years old, so maybe he was dead. The second box contained a tape recorder/player. Tape cassettes filled the third box. Their labels showed them to be mainly popular music from an earlier time—Belafonte, Mantovani, Vera Lynn, and songs from musicals. One of the tapes had no label.

I checked to make sure that everything was as I had found it and went to bed. I lay for a long time trying to understand what I had seen. Of the people in the photos, I could recognize Rose, Mary, and Frankie. I fell asleep dreaming about them and about Mabel ladling leek soup out of a bucket.

19.

THE NEXT MORNING AT CHAPEL, I SAT WITH CLARA AND Frankie, because Mary and Rose were away. The ancient pews were hard and intended to keep the congregation awake. The altar was a simple wooden table with vases of fresh flowers flanking an old brass cross. Frankie enjoyed the hymns and psalms and sang loudly, generally in tune, in a forceful baritone. The rest of the time he played with the knife Rose had given him. Isaac Nancarrow led the service. His sermon was about striking a balance between gaining knowledge and not being too inquisitive. From the number of times he looked in my direction, I became convinced he was addressing it to me. I drifted off into a daydream about my being too nosy. *I'm not paranoid*, I thought. *Hell, I'm going to be a scientist. What do you expect?*

After the service, I gratefully accepted Clara's offer of lunch.

"Frankie, I guess you and Rose have been friends since you were kids?"

Frankie grunted and continued eating his shepherd's pie.

"They've always been close," Clara volunteered.

"I'm still having a hard time understanding who the various families are, and their interrelationships. What other kids were around when Frankie and Rose were young?"

Clara looked bewildered. "You mean like Jagos and Cockings and Nichols and…"

"Yes."

"Young Artley, Roddie Gay, John Anthony." Frankie spoke through a mouthful of mashed potatoes.

"John Trevenna," Clara added.

"Don't like Johnny."

"Frankie, that's not true. He's your cousin, and don't let Jane hear you calling him Johnny. She doesn't like it."

"Caught Johnny with Rose. Had to fight 'im." So that was the reason Frankie didn't like him. Unfortunately, it confirmed that Johnny and Rose really did have something going. *Damn! Was John Trevenna at the same university as Rose?*

"Frankie. When was that? You never told me," Clara cried.

"Just before he and Rose went away."

"Frankie, I've told you a thousand times not to fight."

"Shouldn't have kissed Rose." Frankie shoveled in more potato.

"That's for her to decide, Frankie."

"She told me no kissin', mum."

Clara was looking uncomfortable, so I interrupted, "What other girls were around when you were young? I think I've seen a photograph somewhere with Frankie and Rose."

"None," said Frankie, grumpily, digging into the pie.

"Frankie, you know that's not true. What about…." Clara stopped talking abruptly.

Frankie's knife and fork drummed on his plate. His head was down and he was muttering to himself. I had never seen him so worked up before. "Don't want to talk about it."

He looked up and pointed at me. "Why did Rose do last dance with you? Why?"

"The last dance had started, Frankie. I met her when I came out of the loo. We were both on our own."

"Shouldn't have. I thought you were my friend."

"I am. Sorry."

"I'll get pudding." Clara started to pick up the plates. I helped and followed her into the kitchen. "Don't mind Frankie. Rose is very special to him. I don't know what will come of it, she and John being educated and him being...you know."

I patted her on the shoulder in commiseration.

When I got home, Mary and Rose were in the living room. They were side by side, fitting together the pieces of a jigsaw puzzle on a folding card table.

"You both disappeared pretty quickly after the dance," I said.

Mary nodded.

"Have a good time?"

"What? Oh, yes. Rose, I can't see where this brown and green piece goes."

I gave up finding out what had happened to them. "Can I help?"

Rose pointed to the edge of a partially finished cottage. "You can get a chair from the kitchen."

The picture on the box top showed an idyllic English country scene with thatched cottages beside a village square. People were dancing around a maypole. The stocks on the green made an incongruous contrast. They trapped a sad-looking man who was staring at the dancers. Mary handed me the bottom half of the box. "I'm doing the village green and the Maypole. Rose is doing the cottages.

Why don't you do the sky? It won't matter if you're seeing it upside down."

I rifled through the box and removed the sky pieces. Working from the top end of the puzzle was difficult, but it allowed me to look at Rose. I found it hard to concentrate and made slow progress—even slower when our hands touched as I tried to fit a piece of sky to the roof of a cottage she was erecting. For a moment we tussled to fit the pieces together. Rose looked at me conspiratorially and advanced another piece of roof. I could not see a matching piece of sky and tried to force fit the piece closest to it.

"We'll not get t'puzzle done if you two carry on." Mary looked at us pityingly. "I'm going to make some tea."

"Rose, why did you rush off after the dance?"

"You're very nosy, Andy." Rose sounded irritated.

"Sorry. I wanted to talk to you."

"Talk!"

"You know. Get to know you better."

"That can mean many things, Andy. We country girls can't afford to be taken in by your big city ways." She was laughing at me.

"Like Patsy you mean?" I snapped, in irritation.

"Patsy got what she wanted."

"You mean Artley?"

She nodded.

"Wasn't that all fixed by them being chosen?"

"Andy, you're new here. Don't make the mistake of assuming that you understand us."

"How about you explain it to me, then? So many things don't add up. For example, what happened to Clara Quick that makes everyone say 'poor Clara'? Who was your father?"

I did not catch myself in time. I had gone too far. Rose wasn't smiling anymore.

"I'm sorry. It's none of my business. Too much spare time to fantasize about the island. I should have gone back to the States until the auks returned. I'm getting sick of sitting in the library, writing stuff for the professor. It's lonely, so I go for long walks."

"Poor Andy. Of course, there's Esther Cocking who would love to cheer you up."

"Sure, and she'll get chosen and Jane Trevenna will give me another lecture and threaten me with dire consequences for messing with her."

"I wondered what had happened...seeing you and Patsy." She paused, looking embarrassed. "Mum wouldn't talk about it."

"I really don't fancy Esther. She's not my type." I looked hard at her. "Now you."

"Are you serious?"

"Yes, very."

"People won't like it," she said it tentatively.

"You mean like Frankie? Frankie wasn't happy about the last dance, you know."

"I know."

"So you'll stay away from other men forever, because Frankie doesn't like it?"

Rose shook her head.

"How about John Trevenna?"

"How do...." Rose pretended to find a fit for a piece of puzzle. "Do you have a girlfriend back home waiting for you?"

I thought about Annie, briefly. "Not anymore."

Rose laughed. "Poor Andy. Tell you what. Next time you go for a long walk, if I'm not working, I'll come with you."

"It's a deal."

Mary came in with the tea and a cake, ending further discussion. "You haven't done much," she said grinning. Too much time arguing, I bet."

We finished tea and continued work on the puzzle in silence. I was concentrating now, and I soon finished the sky. Mary noticed and motioned to the box. "Andy, take my place. I need to wash up the tea things. Why don't you finish this bit of the green? The pieces are in the box."

"Can I help?" I started to rise.

Mary shook her head.

I sat next to Rose and rummaged through the remaining pieces. The ones I needed were easy to spot. They showed the man trapped in the stocks. Not an omen I hoped. Rose watched me putting them in place. Although she said nothing, I could sense a suppressed smile.

20.

ONE SATURDAY IN LATE MAY, ROSE CAME ON A WALK WITH me for the first time. We climbed Brown Willy to the highest point above the lake, chatting about inconsequential matters. Inconsequential, because I did not want to ruin being alone with her, although I couldn't suppress thinking about *the dearth of young women*. The day was cold and clear, and for once the wind was not blowing. Breaking waves etched the coastline in white. The island, clad in its winter clothing of dark and pale browns, lay below us. Small patches of green marked the presence of yews and other evergreen trees. Smoke rose from the chimneys of distant cottages and farms. The trees were bare around Jane Trevenna's house and it stood out clearly.

"That's Trewince," said Rose.

"Yes, I've been there. Jane Trevenna's an interesting person."

"Of course. She explained our customs to you."

I nearly raised my concerns about infanticide, but held back. "Reamed me out would be a better description," I said.

"Served you right!" Rose poked me in the ribs, chuckling.

"She reminds me of a teacher I had in second grade, Miss

McIntyre. I can hear her now, 'Andrew Ferguson stop your jabbering and listen.' I learned a lot from her."

"Did you learn a lot from Jane Trevenna?"

"Up to a point, yes. That tough old bi…rd put me in my place. She's smart."

"She's not the smartest one."

I remembered the change in Jane Trevenna when I had described the mating arrangements of the auks. She had let her guard down. "Who is the smartest, then?"

Rose looked into the distance. Her lips twitched. "You might find the information in the library." Then she shook her head and kicked the ground, as if she had spoken out of turn.

We continued our walk in silence for a while. Her comment reminded me about the piles of books and the bundles of music, plays, and newsletters in the shed behind the library. I had been looking for books on birds and had not paid much attention to them. What had I missed? Reading them would give me something else to do during these dull winter months; however, for the moment I was more interested in finding out about Rose.

"Mrs. Trevenna said that the brighter kids like you go abroad to university. She went to Cambridge in England. What about you?"

"Cambridge, England. You mean like Paris, France? Where else would it be?"

"You know what I mean."

"It's hard not to if you've been in the States. When I visited Duke, I had to explain that when I said Athens I wasn't referring to a town in Georgia."

"Aha! So you also went to Duke. What were you studying?"

"Mum said you were inquisitive. I said I visited Duke. I

didn't say I studied there. It would have been nice. I could have stayed with Aunty Mabel and the professor during breaks, but Duke was too expensive."

"That's why you ended up at Manchester?"

"Yes. I've completed just over four years, and I've got two-and-a-bit years to go."

"What did they say when you left in mid-semester?"

"I explained about the problem for the island with the Penseythan having trouble getting around. The university was very understanding. It made me realize how important it is for me to finish my training. Aunt Jane's having trouble seeing sick people like Aunt Flo and Uncle Ernie at their homes, and...."

"Deliveries?"

Rose turned away. I could see her shoulders tense. "The Penseythan can deal with that,' she muttered. She started to walk away.

I followed. "When I talked to Mrs. Trevenna, she mentioned medical courses. I wondered if she'd finished them."

"Aunt Jane wasn't able to finish her degree, but she's good."

"She mentioned that her son, John, was studying engineering. When will he finish?"

Rose looked thoughtful and a shadow of what looked like unhappiness crossed her face. "He'll be coming back to the island at the same time I hope to be leaving."

"Bad timing. You're not pleased about it?"

"Don't know, really. People expect us...." Her voice trailed away as she quickened her pace.

"Expect us?"

"What?" Then, remembering I was there, "Oh, nothing."

"Where is he?"

"London University." Rose still looked distracted.

"You like him, don't you?"

Rose's head jerked up. "Why did you say that?"

"Frankie said he got into a fight with him because John kissed you."

Rose frowned. "Frankie should learn to...." She slowed down. "John Trevenna and I have been friends for a long time. He's one of very...very few island boys who are intelligent enough to keep up with me. Choice here isn't great. Nice enough lads like Artley, except I need more."

"Do you love Johnny?"

Rose hung her head. "Don't know what that means."

"You would if you did. Does time stop when you see him? Do you get butterflies in your stomach?"

"None of your business," she snapped. Her head sank and we walked in silence again.

I had many more questions to ask about the islanders, but Rose was still looking irritated. "Would you like to see where I was doing my studies at the rookery?"

"Sure."

We passed along the shore of the lake on our way down the mountain. Its clear waters reflected the blue sky. Rose saw me looking and gave a mock shiver. "It gives me the creeps."

"It doesn't look so grim today."

"It's not the lake exactly. It's what happened here."

I laughed. "You're not going to tell me, are you?"

Rose made a face and carried on down the path. We picked our way through the gorse. Its spiky branches were as vicious as ever; they tore at my jeans. Like Frankie, Rose managed to negotiate the path without a problem.

The rains of autumn had cleansed the rookery, although it

still smelled fishy. I told Rose about the excess of males, Nellie and her men friends, and the other good time girls.

"You really like them, don't you?" she said.

"Yes, except...." I left the sentence trailing.

"Except what?"

I turned to look at Rose. "I think that the females deliberately starve female chicks to ensure that there are more males."

Rose's face went taut. She clasped her chest and her head sank. She sounded breathless as she said, "I don't think a mother would kill her own babies."

"No," I replied. "But other females could."

Rose walked away. "Let's talk about something else. Frankie mentioned an auk called Fred. What happened?"

I showed her the place where Fred had died, and described how distraught Nellie had been when she realized he was dead. I explained how Dracula had attacked.

"Dracula? Now there's a name." She chuckled.

"Frankie was very upset, Rose."

"You, too?"

"Yes." The scene was still vivid in my mind. My eyes misted.

Rose put her arms around me and squeezed. "Andy Ferguson, beneath your suave American exterior, you're an old softie, aren't you?"

We held for a moment. She moved away when I tried to kiss her. Damn. I needed to be more patient.

"We peed at the skuas and the gulls," I called after her.

"You did what?"

"To get revenge."

"Did it work?"

"No, and the wind was blowing our way."

Rose giggled. "Serves you right. And I thought you were an adult."

"Frankie does it all the time."

"So, Frankie made you do it? I bet he was laughing to himself."

"He seemed serious."

"Watch out! Frankie's a lot brighter than the act he puts on. Watch out for Clara, too."

Interesting, I thought. "You mean they act out plays in real life?"

"Maybe." Rose started down the path.

On the way back to Veryan, I tried to find out more about Clara's plays, but Rose deflected most of my questions and I found myself describing my background. We were approaching the village, when Rose sprung the one question I did not want to hear.

"What happened to your girlfriend in the States?"

"I've had many girlfriends."

"I bet you had a special one, didn't you?"

"Look, there's the Round House."

"Men used to join the Foreign Legion to escape an unrequited love, Andy. Nowadays they go to an island at the end of the earth." Rose prodded me in the rib again. "Come on. Be honest."

"Odd, the Prof said the same thing. Okay. It didn't work out. I'm over it."

"Are you sure? You sound sad. Was it your fault?"

"Yes, it was my fault. Got to move on." I was sure of that since I'd met Rose. She pursed her lips. I couldn't tell whether she was pleased or not.

"How about you and Johnny Trevenna?"

Rose stopped. Her face clouded for a few seconds. "I haven't seen much of him. I don't know. Recently…." She laughed. "Race you to the house."

I won, but not by much.

That night, as I lay in bed, Rose's question about my girlfriends triggered memories of a discussion I'd had with Annie…

"How do you get on with the girls—women you've dated?" Annie had asked.

"Okay, I guess." I wondered where the conversation was leading.

"How many are still friends, bosom buddies?" Annie stopped fiddling with the book.

"It doesn't work like that with men." Better clarify. "I've got golfing buddies."

"Golf!" Annie shook her head. "When you go home, do any old girlfriends call you just to see how you're doing?"

"I haven't been home enough recently to know."

"What about the women you've dated here?"

"Not really."

"So when you're done with a woman that's—?"

"Whatever!" I was getting tired of the questioning.

A shadow passed across Annie's face. She looked closely at me. "Are you saying that there's never more to a relationship than making love?"

I could tell she was serious, and I did not have a ready answer. In reality, most of my previous relationships had been one-dimensional. My relationship with Annie encompassed more than sex. I had never faced up to what it might mean. Then I screwed up and it was too late.

21.

THROUGH MAY AND JUNE, THE DAYS SETTLED INTO A DULL routine of collecting my thoughts on the auks, finishing essays for the professor, watching Laurel and Hardy movies in the village hall, and taking long walks alone. I also began to work my way through the books in the shed behind the library. Generally, the books were old and had nothing to do with Roseland, so I started on the bundles of papers. The first set consisted of sheet music from the 1920s and '30s. The second bundle contained a number of plays by Shakespeare, and it included two by George Bernard Shaw with all the parts separated out—*Pygmalion* and *The Doctors Dilemma*. A flier for performances of *Pygmalion*, for May of 1944, was stapled to the last page. The cast names included Clara Trevenna as Eliza, a Hartley Billing as Doolittle—surely Cap'n Billing would have been too young—and a George Nancarrow as Professor Higgins. I nearly missed the credit at the end, to the director—Jane Nichols! So even before she married Charles Trevenna, she was organizing things.

The absence of a woman in my life was getting to me again, and my frustration progressed to a kind of sexual numbness that continued into July. My main relief was going back to the dance on Saturday night where, at least, I could enjoy the pleasure of holding a woman. Although Frankie came with Clara, he did not dress up any more and spent most of his time chatting to the unattached young men and dancing occasionally with Esther or Rose. Rose danced with me, but never for the last dance, when she played the field. I hardly knew most of the women who collared me at the end of the night, but I learned more about the art of the quick, passionate kiss.

Esther grabbed me for the last dance at the mid-July dance in Portloe. She had tried, unsuccessfully, at previous dances. From the moment I put my left hand on her back, she pressed hard, and when the lights went out, she slid her hand between my legs and opened her mouth wide on mine. No longer numb, I responded. Esther pulled away before the end of the dance and, taking a handkerchief, wiped my mouth. The lights went on. Amazingly, Esther had not lost an earring.

Rose was with Frankie. He had a faint trace of lipstick on his mouth and appeared bewildered. As I led Esther back to pick up her bag and helped her with her coat, she whispered in my ear, "I'm free Wednesday afternoon. I can meet you on the Trewince road at two. Will you come?"

What the hell, I was getting nowhere with Rose. "Sure, where exactly?"

"There's a hill behind the farm...in the woods where the road goes over it."

Before we left Portloe, the Lagonda appeared and Clara and Frankie got in.

On the bus, I sat with Mary, and Esther sat with a girlfriend. Rose had disappeared.

"Mary, where's Rose?"

"Gone to stay with a friend." Mary replied brusquely.

Esther and her friend got off the bus at the school. As she passed my seat she whispered, "I'll see you then?" I nodded.

"What was that about?" asked Mary.

"The next dance?" I replied quickly.

Mary tilted her head, looking skeptical.

Sunday was another miserable day, and after chapel and lunch, I settled down to helping Mary with yet another jigsaw puzzle. By three o'clock, feeling housebound, I went for a walk to the rookery and back, keeping close to the stone wall on the final approach to Veryan to avoid the biting wind. As I approached the Round House, the Lagonda drove into the square and stopped. Mr. Thomas and Frankie got out. They opened the rear doors for Clara and Rose, who ran home shielding their heads from the rain. My list of questions without answers was increasing, and I added to the list why Mary had not told me that Rose was at Trewince. I could understand why Clara and Frankie would stay there, Clara being Jane's sister-in-law. Why Rose? Was Jane Trevenna training her? I didn't like to think about what that might mean. I waited a few minutes before returning to the house. Mary was reading.

"Andy, best get those wet things off. You'll catch your death of cold. Rose was lucky, she had a lift. Got wet anyway. She's upstairs changing."

"I saw the Lagonda leaving."

"I'll take your jeans and shirt and hang them up in the kitchen. They'll dry faster there near the stove." She held out her hand.

"You mean here?"

"Andy, I've seen men in their underwear before. Hurry, before Rose comes down and embarrasses you."

"It's not Rose I'm worried about. It's you." I stripped off and paraded in my briefs.

Mary laughed and smacked my butt. "Get upstairs before I really spank you."

At that moment Rose came downstairs. She looked startled, and I pretended to be embarrassed.

"Your mother made me do it," I shouted and ran up the stairs.

On Wednesday morning, finding it hard to concentrate in the house, I went to the library to work on my dissertation. Visions of Esther Cocking kept appearing in my mind, and she was becoming more and more attractive as the morning wore on. I gave up on work, and instead went to the shed to find the old newsletters. They confirmed that the Penseythan was always a woman. She served for a number, usually three five-year terms. Florence Billing served from 1920-24, 1925-29, and 1930-34 and Agnes Nichols from 1935-39, 1940-44, and 1945-47. I wondered why her third term was cut short. Had she died? For 1948-49, presumably to finish the Nichols term, 1950-54, and 1955-59, Prudence Nancarrow served and from 1960-64, 1965-69, and 1970-74, Jane Cocking. Since 1975, Jane Trevenna had been the Penseythan. As far as I could tell, when there was any mention of a birth, the Penseythan was the midwife, supporting my theory that a key reason they held the post was population control. I thought about tackling Rose again on the subject, but given her reaction to my comment on the auks I decided I didn't want to mess up my chances with her.

I ate my bread and cheese on the way to meet Esther. No pickle, I did not want my breath to smell. The clouds had dissipated, and the day was cold, but the sun had broken through for the first time in days, a good omen. A mile and a half down the road, a cyclist came toward me as I started up the hill. It looked like Rose. For a moment I thought about ducking behind a hedge, but she had seen me and waved.

"Hi, Andy."

"Rose, where did you come from?"

"Trewince. It's a nice day so I borrowed a bike to get home. Where are you going?"

"On a previous walk, I noticed a stile and a path skirting the field that looks like it might go up to the southern cliffs. There's a path just ahead. I thought I'd explore it."

"It's a lovely day. Mind if I come with you? Please, please." She linked her arm in mine and looked at me beseechingly. She was wearing tight fitting jeans and her blue anorak, and looked wonderful.

"Come on, Rose!" I said, laughing. "I'll enjoy the company." I wondered if Esther had seen us. I would have to think of an excuse.

"Great!"

We manhandled the bike over the stile and rested it against the hedge and then followed the path around the field for a quarter mile before heading up through the woods to the ridge. A tough hike through the woods took us to the top of the cliff. This was a little-used path, and on the steep sections we had to walk in single file. Rose's slim, long legs and neatly rounded backside led me. It was the turn of the verb, 'to lust', to come to mind.

The woods thinned as we neared the cliff and the trees became scrawnier and bent by the wind, which gusted strongly as we left the cover of the hill. Praise the Lord, there was no gorse. The cliffs were scalloped in a breathtaking view from the Nare Head to the west to Lands End in the east. The rollers came from the south—probably as far as South Georgia some sixteen hundred miles away—without breaking, and surged against the sheer face of the cliff. Only in a few places had rocks collected at sea level, suggesting the sharp drop-off went far below the surface.

"Spectacular, isn't it?" said Rose, taking hold of my arm to steady herself against the gusts.

"I should have brought my camera. I'm missing some great shots." I wasn't just talking about the scenery. Rose's hair was blowing in the wind. She wore no makeup. Her cheeks were flushed. My heart was beating rapidly. "Thanks for coming with me, Rose." I turned quickly and kissed her.

Rose pulled away. "Andy, behave yourself!" She sounded more exasperated than angry. She walked away, turning to call out to me. "If we go towards the Nare, we'll come across a path down to Anthony's farm. It's a lot shorter."

I followed her and after about a mile, we saw the farm through the trees. A man was working on a tractor in the barn—George Anthony from the band.

We continued carefully down the steep path. Near the farm I said, "I wonder if his brother's better."

Rose looked surprised. "You know Ernie?"

"Band practice. George told me about him."

By this time we'd reached the barn. "Uncle George," Rose said.

He looked up and grinned. "Rosie, Andy, it's nice to see

you both. I must look a sight. Come on into the house. I'll make some tea. Andy, Ernie has been hoping to see you."

George led us into the kitchen. As we entered, I could feel the heat emanating from the black stove that took up much of the inner wall of the house. Water pipes branched from it along the wall and to the floor above.

"Wait here a minute while I get Ernie ready," said George as he moved a ready kettle of water onto a hot plate.

After a while, he reappeared. "You can come in now."

A frail-looking version of George was sitting up on a couch that backed onto the kitchen wall, the warmest part of the room. He was wearing a dressing gown over pajamas and a blanket covered his legs. "Andy, I've looked forward to meeting you. George tells me you play a fine trumpet." Ernie's voice was surprisingly strong.

"Thank you, Mr. Anthony. I've had a lot of fun being in the band. I wish it were under different circumstances."

"Don't you worry yourself about that, Andy. God giveth and He also taketh away...so the Bible says. You were meant to play your role." He paused. "I'd like to hear you play, Andy. Would you, after we have tea?"

"I don't have my—"

"You can use my trumpet, if you don't mind."

"That'll be fine."

George served the tea very strong and hot, accompanied by thick slices of bread and butter and strawberry jam. The hike had made us hungry and we tucked in. Afterward, I played "Lamorna," "The Tennessee Waltz," "Starry Gazy Pie," and lastly, the "Floral Dance" with George and Rose dancing into and out of the kitchen.

"Thank you, Andy. George is right, you play a fine trumpet. You're welcome to play here any time."

"I'll remember that. Now, you get better, you hear." I shook his hand and Rose kissed him on the cheek.

George grasped my hands as we left. "Andy, I can't tell you how much this meant to Ernie." He let go and brushed a hand across his face. "Got to work on the tractor." He turned away so that we wouldn't see his tears.

We headed home. When we were out of sight, Rose turned towards me. "Andy, that was a really kind thing you did, playing for poor old Ernie. I'm afraid he's got cancer. He won't last long. You play a mean trumpet, too." Her arms went around my neck. Her kiss was tender and thoughtful as if she were checking me out. I responded cautiously, not wanting to ruin the moment, and let her decide when to finish.

Late July into August had the worst weather I had experienced on the island. The temperature hovered in the forties during the day and dropped further at night. It rained for days. I forced myself to go to the library and work. In the evenings, I went to the pub more often than before. Jacob Jago was usually there. Whatever he knew about Patsy and me didn't seem to worry him. He taught me to play darts. Though I became quasi-proficient, I was unable to beat him, even when he was tipsy. I have no idea how he made it home on his motorized bicycle. Driving at night had become dangerous, and they cancelled the Saturday dances. I did not have to face Esther, but heard how she felt from Rose.

"I hear you stood Esther up, Andy."

"Where did you hear that, Rose?"

"At the school from a mutual friend."

I smiled at her. "You're to blame. You intercepted me and enticed me away."

Rose looked surprised. "You were going to meet Esther when I met you?"

"Yup."

"Why didn't you tell me?"

A good question and the truth seemed the best way to answer it. "Honestly, I worried that she might be the next girl *chosen*, and frankly, I preferred to be with you."

Rose shook her head. "I keep finding out things about you, Andrew. One minute I see how kind you can be; the next, you aren't very nice."

"Aw, shucks, Rosie." I said, trying to sound like a cowboy in the last movie I'd seen. "I didn't expect to meet you. Incidentally, you never told me where you'd been."

Rose ignored my question. "Charming, but opportunistic," she said as she walked away, turning to add, "Now I can see how you might have lost your last girlfriend."

How could she have known, a lucky guess? Not the time to argue, I decided. "You're right, Rose. I'll apologize to Esther, when I see her."

"Clever answer, Andy, but do you mean it?"

"I wasn't joking when I said I preferred to be with you. It's difficult seeing you every day and not being able to…. You're not my sister, for God's sake!"

"It's not easy for me, either. Mum told me I'd have to be careful. I do like you, but I'll be here on the island when you're gone and I have to worry about my future." She bit her lip and looked at the floor. "It's expected that John and I—"

"You and John Trevenna, how do you feel about it?"

"You wouldn't understand, Andy. We go back a long time.

He's educated like me. We both have responsibilities. It makes sense."

"You didn't answer my question."

"I did. You don't like the answer. You don't understand responsibility. The island needs us."

"That's more important than what you want for yourself?"

Rose came close and looked hard at me. "Yes it is. This is my island, too."

I reckoned I had a chance to win over another man, but fat chance against a whole island. My face must have shown my disappointment.

"Poor Andy," she said again. Compassion or amusement, I could not tell.

"You make it sound just like 'poor Clara.'"

"I pray it won't be."

"What do you mean?"

Rose was silent for several moments before she replied. "I'll tell you what happened, but you mustn't let anybody know I told you."

"Cross my heart and hope to die."

"I'm not joking."

"Nor am I."

"Aunt Clara's first boyfriend was John Nichols. The Nichols work the farm south of the Cockings'. It backs onto the Trewince road. Clara and John were childhood friends and he was the only one for her, as she was for him. Clara was very beautiful when she was young, I'm told."

I nodded. "I've seen signs of it, when she's happy and not worrying about Frankie."

"John's mother, Agnes Nichols, was Penseythan. She and the Seythan picked Clara to be Queen."

"And they didn't pick John Nichols as her King?"

Rose nodded. "They picked Pete Quick and six other men. Mum says that Clara and John were devastated."

"Why did the Seythan do that? Didn't Agnes Nichols like Clara?"

"I've heard word…but I'm not sure. Anyway, the reason she gave was that Agnes Nichols's father was a Trevenna. Clara and John were second cousins. Our rules on intermarriage are strict."

"That makes sense on a small island, but isn't second cousin a far enough separation?"

"I think so, and I'm sure you could find examples if you looked at the register of marriages, births, and deaths in the Seythan House. Nevertheless, Agnes Nichols felt she couldn't be seen as making that decision or didn't want to…or so my mum says."

"Clara ended up marrying Pete Quick?"

"Eventually."

"What happened to John?"

"On the day before the dance, he and Clara met in the woods below Trewince. They planned to hide there until December the 22nd, so that Clara wouldn't have to go through with the dance and all. Agnes Nichols had been worried John and Clara would do something like that. She saw John going to the woods and alerted the Seythan. The men came and found them. They threw John in jail. On the twenty-first, after the children had left, they put him in the stocks. He was there until the next morning, watching the dance, looking at the Round House, seeing the seven men go in to be with Clara and seeing everybody leave."

"Oh shit! The poor guy."

"After they released him, he ran away. A week later, they found his clothes on the shore of Dark Lake. His body was lying near where the stream comes down the mountain. Clara had a complete breakdown."

"My God! I can see why she flipped. Did she do the whole…sex thing…in the Round House?"

Rose looked surprised. "What do you mean?"

"Patsy told me what happens."

"Oh!" She hesitated, obviously worrying about what she could say. The words came out in a rush. "Nobody knows, exactly, although I've heard that Pete Quick persuaded all the men it wouldn't be fair. He was a decent man."

"John Nichols didn't know what had happened?"

"He ran away before Clara or Pete could tell him."

"Clara married Pete?"

"A month later." Rose sighed. "She was already pregnant with John's child."

"Pete didn't mind?"

"I wouldn't say that, exactly. Pete was in love with her. They had a happy marriage for the few years before he died."

"Jesus. Poor Clara! So John Nichols was Frankie's father?"

"They reckon. I shouldn't…." Rose bit her lip. "You promise you won't tell anyone. Mum'll kill me if she finds out, you know."

"Cross my heart…."

"I mean it!"

"What happened to Agnes Nichols?"

"She resigned as Penseythan and never left her house again."

"I wondered why her third term was shorter than normal."

Rose looked startled. "How did you find that out?"

I grinned. "Musty old newsletters in the library; they're full of interesting information."

Afterward, I thought about what I had heard. It explained why the islanders were protective of Clara and Frankie, and it showed how seriously they took their rituals. Agnes Nichols had acted in a positively biblical way in sacrificing her son to protect the islanders' way of life. Crazy though, looked at from the outside. Then there was the fact that they must allow some women to have two female children to compensate for those who only had males. Otherwise the population would have gradually decreased. In turn, that implied that the Penseythan could use prejudice in deciding which women would have that privilege—a frightening power. Jane Trevenna hadn't been joking when she said she would deal with me severely if I continued to mess around with Patsy.

What would happen to Rose, I worried? At least she had not been chosen yet. I did not like the thought and went to the library to submerse myself in my dissertation.

My relationship with Rose was improving. We worked on puzzles together and played chess. She usually beat me. We went for walks now, when the weather was not impossibly bad. We talked about her dream of becoming the island's doctor. Rose was amused by my stories about the auks. She loved the names I had given them and insisted I take her to see Nellie and the other good-time girls when they returned. She flirted outrageously when her mother was not around, and I suspected that she timed her visits to the bathroom so that I would see her scantily clad. Rose was skittish, letting me kiss her but being firm in not letting it go any farther, exciting me and frustrating me at the same time.

22.

BY THE TIME I COMPLETED MY SECOND ESSAY FOR THE PRO-fessor, August was nearly over. During the month, Rose came with me to one dance at Portloe. I had not seen Esther since standing her up, and when I entered the hall she stuck her tongue out. I toured the floor with a number of women, but not Esther, and then Clara picked me.

"I see you came with Rose."

"With Rose and Mary," I said cautiously. "Frankie's avoiding me."

"Don't you mind Frankie. He'll get over it." She squeezed me gently. "You and Rose make a fine looking couple."

"Thanks, Clara." I waited until we had done a twirl or two. "How about Rose and John Trevenna?"

Clara pulled back so that she could look at me. Her face was guileless. "Isn't that for you and Rose to decide?" I caught the flicker of a smile as her head came forward.

I returned to sit with Young Artley and the lads. Frankie moved away. I signaled to Rose to meet me outside. She nudged Mary and they went to the ladies room. I followed.

"Rose, I can see Frankie's upset. Could you...uh?"

"You want me to do the last dance with him, don't you?"

I nodded.

"Okay."

I hugged her.

"But you've got to do it with Esther."

"You're kidding! She's not talking to me."

"Leave it to me!"

Just before the last dance, I could see Esther arguing with her escort. He looked furious when she strode across the floor and grabbed me.

"I'm sorry, Esther. I didn't know what to do when I met Rose on the road."

She pinched me hard. "I'm not forgivin' you, Andy Ferguson."

"I'm sor—" I did not finish, because as the lights went out, her mouth was on mine and again her hand slid between my legs.

She pulled away before the lights came on. She wiped my mouth. "Now you know what you've been missing."

She was right. My wilting erection was evidence, but I would have given it up for being with Rose. Frankie was holding Rose's hand. On the way home he and Rose sat together on the bus. Mary had disappeared. Rose and I returned to the house alone.

"Goodnight, Andy." Rose ran to her room. I wanted to follow, but some instinct told me to be patient. I worked a while on the unfinished puzzle and used the toilet before going upstairs to brush my teeth. On the landing, I met Rose, wearing her baby doll nightie.

"Oh, Andy, I thought you'd gone to bed!"

Her act of surprise was not convincing. "Do I get a goodnight kiss to make up for missing the last dance?"

"If you promise to be good."

"I'll be very good."

She came into my arms and the kiss was more passionate than ever before. I had my hands on her firm round little bottom and was pushing against her. For a moment, she did not resist and her legs separated slightly.

"No! You mustn't do that." She maneuvered out of my arms.

"Come to my room?"

"I don't know, Andy. Are you serious about me?" She was edging away.

"I—" There was a noise downstairs, the front door opening.

"It's me mum. I've got to go."

"But—"

"Quick, go brush your teeth!" Rose shoved me away and scurried to her room. Mary was at the bottom of the stairs. She did not come up.

"I got a lift," she said. "I'm going to have a cuppa. Good night, Andy."

I brushed my teeth for a long time, brooding about what I'd missed. I slept fitfully. Later, there were noises from Mary's room, quieter than usual, but enough to wake me.

I slept with a recurring nightmare. I would be with Rose, feeling her soft body as we melted together when, suddenly, I would not be able to move. The reasons varied: the blind had fallen on top of me or, worst of all, I would be trapped in the stocks looking at the closed door of the Round House—just like poor John Nichols.

I wanted to tell Rose how I felt about her, but we were never alone. We went for a walk only one more time before the professor contacted me; unfortunately, Mary came too.

I was eating breakfast when the phone rang. Mary answered it and called out, "Andy, you need to go to the radio station. They have a message for you and you'll need to reply."

"Do I have to walk to Portloe?"

"Better. You can take the bus. When you get there, take the track to Billing's farm. It's about half a mile or so farther on. Say hello to Uncle Douglas for me. He's the Cap'n's older brother, Young Artley's dad."

After a two-mile hike up the hill from Portloe, I came to the low building that I had seen from the boat. A radio tower, an array of aerials, and various weather meters rose above the building. Inside, I met Douglas Billing, the radio operator and weather recorder. Despite a resemblance to the Cap'n, his face was softer and kinder looking.

"I'm Doug Billing. It's nice to meet you at last, Andy. I don't get out much anymore. What with the work an' all. I've heard a lot about you from Artley." He reached into a drawer. "Here's the professor's message. You be thinking about a reply while I get us some tea. I think I still have biscuits in the larder."

The professor's message was brief:

Return next boat to Capetown. Immediately airmail samples for testing to me at university! Mark package 'Scientific Samples.' I will deal with customs! Use your return airline ticket to get to States. You will return to Roseland on subsequent boat. Please acknowledge. GLJ.

I munched on an oatmeal biscuit before sipping the very hot tea cautiously. "Do you know when the next boat is, Doug?"

"I've heard they're hoping for the day after tomorrow, depending on weather."

"Good grief!"

"Can you be ready in time?"

"Whatever!" I replied without thinking.

Douglas shook his head. "You young people. I can't keep up with your lingo."

"It's from *Peanuts.*"

Douglas's face was uncomprehending. "Whatever." He looked pleased with himself. "Now, what do you want to say?" I handed him my reply.

Will come. Got many good samples. Regards to Mabel. A.J.F.

I retrieved my cartons from Mary's icebox and transferred the frozen auk parts to thermos flasks loaned to me by Arthur. Three days later, the weather was decent enough for the boat to go to sea. Mary and Rose came to Portloe to see me off.

Both gave me a hug and Rose whispered, "Safe trip, Andy. I'll be thinking of you."

Mary had turned away to talk to Cap'n Billing, and Rose gave me a quick kiss. She was still standing on the jetty watching when the boat cleared the harbor entrance.

The weather might have been improving, but the bitterly cold wind was strong enough to make white caps and blow cold hard spray as the boat lurched on the giant waves. Neither Frankie nor his replacement had sailed with us, so I did odd jobs to help the crew. It took my mind off the nausea induced by the engine fumes below. Other than that, I spent as much of my time on deck as possible, and returned to my diet of oatmeal and hot tea.

After two days in Cape Town, I flew back to the States, arriving September 7th.

* * *

Mabel met me at Washington's Dulles airport. "The professor has to teach," she said. "You'll have to make do with me."

"It's a pleasure to see you, m'dear," I replied in my best island accent.

Mabel laughed. "You'll never pass for one of us." Her face turned serious. "I heard Jane Trevenna had words with you."

"You could say that."

"You need to watch your step with her, young Andy."

"You're not kidding. I heard what happened to...." I was going to say Clara, when I remembered that anything I said would likely get back to Roseland.

"What happened to who?" Mabel asked casually.

"Oh, nothing."

When we reached the house, Mabel pointed me up the stairs. "You'll be in the same room, m'dear," she said. "I'll serve tea shortly."

The professor returned while I was having tea and scones.

"It's good to be back in warm weather. It's been really bad on the island."

"I always tried to avoid their winter." The eyebrows showed sympathy. "You mailed the auk samples as soon as you arrived in Cape Town?"

"Yes, sir."

"Hopefully they left on the plane with you."

"I think so. Will customs be a problem?"

"The problem is the Department of Agriculture, if you

don't make arrangements in advance. Forewarned is fore-armed. I expect to hear from them soon."

"I'm glad you told me what to do. By the way, I have my second essay for you. I was going to send it when your message came.

"The first essay was excellent. I can tell you don't like skuas." The professor's eyebrows exhibited horror. "Nor I. Nasty birds."

I described in detail what had happened to Fred.

Mabel, looking upset, said, "How awful."

"Typical behavior, Mabel. Skuas are vicious creatures. But it's their role in life." The professor's eyebrows shrugged.

His use of the words "vicious creatures" reminded me of the question I wanted to ask about infanticide. But I held back until Mabel had left.

The professor continued. "Now to business. I expect you'll want to see your parents, Andy. We don't have a lot of time for our work."

"I thought the boats only went every two months or so in the summer?"

"Generally speaking, yes, but I hear that with this bad winter, fuel supplies on the island are low. The boat will go back to Cape Town and will return to Roseland the first week in October."

"What do you want me to do?"

"We need to go over your ideas about the auks. I suggest you visit your parents as soon as we've discussed the tests you should do on the samples. Then I need time to digest your written work and thoughts. Let us say you will go for three days."

"When I come back, there's something I need to get your advice on," I said. "You won't believe what they're doing."

The eyebrows showed interest. "Certainly. The subject?"

"How the islanders limit their population," I blurted out. "Just like the auks."

The eyebrows sagged. "I wondered if you would notice that issue, Andrew. We will discuss it when you return. The auks too, eh. Most interesting."

"It's barbaric."

"When you return from visiting your parents, Andrew," the professor said firmly.

23.

MY PARENTS CAME OUT OF THE HOUSE AS I DROVE UP. MY mother hugged me for a long time. Even my father appeared relieved to see me. Big surprise. In a strange way, I felt relieved.

"I read your essay, and the work on the auks was most interesting." He seemed amazed that I could put my thoughts on paper. "You seem to believe this business about their… um…sex life?"

"You should see them, Dad. Nellie is real clever at handling—"

Dad rolled his eyes. "Really clever!"

"Yeah. She's really clever at handling her gentlemen friends."

My mother gave me another hug. "I love the way you call the females your good-time girls."

My parents and I talked for hours that afternoon and evening. I told them about Roseland, its isolation, the apparent surplus of men, and the kindness of the islanders. I talked about Mary Pascoe and Cap'n Billing, and Frankie and Clara. I described playing in the band, the pub, and the dances, with the custom of turning the lights out during the last dance.

"I remember that when we were young," my father said, looking at my mother.

She smiled at him, fondly. "So, how did you fare?"

"I feel like I've been kissed by half the women on Roseland."

"Any in particular?" my mother asked, looked at me intently.

"Two girls, Patsy and Esther, came on strong. Patsy's married now."

"I hear you. It nearly got me into a fight once." My father laughed. "If what you say about a surplus of men is right, you can't be exactly popular?"

"I have to be careful." I told them about the Seythan and Jane Trevenna's comments on their determination to keep the population under control. I left out the part about the warning.

"So is Esther the girl?"

"Mom, let it go!" I continued talking, while working on an answer to her question. I started by describing the various summer festivities, leaving out what happened in the Round House. I talked at length about the auks. My description of Fred's death upset both of them. My mother continued to look at me expectantly.

"Okay, Mom. I can see you won't wait anymore. It's my landlady's daughter, Rose Pascoe. She's beautiful and smart, and she's going to be a doctor. When I went with her mother to collect her from the boat, everything stopped. For a moment I couldn't breathe, and—"

"I know what you mean," my father said. "That's how I felt when I met your mother." For the moment, he and my mother were in their own world.

"I'm going to make some coffee." He left. We had reached the limit of how much personal chat he could stand.

"You were going to say something else?" My mother said, reading me correctly as usual.

"Right." I couldn't mention the babies, but John Trevenna was another matter. "Unfortunately, I think she's going with someone else. Also, she's adamant that when she finishes her training she'll go back to the island."

"But I sense you believe you have a chance." My mother looked hard at me. "If you were successful, would you go and live there?"

"I don't know. What would I do to contribute?"

My mother sighed. "Andy, I don't want you to leave. But if you really care, you should come up with something the island needs. I'd better see what your father's doing." She stood.

I went over and gave her a hug. "Thanks, Mom." She clung to me briefly before heading to the kitchen.

I knew that Rose's sense of duty would never let her leave the islanders without a doctor. Thinking about what I could do had already led me to modern agriculture, and now it spurred me to find out more about my father's plans. I spent most of my remaining time with him, learning about environmentally responsible farming. He'd taken a course at North Carolina State. His new dream was to raise pigs, collect the manure in a tank, and use the methane from anaerobic digestion to make heat and electricity. When I returned to Elkton, I had a copy of his course notes and suggestions for books to read.

24.

JUST AS ON THE FIRST TIME I HAD VISITED 6 GROSVENOR Drive, the professor was working in the garden. He waved and came forward as I drove in and parked.

"Come on in, Andy. Let me help with your bag. Mabel will make us some tea." His eyes widened and his eyebrows lifted. "Andrew, when you're settled, you and I will have our talk. Let us say in the library in fifteen minutes." He headed for the house.

I returned to a distant bedroom on the third floor that must at one time have been servant's quarters. I unpacked, went to the library, and pretended to read a book on albatrosses while waiting for the professor.

At the appointed time he stuck his head around the door. "Good," he said, closing the door.

I explained that we had much to talk about. His small dark eyes stared at me quizzically. "I presume that you have not mentioned the matter of the island's population to anyone else."

"No, sir. I don't even like to think about it. It's horrific."

"Right, right." He sat across the table from me. "Since you

raised the topic, I have given much thought to what to say to you. I was not exactly straightforward when I told you that the reason I had stopped my research was a difficulty in scrambling around. The fact is that I was thrown off the island."

"Why?" I blurted out. There was a lot more I wanted to say, but it was more important to prod him into telling me all he knew...or suspected.

"Like you, I wondered how the island constrained its population, and had semi-developed ideas about the auks." He sighed. "When I was on Roseland I stayed at the Jago farm. Mabel's father, George Jago, was interested in birds and helped me in my studies. I got to know him and his wife, Emily, very well. When I arrived, they had two children, Jacob and Miriam, and Emily was pregnant. I could tell they were worried about something as the due date approached. Finally, Emily explained the sad truth to me. If she had a girl the chances were that it would die. The decision would be up to the Penseythan, Prudence Nancarow."

"Not the Seythan?"

"In principle, yes." The professor shook his head. "In practice, nobody else likes to be involved."

"But the Penseythan has to allow it sometimes."

"Yes, but I also realized from various comments that there was a long-standing feud between the Jagos and the Nancarrows, an argument about land. George and Emily were not optimistic about the outcome." The professor looked at the ceiling. "Prudence Nancarrow...the name evokes images of a maiden aunt. It should not. Lucrezia Borgia would be closer to describing that manipulative, cruel woman."

"What did you do?"

"I had planned to take the next boat to Cape Town to pick

up supplies. At the time, Captain Hartley's father, a good friend of the Jagos, was the skipper. Emily came with me. I arranged for her to stay in Cape Town and have her baby."

"Which was...I've got it...Mabel."

"Yes." The professor smiled. "Shortly after I returned, the governor visited. I asked to talk to him privately. We went for a walk and I explained what I believed to be happening.... I don't know whether he didn't believe me or didn't want to know about it, but I can still see his hard face and his eyes looking into the distance. 'Llewellyn Jones, you are a guest here. This island is strategically important to our government. It is a model of reliability and stability. You tell me that someone told you this...this business of infanticide, yet you have no proof of what you say, and will not divulge the name of your informant. If you insist on pursuing the matter, I suggest that you do so with the appropriate authority... the Penseythan.' He turned his back on me and returned to Veryan."

His comments brought back memories of my visit to see Jane Trevenna. "And you went to see her?"

"I didn't have to." The professor's eyes closed briefly, as if he were remembering the scene. "The governor had mentioned our discussion and by then she had understood my role in helping Emily." He drummed his fingers on the table. "Only after I swore on the Bible to keep their secret did she allow me to leave. She agreed that Emily and Mabel could return to the island. Having me die would have been awkward, seeing that the governor knew about my concerns. Eh, boyo?"

"But Mabel lives here?"

"Part of the agreement was that Mabel could remain on Roseland only until she was sixteen."

"That explains a lot, but after what happened to you, why did they agree to let me come to the island?"

"It was difficult for Mabel coming to live here. I encouraged her to call her sister Miriam every month." The professor smiled. "I began to get requests for help. Helping support studies abroad. Other than that, small things most of the time, you know, but important for the islanders. Letting you complete my studies was their way of paying me back."

"So, what should I do?"

"Well, Andrew, you must make your own decisions. But if you plan to confront Jane Trevenna, we should reconsider the wisdom of your returning. From all accounts she can be a vindictive woman. Let me tell you something: she married Charles Trevenna because of his status on the island."

"Owning Trewince you mean?"

"Yes. In reality she was in love with Charlie Gay, but he had married Petunia. From all accounts, Jane has tried to make life difficult for Petunia ever since."

I half-listened to what he said. My mind was on Rose. *Not see her again? No way.* I had anticipated, somewhat, the prof's reaction, and had rationalized a solution in my mind. I would go back and pursue Rose. Not for the professor, so back to our discussion. "I know it would be difficult, but I suppose I could contact the governor on St. Helena. And—"

"And what?" the professor retorted sharply. "You are a student and not even a British citizen. I suspect that you would be politely asked to…how does the modern expression go, boyo? Shove it."

I acted as if I had not thought of that response. "I'm sure you're right, sir." I tried to sound rueful. "So, I guess I'll go back and keep my mouth shut."

The professor shook his head and his eyebrows expressed sadness. "Unfortunate conclusion, but I suspect the correct one." He paused. "I have some photographs somewhere that might help me to explain more about the islanders and there customs. I'll get Mabel to track them down."

25.

FOR THE NEXT FIVE DAYS, I SPENT MOST OF MY TIME AT THE university. The professor had arranged for me to use equipment in a physics department laboratory. I mounted my auk's beaks on stands and studied them under white light using a hand-held spectrometer. At first, I could see few differences. Then, in the way that many scientific discoveries are made, I found an effect. While I was peering at Fred's beak, my sleeve caught on a second stand causing it to move Fred's stand. I saw a subtle effect. The spectrum changed. I then tried rotating each beak quickly in front of the spectrometer. In the case of the men friends, the spectrum changed very little. But on Fred's beak, the spectrum flickered. In fact, once I had found the effect I could see it by simply looking while rotating the beak. It made sense. I had observed that during courtship the males waggled their heads. Ergo, the females responded to the changing colors.

"Wonderful discovery, Andrew. It's the kind of thing that keeps us scientists going." The Prof's eyebrows mirrored his excitement. "We must celebrate. At dinner, I will open a bottle of a fine red wine that I have been saving for just such an event."

Further results on the auk samples came in the next day, showing little difference in chemical emissions from the organ samples between the principal males, like Fred, and the gentlemen friends. Also, from the chromosome tests on the auk parts I could not detect any consistent variation between the gentlemen friends and the dominant male auks, like Fred. The sperm counts, though, were very interesting. The gentlemen friends did not do well in that regard. It seemed that the good-time girls were wise in their choice of lovers. I called the professor. He urged me to try to get more samples when the auks returned to Roseland.

In the afternoon, Mabel appeared with three photo albums. Her attempts to clean them before dumping them on the dining room table had not been successful. Dust covered our working surface. Most were of the scenery—Portloe, the square at Veryan, Brown Willy, Trewince, and a few of the farms—looking much like they did today. But some showed Guy Fawkes and Mid Summer's Day festivities. I concentrated on them. I gave up trying to work it out and turned to the other photos. I could recognize a young Mary Pascoe—gorgeous as ever—and a young Mister Thomas, quite handsome looking.

One in particular caught my eye. It showed a young woman apparently flirting with a young man. The caption said, "Jane Trevenna and Charlie Gay enjoy the festivities." I remembered the professor had told me that Jane had never forgiven Petunia for taking Charlie.

As I replaced a photo of the square in Veryan, I spotted something odd—there weren't any stocks. The date on the photo was June 1953. At dinner, I mentioned it to the professor.

"The stocks, eh. Do I remember stocks? Yes, I do. They used to be in the square. Then they were taken up and put in a shed behind the Seythan House, I think. They must have decided to put them out again. The islanders have many customs they don't talk about."

"Why would they do that?"

"Maybe they put them out when they think they'll be needed, eh."

I ignored his warning look. His comment on customs had reminded me of the pagan costumes I had seen. "Prof, what's with the weird costumes and masks, like for Guy Fawkes and the day of the Floral Dance?"

The professor flexed his eyebrows and looked at the table. "The Cornish have been around a long time, Andrew. Their oldest monuments are at least three thousand B.C. On Roseland, as in my homeland, Wales, the old ways have not been forgotten. I have often wondered whether Christianity is merely a thin covering over the more ancient religions. To many of them, the devil is very real; hence the round houses. The wearing of the costumes and the devil's masks is their way of acknowledging the past and, if you like, hedging their bets. Such carnivals in their various forms are practiced in many parts of the world."

"You think that's all there is to it?"

"I am not sure. Halloween, October thirty-first, is an ancient Celtic festival—Samhain—a time to worship the lord of the dead; it is a great *sabbat* in witchcraft. Their Druids, their priests, organized the celebration. You Yanks didn't invent it!" His Welsh accent thickened. "Of course they didn't have pumpkins back then; turnips or skulls with lighted candles were the custom. They lit bonfires to help the light of the sun continue through winter. People wore masks and danced around the fire. On Roseland, they combined Halloween with Guy Fawkes Day."

That explained why the women were dressed like Druid priestesses. It made sense, except they were in the wrong hemisphere. "Isn't it the wrong time of year?"

The professor smiled appreciatively. "I thought of that, too. There's an explanation in another Celtic festival called Beltine, which has the same kind of activities. This occurred at the beginning of summer on May first, somewhere between October thirty-first and November fourth in the southern hemisphere. Close enough, eh, boyo?"

"I should not have been surprised. There are carnivals all over, in Rio, New Orleans—"

"Right! The custom is far more widespread than most people realize. You could have added Bolivia, Trinidad, and even Iceland. Many years ago, I went to Bolivia during the pre-Lenten period. High up in the Andes on a hill in the Altiplano we came to the silver-mining town of Oruro. The mining is more or less over now, but the tunnels still exist. In fact, an entrance to the mines can be reached through the large Catholic church. During carnival time the procession of dancers and bands makes it way through the town to the main square and up to the, let me think…*Iglesia de Cunchupata* to honor the…*Virgen del Socavon*. In the church are the statues of the Virgin, the Christ child, and various saints. However, in the mining tunnels under the church there are the effigies of the ancient gods. Lighted candles and gifts honor all of them equally."

"The islanders also wore the masks on Midsummer's Day."

"Same kind of thing, if I…." The professor scratched his

head. "Yes, I remember. In Cornwall, around Christmas, there are the goose-dancers who also wear masks and wander the streets frightening people."

"Does this darker side go farther than witchcraft? I could swear there was a real sheep's skull in the remains of the bonfire on Guy Fawkes Day."

"You are asking about Roseland. Honestly, I don't know. Their society is very isolated. Who can say how such beliefs might evolve when uncoupled from the greater society. In Britain, there are still people who practice witchcraft and pretend to be Druids. My only advice to you is to be careful. I have no personal experience yet, like you, I saw some strange behavior on Roseland. A word of advice: do not test the system! You may regret it. Remember, you are a guest there."

"The women are off limits."

"Yes."

I wasn't going to tell him about Rose, and the topic ended there. We finished dinner with small talk. The professor reminisced about bird watching trips. It appeared that he had been to most parts of the world. I declined the customary glass of brandy and went to my room.

The next morning when I went downstairs, Mabel was in the kitchen preparing breakfast. This time, she spoke before I could ask her a question. "There's someone on Roseland, isn't there? Who?" Mabel turned and busied herself whisking the scrambled eggs. "It wouldn't be Mary Pascoe, she's accounted for. I heard rumors about young Patsy, but she got married, and young Esther's got a boyfriend."

The professor hadn't gone beyond a warning about women in general. It looked like Mabel wasn't going to let it go. I tried anyway. "She does? Who?"

Mabel looked as if she had spoken out of turn. "Never you mind." She turned. Her face was triumphant. "I know who it is." She slammed the bowl down and grabbed my arm, speaking angrily, "Rose. I should have realized there'd be a problem when she had to go back. I hope I'm not right, Andrew. Don't—"

"Do what? I'm going back to study the auks."

"Make sure that's all you do. I'm warning you."

I was trying to look innocent. Again, it didn't work.

"If you mess with Rose, there'll be trouble."

"Rose? She's a nice girl and we do jigsaw puzzles…that's all, and—"

"Rose is promised," Mabel stated firmly.

"John Trevenna. I heard. What if Rose doesn't want him?"

"She told you that? I don't believe it. You men are all the same. There's more important things to life than what's dangling between your legs." Mabel raised her arm as if she wanted to hit me. "You're already on Jane Trevenna's bad side. She'll get you like she'll get Petunia."

"What do you mean?"

"You'll understand when you see Petunia." Mabel snorted. "But you stay away from Rose! If you don't, it will end badly. I guarantee it."

What about Petunia? Damn secrecy and another warning. But it didn't make any difference. I was going back to pursue Rose.

26.

THE SEA, VIOLENT AS WHEN I LEFT ROSELAND, MADE STUDY-
ing on the boat impossible. The rocking motion and fumes
below deck made me want to throw up, and the strong wind
made it hard to work on deck. Relief came when the boat
turned back to the east and the dock at Portloe came into
view. There we entered the calm waters of the harbor. I helped
carry the island's supplies onto the dock. Not until we had
cleared most of the cargo did I see Rose's slim figure waiting
in the background. She was simply dressed, as usual, in jeans,
sneakers, and an anorak. The hood was down and the breeze
ruffled her black hair. When I got closer, I could see that she
was wearing a trace of lipstick. As I had told my parents about
the previous occasion, everything stopped and for a moment
I could not breathe.

Rose smiled radiantly, "Welcome back, Andy."

"No Frankie?"

She made a face and walked toward the bus.

"I got him a present," I called after her.

On the ride to Veryan, she quizzed me about what I
had done back home. I told her about everything, visiting

my parents, the Professor and Mabel, and the results from the auk tests. She appeared most interested when I told her about my father's interest in using animal wastes to provide energy.

Mary greeted us at the door and hugged me. "It's nice to have you back, Andy. We've been talking about nothing else for days."

"Mum! You'll give him ideas."

They were both looking at me expectantly. I acted as if I didn't notice. "Should I take my stuff upstairs?"

"Of course, Andy," Mary said briskly. "Rose, help me make tea, would you?"

The presents were at the bottom of my backpack and I had bought women's magazines at Kennedy airport. I left them on the stairs. When I entered the kitchen empty handed, they looked so disappointed I started laughing.

"Okay, you win." I reached up the stairs and produced the magazines and two of the silk scarves that Mabel had helped me select. She had balked at my getting something for Rose, but I had persuaded her it would look odd if I only brought presents for Mary and Clara. Mabel shouldn't have worried. After polite purrs of appreciation, they showed far more interest in the magazines.

"I'm real glad you're back, Andy. I wasn't looking forward to being on my own again." Mary's comments dashed any hopes I had of having time with Rose that evening. "What do you mean?"

"Rose, didn't you tell him?"

"Sorry, mum, I forgot." She shrugged apologetically. "I'll be helping Jane Trevenna."

"Where will you be, then?" I asked.

"Out at Trewince. Uncle James will drive me to the patients."

Damn for a number of reasons, I thought, yet what I said was, "I'll miss you, too. I brought a new, very difficult jigsaw puzzle. It can wait until we're all here."

Rose's face showed a mock sadness. I managed to get a quick hug from her as we passed on our way to the bathroom that night. That and an image of her silhouette, through her nightie, as she entered the bathroom were all I would have to keep me going until she returned. She was being groomed to take over from Jane Trevenna, and that meant dealing with the babies, too. I wondered if she'd already assisted at a delivery. Not a good topic to raise until I had a chance to try and persuade her to leave the island with me. I would just have to grab every opportunity to make her take me seriously. In the meantime I would concentrate on my studies.

Charlie Gay came to see me soon after I returned. "Andy, we've missed you. Ernie Anthony is hanging on, but he's far too frail to come back to the band. We're hoping you'll continue on the trumpet for us."

"I'll be happy to. I really enjoyed it before. Is it still the same group?"

"Basically. We see less of Patsy now, her being pregnant-like. Paul is doing fine. I think he'll be permanent." He paused. "And Petunia'll be taking a break after Mid Summer's."

"Any reason?"

"We're expecting." He didn't sound happy.

"Congratulations," I said. So that was what Mabel had meant about finding out when I saw Petunia. Back to business. "Same music?"

"More or less. We added the *Imperial March* from *Star Wars*, you see. The music came on the boat when it returned from dropping you off in Cape Town." Charlie chuckled. "Got to keep up with the times." He rummaged in a bag and handed me the music for my part. "I brought this so you'd have time to look at it before practice Wednesday evening in the hall."

I glanced at the music quickly. "I'll try."

"One other thing, Andy. If you have time, Ernie would really like to see you. He hasn't got long, you know."

"Sure. Should I arrange it with George?"

"Better, so he can get Ernie ready."

In the excitement of returning to the rookery in the second week in October, I even forgot about Rose for a while. Frankie helped me carry the materials for the blind and we rebuilt it on the old site. I brought back my note pads, pencils, and the binoculars. Nellie was in residence with her new boyfriend, "Dapper Dan." Two of the original gentlemen friends, Tom and Harry, were in attendance. Dick had disappeared, probably a victim of the bitter winter months. Sydney, a sprightly young auk, had replaced him. Syd, it turned out, aspired to more than the fake sex, but Nellie would have none of it. I wondered how long Syd would hang around. It seemed that some of the males fit between the two types—lover and gentleman friend—another category to research for my dissertation. I sat in the blind for an hour and practiced the new march with my muted trumpet as I considered this new wrinkle.

On the way back, as arranged, I took a detour to the Anthony's farm. George came out to meet me as I approached the house.

He grasped my hand warmly. "Andy, I can't explain how much this means to Ernie." His eyes were teary.

"You have, George. I brought my trumpet and some new music. Is that okay?"

"Wonderful. Ernie'll love it."

Ernie was lying on the sofa in the living room. His handshake was limp and his formerly strong voice was a whisper now. "Thank you for coming to see a sick old man, Andy. I see you have your own trumpet this time." He gave a weak smile.

"Charlie's started us on a new piece, the march from *Star Wars*."

"Star Wars?"

"It's a very successful movie. I think it's been shown here."

"George may have mentioned it."

I played the march.

"Very striking," Ernie whispered. "The children'll love it."

While I was playing, George had made tea. He was pouring me a cup when the phone rang. He handed me the teapot. "Put lots of milk and sugar for Ernie."

When George was out of earshot, Ernie beckoned for me to come closer.

"Andy, I shouldn't be saying this, but you've been very kind coming here. Watch out. There are people on this island who like to play games. Some of them mean to hurt you. It's happened before. Maskers…."

"You mean like with Pavlov and—"

"So you've heard. That was a long time ago. Not the maskers…." He looked away for a moment. "I don't get out at all nowadays. Petunia came to see me. I asked her how you were getting on. She said fine. She, Charlie, and the rest of the band really like you. And…."

I noted the hesitation. "And I like them." I grinned. "But you were going to say something else."

Ernie took a moment before replying. "When I talked to Petunia she looked guilty…she wasn't telling me everything. She thinks someone may be setting you up." We heard George returning and Ernie motioned me away. "I don't know what…."

George came in looking thoughtful.

"Is everything all right, George?" Ernie asked.

"Fine, Ernie. Seythan business, I'll tell you later."

After tea, from a somewhat hazy memory, I took a stab at the old favorites, finishing with "The Floral Dance."

"*Rum tum ti tum tum tum*," Ernie squeaked. He was smiling now, broadly. "I remember when it was my turn," he said. "Jane Nichols was very proficient. Pity she married Trevenna." He was still smiling as he fell asleep.

"You didn't hear that, Andy, did you?" George failed to keep a straight face.

"Hear what?" I said, grinning back.

The sun was setting by the time I reached the road. Shortly afterward, I heard the sound of a car approaching from the direction of Trewince. I stepped close to the hedge to let it pass, only to hear it stop behind me. I turned and saw Rose getting out of the Lagonda.

"I'll walk the rest of the way, Uncle James. Thanks for the lift."

Rose ran up and faced me, smiling. "I'll walk with you. You don't mind?" She looked at me expectantly.

"Of course not."

"I could ask Uncle James to take you."

I leaned forward, conspiratorially. "I'd prefer to walk. I don't think he approves of me."

"Andy, he's only being protective of me. Now, where have you been?"

I held up my trumpet. "Visiting Ernie Anthony. He hadn't heard the *Star Wars* march."

Rose linked her arm in mine. "That was a kind thing to do, Andy." She squeezed my arm and tilted her head briefly onto my shoulder. I was going to kiss her, when I heard the Lagonda coming up to pass us.

"That was good timing, meeting like that," I said, as the Lagonda disappeared toward Veryan. The moment for a quick kiss had gone.

"Uncle James has to pick up my mum. She and Aunt Jane have stuff to talk about."

Did that mean Rose and I would be alone in the house? I must have been smiling for Rose stopped, looking up at me.

"What's so funny?"

"I was just thinking about something Ernie said."

Rose looked at me expectantly.

"*Rum tum ti*, you know."

"Andy, behave! What did he say?" Rose giggled.

"That's for me to know and you to find out, to quote—*oof!*" Rose had pinched my arm hard. "Let's change the subject. What's it like, working with Jane Trevenna?"

"Really interesting, though I'm finding out more about people's personal lives than I'd expected. People use the visit like a confessional."

"You mean there are even more secrets than the ones nobody talks to me about?"

Rose stopped and turned me to face her. She was stronger

than she looked. "You're too nosy, Andrew Ferguson. Worry about your auks. Leave us alone!"

"You're serious, aren't you?"

"Yes. I've heard about other foreigners who came here, prying into our lives and customs. The Seythan dealt with them."

"I hear you. It'll have to be auks…and you." I avoided her attempt to pinch me.

She stayed behind for a while like an Indian wife, before I heard her footsteps quicken and she took my arm again. "What did you mean?"

"About what?"

"You said, 'and you.'"

I stopped and faced her. "I like you Rose, and I'm not going to give up."

Rose was standing with her arms crossed, hugging herself. Her head was down and her hair covered her face. She stayed behind me the whole way to the house, came in a few minutes after me, and went into the kitchen. I pulled the curtains in the living room and then went into the back yard to get coal and wood for the range. Rose ignored me as I went by. I decided to leave her alone, took my puzzle from the cupboard, and started looking for the edges.

"Mum said I should cook dinner for us," Rose shouted from the kitchen. "Fish and chips and the left-over apple pie, okay?"

"Fine. Do you need any help?"

"You could peel the potatoes."

I went into the kitchen. Rose was making batter and looking cute. She had flour on her cheeks and a small smudge on her nose. "Let me wipe it off." She put her face up. As I wiped her cheeks, she closed her eyes like a child. "All better now," I said.

"Yes."

I kissed the remaining flour off her nose.

We ate the fish and chips the British way, with pepper, salt, and vinegar, off a plate because there was no newspaper. For dessert we had another British tradition with the apple pie, Bird's Custard.

Although I had only been away from the States for a short time, I had a craving for a hamburger. "Craving" was a poor choice of words. "Wishing" was more accurate. Craving was what I felt for Rose; it was hard to keep my hands off her as we washed the dishes.

Rose followed me into the living room. "I'll see you to… oh, you're doing the new puzzle. Can I help?"

Our fingers touched as we scrambled for pieces. After a few times, I could see she was smiling and looking at me across the puzzle box. The next time, I held on. Rose became still. She did not resist as I took her hand and bent down and kissed it. She came into my arms and we kissed. I was careful not to rush her and let her take the lead. It soon became more intense, with hands exploring and her gentle touching with fluttery fingers. She let me lift her sweater and undo her bra before she lay back on the sofa. Her breasts were small and firm, and the nipples pink and hard. I kissed and nibbled and she held my head against her, stroking my hair.

"No love bites!" she whispered. I pretended to bite. A hand went between my legs and she squeezed hard.

"Ouch!" I lifted my head, quickly.

She was grinning at me. "That's enough." She pulled her sweater down. "I've been going to dances here since I was fourteen. After that, and four to five years at university, I can handle rougher men than you, Andrew Ferguson.

I tried to put my hand back under her sweater. She slapped it, reminding me of dates when I was fifteen or so. I dropped my head. I had gone too far. "When will it be okay?"

Rose looked at me hard. "If I could be sure of you."

"You're not?"

"What are your plans? Would you live here? What would you do, study birds? Is your interest in agriculture a pretense?" She shook her head in exasperation. "Am I just a quick fling because you're stuck on our island? Like with Patsy?"

Rose was right. My needs were immediate. I was crazy about her—frustration, lust, love, who knew—but I hadn't thought about staying on the island for good. Plan A was still to get Rose to leave the place. Plan B was to learn about agriculture. "I only know that I really"—I nearly said "want you"—"like you a lot and want to be with you. Making love is an expression of that." I think the line came from some movie. I hoped Rose had not seen it.

"I like you too, Andy. But I'm not ready for going further." She looked embarrassed. "It sounds old fashioned, but I'm saving myself."

"For Johnny Trevenna?"

She raised her hand as if to hit me. "Stay away from that subject. I'll see you tomorrow." She hooked her bra and went upstairs.

Doing the puzzle was poor relief for my frustration. About thirty minutes later, I heard the sound of a car stopping.

I met Mary at the door. "Would you like a cup of tea?" I said.

"Thank you, yes. Where's Rose?"

"We were doing a puzzle. Then she went upstairs."

Mary looked at the table. "Good, you're doing the new one.

I'll help you when the tea's ready. Be down in a minute." As she turned toward the stairs, her face bore a strange look. As I returned to the kitchen, I heard the sound of a door opening upstairs and then voices.

That night, a dream/nightmare picked up where Rose and I had left off. Of course, the conclusion was different.

"Now take your shirt off and lie back!"

Rose knew how to get a man excited, and I was having a hard time controlling myself. After more passionate fondling, we ended up on the floor with her lying on top of me. When I reached down, her hand came with mine. She slid off me and her legs parted, slightly. We kissed and caressed. She led the way in loosening our belts and unzipping. I could feel the soft hair beneath her panties as I stroked gently.

She moaned softly and whispered, "Take them off!"

I lifted and started to pull her jeans down.

"Yours first!"

She watched as I stripped. "You're ready, aren't you?" She stood, pulled her sweater off, dropped her jeans, and then stepped out of her panties.

I reached between her legs. The lips were parted and wet. "You, too."

"Have you got protection?"

"Upstairs."

"Can you get one, and bring a towel? Better down here, it's warmer."

"Only one?"

Rose pulled away and looked at me, shaking her head. "You men!" She smacked my retreating butt, then went to the window and pulled the curtains closed.

At the sight of her small firm behind and lean, athletic legs, my earlier impression of her frailty disappeared quickly.

When I returned, she took the towel and put it on the carpet in front of the fire. We lay down and started to make love again.

I was close to the point where I could not hold it back any more when she whispered, "I'm ready. Now! Please, now!" While I put on the condom she stood up and straddled me, and then I heard the faint sound of a car. Rose froze above me. I had my hands between her legs to guide her down. She did not move. A car door slammed shut.

"Oh, shit!" She cried, jumping up. "It's me mum. Quick, get the clothes and the towel!"

I followed and went upstairs. Rose's door was already closed. As I stood trying to decide what to do, I realized the condom package was still on the floor, and woke up sweating.

The next morning, when I left the bathroom after shaving and brushing my teeth, Rose came out of her room. I could hear Mary downstairs making breakfast. Rose came into my arms quickly, whispering, "I'm sorry, Andy. I don't know when I'll see you again."

"Sorry. Me, too." My reply was heartfelt. "Where are you going?"

"To work in Portloe, then back to Trewince."

That did not sound good. "How long?"

"Until Christmas."

"Breakfast's nearly ready," Mary shouted. Rose gave me one quick hug and was gone.

* * *

In a frustrating way, having Rose out of the house was a good thing. I spent plenty of time with the auks, thinking about the auks, photographing the auks, taking samples from the unfortunate dead auks, and writing about the auks. With the help of Arthur and Mary, I was able to store more auk samples for later analysis.

Nellie and Dapper Dan were having a good sex life. Tom and Harry seemed to be content with their version. Sydney was not a happy camper. He showed his frustration at Nellie's lateral arabesques by turning and pecking at her. Syd's attempts to act menacing were unimpressive. I took some terrific photos, showing Nellie and Dapper Dan shooing him away. Sometimes, Tom and Harry would join Dan and they would strut together with their chests stuck out. Syd came to Nellie less and less, and eventually he moved away, presumably in hope of finding a mate in another part of the colony. At the end of October Nellie laid an egg in the nest. I checked, using my mirror on a stick, and could see only one. What a relief—it would have been hard to feed twins with only two gentlemen friends and Nellie, showing her age, catching less fish.

My research was going well. I ought to have been having fun, yet I was edgy. Rose was still away, in Portloe. Frankie, on the other hand, was omnipresent at the rookery. For some reason, he wasn't working. When he was not watching me studying the auks, he collected gulls' eggs and peed at the skuas; particularly Dracula, who was still prowling, stealing fish from the auks. While he asked many questions about the auks, he never seemed to retain the answers. Despite his seeming mental inadequacies, he had an uncanny ability to spot the differences between the auk husbands and the gentlemen friends. He must have understood the differences between their beaks all along. If only I had been smart enough to ask him at the beginning of my research.

"You can see the colors changing as their beaks turn, can't you?"

"Maybe can."

"Is there anything else about them you can see?"

"Not see. Hear."

"You can hear differences?"

Frankie nodded his head. "Listen when they talk to Nellie."

I spent many hours listening before I could detect the subtle differences in the chatter of the main men and the gentlemen friends. I borrowed a tape recorder from Nancarrow's and made tapes to take back to the States for analysis.

As he had done the year before, Frankie tried to persuade me to collect gulls' eggs with him. I went one time.

"Okay. I'd like to see the gulls' nests. Maybe there's something in it for my dissertation. Not too far down, though!"

"Follow me. Do what I do and you'll be fine." Frankie led me alongside the rookery, down a well-worn path. The tussocks of grass gave way to bare layers of rock and the path zigzagged as it dropped to the top of the cliff. Frankie turned around and lowered himself over the edge, using protruding rocks as handholds.

I crawled to the same point and looked down. Ropes hung at intervals along the cliff, and others spread horizontally under the rookery to my left and right toward Brown Willy. The cliff was not quite vertical and I could see a series of descending ledges. Frankie had already reached the third one down. The sea surged with the swell in successive blue bands toward the cliff, and a gentle breeze ruffled my hair. This quiet was disturbed only by the screeching of the birds that circled above and behind me and the thumping of my heart as I tried to follow Frankie.

"Come on!"

I turned around and lowered myself over the edge. The start of the descent was tricky. The rain and wind had eroded the ground and the handholds rocked precariously. The footing felt unstable. A single rope, anchored at the top of the cliff, helped me to negotiate the descent. I managed to reach the second ledge and could see the first of the gulls' nests a few yards away. The gulls started to circle near me and make darting moves at my head. I could hear Frankie singing "Starry Gazy Pie" below and to the left of me. I looked down but could not see him. An oily swell slurped the dark waves onto the rocks below. The scene was beginning to blur, my stomach felt hollow. I turned quickly to face the cliff, concentrating on a bug that was marching around a small plant, before starting the slow climb to the rookery.

Twenty minutes later, Frankie appeared, carrying a bag of eggs.

"What happened to you?" he asked.

"I got dizzy and had to climb back."

"You're okay?" He looked genuinely concerned.

"I guess so. You're not going to make fun of me?"

"There's a time and place for everything, Andy." He seemed to have stepped into a new character, concerned older brother. "I should have warned you not to look down."

"It's a pity, because I'd like to take a closer look at more of the auks' nests."

"I could put another rope for you. Tie it to a stake at the top of the cliff."

"That might work."

Frankie grinned. "Day after tomorrow it'll be Guy Fawkes. Are you playing?"

"Yes, I've got practice tonight," I told him for the tenth time. It had been his main topic of conversation for the past week. "Do you think Rose will come?"

"Dunno." He looked at me sideways. "She's my friend."

"I know. That's why I thought you might have heard."

"You get the rope. I'll help." He loped away with his eggs doing a little jig as he disappeared out of sight, back in his normal character.

Surprisingly, Patsy turned up for band practice, the first time since I had returned to the island. She gave me a toothy grin and patted her bulging belly.

"So, what have you been up to, Patsy?"

"You know darn well." She came closer and nudged me in the ribs. "Artley's not as good as you."

"Good enough, though! He'll learn."

"Yeah, and it won't take long, neither. We do it ev'ry day." Patsy punched me lightly on the arm. Her voice showed no doubt that Artley would learn quickly. "Esther is looking forward to seeing you at Guy Fawkes." She grinned. "Esther has plans for you, behind the toilets at bottom of field."

"Patsy, I don't—"

"I hear Rose won't be there."

I reacted too quickly. "Why not?"

Patsy gave a knowing grin. "That's for me—"

"—to know and…. I've heard it before. Give me a hint!"

Patsy picked up her clarinet and played the first bars of *The Floral Dance.*

"Shit! You're kidding?" I couldn't hold my feelings back. My legs felt weak. I turned away to hide the misting in my eyes, pretending that I needed my trumpet. Was Patsy playing games or had Rose really been chosen? A void sucked in my stomach. I played the next part of the *Floral Dance* with difficulty. A futile attempt to show I was not concerned.

Patsy shook her head as if in sympathy, but she was grinning. "You keep picking the wrong girls, don't you?"

I could not concentrate and the practice did not go well for me. At the break, Charlie Gay came up. "You feeling okay, Andy?"

"Sorry. It must be something I ate. Stomach's a bit queasy. I'm going to the loo."

When I returned from the rookery the next evening, Mary met me at the door. "I hear you've not been feeling well. Do you need to see the doctor?"

"No, it's better now," I answered too quickly. The doctor meant Jane Trevenna, and it might have been a chance to see Rose.

"Like some tea then?" Mary asked as she went into the kitchen.

I followed. "That reminds me. How's Rose doing?"

"Just fine. She helped at Jean Nichols's delivery. You've not met her. Beautiful baby brother for Edward and Susan."

Thank God it wasn't a girl.

"You all right, Andy?"

"Sure. Just wondering what else Rose had been doing."

"Main thing taking her time has been nursing some old people around Portloe. Auntie Florence, Cap'n Artley's mum, is confined to her bed."

I remembered something that had bothered me. "I was wondering. Aren't there people other than the Penseythan and Rose who can help if there's an emergency…medical problem?"

Mary smiled. "We're not completely helpless you know. All of us learn first aid in school, and Martha Nancarrow is trained as a nurse."

"I see." Now to the second question. "Will Rose come to Guy Fawkes?"

Mary shuffled the cups and saucers and moved the kettle before answering. "She's not sure. Depends on how Auntie Flo's doing, you see."

It sounded like an excuse, since Martha Nancarrow could have handled the problem. "Any other news?'

Another long silence while Mary fussed over the tea. "No, I don't think so."

That evening, Mary produced a new puzzle. It showed a fishing boat leaving a harbor in stormy weather. A raven-haired woman was standing on the stern waving to people on the dock. "Is that you?" I laughed, pointing at the box lid.

"Rose going back to university, I hope."

"Can you get the funding?"

"We're working on it. I think so."

"You happy about it?"

"I'll miss her, Andy. She's all I've got." Mary turned away. I put my arm around her and she buried her head on my shoulder. She was crying.

"Does she have to go?"

"Island's got to have a doctor. Jane Trevenna's getting old. She won't be able to handle all the work forever. Rose is our only hope, and she wants to do it."

"When she's graduated, she'll be here for good."

"Better be, unless something or somebody persuades her not to come back." Mary busied herself looking for puzzle edges.

Did she mean me, I wondered?

27.

GUY FAWKES DAY WENT AS BEFORE. WE PLAYED OUR STAN-
dard songs and then launched into the *Star Wars* march as we
circumnavigated the huge pile of wood. The children marched
behind us. A few of them had light sabers—deep in the southern Atlantic! *What a connected world we live in,* I thought. At
the break, we drank and drank. Only beer for me—I had
learned the dangers of mixing it with what they called cider. I
found the stall selling pasties and bought one. Esther hovered
around, smiling in my direction when nobody was looking.
By the time I had finished eating, the Seythan had appeared
with Jane Trevenna in the lead. Although she used a stick, she
seemed to be walking better. Isaac Nancarrow, carrying his
mask, followed. Sam and Sandy Nancarrow stood back to let
the Seythan pass. They noticed me and pointed their masks in
my direction. Albert Pascoe, Rose's uncle, was now a member.
He lived in Portloe and I had met him once at a dance.

I stood with the band, no time for a pee. Penseythan Trevenna, wearing her red gown and pronounced makeup, spoke
about the lesson to be learned from Guy Fawkes: a society
must work together for the common good, and disruptions to

the proper order would not be tolerated. She was looking at me when she finished. *Oh God. Here we go again.* I had a hard time concentrating as we played the National Anthem.

The Penseythan walked over with Cap'n Billing. He handed her a firebrand and she lit the woodpile. It had been laced with tar and petrol, and it erupted in a *whoosh* of flames and smoke. When we started on *The Oggy Man*, Frankie joined the masked figures dancing around the fire. I didn't stop to see if there was a skull in the pyre. The moment we stopped playing, I rushed to the bottom of the field.

Oh, shit! Esther was waiting for me. "No time, Esther."

I went behind the canvas wall that faced the hedge. Before I could zip up, Esther's hand came from behind me, stroking gently and expertly. I was tipsy and still feeling the frustration of missing my chance to talk with Rose. Assuming that she had been chosen, this might be my last chance. I reached behind me and rubbed my hand against Esther's soft belly.

"Best not here, Andy. Other side of hedge."

She led me to a place where the bushes had been damaged and we scraped through and then went a little farther down the hedge, away from the bonfire. We kissed and she stroked again. I started to pull her shirt up. Her long earrings caught on the fabric. She removed them, her shirt, and her bra and dropped them on the ground. When she stood, her pendulous breasts swung toward me. I kissed them.

"No marks now!" she said softly.

It reminded me of what Rose had said. An image of Rose, naked and poised above me, cut through my alcohol-induced euphoria. "Esther, I can't do this. It's not right."

"Why not, Andy? Don't you fancy me?" She pulled away, scooped her breasts together and held them towards me. The

237

fireworks started, making colorful patterns on her body. Both were awesome sights. "I'll make it good for you." She came back, pushed against me, and her hand became more insistent, but I was losing the excitement. She stopped. "What's wrong? I know how to do it. I've been trained."

"Like you've been chosen," I said.

"What are you saying?" She sounded scared and moved away. "Patsy told me what to do."

"Sorry, but I got into trouble before. I can't risk it. You're a sexy girl."

"Not as sexy as Rose." She snorted. "You'll never have her. They'll see to that."

"What do you mean?"

"More important things to do than…." Esther put her bra back in place and pulled her shirt over her head. "I've said enough." She picked up her earrings and was gone.

As I started walking the long way around the outside of the field toward the main gate, I heard the noises of people coming through the hedge. I turned to see masked figures bearing down on me. Before I could react, I was wrestled to the ground, and someone jammed my face into the grass. I could feel the pressure of a boot on the small of my back.

A muffled voice said, "Stay away from our women. We don't need you foreigners."

The pressure was maintained as the speaker—I think it was the speaker—grabbed my hair and pulled my head up.

"Understand? Next time could be the last time!"

"Yes."

"Stay where you are for five minutes, and don't say anything to anybody. Right."

"Okay." Just like Ernie had warned, maskers I bet.

I heard them go back through the hedge, waited, and then brushed grass and dirt from my face, cleaning up as best I could. When I reached the main gate, some maskers were cavorting around the blazing bonfire, and the effigy of Guy Fawkes was disappearing rapidly. I could not tell whether the maskers were the ones who had assaulted me.

Looking around, I saw Esther talking animatedly to Patsy. She and Patsy started laughing. Cap'n Billing appeared. He motioned at them with his hand and then guided them to where Jane Trevenna was standing alone. The light from the bonfire allowed me to see them clearly, while they could not see me in the shadows. The girls looked subdued as the Penseythan spoke. They were grim faced when the Penseythan stopped.

While I was buying an orange drink and another pasty, Frankie came up.

"Can I get you a beer?"

"Don't drink," Frankie snapped. "Your face is dirty. I'll have a pasty." He grabbed one.

"I tripped on my way to the toilet," I replied, spilling some orangeade on my handkerchief and wiping my face. The resulting stinging sensation made me realize that my face had been scratched.

"Good fire. Pity Rose couldn't be here," I said as I tried to clean up.

Frankie spoke through a mouthful of food, "She's with her mum."

"Rose is here? Where?"

"Over there." He pointed at the gate to the field. Rose, wearing her low-cut white dress, was with Jane Trevenna, Mr. Thomas, and Mary. They were leaving. I felt sick. Had Rose seen Esther follow me to the toilets? I ran up the field. Rose had moved ahead and was getting into the Lagonda. She saw me. I waved. Her face was set in a hard expression as she sat down and closed the door.

Jane Trevenna noticed me and motioned for me to come over. "Andrew, we haven't spoken in a while. I would like to hear more about your progress with the auks. Would you be able to come to Trewince for lunch?"

My heart was beating hard. Rose might be there. I did not answer immediately.

"Did you hear me?"

"Yes, ma'am, I'd be pleased to come."

"Good. Mr. Thomas will pick you up tomorrow at twelve." She went to the car.

I started to follow

"Slow down, Andy." Mary said.

"You didn't go with them."

"Jane and Rose have gone to check on Auntie Flo. She's not well."

"I thought Rose was going to stay with her today."

"Flo wouldn't hear of it. Insisted she didn't need help and said that Rose should see the bonfire and fireworks."

"Oh!"

Mary reached over and brushed my collar. "Lipstick, Andy! And what have you done to your face?"

"I tripped near the toilets and fell into the hedge."

"I see." Mary looked doubtful.

"Then Esther came after me. I told her to go away."

"But not immediately." Mary chuckled.

"I'd been drinking."

"Stay away from her or there'll be more problems." Mary's face was grim.

I tried to make fun of it. "Not again. What's a guy to do?"
Mary's eyes misted. "I like you, Andy. Rose likes you. But it
can't be. What would you do here anyway?"

Mary was right. I had little to offer the island. "Teacher? I could do science," I replied tentatively. "Also, I do know
something about farming. My Dad's a nut about recycling.
When I visited last, he was talking about raising pigs, putting
the manure into a covered tank. When the manure rots down
it produces methane. He plans to collect the methane and
use it to make heat for the piglets and electricity to run the
farm. He had other ideas, too…like growing tomatoes and
fish farming, I think."

"I don't think we'd need fish farming." Mary looked
thoughtful. "But if you could help bring modern ways that
increased the yield and the other stuff we wouldn't have to…."

I wondered if she was going to say, *limit the number of females*. Not a good time to ask.

"You should go talk to Morley Thomas. He might be interested." She looked at me searchingly. "Andy, teaching or farming, is that really what you want to do for the rest of your life?"

I had no answer, but it was worth checking out. I'd already
worked out that Morley was James Thomas's brother. "Is
Morley like his brother?" I said.

Mary chuckled. "No. He's very easygoing."

* * *

"Andy, I'm sorry I spoke so rude last night." Mary said at
breakfast the next morning. "I was upset about Auntie Flo
and Rose being gone again."

I looked up from my scrambled eggs. "Don't worry about

it. I guess I don't need distractions while I'm finishing my research."

"You mean like Rose."

"Things don't always work out the way they're planned." My reply sounded weak.

"Well, it's good you won't have to worry about that any more."

"What do you mean?"

"You'll see." Mary ate the last piece of toast and put her plate in the sink. "I've got to get to work. Can you finish up?"

"Yes. Before you go, why was Rose wearing her white dress last night?"

"Keeping me company and joining in the fun."

I hoped there wasn't more to it.

* * *

Mr. Thomas picked me up and took me to Trewince, where his wife, Miriam, ushered me into the living room. A tray with a decanter of sherry and two glasses sat on the coffee table. Jane Trevenna stood by the binoculars. Her cane was lying on the floor by her chair. The hound, Winston, eyed me warily under hooded lids.

"I wish I had a better view of the rookery, Andrew. May I offer you a sherry?"

"Thank you, ma'am. I see you're feeling better." I nodded at the cane.

"Yes indeed, Andrew. I'm hoping that I will be fully recovered before Christmas, so that Rose will be able to return to university. Until then, there are important things for her to do."

Her look implied that I should leave Rose alone.

After Miriam handed us our drinks, Jane Trevenna turned and looked through the binoculars. "The most I can discern is a cloud of birds, seagulls mainly, I suppose," she said, ending the discussion.

"Yes, gulls and skuas. The auks come in close to the ground. The skuas are the worst at attacking the auks."

"I remember now, Rose told me what happened to one of your favorites…Fred was it?"

"Yes, ma'am." Even this long after Fred's death, I could feel my eyes misting.

"I can see that it would be hard not to get fond of them, and hard to have to deal with reality when they have problems." She became silent for a moment. "You have to let nature take its course. Just like with my patients."

"You mean like Auntie?"

"What? Yes, it's hard watching her fade away. Florence Billing was Penseythan once you know, a proud, strong-willed woman."

"Still is, I hear. She insisted Rose watch the fireworks," I said, angling to find out if Rose was at Trewince.

"Yes. Of course, we should not have agreed. She took a turn for the worse in the short time Rose was gone. I won't let that happen again."

"So, Rose is back with Auntie Flo?"

"Yes, Rose is back with Mrs. Billing," she replied pointedly.

I smiled ruefully. Apparently, I wasn't allowed to call her Auntie Flo. Unfortunately, my prodding led to the discussion I was hoping not to have.

"While we are on the subject of Rose, let me give you some advice, Mr. Ferguson. Rose has been chosen for important things and I…that is, the Seythan…do not want her distracted. I made the mistake of failing to caution you early enough before the unfortunate business with Patsy Jago. I am not making that mistake again."

Chosen! That word again. I felt cold. I had many questions, but I was still confused about whether the islanders were playing me for a sucker. I decided to ask a general question. "Are you telling me that I can't have a relationship with any woman on this island?"

"You are a foreigner. From past experience we know that men from outside our community can cause problems; Pavlov, even the professor.… I doubt you plan to live here for the rest of your life. What would you do, watch the birds?"

"I know something about farming. I could—"

"We have our own experts who know how to work Roseland. This is not the United States."

End of conversation. Irritating. "How about the professor and Mabel? He doesn't—"

"Mr. Ferguson, I am speaking as the Penseythan. I am not interested in a debate on matters that do not concern you." Jane Trevenna had risen to her feet and looked truly angry. She paused, catching her breath. "Lunch should be ready by now. Let us retire to the dining room."

The lunch consisted of a chicken salad and apple pie and ice cream. I enjoyed both the lunch and talking about the auks, but I did not mention my conclusions as to how they limited the number of females. Jane Trevenna was an attentive and intelligent audience. She did not seem surprised when I told her how Frankie had alerted me to the different noises made by the male auks.

"It is interesting how nature can compensate a weakness

with a strength." She did not elaborate. "About the way the beak colors change when the auks tilt their heads. You seem to have found something important there. How does it work?"

"I studied the beaks under a microscope. The surface is not as simple as it looks from a distance; there's a fine structure. The best way I can put it is that it's like the structure of peacock feathers or my mother's opal earrings: they reflect differently from different angles."

"A well-known ploy," said Jane Trevenna. "Gaudy colors are often used to attract the opposite sex."

I used the comment to bring the discussion around to something I had been waiting to ask her. "Is that the reason for the heavy makeup I've seen at Guy Fawkes and Midsummer's Day?"

A brief look of irritation was followed by a tilting of the head and a smile. Not so much a friendly smile as a smile of resignation. "You have answered my questions. I suppose, in fairness, I should answer some of yours. When our great great- and great-grandparents left Cornwall, they brought with them many things to remind them of their past. We remain Protestant, somewhere between Baptist and Congregational with a touch of Church of England. We make our own Cornish beer…under license for the St. Austell brewery. They kindly ship the ingredients. We eat much as they do in the home country: meat and two vegetables, fish and chips, pasties, fruit pies, saffron buns at Christmas, even stargazy pie; I hear Clara and Frankie had fun with you." Her smile was genuine.

"The first islanders recreated the round houses, and they brought the stocks; fortunately, they did not bring a gibbet." The last comment seemed to be directed at me.

"A gibbet?"

"Old English. You probably call it a gallows."

"Oh, I see."

"And they brought the old customs for Guy Fawkes Day and the Summer Solstice. We live in isolation. It can get boring. People need pleasurable things to anticipate: the dances, Clara's plays, the bonfire, and the Floral Dance festivities complement the standard religious festivals. Dressing up, the makeup, the colors are part of the fun and, yes, they do have a sexual content, as they do for the auks, and as they did for our pagan ancestors."

She was looking out of the window when she continued, nearly to herself. "Must keep things in perspective. Easy to regress."

She turned to look at me. "The Seythan, under the leadership of the Penseythan, has responsibility for Roseland. For a time, the island faced the possibility of another, older authority holding sway. Fortunately, my predecessors were able to contain the cult. However, there remain some who would like to see that situation reversed. Do not give them an excuse to deal with you!"

Was she serious? What had happened on Guy Fawkes Day suggested that the threat was real. And the professor had said something about an ancient cult—Druids, devil worshippers. Alternatively, it was another part of the game I suspected was being played on me.

"I'll try to keep out of their way, ma'am." I tried to hint at my disbelief.

Jane Trevenna's face was stony. "I have said enough about us. Let us return to the auks. Many years ago, a Penseythan restricted fishing in the waters below the rookery. A wise decision, I think."

"Yes, ma'am. I've seen pictures of the northern auks with mouths full of little fish, when they return to feed the chicks. In Roseland, it's rare for an auk to return with more than two or three. The competition for food is fierce. I'm coming to the conclusion that it is a major reason for having auk drones to supplement the parent's catch."

"Auk drones! I like the analogy to a beehive. Ah, I see Miriam has brought the coffee. We will take it in the sitting room, I think."

We continued our discussion over coffee. Winston studied my ankles the whole time. I left feeling good. Despite the warnings to leave Rose alone and to watch out for some cult, our meeting had gone better than I had anticipated.

I declined the ride back to Veryan, saying I'd prefer to walk. After covering about three miles, I headed down the road that branched toward the Thomas farm. Halfway to the schoolhouse I came to the hand-painted sign that read THOMAS and pointed down a rutted track to my right. Scattered cows—Jerseys I guessed—munched contentedly on the grass on the north side of the track. On the south side, the grass had been allowed to grow tall—hay for the winter, likely. After covering about half a mile, I reached a two-story farmhouse. A large barn and low open-sided sheds formed the other sides of the farmyard—a clean concrete-covered area. In one of the sheds, a man with gray hair was bent over an ancient tractor working on the engine. He looked up when he heard me approach.

"Mr. Thomas," I said. "I'm Andy Ferguson."

"I've seen you around, Andy...and heard about you...and the auks and all." He grinned.

"Some good, I hope?"

"George Anthony and Charlie Gay speak well of you," he

said, wiping oil off his hands. "I also heard recently that you have an interest in farming." He held out his right hand and we shook.

"I grew up on a farm. My father's passionate about environmentally sound approaches."

"But you?"

"My father got me hooked on ornithology." I hesitated before continuing. "But, until recently, I didn't feel the same way about his love of agriculture."

"What changed your mind?"

Morley seemed to be very different from his stern-faced brother. I decided to trust him. "When I finish my PhD, I'd like to come back to the island. I told Mary and she asked me what I could do here."

Morley chuckled. "And what did Rose say?"

No secrets on Roseland. "I haven't been able to speak to her recently. I'm not sure what to say."

Morley patted me on the shoulder. "Don't give up. Now back to business. We live on a small island. What you can do in the States may not be practical here. We can't afford much in the way of expensive fertilizers. We have to do conservation farming." He motioned for me to follow him and headed off toward the house. His wife met us at the door.

"Andy Ferguson's come to see us, m'dear," Morley said. "My wife, Hilda."

"Pleased to meet you, Andy," she said, smiling. "Petunia's told me all about you. Would you like a cuppa?"

"No thanks, I just finished lunch," I replied.

"Well then I'll leave you two men alone." She left.

Morley pointed at a chair by the kitchen table. "Now, tell me about these new approaches."

"Up till now my father's been raising chickens and planting corn and soybeans. But his dream has always been to make our farm completely self-sufficient in energy. When I went home a few months ago I found out he's getting ready to raise hogs. He told me about some neat ways to use manure to make methane and still keep the phosphorus and nitrogen for fertilizer. Then he'll use the methane for making electricity and process heat to keep the sows and piglets warm in winter."

"That means you have to keep them indoors, right?"

"Yes, but if you put the manure in a pool and cover it, you don't get that smell, like at the Jagos'. I can often smell the pigs when I'm going to the rookery."

"How about with cows? As you saw coming in, they're out in the fields. Makes it harder."

"Well, you'd have to keep them where you can collect the manure easily."

"Might work in winter." Morley looked thoughtful. "I usually put them in the barn. The bullocks and extra heifers go across the road to the Cockings to fatten up. Might work there." He scratched his head. "How much electricity do you reckon you'd produce?"

I fished for the notes I'd had the foresight to put in my back pocket. "Dad gave me these numbers. A 1000-pound cow produces about ten ponds of manure a day. That's dry weight. With anaerobic digestion the biogas can produce as much as two kilowatt-hours of electricity. For 1000 pounds of hogs it's maybe 1 kilowatt-hour."

Morley looked at the ceiling. He seemed to be calculating something. "That's not bad," he said, eventually. "I could use it to run the dairy...and a refrigerator. Keep the milk longer."

"Milking machine, too."

"Nice idea, but can't afford it." He chuckled. "Anyway, what with me, Hilda, Nicholas, and Susan we've got enough hands." He pointed at my scruffy piece of paper. "Now, how much do you really know about all this?"

"Not enough," I said, ruefully. "But North Carolina State's Agricultural College offers courses. I'll need to take them."

"You could be a big help." Morley looked at his watch and stood. "Sorry, I need to get back to the tractor. Now, you go and tell Jacob Jago what you told me. I'll talk to Edgar Cocking."

I left the farm and headed for the school and then on to Veryan. It didn't take me long. I had a spring to my step. Maybe there was something useful I could do on the island. I needed to tell Mary and Rose.

28.

I WAS AT THE ROOKERY IN LATE NOVEMBER WHEN NELLIE'S
egg hatched. The arrival of the new chicks initiated a period of intense feeding. Dapper Dan, the supreme fisherman,
returned every time with three or four small fish. The serrat-
ed edges of the auk's beak allowed the birds to hold the fish
crosswise, which let me easily count the catch. Although Tom
and Harry were not as effective, Nellie would congratulate
them equally when they flew in.

If they were like the Atlantic puffins, the Roseland auks
would have a twenty-five year lifespan. I guessed that Fred
and Nellie had probably been together for more than ten
years, which explained her grief when he was killed. Sadly,
Nellie fished less now and, I suspected, mainly for herself.

The skuas were an ongoing concern, always out in force,
dive bombing the auks. I could not get the images of Fred
dying out of my mind, and I thought of asking Frankie if he
knew where I could borrow a gun, to shoot any skua that attacked Nellie. But my life's work was birds, and I reluctantly
accepted that even skuas like Dracula had their place.

Studying the auks brought back memories of my conversation with Jane Trevenna, particularly the fact that Rose had

been chosen for important things. She had said, "I," and then corrected herself to say, the "Seythan." Did the "I" refer to Rose being chosen for her son John? *Unlikely.* Assuming, as Patsy had hinted, that the Seythan had chosen Rose to be Queen, how did that square with John being away? Similar to Agnes Nichols and her son—maybe this Penseythan did not have the power to decide her son's role either. Rose, chosen to be the next doctor, could be a part of it. Not knowing was frustrating. My stomach became queasy again.

I chuckled, remembering that we had played the *Star Wars* march on Guy Fawkes Day. If I took Jane Trevenna seriously, a dark side of the force existed on Roseland. What about the cult business? Obviously, the masks and costumes had not been created for my benefit. I had seen pictures of dancers around the bonfire in old newsletters. Were particular people a part of the cult, or was it a part of all the people? The latter possibility seemed more likely. Mary, Petunia, Rose, and even Jane had all worn white dresses, old-looking jewelry, and heavy makeup. Were Clara, Cap'n Billing, Mr. Thomas, Isaac, Arthur, and George behind the masks?

I went for a hike up the base of Brown Willy to clear my head. The sea had changed again, showing a small chop, and myriads of white caps flecked the surface. The wind was picking up and to the west a line of dark clouds indicated the approach of a storm. Motor boats that had been fishing outside the bay were making their way back to the safety of Portloe harbor. I hurried back to Veryan to avoid the rain.

The next day, in between taking photos and notes, I thought about names for Nellie's chick. When Frankie made one of his random visits, I made my decision.

"What's the chick's name?"

"We don't know if it's male or female."

"Well?"

"How about 'Rose' for a girl and 'Gareth' for a boy?"

"Rose, I like that. Who's Gareth?"

"Prof Llewellyn J.," I replied.

"His given name's Gareth?"

Frankie showed me that he had lost interest in the subject by leaving the blind and peeing at the gulls. When he returned, he sat quietly for a while. I was busy consolidating notes, and at first, I did not hear what he said. He repeated it.

"Midsummer's Day, I'm going to be one of the chosen men."

I tried to control my hands, but the pencil made a jagged mark on the page and the tip broke. Rose would have to service Frankie in the Round House. Weird, if Jane Trevenna arranged it for her nephew, given the expected marriage with her son? Maybe it wasn't true, but if a reality, at least he had not said he would be the king.

"You broke your pencil." Frankie looked at me sideways. He was grinning.

"My hand slipped." My chest had tightened and I continued with difficulty. "When did you hear this?"

"Mum says. It's not official-like."

"I'm pleased for you, Frankie," I lied. "You deserve it." *Why not me?* I thought; although, I wasn't an islander and could not imagine sharing Rose's attention with six other men. "When will you hear officially?"

"Another week, my mum says." He frowned. "Now don't you go telling *no one*. I told you because you're my friend."

"Cross my heart and hope to die." Frankie looked hard at me. I went through the motions.

"See you." He was gone.

My unfinished notes needed more attention, but I couldn't concentrate, and put my stuff in the backpack and left at mid-morning. Returning to the empty house held no appeal, so I started out along the cliffs toward the Nare Head with no plan of where to go until I reached a fork in the path. The right branch continued to the Nare. The left followed the cliff top leading, eventually, to Trewince. I took it. The view from the cliff top was stunning and scary. The sea was battering against the southern shore of the island. This outpost of civilization always appeared fragile, rising out of the ocean depths and facing the constant onslaught of the waves that came unimpeded from the Antarctic. I stopped to take photos and spent an hour and a half getting to where Rose and I had hiked the day I stood up Esther. I found a dry spot and sat and ate half a sandwich. A faint sound signaled a car driving on the Trewince-Veryan road, probably the Lagonda.

Decision time. Should I go down to Anthony's farm and visit Ernie, or should I carry on to Trewince? Getting near Trewince and then back to Veryan would be a fourteen-mile hike, with little chance of getting a ride. But I needed to work Frankie's news out of my system before talking to anyone. I walked rapidly, no time for more photos, and after one and a half hours reached a part of the hill from which I could see Trewince about a mile or so away.

The path was above the tree line, and it gave an unobstructed view of the front of the house and the lawn and gardens that descended towards the gorge. When I looked through my binoculars, I saw Rose and Jane Trevenna seated on the patio having tea, I guessed. The Penseythan was gesticulating at her. Suddenly, Rose stood and ran toward the house. Winston started to follow and the Penseythan restrained him.

What was that about?

I finished the other half of my sandwich and some orange drink and left. I cut down through the woods to the road and walked to Veryan. When I reached the house, I found Mary eating dessert.

"You look exhausted, Andy. Where have you been? I was getting worried."

"At the rookery and then I felt like a hike so I went to the Nare and then along the cliffs. I thought of visiting Ernie, but I didn't have my trumpet." A lie, I could have borrowed Ernie's.

"Sit down. Anyway, I cooked for both of us—shepherd's pie and peas." Mary took my plate and scooped food on it. "Oh, it's cold. Would you like me to reheat it?"

"No, that's fine. I'm hungry." Mary let me eat for a while before asking the question I had been expecting.

"How far did you get on your ramble?" She was pushing the remains of apple pie around with her spoon.

"Somewhere between Anthony's farm and Trewince, I'm not quite sure where. The woods blocked the view." *Time to stir things up,* I thought. "Why did you ask?"

The spoon was busy again. "Oh, I was just thinking you could have gone to see Rose. It's a long way, though."

"Yeah, I walked far enough as it is. I'm beat."

"Got time for a puzzle? It's one we did before."

"Sure."

Mary emptied the puzzle on the table. "I'll look for edges; why don't you look for pieces of buildings."

I picked up the lid and caught my breath. The man in the stocks faced me, again. I started collecting my pieces. "Where do you get these puzzles, Mary? All of them are of places on the island."

Mary laughed. "I wondered when you'd ask. Clara does the original painting, makes copies, and converts them into puzzles. Years ago someone bought a puzzle-cutter from England. You didn't notice that they're all the same pattern?"

"Now you mention it, I guess I do. How does she pick the subjects?"

"I think they are topical things that interest Clara. As you know, she's very imaginative. You've seen one of her plays."

"When I was helping Clara sort through stuff out back of the library, I had the impression that Jane Trevenna was often the director."

Mary looked surprised. "Jane might have directed once or twice over the years, but normally it's Clara. Don't be misled by the way she behaves. She's clever."

"It didn't look like an act when I was helping her in the library. She didn't seem to be able to concentrate."

"I agree she can appear a bit scatty. Watch out, there's usually a reason for it!" Mary's face looked sad. "Clara goes through phases. The Australian aborigines have words that fit. When they leave wherever they're camped and move on, they're 'going walkabout.' Clara's mind sometimes 'goes walkabout.' That's what you've seen. It got worse after the problems, those many years ago."

"You mean with John Nichols?"

"How did you...oh, Rose told you, did she?" She pursed her lips. "She shouldn't have."

"People in masks will come and get me?" My expression was designed to show how absurd the idea was.

Mary looked horrified. "Don't even joke about it! You have no idea what you're getting into. How on earth—"

"Jane Trevenna warned me."

"I hope you listened."

"Who are they?"

Mary shook her head and pretended to be looking for a piece of the puzzle.

"Okay, enough said. I'll be careful." I searched for pieces of the Round House.

I lay in bed thinking about comments in my school year book about being too suspicious, even a sneaky suggestion that I was paranoid. In my head, I again went over all the events that had occurred since I had arrived on Roseland. Ernie Anthony had worried that I was the victim of a game. It would explain many strange events, the noises, the puzzle pictures, Patsy's coming on to me—a set up? I did what all scientists do when presented with a challenge: I decided to formulate a theory. I turned on the light, found a pad and pencil, and started a list:

- The islanders sometimes played games with visitors, as shown by Throgmorton's notes and the comments about the Russian, Pavlov. Even if those stories were made up, some people were playing a game with me. As Jane Trevenna had told me, life on the island could be boring, and a game gave them something else to do.

- If this were true, it implied that a large number of islanders would play the game over an extended period of time, and nobody would let on. Unlikely. But clearly the Seythan and the Penseythan wielded enormous power; how else could they get the islanders to agree to the business of a Queen and seven men? If the Seythan supported the games, it seemed possible that they could get everyone to toe the line.

- The business of the puzzles was very strange. They were not simply pictures of island scenes, but pictures that might connect with me. What about the puzzle with the stocks connected to Jane Trevenna's warning? If I misbehaved would I be put in the stocks? Had the stocks been taken out of storage and placed in the square to convince me? Was Jane Trevenna's comment about an underground cult that could do me harm simply using the fact that they liked to dress up as a way to pull my chain?

- In total, it implied that at least Clara, Jane, Cap'n Billing, and Patsy had to be involved, and a nasty thought, Mary and Rose also. The list would have to be huge. Then there was Frankie, acting the idiot, but twice he had shown a different character. As I had been told a number of times, in a number of ways, he's not as dumb as he appears.

- It seemed like the business with Mary's phantom lover was a clever trick to increase my frustration so that I would more easily respond to Patsy and Esther. Was all of that designed to set me up to fall for Rose and then get rejected in a way that would bring me to my senses? It might explain why every time I got close to Rose, Mary appeared.

I felt very cold and started to shiver, so I climbed into bed and pulled the blankets up to my chin. For some time I lay, feeling numb.

In the early morning, two key questions had me brooding.

- If I was right, who was masterminding the real-life play I'd been tricked into; and if I was wrong, what other explanation could there be for the odd events?

- Was the game-playing connected to the dark side i.e., the maskers, and who led them—the Nancarrows?

I ate breakfast quickly and then went to the rookery. Despite the noisy chatter of the auks, there was something soothing about the place.

I considered the question of a mastermind first. The main candidates appeared to be Jane Trevenna—tough enough, intelligent, and organized. She was the Penseythan and sometimes directed plays. Who else? I discounted Cap'n Billing, Mr. Thomas, and the other men I had met. None of them seemed to have the right aura of power that I expected.

Directing plays led me to think about imagination as a crucial characteristic. In turn, that led me to consider Clara Quick: gifted (once or maybe still), an actress, and director of plays. Was her vagueness an act? Did Rose and Mary feed me the stories about her thwarted marriage and her tendency to go "walkabout" to convince me she was not always a part of the real world—harmless? In fact, on reflection, she was the best candidate if my analysis was correct. She adjusted plays, and she could create real-life ones.

What if my analysis was nonsense? In that case, everything

that I had heard about the islanders was true: more males than females; Midsummer's Day events were a regular part of their life; and an ancient cult lay just below the surface. Sometimes they did play games on people—Throgmorton and Pavlov—but rarely, and maybe they played a little with me. Clara and Frankie were somewhat out of it. Jane Trevenna was not playing games when she warned me about Patsy and Rose and the cult. Mary did not have a phantom lover, and Rose really did like me, but her obligations to Roseland outweighed that. This picture made the most sense. How could I prove anything? I decided that I would set up a number of tests, but first I had to do more work with the auks.

29.

IN BETWEEN WATCHING NELLIE AND HER MEN FEED HER
male chick— the other females didn't interfere—taking notes
on auk behavior and collecting samples of dead auks, I brooded about whether I was an unwilling actor in a play. This led
to a list of action items that I wrote in my note pad:

- Go to the library and look more carefully at the old docu-
ments in the shed. Look for more evidence that the Midsummer's Day activities and the masks and costumes have
been around for a long time.

- Watch Clara to see if she is putting on an act.

- Find an opportunity to check in Mary's room again—photos and tapes.

- Visit Ernie Anthony and ask him about Throgmorton and
Pavlov…and me?

Time was pressing if the game would play out on or by
Midsummer's Day.

I started with the library. Although Clara was away, the shed was unlocked. The stacks of newsletters and plays were where I had left them. A quick scan showed that there had been a queen and kings on Midsummer's Day at least as far back as the 1920s. I found little information about what they did other than take part in the Floral Dance and play around the Maypole. The few grainy pictures showed people in masks, obviously not something invented for my benefit. One comment from the 1930s said that it had been a satisfying experience for the kings. *Rum tum ti*, I thought. A later photograph showed Throgmorton watching the dancers. The caption read, "Mr. Throgmorton enjoying the festivities."

The professor and Gwyn were the subjects of numerous bylines in the earlier editions. The professor's interest in birds was mentioned, as were compliments about his acting as Petruccio in a 1948 production of the *Taming of the Shrew*, opposite Jane Nichols as Katherine. I chuckled.

"What's funny, Andy?" Clara asked.

I wondered how long she had been there. "Was Jane Trevenna playing to character as Kate in *The Taming of the Shrew*?"

Clara smiled wistfully. I could not tell if she shared my amusement. "That was a long time ago, when…."

"I didn't ask you before. Why do you make changes?"

Further silence as she edged toward the door. "To make the plays more enjoyable for Roselanders."

"Oh."

Clara shuffled out. No chance to ask more questions. Instead of following her, I went to the stack of scripts. They were dated back to the 1900s, and most had changes, like I had seen in Clara's production of *The Tempest*—presumably to fit what was easy to do in Roseland. I decided that it would take too much time to understand the purpose of changes to the dialogue, when I realized that I had no idea what I was looking for and put the scripts back on the floor.

The articles on the Russian Pavlov in newsletters from October through January 1952 were more interesting. As the professor had told me, the Russians had sent an agent, Dmitri Pavlov, to Roseland. The first newsletter described how the Seythan had welcomed Pavlov and held a meeting to find out about his interests. The article explained that he had claimed that he wanted to set up a place for rest and relaxation for Russian sailors working in the Antarctic, whaling and harvesting krill. The sentence was concluded with three exclamation marks. A photograph showed the members of the Seythan with Pavlov—a handsome, stocky, fair-haired man—smiling broadly in the middle of the group. The second newsletter mentioned an unfortunate event at a dance in Portloe, in which an inebriated Mr. Pavlov had behaved improperly with the women. The third newsletter had an article explaining that Mr. Pavlov had ignored the warning of the Penseythan and had assaulted Petunia Quick, the Midsummer's Day queen. A photograph showed him sitting in the stocks, looking at the Round House. The January newsletter concentrated on the British government's response to the Kremlin, reminding them that Roseland was a British dependency.

I tried to remember what the professor had said, something about, "Life can get boring for the islanders. A little fun whiles the time away. Mind games to teach Pavlov a lesson. They led him on a merry dance. *Rum tum ti tumpti....*" While it sounded like Pavlov had acted like a drunken boor, I wondered if Petunia had led him on deliberately. That brought me back to whether Clara had encouraged Patsy to make a pass at me.

The next set of newsletters had little useful material except that, in 1954, Mary Billing was the Queen of Midsummer's Day. David Pascoe was the king—Mary's missing husband. A grainy picture showed them in their finery. He was the man whose photograph was in Mary's room. Why Mary and Rose would not talk about him remained unclear. Anyway, it told me that Mary must be related to Cap'n Billing. From the way they carried on, it was unlikely to be too close a relationship—cousin or second cousin maybe. Nevertheless, it might explain why they were not married.

"Still trying to understand us?" Clara had crept in again.

"Something to do, Clara, when I'm not studying the auks."

"We're more interesting than those auks."

"So I'm finding out. The birds don't play games with me." Clara's mouth was shut tight, but a smile flickered briefly. *I might as well go for my question,* I thought. "The maskers are real interesting. The Prof told me it's an old pagan custom. Anything in the library on them?"

"Might be." Clara, looking shifty, edged out the door.

I caught up to her outside the shed. "Would you show me? Please."

Clara went to her desk in the library and started to sort a pile of returned books. "You're not one of us," she said, not looking up.

"Please!"

She shook her head.

"I'll look for it myself. I bet it's in the shed."

"Suit yourself." Her mouth was now shut tight as she arranged the books into stacks.

I acted as if I was going to the shed but stopped outside the back door, leaving it ajar. I watched as Clara stopped sorting and picked up three books for filing. She put them away and then took a detour past a cabinet in a corner, patting it before returning to her desk. I walked quickly to the shed and continued scanning old newsletters.

I was still reading when she came by. "I'm going, Andy. Frankie will be home soon. Shut the door when you leave."

I waited fifteen minutes before going into the library. The cabinet was unlocked. It contained notebooks. A quick glance showed that they were records—mainly data on fishing, farming, and finances—prepared for the governor. Dull reading. I was about to give up when I saw a thinner notebook behind them, flat against the backboard. Part of the cover was torn off, and the remains of a date started with an 18. The title read, "Maskers: a serious issue or not?" The author was Maude Trevenna, once a Penseythan, and the grandmother of Jane's husband, I assumed. She had penned her thoughts in neat copperplate writing. I scanned it quickly. The first chapter summarized very much what the Prof had said about the Celtic Festivals and the goose dancers. I wondered if the Prof had read it.

The second chapter reviewed anecdotal evidence that, in some parts of the southwest of Britain, the maskers had enjoyed a more powerful, secret role in society than merely hopping around on festival days and after Christmas. Maude Trevenna noted her concern that there were signs that this might occur on Roseland. She stopped short of mentioning names, but I am sure that had I lived in that era I would have known who she was talking about.

As I dug into the third chapter, it became clear that she

was referring to the men in masks as being the problem. In fact, at one point she referred to a brotherhood of maskers. Her description of the role of women in the festivities related to the costumes and dances. She did not use the word "sex," but that seemed to be the reason for the women dressing up, as I had seen on Midsummer's Day.

By the time I got through the fourth chapter, it occurred to me that what she was writing about was a battle of the sexes. By tradition, the Penseythan was a woman, and some of the men were using the brotherhood of the masks as a route to challenge that authority.

Her final chapter discussed crimes she believed had been committed by the brotherhood. Again, without naming names she mentioned theft, rape, and even murder. She ended by saying that she would do anything to stop the butchery and prevent them from usurping her power. *Butcher*, a strange choice of words. Did it refer to the abattoir? And who was the butcher back then?

The book looked old enough to have come from the nineteenth century. However, when I returned it to its hiding place, I was still uncertain about whether to take the maskers seriously. Had Clara known I would be watching when she gave a sign as to where the book was hidden? Was the book another of Clara's doctored creations?

* * *

The next day was market day in Portloe, a good time to visit Ernie, assuming George would not be home. In the morning I went to the rookery with my trumpet. I stayed only a short time before heading over to the Anthonys' farm, acting as if

I were looking for George. The front door was unlocked so I opened it and shouted, "Ernie, are you home?"

There was a voice from the living room, "Is that you, Andy? Come on in."

Ernie was lying on the sofa bed. He looked even frailer than before. I helped him sit and propped him up with cushions.

"George is gone to market," he said. "I'm sorry I can't do very much. There's hot water on the stove. Tea's in the tin box on the shelf. I'll have mine with lots of milk and sugar."

We drank our tea and then I played the trumpet, finishing with an extended rendition of *The Floral Dance* that I had been practicing for the occasion.

"You like that tune, Andy." Ernie chuckled weakly.

"I like the whole day, Ernie. Pity I don't get to play like the other guys." I grinned.

Ernie took the bait. "You do play...oh, I see what you mean. Sorry. It isn't for foreigners, though some have tried."

I tried to look quizzical.

"I remember that Russian, Pavlov...a nasty piece of work. I suppose I shouldn't say."

"Ernie, surely you can tell me?"

Ernie looked hard at me. "You've been a good friend to me, Andy, so I'm going to tell you some things, but you must keep them to yourself."

I nodded agreement.

Ernie scrunched his eyes as if he were visualizing the events. "Back in the '50s...I don't remember the year...Pavlov came on a trawler with some pretext that the Russians sailors would like to be able to stop here on their way to fish down south. He even suggested that they would blast out a port on the north

coast, near the Bodmin River. The Penseythan alerted White-
hall and they had strong words with the Kremlin. The Russ-
kies recalled him eventually. He behaved badly at the dances,
tried to take advantage of our girls when the lights went out,
and made lewd suggestions. Offered to pay. He was a drunk.
The Seythan decided to teach him a lesson. They asked—never mind who, someone who is good at organizing things—to
come up with a plan. She reminded them of something she
had done before, and…er…suggested that Petunia should lead
him on. Petunia was queen that year. The Penseythan would
warn him to stay away from her. Then, when Mr. Pavlov was
drunk, she would go to him all innocent-like. He would try
to do…you know what…and some member of the Seythan
would arrest him. On Midsummer's evening, after the children had gone to bed, they would put him in the stocks and
let him think about what he was missing."

"Did it happen like that? Wasn't it a bit dangerous for Petunia?"

"In hindsight, the plan assumed too much about Mr. Pavlov's good nature. When *she* set up the plan, *she* believed he
would take his time. He didn't, and immediately started to rip
off poor Petunia's clothes. The Seythan member assigned to
look out for her was slow in going to help. Fortunately, Petunia
wasn't hurt too bad." Ernie seemed to be picturing the scene.

"Why did…'she'… not think of that possibility?"

"The game was played earlier. I heard later that it hadn't
ended up like that with an English visitor, some years earlier.
Of course, he was a gentleman."

So tha's it, I thought, *confirmation that the islanders had
played sexual games with Throgmorton and Pavlov.* It sounded like the same woman was the prime mover in both cases.

Could I attribute the game to the Clara whose lover had committed suicide? Not unless the Throgmorton affair occurred before John Nichols' death.

"You're very quiet, Andy."

"Just thinking about it, Ernie, trying to work out who the 'she' is."

"You'll never guess."

I faced him squarely to make sure I would see his reaction. "It was Clara, wasn't it?"

"How did—" Ernie looked troubled.

"Ernie, don't worry. This is between you and me and you never told me."

"I'm not worried about me, Andy. Like I said before, I'm worried about you. From the way Petunia acted, I think you're Clara's latest target. Watch out for Frankie, too. He takes after his mum. She's very clever, and since she lost John, then Pete Quick, and then someone else, she hasn't been quite…normal. She goes through phases of being rational and phases when she's in another world."

"Walkabout," I said. "Aborigine expression, Mary told me."

"Yes, that's a way to look at it, but she can be cruel when she's in one of her moods." He looked down at his hands as if they would advise him what to say. "Clara isn't the main one you should be worried about. Be very careful."

"You mean the maskers?"

Ernie's face adopted a strange expression for a moment. He appeared puzzled.

Not the maskers, then? That leaves Jane Trevenna. "The Penseythan?" I asked.

Ernie put his fingers to his mouth and made a closing gesture.

That made sense if she was determined that Rose marry her son. I remembered what the prof had said. But how far would she go? I realized I wouldn't get anywhere on that topic and said, "Did Clara set me up with Patsy?"

"Probably." Ernie grinned. "From what I heard, Patsy wouldn't have needed much encouragement. Poor Artley wasn't very happy."

"He seems to have forgiven me."

"Now that he's getting it regular-like, he doesn't care."

"I see what you mean." I grinned. "More seriously though, how about right now with…" I was going to say Rose, then changed my mind, "…with Esther."

"Esther?" Ernie sounded puzzled. "I need to lie down. Can you help me, please?"

I rearranged the cushions, and when I took the tea-cups out, he was asleep or pretending to be. I had a lot to think about when I walked home, especially why Ernie had seemed surprised when I mentioned Esther. Did that mean that there was no game? Or did it mean that Rose was in the game? I was brooding about this when George cycled up.

"Hello, Andy." George stared at me expectantly.

"I've been visiting Ernie. I made some tea and played some tunes for him."

"Was he all right?"

"Yes. He's sleeping now."

He shook my hand. "Thank you, Andy. He appreciates your visits."

I walked on. When I turned, George had stopped and was watching me. I waved. He waved back. I could see that he looked worried.

I returned to the house, went to my room, and sorted out my notes, hiding them in my backpack, before joining Mary for supper.

"It's bangers and mash and lemon curd tart for supper, Andy. Did you have a good day?"

"Yes. I worked at the rookery and then went to see Ernie."

"How's he doing?"

"Getting frailer." I speared a sausage and toyed with the fork to get her attention. "I found out some interesting stuff in the library."

"Like what?" Mary said, cautiously.

"About the game with Pavlov."

Mary took a mouthful of food and chewed on it.

Seeing that she was not going to say anything I raised the stakes. "I worked out that Clara organized the game."

Mary took another mouthful. She was chewing and shaking her head.

"I also read some of those old newsletters. I learned a lot. Your maiden name was Billing. I've worked out that the Cap'n is your second cousin, and David Pascoe was your husband."

"Andy, I don't like you prying into my affairs." She poked at me with the fork. "It only hurts me to be reminded of David's death."

"Sorry. I wasn't thinking."

"Sorry doesn't change what you said." Mary spoke angrily. "But it's the other stuff I'm worried about. I've warned you before. You go nosing around, you'll get into trouble. We have our own ways of dealing with some problems, some old customs, too. Best you don't find out."

"Find out what?"

"That's your problem. You can't tell what's real from what's part of the—"

"You were going to say play, weren't you? Clara's play."

Mary stopped fooling with her food and stood up. "You're not listening, Andy. Living on an island…isolated like this, we have to do some things different from a big country. A long, long time ago, when Ruth Trevenna was Penseythan, the island had problems. Ruth proposed ways to deal with them. The Seythan accepted her ideas. We all have to make some sacrifices. It's worked for a hundred years. We aren't going to change. It's none of your damn business what we do!"

"Is that why there are more boys than girls?"

Mary looked like she might reply, but she didn't. Instead she shook her head again and went to the sink to wash the plates. I finished my piece of tart and helped with the drying. I could see tears on Mary's cheeks.

"I'm sorry, Mary. After I've done my work on the auks, I have too much time to think about things, girls, and how this place works." I put my arm around her shoulder. "Patsy was a useful distraction. I'm trying to stay away from Esther and Rose—"

"Would you stay on this island if Rose…." She moved away.

If Rose what? I wondered. "If Rose and I got married?"

"You hadn't thought about that, had you?" Mary sounded bitter.

I did not say that, in my fantasy, I had earlier assumed that if Rose wanted to be with me, she would come with me to the States. "You mean I have a chance with Rose?"

"You know what I mean."

"I have to finish my PhD. After that, I've nearly decided to go to agricultural school. Morley Thomas seems real interested in the kind of things my dad's doing. My dad'd be pleased, too."

Mary frowned.

"I guess that would work here." I said. "But if Rose would...."

"If Rose?" Mary spoke sharply and fussed around the sink, wiping vigorously. "We've found support for her to finish medical school. She'll come back after graduation. The island needs her. When Jane Trevenna is gone we will not have a mid...." Mary stopped and threw the dishcloth down.

"You were going to say midwife, weren't you?"

"Doctor! I've said enough." She ran upstairs and I heard her door slam shut.

That night, I had a terrible nightmare. Rose and Frankie were in the Round House on Midsummer's night making love, and when they finished, Frankie was helping Rose drown babies, as if they were unwanted kittens. When I tried to stop them, figures in devils' masks held me back. I woke in a cold sweat telling myself that it could not be true—Rose could not do it. It had to be the game, a sick fantasy of Clara's warped mind. But I had to admit that rationalization did not seem credible either. So what did it all mean? The one thing that seemed real was that they were worried I would seduce Rose away from the island. With their investment in her becoming the next doctor, they could not afford to lose her. But again, why go to such lengths—the Midsummer's Day activities, the stories about Clara, Throgmorton, and Pavlov, the noises at night— purely to get this point across to me? Confused, I decided I would have to think of some more tests to find out the truth.

30.

THE REST OF THAT FIRST WEEK IN DECEMBER WENT SLOWLY.
I tried to concentrate on my studies but could not stop thinking about what I had learned. Mary was rarely in the house,
and I concluded that she didn't want to speak to me. George
had probably guessed why I had visited Ernie, and even if
Ernie had not ratted on me, that source of information was
lost. I knew the newsletters held more important information;
however, when I scanned them again I couldn't find anything.

At band practice, Charlie Gay started rehearsal before I
could ask him about Midsummer's Day. We worked hard for
two hours, with only a fifteen-minute break, and then went to
the pub. I made a point of sitting with Charlie's wife, Petunia.
After the third round of drinks, when Charlie was playing
darts, I asked my question. "I was reading some of the old
newsletters and one of them referred to a Petunia Quick. Was
that you?"

"What did it say?"

"Something about problems with a Russian."

Petunia chuckled. "Bloody fool. We showed him." She
turned to look at me. "Why were you reading that old stuff?"

I lied. "Curiosity about the island and seeing if there was anything about the auks."

"Huh," Petunia said dismissively. She finished her drink looking at me pointedly.

I picked up her glass. "Let me get you another." I went to the bar.

"What'll you have, Andy?" Mary was wearing her low-cut blouse.

"I know what I'd like but I'll settle for a brandy and lime and a half of bitter. Can I get you something?"

Mary shook her head, leaned across the bar and patted my cheek, not so gently. "Andrew Ferguson, you keep your sweet talk to yourself." She was not smiling. "What are you asking Petunia about?"

"This and that, and was it true that Patsy wanted to call her baby Andrew?"

She turned to look at the man who had just come in—Cap'n Billing. "Watch the 'this and that!'" She patted me on the cheek again.

I handed Petunia her drink.

"Thanks, Andy."

"I saw something about Pete Quick. What happened to him?"

"Collecting gulls' eggs, he was. Fell off that cliff near your auks."

"So that's why Clara doesn't like Frankie going there."

"Yes, and I didn't like Pete doing it, neither."

"Was Pete your brother?"

She took a big swig of the brandy and lime. "Yes."

"Poor Clara, losing John Nichols and your brother."

"She's not been quite right since."

275

"Who hasn't?" said Charlie, sitting down.

"We were talking about Clara's bad luck with men."

"Andy, it's your turn at darts." Charlie handed me his set and motioned for Paul to play with me. While I was playing, he was bent over talking vigorously to Petunia. She did not look happy. By the time I finished my games, losing handily, Charlie and Petunia were gone. I said my goodbyes and went home. Mary was out. I made a cup of tea, worked a bit on the jigsaw puzzle, and then went upstairs. The door to Mary's room was open. I didn't hesitate.

I now knew that the previously unknown man in her photographs was David Pascoe. I was interested now in only one item, the unlabeled tape. I removed the tape player and tape from the wardrobe and played it. My theory was that it would contain the sounds of sex, designed, along with the banging on the wall, to make me frustrated. The tape was of the Roseland band playing the old favorites. The noises had to be Clara manipulating me.

* * *

By the end of the week, my auk samples were beginning to overwhelm Mary's icebox, so I went to see Arthur. I found him in the clothing store. A customer was just leaving, carrying a large package. Arthur looked pleased with himself.

"You look happy."

"Not often I sell a suit." He smiled. "What can I do for you, Andy?"

"I've got too many auk pieces for the icebox. I need some other way of storing them. Any suggestions?"

"I'd like to say you could store them here, but Isaac would

never agree." He scratched his head. "You could pickle them-like. I think we've got formaldehyde somewhere."

"I guess so. I hate the smell of that stuff, but it would work for some of the pieces. Also I need to borrow a rope."

"What for?"

"I want to look at the auk burrows nearest the cliff edge. I'll get Frankie to help me. I can't free climb like he does."

"Good luck with that." Arthur laughed. "Let's look. Come out back!" While we were hunting for the bottles, Arthur quizzed me. "I hear you've been getting around, Andy."

"I have? Oh, you mean seeing Ernie?"

"More like reading in the library." Arthur rubbed his head with his right hand. A nervous habit I'd noticed before. Red light reflected off the carved stone in his ring.

"I'm interested in the social life and connections between the different families. I find it hard to keep up with who is related to who…m." For a moment, I had heard my father censuring me. "You have an amazing society here. The old newsletters are fascinating."

"What did they tell you?"

"I learned about all the plays that Clara has staged, with her little adjustments."

Arthur grinned. "You mean like putting *The Tempest* on Tristan. We like to make fun of those people."

"Yes, and about the various Seythans and Penseythans and their roles. Marriages, births, deaths, and—"

"What did you learn?" Arthur asked abruptly.

I took a moment to think of a safe answer. "I always wondered who Mary's husband—Rose's father—was. It's in the newsletters. What happened to him?"

Arthur was silent for a while. "Died at sea, a bad thing." He paused, obviously trying to decide whether to tell me something. It came out in a rush. "Don't believe everything you read in the newsletters, Andy."

"Why not?"

"Some of the stories are like the plays. They've been adjusted."

"Who wrote them then?"

"Mostly Clara."

"Oh. I see." It sounded like more of my set of facts and conjectures were questionable. "How can I find out which are real and which have been changed?"

Arthur patted me on the shoulder, in commiseration. "I'm not sure you can. Some things are best left alone. If you want to learn the truth about something on this island, concentrate on your auks!

There's some nylon rope over there. Good for climbing. Do you want to take it now?"

"It can wait until I've talked to Frankie."

"All right, now here's the bottle of formaldehyde. I'll get you some jars with seals. Bring back what you don't use."

Arthur's comment on David Pascoe's death drove me to recheck the newsletters that followed his marriage to Mary. After taking my stuff to the house, I went to the library before trekking out to the rookery. Mary and David were married in early 1955, and Rose was born the next year. The most interesting part was the section from marriages, births, and deaths from February 1958. It included a one-liner that offered condolences to David and Mary Pascoe on the death of their baby, Daisy, who suffered breathing problems and died shortly after birth. I went back to the earlier newsletters and scanned the infant deaths quickly, taking notes. Between 1921 and 1970, there were 375 births, and 30 infant deaths. About ninety percent of the infant deaths were of baby girls. Various reasons for their demise were given by the midwife: stillborn, breathing problems, severe fever, and so on. It agreed with what the prof had told me. The islanders had a simple solution to population control—limit the number of girls. If Rose was being trained to carry on the tradition, it would explain why Mary did not want to talk about it. It was hard to believe though. I suppressed images of Rose as I reread an item from 1959. It expressed sadness that David Pascoe had been swept overboard and drowned at sea while fishing near South Georgia.

As I walked to the rookery, I reassessed my "facts." The Penseythan, supported by the Seythan, had likely been responsible for constraining the number of females on the island by killing excess baby girls—younger sisters. Consequently, there would be fewer sisters than normal. One question that bothered me was why the men didn't just up and leave. Maybe some did, but it wasn't so easy to get off the island unless you were a sailor and jumped ship. What about the practices today? I had seen the birth control pills in Mary's room, and heard Arthur Nancarrow's comment on the cupboard for women's things in the store. Now that contraceptive pills were available, the problem might not exist anymore. Maybe they did not need to eliminate girl babies. I hoped so, since Rose had been designated to become the doctor/midwife and, most likely, Penseythan.

This still left me with Patsy's comments to fret about; Rose would be the Queen on Midsummer's Day. As to the rest of my concerns, some of the information backing my theory came from the newsletters, and apparently, Clara adjusted them like she did the plays. However, the information about Mary's husband, the death of her second daughter, and David's subsequent death was consistent with Mary's unwillingness to discuss them. I concluded that Mary and Cap'n Billing conducted their affair elsewhere. The persistent banging on the wall and sounds of sex didn't come from the unmarked tape, but from Clara next door. Assuming she was playing a game with me, she was orchestrating the noises to frustrate me. It must have been irritating for Mary, too. Why didn't she complain? The only answers I could think of were that she was inured to putting up with "Poor Clara's" shenanigans or that Mary was part of the real-life play in which Clara had cast me as a—a what? Most likely as an idiot. Clara had set me up before with Patsy. I was determined that Clara would not fool me again.

Nevertheless, my first priority had to be completing my study of the auks. I was close to having all the data for my PhD. The auk remains that I had collected would be enough to settle a few questions about color, feather structure, and smell. My main effort now would be photographing the auks while they looked after their chicks. During that time, I would decide how to act in Clara's real life play.

31.

A large number of chicks had been born this year and the auks were spending most of the daylight hours fishing, including Nellie and her male attendants, Dan, Tom, and Harry. Harry had become very effective and Nellie made a big fuss over him, to the apparent irritation of her main man, Dan. I do not know whether auks have such feelings, yet that is what it looked like to me. The chick was beginning to show itself at the entrance to its burrow, definitely a male. I labeled him Gareth. Nellie still fished occasionally, eating most of her catch. Her feathers were not as carefully groomed as before and I had the sad feeling that she would not survive the next winter.

The weather was good for the next couple of days so I left the blind and roamed the edges of the rookery, photographing the families of a number of the good-time girls. The path had petered out and I was severely scratched by the gorse. It paid off for I could see subtle differences in the ways in which the families worked. Nellie's family was a model of efficiency; she had picked most of her men well, except in the case of Syd. However, in some other families, the gentlemen friends were not very energetic and the good-time girl and her man did most of the fishing. I hoped that some subtle difference would show up in the photos or on the films, to explain the deviations in behavior.

On the second day, Frankie arrived to collect gulls' eggs. He saw me on the far side of the rookery and waved before descending the cliff. The rookery was on a part of the cliff that curved gently towards the west. I could see where I had followed Frankie down the cliff on the north side of the rookery. In fact, a series of ledges descended down the cliff; it was not as vertical as it had seemed when I was on it, but it was still scary as hell. Various handholds allowed a climber to go from one ledge to another as he worked his way along the cliff. The focus of circling angry gulls showed where Frankie was. I watched as he put eggs into a bag slung by his side from his belt. By the time I returned to the blind he had climbed back and was waiting inside for me.

"What were you doing on t'other side of the rookery?"

"Taking pictures of some other families."

He appeared disinterested. "Hot work. Got a drink?"

I handed him my flask. Distracted by thoughts about being made a fool of, I had forgotten to bring two. Frankie slurped it noisily, dribbling orangeade on his chest.

"Anything to eat?"

I nodded and handed him a sandwich. He crammed it in, munching open mouthed with wet crumbs spattering onto his jaw and shirt. He looked a mess.

"I'm going to be King," he said, his mouth full.

I made a pretense of doing something with my camera.

"Your hands are shaking."

"Cramp from operating the camera too many times," I said, squeezing the words out.

"I'll get to do it real."

I had a hard time getting out my question. "Who's the lucky queen?"

Frankie looked blank. "I dunno. Mum didn't say." I must have shown my surprise. "Do you know?" Frankie asked.

"Nobody tells me anything. Who do you think it might be?"

"Could be Esther." He licked his lips. "I like big girls and Esther's big." He moved his hands, expressively.

"Certainly is."

Somehow I'd not thought of Frankie with women, other than a fear he would be King to Rose's Queen. "How do you know that?"

"At the dance. You can tell."

"Thanks for the drink and stuff." Frankie picked up his bag of eggs.

"Will you be here next week…say…Wednesday?" I asked.

"Why?"

"I need to take some pictures of the burrows and I'd like your help."

"It's a bad part of the cliff."

"Arthur's lending me a rope. I'll tie it round my waist and you hold it while I go down."

"Auks won't like it."

Stop finding arguments against doing it, Frankie. "I know, but it's the last thing I need to do and it will only be on this side of the rookery," I said testily.

Frankie looked surprised. "I'll be working at Jago's," he said. "Could do it Tuesday."

"Fine, it's a date."

Frankie giggled. "Dates are with girls."

"It's an expression."

Frankie looked incredulous. He left, picking his way through the gorse, effortlessly avoiding the prickles. I felt a lot better than when he had announced his pending coronation. Maybe Rose was not the Queen. That would mean that Patsy had lied. Prompted by Clara? The only way to find out was to get Mary to tell me or find some way to speak to Rose.

Mary greeted me at the front door. "How are the auks doing?"

"Fine. Nellie's chick, Gareth—"

"Like the professor?"

"Yes."

"Gareth! What will you think of next?" Mary laughed.

"Actually, I'm not sure yet. I'm just betting he's more likely to be male than female. Like the...." I was going to say babies.

Mary's smile disappeared. "Like the...?"

"Like the other auks," I answered, quickly.

"I'll fix supper."

I needed to find out more about Midsummer's. "Can I help cut up anything?"

"No thanks," Mary replied. "It's cold chicken and salad. But you could set the table."

"How's Rose doing?" I tried to sound casual.

"Studying hard." My face must have shown my disappointment. "Come on! It's not the end of the world. She'll be here for Christmas."

"What about Midsummer's Day?" I asked, picking cutlery out of the drawer.

"What do you mean?"

"Will she be there?"

"You'll see."

"Frankie says he'll be King."

"Frankie says many things."

"Who'll be Queen?"

"It's not for me to say." Mary looked away.

"But you know, don't you?"

"You've got too many questions, Andy," Mary said, angrily. "I've told you before. It won't do you no good prying into our affairs."

"Sorry. I don't have much else to think about."

"Oh." Mary went out into the backyard.

If Mary was not going to say anything, I would have to find a way to talk to Rose. There might be a chance after chapel on Sunday.

For the first time in a few weeks, I went to chapel. At previous services, I had seen Jane Trevenna sit in the front left pew. I arrived early and took a seat near the front on the right side, hoping it would be easier to look at Rose. The islanders filled all the seats, leaving six at the front by the aisle. Jane Trevenna came in accompanied by James and Miriam Thomas. They were followed by Rose with her hair up in a Grecian style, Mary in a floral dress, and Cap'n Billing in a dark suit. Rose turned as they reached their seats and gave me an uncertain smile. She sat between Mary and Jane. I paid little attention to the service, singing perfunctorily and thinking how graceful the back of Rose's neck was. She was wearing small gold earrings that highlighted the delicate shape of her ears.

Isaac Nancarrow's sermon dwelt in part on 2 Corinthians 6:14: "We are to separate from, not tolerate paganism." It seemed to be a warning to the people who wore masks and danced around the bonfire and maypole. However, as in a previous sermon, he seemed to be looking at me when he commented that sometimes their rituals could get out of hand. Was it a follow-up to what had happened on the last Guy Fawkes Day—another warning? After having paused to look at me, he continued with a totally different subject, the connection of the perils of the sea to walking on water. I could not tell what the connection was. The ability to walk on water did not seem to be a very useful ability for the island's fishermen who, normally, were hundreds of mile from land. I tried to picture walking on the waves I had seen around Roseland, and concluded it would be difficult. Finally, he made some comment I half heard about taking a woman away.

I timed my exit to place me just ahead of Rose, turning to face her in the doorway.

"How's the studying going?"

"It's tough, Andy. There's so much to review. What about the auks? How's Nellie?"

"She has a new chick. I'm guessing he's male. I call him Gareth." We continued toward the square.

"The professor will like that. Good, good, good, eh?" Rose did a creditable imitation of the professor's Welsh accent.

"When will I see you? We need to talk."

"We are talking."

"You know what I mean."

"I can't say. I've got to study."

"How about Midsummer's Day?"

There was a long silence. "I don't—"

Mary interrupted her. "Rose, we've got to go. The car's waiting. Jane's impatient."

"Andy, I…." Her hands were expressing something, unhappiness I hoped, as Mary led her away. She looked over her shoulder. "Midsummer's…I'm…it won't work."

I watched Rose leave. Mary walked back to the house with me. "Sorry, Andy. I had no choice."

"Jane made you do it," I muttered bitterly.

Mary stopped and turned to face me. "You know how this island works, Andy. Stop fighting it. The Penseythan has to make the tough decisions and we have to support her."

"I've worked out what those tough decisions are. She's training Rose to make them in the future. Isn't she? Are you happy with that?"

"I'm proud of Rose and so is the whole island. If you care about her, support her too!"

"Hard to do if I can't see her."

"You don't listen," Mary retorted, angrily. "I don't want to talk about it anymore. I'm cooking lunch. You can fix the vegetables."

In the kitchen, Mary handed me a handful of potatoes. I started peeling. "When Isaac Nancarrow spoke about taking a woman away, what was he talking about?" I asked.

"Could have been Mabel not coming back." Mary's lips were pursed. "Protecting the island's ancient ways. That pious old hypocrite...."

Ancient ways, hypocrite? Curious. I remembered having to study an Ibsen play in high school. "Isn't he a pillar of the community?"

"You didn't hear that." Mary looked worried. I wondered why. Unlike Arthur, Isaac had been unfriendly, but her comment implied more than that he didn't like foreigners.

"What did you think of the business about the governor?" Mary asked.

"You told me the governor only comes once a year. Is that enough?"

"Yes. We're a long way from St. Helena. We govern ourselves."

"What if there's a major problem?"

"Unless it's international, like that business with Pavlov, he won't hear about it. We like to handle our own affairs."

"The Penseythan has near absolute power?"

"Along with the Seythan, yes."

"What if there's a murder?"

Mary looked wary. "We don't have murders."

"Hypothetically."

"Seythan would deal with it."

"So the governor's role is mainly ceremonial?"

"Yes."

"Incredible!"

* * *

The next Saturday night, when I reached the hall, the normal crowd was at the dance—Mary with the Cap'n, Patsy with Young Artley, Clara without Frankie, and Petunia Gay. Charlie had been ill, and had cancelled band practice that week. I went over to Petunia, who was now showing signs of being pregnant. "How's Charlie doing?" I asked.

"He's nearly over the cold, Andy. You'll be at practice on Tuesday?"

"Sure. It's more fun than watching the auks."

"That's not what I've heard. They do strange things I'm told…like us." She chuckled.

I nudged her in the ribs. "So you have two or three other gentlemen friends?"

"Andy, you know what I mean. *Rum tum ti…*I hear you have names for the auks."

"Yes. My favorite is Nellie. Her main man is Dapper Dan and her men friends are Tom and Harry."

"Only two of them?"

"There was another one, Sydney."

"What happened to him?"

"He wanted the real thing, and got rough. The other guys helped Nellie push him out. I should have called him Pavlov, shouldn't I?"

"It wasn't funny at the time." Petunia poked me in the ribs. "You need to get a seat. The band's starting."

Artley made room for me on the bench. As Ernie had said, now that he was getting it regular, he did not worry about me.

"How's the baby?"

"Grand. He's lovely."

"Who's looking after him?"

"Esther. Can't keep her away."

"I thought she'd be here."

Artley looked surprised. "Not hardly."

I was going to ask him why, when Petunia grabbed me for a dance. She seemed to be flirting as we progressed around the floor. After a few turns, I concluded that the occasional tightening of her grip and the pressing against me were done subconsciously. I could imagine how Pavlov might have felt when she had done it seriously, shades of Patsy. In fact, Patsy took the next dance.

"How are you and Rose doing?"

"I haven't seen her. She's studying."

"I bet she is." Patsy sang a few bars of "The Floral Dance" in my ear.

"Rose is doing medicine; I'm sure she knows what it's all about."

"You haven't done it with her, have you?" Patsy sounded surprised.

"Not everyone is as forward as you, Patsy. How did it go in the Round House?"

Patsy tensed. "Not like with you. I felt cheap." She pressed her head against my shoulder. "Couldn't wait to get to Artley."

"You happy now?"

"Yes."

"How can I get to see Rose? Any suggestions?"

The dance ended. "Chapel on Sunday or you could try going to the front door," Patsy said, smirking. "Good luck!"

Patsy was right. I decided to follow her advice. The rest of the evening was a blur. I danced every dance. Even Mary took me through a perfunctory turn at the Gay Gordons after she had done her customary circuit with the Cap'n. At the end of the dance, I returned Mary to her seat.

"I won't be home tonight, Andy. Tomorrow, I'll cook lunch after chapel." I wanted to ask if Rose would join us, but decided that might tip the balance against it. *Still no chance to talk. Damn.*

Petunia chose me for the last dance. This time the little pressures were more overt. When the lights went out, she kissed me passionately, pulling away to wipe my mouth with a handkerchief just before the lights came on.

"Don't read anything into that, young Andy. We women like our bit of fun."

"Poor Pavlov," I said. "He didn't stand a chance."

"Poor Pavlov, my arse! He tried to rape me. Broke my nose!"

Now I knew what had happened to her flowerlike face.

32.

THAT AFTERNOON I WENT TO THE ROOKERY, WROTE MORE notes on the auks, and reworked the outline of my dissertation. I remembered what James MacDonald had said about dissertations:

"If I haven't come to the main conclusions early on, I send it back. Remember that when it's your turn, Andy."

I considered various versions of my first page. The one I preferred started with:

The Roseland auk—Fratercula Roselandis—is unique among birds. Careful study has confirmed earlier work [1,2] in showing that there are far more males than females: two or three times more. In this dissertation, the reasons for and consequences of this imbalance are discussed. Most of this dissertation will be devoted to the consequences. As to the causes, while further work will be needed to determine them fully, one contributory element appears to be the relatively limited availability of food for this isolated rookery. This is seen in the relatively small catch taken each time a bird goes to fish—that is, relative to catches normal in the case of the northern Atlantic Puffin. An intriguing feature of the courtship is the way in which suitors bring fish: Is it a method of demonstrating their competence to be a father? Did this approach lead to their evolving to handle the problem of a poor supply of food by opting to provide more birds to feed the chicks? As to the consequences, this situation has led to some unusual mating behavior.

The nearly sexual pleasure that comes from conquering a scientific project should have made me happy. There were just a few loose ends to tie up for my PhD—"Dr. Andrew Ferguson" sounded good. But all I could think about was talking to Rose. Patsy had said, "Go and see her." That's what I would do tomorrow. I would have to chance it that she was not out tending to the sick.

* * *

I told Arthur Nancarrow I wanted to go to Portloe, and he lent me his bicycle. I headed off down the road past the last of the homes and the two small round houses. Some islanders were preparing them for the festivities, now four days away. I couldn't see anybody at the road junction by the schoolhouse as I left the Portloe road, pedaling deliberately around the bend towards Trewince. When I reached the tracks that led to the Cocking, Nichols, and Thomas farms, I slowed and walked, checking for people. Again I was lucky; nobody was around. I remounted and cycled hard the remaining four or five miles to the Trewince gates. Up to that point, I had been confident in my plan. Now, faced with executing it, I was not so certain. I entered the grounds and left the bicycle in the woods near the gate. From the bridge, the view of the gorge was spectacular. Below the house, looking north, the gorge narrowed with steep walls rising to the woods on each side. The River Fal descended in a series of small waterfalls. Through the trees, I glimpsed a path with a wooden fence that circled around the cliff from the lawn. Above the house the stream tumbled violently over moss- and lichen-covered rocks. I noticed one place where the cliffs had washed out. Signs of a track were visible leading down from the woods, across the river, toward the house. The sun disappeared behind a cloud, making the scene dark and intimidating. I nearly turned around. The cloud moved on. The road ahead was dappled in sunlight, and the front of the house came into view. *Now or never,* I thought, but before going to the door, I checked for the Lagonda. The good news, the car was there and that implied that Rose was in. The bad news, the car was there and so, likely, were Mr. Thomas and Jane Trevenna. I walked quickly to the door and knocked before I could think anymore about the wisdom of my plan.

"Mr. Ferguson, we were not expecting you." Miriam Thomas said, as she opened the door.

"I know. I wasn't sure what to do. Can I speak to Rose, please?"

"I'll ask. Please take a seat in the living room."

I did not sit, but went to the binoculars. I was curious about what else could be seen through them to the left of the Jago farm. I think I already knew I would not be allowed to speak to Rose, and was subconsciously formulating another plan. The path to the rookery was clear as was the path from the farm. Fortunately, above and to the left of the farm only a short part of the cliff top path was visible, and from then on the woods obscured the view all the way to Trewince. I had turned the binoculars to look toward Portloe when I heard someone enter.

"Mr. Ferguson, you are very persistent," said Jane Trevenna. She did not look pleased.

"I didn't know what else to do. I have to talk to Rose."

She sat and motioned me to take a chair opposite her. "Why?"

"I want to understand if I have any chance with her."

"Are your plans to live permanently on the island?"

Mary's question, I thought. "Not exactly…I need to finish my PhD and then—"

"And then, what? Your skill, ornithology, is not needed here."

I decided not to mention agriculture, although she'd probably heard about my visit to see Morley Thomas. "We could live here part of the year."

"You are comfortable that the islanders will suffer no illness for the rest of the time?"

"I didn't mean that. Rose isn't the only one who can provide medical care. Is she?"

"For the time being, you are correct, however you know nothing of our situation in the future. Someone has to lead and make the difficult decisions, as I do. It takes time to train a person for such responsibility. We have invested heavily in Rose."

"You assume Rose wants this responsibility."

Jane Trevenna stood up. "Mr. Ferguson, you are on dangerous ground again. Do not pursue this line of argument. You may not speak to Rose. She has more important things to do than waste her time on a lovesick young man. The island needs her."

"What if she doesn't want to be the person to control the population? That's one of the jobs for your doctor, isn't it?" I retorted angrily, losing my temper. "You won't trust her to make her own mind up about me. What century are we in?"

"You are in the twentieth, Mr. Ferguson. We are in the nineteenth in many regards. That is when our system was established. Now please leave. I do not want to see you on my property again. If you come back, I...the Seythan will deal with you *severely*. Mr. Thomas will see you out."

"I can find my way," I said to her retreating back.

I covered the eight miles to Veryan in well under an hour, taking out my frustration on the road.

"That didn't take long," said Arthur, grinning, when I returned his bicycle.

"Waste of time," I replied, tiredly.

"Didn't get to talk to Rose?"

"You knew?"

"Andy, it's hard to do anything on Roseland without people knowing."

"I guess so." Angry at my failure to see Rose, I was already thinking again about how to get to Trewince undetected. I did not worry about whether I was being set up again.

* * *

On Tuesday, I rented two nylon ropes from Arthur and took them to the rookery. Arthur told me that the wind would be blowing hard, but it might die down a bit on Wednesday afternoon. He was right. This was not the day for me to go down the cliff to look at the auk's nests. I walked down the hill to Jago's farm. Even with a strong wind blowing from the west, I could detect the sour smell of pig manure well before I reached the pigsties. Anaerobic digestion in a covered tank would sure help. Frankie, sweaty and smeared with oil, was in the yard cleaning a tractor.

"I'd like to look at the nests tomorrow afternoon. Remember, you agreed to help?"

Frankie nodded. "Bad part of cliff, you'll need a stake. I'll bring it."

"Thanks. I'll see you then."

"How much will I get?"

I had not considered payment, but I needed Frankie. If I got in trouble, he was one person capable of rescuing me. "A pound okay?"

Frankie's grinned. "Yes. I've been saving to get something for my Queen."

I did not ask him what. He returned to cleaning the tractor. *Something for my Queen. Shit.*

"Hi, Andy, what are you doing here?" Patsy's voice interrupted my misery. She held out her baby. "Say hello to William!"

Like many babies, he looked ugly to me, but I said, "Nice looking boy. I heard you were going to call him Andrew."

Patsy giggled. "Who told you a thing like that?" She looked at me slyly. "Looking forward to Midsummer's?"

"The band's fun."

"I bet you wish you'd been chosen."

I tried to suppress an image of Rose, lying naked on the bed in the roundhouse. "Not unless I was the only one."

Patsy giggled again. "I'm sure Frankie'll do right by the

Queen. You'll have fun, won't you, Frankie?" she said, raising her voice.

Frankie looked up, grinning. "*Rum tum, ti, tum tum tum,*" he sang.

The image now included a sweaty, dirty, naked Frankie lying on top of Rose. I walked away, shaking my head, trying to stop the tears of frustration. "Got to get back to the rookery."

"See you Friday," shouted Patsy. "Have fun!"

I left the ropes in the blind before leaving the rookery and trekking up to the top of Brown Willy. In my misery, Dark Lake looked inviting for a moment. I had begun to understand why John Nichols had drowned himself. The day was fine, except for the wind, and the island—with all of the farms and their surrounding houses, hamlets for families—lay in clear view below me. I suddenly realized that for its size and the amount of arable land, relatively few people lived on Roseland. Large areas of woods and numbers of fields were not being used. Back in the States I had read about the other islands that constituted the St. Helena Territory: Ascension, St. Helena, and Tristan. They all had larger population densities. The largest and lushest, St. Helena, had a density ten times larger than Roseland. Ascension had very poor land, and it still had twice as many people. Now, Ascension had an airbase and perhaps food was sent in. Nevertheless, all of the islands had abundant sea life, relative to their populations.

In my misery I turned to fretting again about how much of what I had heard was still true. Surely, Roseland could support far more people today. In the nineteenth century, isolated from the rest of the world with no contraceptives available, the birth rate would have been higher. The fear of overpopulation more justified. More recently, from what I had seen in the newsletters, the number of babies per woman was only slightly over two, probably the result of better contraception. If they had all lived, the population would have increased quite slowly. Killing girl babies was wrong in any case and didn't make sense any more. Maybe my fears were unjustified. Rose would know. I had to talk to her, but not today. I could do it after I had filmed the auks on Wednesday or, at the latest, Thursday—the day before Rose had to be the Queen.

Back at the rookery, the auks were in a feeding frenzy. From the side of the nesting area, I could see many of the older chicks sitting at the front of their burrows, fussing for food. The burrows descended in layers of hummocky grass to the point where the cliff had crumbled and dropped precipitously a hundred feet to the sea. It looked scary, but I was determined to take photographs. I hoped that Frankie would find a good place for the stake. I spent the rest of the day observing the birds, writing notes, and taking photographs of the other bird species. In addition to taking pictures of the ubiquitous gulls and skuas, I snapped yellow-nosed and sooty albatross and petrels. I had seen a wandering albatross a few weeks earlier when, unfortunately, my camera was not handy.

The house felt empty when I returned. A note on the kitchen table stated that Mary would be away that night and that I should make my own meals. I had the unhappy thought that she must be with Rose, preparing her to be Queen. My supper of fried mackerel, boiled potatoes, and cabbage was more or less edible. I knew it would taste better with some kind of sauce, but I did not know how to make one. I tried to stop thinking about Rose, gagged on a piece of mackerel and dumped the rest of my meal down the hole in the outhouse. In a childish way, I craved something sweet, and baked apple with Bird's Custard was my solution. Later, I baked a second apple to eat while I reworked the puzzle that showed the man in the stocks. Had Clara been warning me? I hoped not.

33.

THE NEXT DAY, FRANKIE ARRIVED IN TIME TO TAKE PART OF my lunch. He had not bothered to clean up much, and smelled sweaty and oily. The images of him and Rose came back to haunt me. I felt angry and said nothing as we sat in the blind and ate.

"Where do you want to go?" Frankie pointed at the hooked metal stake and sledgehammer.

I took him to the edge of the rookery and pointed. "I want to take photos of the lower burrows. See how many chicks are old enough to go to the entrance of their burrows."

"You really need a rope for that?" Frankie looked disgusted.

"You don't, Frankie. I do."

Frankie drove the stake in among the gorse bushes and tied the rope to it. "This'll do. Tie this around your waist!" I did and he held the rope, releasing it as I went down. When the idea had come to me it had seemed simple. Now doing it didn't look like a good idea. The edges of the grass hummocks were slippery with droppings. The ground became more and more crumbly as I approached the edge, until it began to give way in chunks as I reached the cliff. I suppressed my fear and concentrated on the burrows. The arc in the cliff allowed me to see the whole rookery, with its eight layers of burrows, extending in a few places to as many as eleven. When I started my descent, the auks fussed at me, and most of the chicks scuttled back undercover. I steeled myself and waited. The chicks started to reappear. I was feeling nearly secure, when Frankie tapped me on the shoulder.

"What the hell!" Some of the closer chicks disappeared again.

"Haven't you finished yet?"

"What did you do with the slack?"

"Tied it off."

"I'm waiting for the chicks to come out. I was doing fine. You scared them," I whispered angrily. Frankie shrugged. "Please go back up. I'll be done in about fifteen minutes, if nothing else scares them." Frankie left, keeping low. One by one the chicks reappeared. I finished two rolls of film and climbed back.

"Get what you wanted?"

"Yes, thanks, Frankie."

"You take the rope off. I'll get the stake out."

We finished, went back to the blind, and finished the sandwiches. Fortunately I had made plenty. "*Rum tum, ti tum,*" said Frankie. "Only two days and I'll be the King."

I put down the sandwich. My stomach felt hollow. I acted as if I had not heard.

Frankie crouched and did a little jig, moving his hips, suggestively. "*Rum tum ti tum tum tum,*" he chanted.

At that point I could readily have hit him with the sledgehammer.

"I'm going for gulls' eggs," he said as he strutted away.

I worked on some weak sections of the dissertation and make several changes, noting that a number of empty burrows existed, not because they were unused but because the egg-laying season was longer than I had realized. Some of the late arriving auks were still preparing their nests. Vague mental images of Rose and Frankie appearing in different sexual positions made it hard to concentrate. Nevertheless, by the time I had finished correcting and adding material, an hour had passed. I decided that tonight would be the time to try to see Rose. If that did not work, it would still leave me one more chance before Midsummer's Day.

Frankie had not returned. I walked to the top of the cliff and shouted. The noise of the birds, wind, and surf made it difficult to hear a response. I tried again and this time I heard a cry. I crawled to the edge of the cliff and looked down to the right. Far below, I could see what looked like a hand clutching a protruding rock. I edged along the cliff top to get a better look.

"Frankie, are you in trouble?" I shouted.

"Can't move. Ledge gone. Where've you been?"

"Too much noise, and I couldn't hear. If I lower a rope, can you grab it?"

"Yes."

"Hang on!" I crawled back from the cliff, into the gorse. By the time I reached the blind my hands and legs were bleeding from multiple tiny cuts, a Chinese torture. I felt miserable from the pain and from the continuing thoughts about Rose. I started to pick up the stake, sledge, and rope. The thought came that I should leave Frankie, but a different image came to me: Clara weeping uncontrollably. Poor Clara, who had lost John Nichols, her daughter Primrose, and now all that was left to her—Frankie. She was the one who was playing games with me, yet faced with a chance to get revenge, I could not do this to her, or for that matter, to Frankie. I took the stake, sledge, and rope to the cliff top and, following Frankie's example, drove the stake into the ground in a thick patch of gorse. I tied a loop in the rope and lowered it over the cliff edge. After a while Frankie's head appeared, and I helped him over the last part to flat ground. He lay down, looking exhausted. His shirt was torn and his hands were scratched from clinging to the rocks.

"Please don't tell me mum," he whispered breathlessly.

"I don't know." I was telling the truth, my desire to protect Clara and my anger at her games competed for a moment. "Okay, I guess."

"I won't forget." Frankie held out his bag. "Look! Gulls' eggs."

I shook my head. Frankie was incorrigible. "Let's go. I need to take the ropes back to Nancarrow's. You okay?"

"I'll be fine," said Frankie, adding the stake and sledge to his load. *A quick recovery,* I thought. I had to run to catch up. When we reached the farm, Patsy came out with the baby.

"You two look a right mess. What have you been doin'?"

Frankie was looking at the ground. "Climbing," I said.

"You too, Andy?" Patsy looked amazed.

"Frankie was helping me photograph the auk burrows. I had to go to the edge of the cliff. I helped him when he went for gulls' eggs. See!" I pointed at the bag.

As I left, I heard Patsy arguing with Frankie.

I made my decision on the way home. Sleep would not be possible. The visions of a disgusting-looking Frankie with a naked Rose were becoming more and more lurid. My stomach hurt and I wanted to throw up but could not. I had to talk to Rose, and that meant going to Trewince tonight. Mary was in the kitchen getting ready to cook dinner.

"I hope this doesn't cause a problem. I'm going back to the rookery."

"Now! Why?"

"I need to study the behavior of the auks. I may spend all night there, so I can also catch them early in the morning. Okay if I skip dinner and take some sandwiches and a drink?"

"I suppose so." Mary looked puzzled. "Don't they go to sleep, like us?"

"Eventually, but on the few occasions I've been there late I've seen some odd behavior," I lied. "I'm going to wash up and change into something warmer."

"Off you go. Take the kettle! The water's hot. I'll see what I can fix for you."

I stripped, washed with a washcloth, and shaved. I put on my one decent tee shirt.

When I came down, Mary was putting the bread away. "You said you'd seen some odd habits. Like what?"

"I've seen more fooling around between the 'good-time girls' and their gentlemen friends."

"Like shaving and putting on your best shirt." She prodded my chest with a finger. "I hope this study of strange behavior won't involve Esther or—"

"No, I'm keeping away from her." I answered quickly. My laugh was genuine. "This was the only clean shirt I had. You should smell the one I took off...auk poop."

Mary made a face. "Had to ask. You ornithologists are

pretty strange sometimes. I've made you some ham, cheese, and tomato sandwiches. You can fix orangeade yourself."

On the way to the rookery, I thought again about what route to take to Trewince. I needed to get there early enough to have a chance to see which room was Rose's. Fortunately, in summer this far south it remained light until late. I kept to my earlier decision to cut through the woods above the Jago and Anthony farms to the Veryan-Trewince road, beyond the junction with the road to the schoolhouse. If I was careful, I would not be visible to Jane Trevenna's "all-seeing" binoculars. From there on, if I heard anyone on the road, I could duck behind the hedge.

I stayed at the rookery for an hour before starting out, taking half of my sandwiches, the drink, and my binoculars. The path was rough, skirting the trees on the slope and that, coupled with checking to see if anyone was around, made it take over an hour to walk the five miles to the road. As I was about to climb over a gate, I heard the Lagonda leaving Trewince. I dropped behind the hedge and waited a few minutes before continuing on.

Near the gates to Trewince, the woods were now on both sides of the road. I had to leave the road or I risked being seen from the house and garden. I decided go back up the hill to where the gorge of the River Fal would be easier to cross. The rocks in the riverbed were slippery, and I managed to fill one shoe with water before making the traverse. Trees lined the top of the bank, but a short way on they thinned out, and I had a clear view of the south side and front of the house, the terrace, and the lawn. People sat around a large table on the terrace. With the binoculars I could see that the group had just finished their dessert. That is, except for Frankie who was taking a second helping. Miriam Thomas was collecting plates and Rose and Clara were helping her. Jane Trevenna was seated looking at the garden. She appeared to be arguing with Frankie. I wished I could have seen his face. He was nodding his head, but probably not paying attention. He rarely did with me. Soon afterward, Miriam and Clara appeared with a tray of cups, milk, sugar, and a coffee pot.

I was wondering where Rose was, when a light came on in an upstairs room at the rear on the south side of the house. A large tree stood in a flowerbed by the drive. Its branches spread over the drive toward the side of the house. If this was Rose's room, it would give me a way to get her attention. I was not thinking and stood up to look for pebbles. Frankie turned quickly, staring in my direction. I froze and then edged slowly behind a tree. After a while, Frankie looked away. My heart stopped thumping. I picked up a handful of pebbles on the bank and put them in my pocket.

Later, the Lagonda returned. Mr. Thomas drove to the back of the house, and I could not see who got out. As the sun set, the lights were turned on in the living room. The only light upstairs was coming from what I had worked out to be Rose's room. I walked carefully, keeping low, down to the tree by the side of the house. I started to climb. The going was harder than I had expected and it took me ten minutes to work my way cautiously up to and along the branch that hung in front of the window. Rose was sitting at a table in front of the window. Her door was closed. *Thank God!* It would make it harder for people to hear the pebbles. I started to pitch them at the window. On my third attempt, Rose looked up. I pitched another one. A frown appeared. Apparently, she could not see me. She leaned forward and opened

306

the window before I could pitch another pebble. This time, she saw me.

Rose gasped. "What are you doing here, Andy?"

"I came here Monday. Jane Trevenna wouldn't let me talk to you. Mary won't say anything. I have to find out."

"You shouldn't be here." Rose looked panicky. "Find out what?"

"They're playing a game with me. Why won't they let me see you?"

"I don't know about a game. Aunt Jane says I've got to study."

"What about John Trevenna?"

Rose spoke carefully. "I've known John all my life, Andy. We've been good friends. People expect us to—"

"Get married." I finished the sentence for her. "People! You mean like Jane Trevenna? Is that it? How about your mum?"

"Mum says I should follow my heart."

"And what does your heart say?"

"It's confused." Rose looked as if she might close the window.

I had to prevent it. "I miss you, Rose."

"I miss being with you, too." Rose looked sad. "It's not been easy. Where would it end?"

"You and me together."

"Where would we live?"

Fortunately, following Mary's comment, I had thought of an answer. "Here."

"What would you do?"

"I'm going to learn about agriculture. Things that would help the island. I've talked to Morley Thomas and others. They're interested."

"So that's what Morley tried to tell me after chapel." Rose looked thoughtful. "And that's why Jane pulled me away before he could."

"Andy, I'm going to be the doctor, and later the Penseythan," Rose said firmly. "Could you handle being like Prince Philip with the Queen."

"Not with her." I wanted to laugh but my chest felt tight. "But I could with you."

"There will be things I have to do…emergencies."

"Emergencies like too many girl babies!" I spoke without thinking.

Rose closed her eyes and gripped the windowsill hard. "You don't live here, Andy. You come from a huge country," spoken loud and angrily. "You don't understand how difficult it has been to protect this little piece of land."

"I'm trying to understand, Rose. I realize the birth rate would have been too high in the nineteenth century. I looked at the more recent birth statistics in the newsletters. The natural population growth rate is small. You all go too far."

"That was set up some time ago. We have a system. It'll take time to change completely."

"Better farming could help support more people—"

"Andy—"

The door behind Rose was opened so hard it bounced off its stop. Jane Trevenna stormed in. She looked furious. "Rose, who are you talking to?"

I slid down the branch quickly, let go, and dropped to the ground, missing Rose's answer. I was lucky to land in the flowerbed, just avoiding the hard gravel drive. By the time Jane Trevenna got to the window, I was up the hill watching from the cover of a bush. She looked vainly for me, and then turned to Rose. I could see them arguing. When Rose hung her head, I could not tell if it was because she had refused to admit she had been speaking to me or because she had ratted on me. Either way, I was in a bad position. As I headed for the gorge it got worse. I could hear loud voices and the baying of the hound. Winston had been released. I slid down the bank to the tumble of water. *Don't leave a scent*, I thought. *Stay in the water.* Up or down stream? I started down and then re-alized I would have to go under the bridge. They would be waiting. I had the intelligence to come out of the water and go up the bank before retracing my steps and heading upstream. I hoped this would confuse both Winston and my pursuers, and make them believe I was on or close to the road. If I was lucky they might assume I had come by bike, as before. The fast flowing water was cold and my feet were numb by the time I struggled to a point high above Trewince. I left the stream and headed rapidly to the cliff-top path. I could hear shouting and Winston's occasional bark. They were following the road. A short time later I saw the lights of the Lagonda. By now, I was gasping for breath and felt cold and sore. The adrenaline rush had abated.

I sat for a while before heading back at a steady pace. The clouds were intermittent, and I could see the path in the moonlight. With stops to check that I was not being followed, it took me more than two hours to reach the rookery. I half expected to find a welcoming committee but only the surf and the muttering of the birds heralded my arrival. I finished my sandwiches, leaving a small amount for the morning. Al-though it was only just after ten, I slept from exhaustion—a troubled sleep, punctuated by disjointed visions of birds and dogs and people in odd costumes.

* * *

Before daylight, I gathered my belongings and started down the path to Veryan. I was not too tired to feel frightened, and I had the feeling that I would not see Nellie and the other "good time girls" again. I had tried to kid myself that they could not prove that it been me at Trewince. Even to me the arguments were not convincing. Certainly, Frankie had seen me earlier. He had not done anything about it at the time, but he might have talked later. Rose might not have talked, but Jane Trevenna was smart enough to work it out, and my footprints were in the flowerbed. By the time I could see the Round House I had had more or less switched off all thoughts. I felt the kind of numbness I could imagine being felt by a man going to the gallows, the inevitability of my fate.

I heard a noise from behind the wall. It took an effort not to turn. I saw the horns first as a figure clambered over the wall in front of me. He was dressed in black and his devil's mask leered ominously. Two men in masks followed. They blocked my path. I stopped, and when I turned, the man behind me grabbed my arm. The men in front moved to assist him. A tall figure in a white dress that draped to the ground—Druid—appeared around the side of the Round House and motioned me to approach. She—I assumed it was a woman—wore a witch's mask. The masked men marched me into the building.

The set-up for Midsummer's Day had been pushed to the side. I was forced to my knees in front of a table with a red cloth covering and red candles at each end. The door was closed. The witch faced me across the table. She was flanked by two of the men. I was expecting Jane Trevenna. When she spoke, she didn't sound like the Penseythan. Another role for Clara, I guessed, with a mask and a different voice.

"You are not the first man who has tried to subvert a person chosen for high office. Punishment is severe for those who have violated our trust."

I was having a hard time believing the charade. "What about the law...the Seythan?"

"This is beyond the Seythan. We protect the ancient ways."

"How do I know you aren't the Seythan, all dressed up?" My attempt to sneer failed. I pointed at one of the devil's mask figure. "Mr. Thomas isn't it?" The figure did not move.

The witch responded angrily. "For John Nichols, death was the punishment."

"This is getting ridiculous. John Nichols drowned."

"Do you have anything else to say before I sentence you?"

"If I have done something to offend you I am truly sorry. I believed...believe that I have been the victim of a monstrous practical joke. I did not take seriously the warnings to stay away from Rose. I was...am in love with her and the thought of Rose being Queen tomorrow was more than I could stand." The witch's mask turned toward one of the men. His mask rocked from side to side.

"Someone told you that Rose Pascoe would be Queen?"

"Yes."

"Nevertheless, you tried to see her even though you had been warned?"

"Yes. I had to talk to her."

"She is not for you. It makes no difference. Take him away! You know what to do."

The door was opened before we reached it. I'd been wrong about the Druid's identity, and I wasn't even sure if it was a woman. The door framed Clara. "I heard what you were going to do. You can't! He saved my Frankie's life." She looked frantic. "Andy rescued him from the cliff. He was going to fall. You know the rule, a life given back for a life saved."

The witch looked at the other masked figures and pointed with her right hand at one of the maskers. He raised his hand, showing an ornate ring on the pinkie finger—Arthur Nancarrow. I kept quiet. In turn each masker raised his right hand and extended the thumb up. The Druid looked at me before doing the same. "So be it, we will leave it to the Seythan. Take him to the Seythan House! Throw him in the cell and lock the door! Let the other court deal with him. Our business is over."

Clara patted my back as we passed her. "Thank you," I said.

"You played your role very well." She gave a sweet smile. "All the world's a stage and…."

"You're not the butcher's are— "

Clara gave no reply as she sashayed away, but her head was shaking from side to side. I was sure then that Ernie had been right. She had set me up. Why? Bloody-mindedness, or had someone asked her to play a game on me for some other reason?

34.

THE CELL IN THE SEYTHAN HOUSE, WHERE THE MASKERS had left me, was small and dank, with a concrete floor and wooden planks on the walls and ceiling. A sink and a wooden toilet that smelled bad were tucked into a corner. A window, apparently a porthole from a ship, faced the edge of the Round House and the road to the rookery. Two bunk beds were built against one wall. Despite the grim atmosphere the cell was a safe haven compared to the Round House.

The feeling of relief dissipated quickly when I lay face down on the lower bunk and thought hard about my situation. I felt despair. My fantasy about Rose had been just that, a fantasy. The island meant more to her than I did; it always would, and I was not prepared to be a stay-at-home husband. This was far more my problem than the obvious fact that the islanders did not want to risk my wooing her away.

Thank God I had enough material to finish my PhD…if I ever got out of here. My eyes misted and I buried my head into the pillow and drifted into a troubled sleep.

Well after sunrise, I heard the key in the door. Arthur Nancarrow, looking somber, came in carrying a tray. The red stone in his ring glinted in the light. Mr. Thomas was standing behind him. Arthur handed me the tray. Breakfast was oatmeal with sugar and milk, buttered toast, and a mug of tea.

"Thanks, Arthur," I said, adding, "Was that you in the Round House?"

He ducked his head and left.

At ten, they returned and took me to the Seythan room, placing me on a chair in front of a long table. It had a cloth on top, draped to the platform on which it sat. The seven members of the Seythan were looking down at me: George Anthony, Captain Billing, Petunia Gay, Jane Trevenna, Jacob Jago, Isaac Nancarrow, and Albert Pascoe. A setup designed to intimidate, I thought. It worked; I was scared.

Jane Trevenna's face was grim as she spoke. "Andrew Ferguson, our island welcomed you here. Now you come before us on a charge of trespassing, breaking and entering—"

"Ma'am, I did not break in, I—"

"Mr. Ferguson, silence," the Penseythan barked, her face red. "You will be permitted to speak only when I tell you. As a student of Professor Llewellyn Jones, you have been treated well. Unfortunately, despite repeated warnings from a number of us, you have chosen to meddle in our internal affairs. Though it may not be apparent to you, this island's society is a fragile one. It has taken great skill to keep it both cohesive and vibrant. You are not the first foreigner to cause problems. If you have some notion that being a foreigner gives you some right to contravene our laws, I advise you to rethink that view. On Roseland, the Seythan is the law. We dealt with previous foreign offenders, and we will deal with your case. Fortunately for you, we stopped flogging offenders many years ago. Our punishment, beyond time in jail, is the stocks. My inclination is to put you in them for a number of days. It will give you time to consider the foolishness of your actions. However, some of my colleagues are concerned that would be too harsh a punishment. George Anthony will present that viewpoint. George, have your say!"

"Mr. Ferguson, Andrew, you have done many good things. Played in the band. Discovered valuable information about our auks. Visited Ernie. I can't tell you how...." George Anthony looked down at the table and wiped his eyes, "...how much it meant to him. He will not be with us long."

George paused and when he spoke again, his tone of voice was different. "Why couldn't you let it be? Why ask all those questions? Why check on us in the library? We trusted you. We have our own way of doing things. How we handle our affairs is none of your damn business! Sorry, ladies."

I raised my hand. Jane Trevenna motioned me to lower it. "Not now, Mr. Ferguson. Wait until Mr. Anthony has finished."

"I do not agree with the Penseythan about condemning you to a number of days in the stocks. It's not a good image, and the children will see you. After my young son saw Mr. Pavlov, he couldn't sleep. I recommend jail for the rest of your stay, and to put you in the stocks Midsummer's night, after the children have gone."

Jane Trevenna turned to scan the members of the Seythan. "Does anyone else wish to comment?" They shook their heads. "Now it is your turn, Mr. Ferguson. You may stand."

Lying in bed, miserable and angry, I had thought about what I would say. But after hearing George, I knew my planned speech would not work.

"Mr. Ferguson, What have you to say?" The Penseythan spoke sharply.

"I am deeply sorry to have let you down. I like the people of this island. So many of you have been kind to me, Mary, Clara, Frankie, Arthur...er...Young Artley, Charlie, Ernie and George...I could go on. As George said, my studies of the auks have gone well. I think I have everything I need for my PhD. I hope Professor Jones approves." I looked for a glimmer of friendliness and saw none in the row of stony faces. "The professor isn't responsible in any way for what I've done, but I need to explain."

"Yes, Mr. Ferguson, what is responsible for your ridiculous behavior?" Captain Billing asked irritably.

Since I have been here, a number of odd things have happened. Masked figures threatened me on Guy Fawkes Day." I looked hard at the members of the Seythan. Seeing no reaction, I pressed on. "Then there's what happened last night with the masked figures in the Round House."

"I have no idea what you mean about the Round House last night," Jane Trevenna snapped. "Tell us how this all started."

Might as well tell the truth, I thought. "A year or so before I came here, I was in a messy break-up with my girlfriend. All my fault. Later, I was finishing my degree and trying to find a university to do my PhD. That was when I heard that Professor Llewellyn Jones was looking for a student. I applied and shortly afterwards, I ended up here. I have enjoyed my studies. Auks are fascinating, but I felt lonely and frustrated."

"Auks not fascinating enough, apparently," muttered Jacob Jago.

"Mr. Jago, I didn't understand about the Queen and Kings... I'm glad it worked out for Patsy and Artley. You've got a fine grandson." Jacob looked down at the table.

"I still don't know what the hell you're talking about!" Cap'n Billing said angrily.

"Captain Billing, can you explain the banging on my wall at night and the sound of people having sex?" I retorted. "I thought it was...well, there wasn't anyone."

Jane Trevenna looked hard at the Captain. He shook his head. "What are you implying?" she said. "Is it still going on?"

"Yes, and I think someone has been trying to make me more frustrated."

"Mary tells me that noises carry in that row of houses," said Albert Pascoe.

"In my bedroom, I share a wall with Mary's room and one with Clara's house."

"And one with Rose," said Albert, cautiously.

"She wasn't home when this started."

"I don't have all day, Mr. Ferguson," said Isaac Nancarrow. "Is there more?"

"Other than my misunderstanding with Patsy, everything was going fine. Then Rose came home. You called me lovesick, Mrs. Trevenna. Yes, I was. Rose is—"

"Not for *you*, Mr. Ferguson," the Penseythan said with emphasis. "We understand how you felt. It still does not explain why you believe you are part of a game. Everything you have said is circumstantial and is a weak excuse to justify your actions."

"I made a list of odd things. Please let me go over them."

Jane Trevenna looked reluctant.

"I would like to hear what he has to say, Penseythan," George Anthony said firmly. The Penseythan looked as if she would tell him to be quiet before nodding agreement.

I took a deep breath and continued, "I've read Throgmorton's notes and the stuff about Pavlov. You islanders sometimes play games with visitors. I think I know who orchestrated the real-life play with both Throgmorton and Pavlov. I don't know how many of you got involved."

"Who is supposed to be organizing these games?" Jane Trevenna asked.

"I thought of you, Penseythan, until I realized I was looking for more of a sense of humor."

Some members of the Seythan were trying not to laugh. Jane Trevenna's face was stony as she asked, "Who then?"

"Clara Quick."

"How did you arrive at that conclusion?"

"I've heard that Clara organized the game with Pavlov. She directs and acts in the plays. She changes them. She puts out the newsletters and makes subtle adjustments. She makes jigsaw puzzles and gives them to Mary. They always show something that may happen to me. She likes to play jokes...feeding me stargazy pie, and I don't know who else could be banging on my wall."

Jane Trevenna's eyes narrowed. "Why would Clara do those things?"

"I'm not sure I want to answer."

"This is your only opportunity."

I took another deep breath. "Okay, you asked for it. Clara is brilliant and imaginative. Look at her paintings and the way she does the plays." I remembered her comment in the Round House. "After she had saved me from the maskers, she said, 'You played the role very well.' Except for the last bit with the maskers most of what happened to me must have been her game. I'm lucky I saved Frankie—"

"You what?" Jane Trevenna looked puzzled. "No matter. I'll find out later what you meant. Carry on!"

"Is there more of this fantasy?" Cap'n Billing asked curtly.

"I thought you were here to do a PhD on the auks. Not to be snooping around checking up on us." George Anthony sounded disappointed. "I'm not going to comment on Clara. She has her funny ways."

I tilted my head. "Would you say that Clara also has reasons to keep me away from Rose?"

I saw Petunia Gay looking at me, pleadingly.

"That's it, but—"

Isaac Nancarrow stood again. "Penseythan, I have had enough of this nonsense. The charge is trespassing. None of this is relevant. I ask for a vote, now."

"I second Isaac," said Cap'n Billing.

George Anthony tried to speak. "I think we—"

Jane Trevenna cut him off. "I agree. We have heard enough. Even if it were true, it does not justify Mr. Ferguson's actions. We are all agreed that he stays in jail until he leaves. We will now vote on the time in the stocks. Those in favor of, let me suggest five full days, please raise your hands." She joined Captain Billing and Isaac Nancarrow.

"Those in favor of Midsummer's night after the children have gone to bed." George Anthony, Petunia Gay, and Albert Pascoe raised their hands.

"It seems that we are tied, and Jacob Jago has not voted," Jane Trevenna said, showing her exasperation. "Jacob you must decide or offer another option!"

"Give me a moment please. Some things are coming back to me. I had a long talk with Patsy after the business last year. She said that Clara—"

Jane Trevenna held up her hand. "Jacob, there can be no more discussion. It is Mr. Ferguson on trial, not Clara Quick."

Jacob Jago closed his eyes, his lips pursed, and he said firmly, "One night in the stocks."

"So be it, Jacob. Tomorrow night it will be. We have other business to attend to. Take him back to his cell."

"What about last night? Clara knows," I pleaded.

"Enough, Mr. Ferguson, our business with you is over."

Unfortunately, I lost my temper again. "It's about your son, isn't it?" I said, glaring at the Penseythan. "You want Rose to marry him. Keep power in the family."

I had gone too far. Jane Trevenna's face was a mask of fury. "How dare you try to involve my son! I am inclined to—"

Jacob intervened quickly. "Penseythan, this session is over, take him back to the cell!"

I took one last glance at the Seythan. All were looking away except George and Petunia. Both smiled sympathetically. As the door closed behind me, Jacob, Isaac and Jane Trevenna were talking angrily.

35.

BY TEN IN THE MORNING, I HAD SPENT TWENTY-FOUR HOURS brooding about my plight before the start of the Midsummer's Day's festivities, and some thirty-three hours remained until I would be placed in the stocks. I went over my *facts* again. If anything, the debate in the courtroom had added to my conviction that Clara had set me up. To be honest, I knew Patsy would not have needed much encouragement. I reckoned that the maskers in the Round House had not been the evil ones I'd heard about. Arthur Nancarrow didn't fit the bill. Now Isaac Nancarrow, that would have been different. What I couldn't tell was whether the Penseythan's reactions to my story were because I was right, or because she was protecting the interests of the island and her precious son, John.

I could feel the acid rising from my stomach as I stumbled off the bed to the toilet, knelt, and threw up. I stayed on my knees, ignoring the stench, a kind of penance for my stupidity. In a strange way, I felt cleansed after I washed out my mouth and returned to the lower bunk. When I closed my eyes, Rose appeared, seemingly on the back of my eyelids. I felt silly and giggled. The image was replaced by a comforting image of Nellie with Fred and her men friends.

Arthur Nancarrow brought me lunch and supper. Each time, he opened the door, slid the tray along the floor, and avoided looking at me. I toyed with the food, remembering the smell of the toilet. I could not sleep and spent various parts of the night pacing the cell. Breakfast came and with it the first sounds of Midsummer's Day: the clip-clopping of ponies and horses being brought to the field next to the chapel, followed by the excited sounds of children playing in the square. I lay prone on the bunk, pushing my face into the hard pillow, hoping unsuccessfully that it would prevent unwanted images.

"Auk, auk, auk." The voice was accompanied by a rapping on the porthole. Frankie's grinning face appeared. "*Rum tum titti tum tum tum.*" His face disappeared. I went to the porthole. He was jigging away from the Seythan House, aping the Floral Dance. Frankie turned, and I gave him the thumbs up sign. He bowed mockingly and was gone. All night, I had succeeded in preventing scenes of him and Rose appearing in my head. Now, they came back persistently until lunch distracted me, and then I heard the start of the first Floral Dance. I spent the rest of the afternoon lying on the bunk feeling miserable. The sounds of people in the square having fun made it worse. At what I guessed to be six o'clock, Cap'n Billing, Mister Thomas, and Arthur came to my cell. The Captain did the talking.

"We'll be taking you out at ten to seven. Best use the toilet while you have the chance. You won't be back here until seven tomorrow morning."

"Will I get any water to drink over night?" I had been brooding about it.

"No," Arthur said. "Best finish what you've got." Arthur was looking away as he spoke.

The square was nearly empty when they returned and took me to the stocks. I considered trying to escape, but I had nowhere to go. Cap'n Billing motioned for me to sit on the baseboard and lifted my legs into the grooves in the wooden bar that was bolted to it. The second bar was lowered, trapping my ankles. Then a spacer and the third bar were put in place. The fourth and third bars trapped my wrists. A large padlock secured the whole ghastly contraption. The position was horribly uncomfortable, sitting with my knees raised, leaning forward to bring my wrists above my ankles. I knew I would have to relax or run the risk of cramping. I closed my eyes and tried to think of something to distract me from my miserable plight. I concentrated on the auks—visualizing them one at a time. After a while that ploy palled. I heard the band start up the second Floral Dance. As the band and the dancers approached the square, I opened my eyes and tried to look back toward the Portloe road; it was a waste of time, because the crowd gathering in the square blocked my view. A few of the dancers pranced by me, dipping their leering masks, but mainly people ignored me. I managed to turn enough to see the maypole for a brief moment, and glimpsed Rose, in a white dress, dancing around it. I put my head on my arms. I knew what would follow. The Queen—Rose—would go to the Round House. The Round House was in front of me, but again, most of the time the crowd blocked my view and I did not see her enter. I caught glimpses of Jane Trevenna and Mister Thomas by the door and some of the young men being ushered in. I could tell when they came out by the raucous shouts.

Suddenly, the music slowed, and the dancing stopped; the six kings had been serviced. Now was Frankie's turn. I kept my eyes closed, but I could not suppress the image of Rose looking frail and beautiful as Frankie shambled in doing his customary little jig. As he disappeared through the door, my image of Frankie turned and looked at me. He was smiling triumphantly. The image of Rose, naked, pale legs spread, available for Frankie to do what he wanted, came into my head. I wanted the whole set-up to be a fake. An insane invention of the game designed to frustrate me. I escaped to my imagination.

I was free of the stocks and no one was paying any attention to me. I grabbed my camera and ran to the Round House. The door was locked. The music stopped. Through the door, I could hear tremulous sounds. I felt a touch on my arm.

"You have to know, don't you?" said Mary.

"Yes," I said. "It's a fake, isn't it?"

"The door's not locked."

I wouldn't turn to see, but I knew the islanders were all looking at me. I didn't care. I opened the door and went in, camera ready. The flash lit up the small room. Clothes were strewn on the floor. Rose and Frankie did not notice me. Their naked bodies were entwined on the bed. Rose's legs were wrapped around Frankie as she ground her body against him. She was moaning. Not a fake. Not Nellie and a gentleman friend. This was for real. Like Nellie and Fred. When I tried to run away, I could not move. The islanders stared at me, saying nothing.

Even my imagination was being cruel to me.

I don't remember what happened after that. Maybe I fainted. When I opened my eyes, the crowd had gone. The Round House door was closed. A faint light emanated from the slit windows. My wrists and ankles were sore from straining against the stocks. A drizzle started, and the water formed a pool around the wooden base of the stocks. I felt despair as I rested my head on my arms and wept. The water dripped off my nose and ears. An uncomfortable kind of sleep came later.

I did not hear the person come up behind me, and only realized someone was there when I felt a hand brush across mine. I tried to turn my head but a firm grip stopped me.

"Don't turn! I'm going to let you out. There's some food and drink in this bag."

It sounded like a woman, but I could not recognize the voice.

"When I let you out, wait a couple of minutes before you move. Eat, drink, and stretch. You must be back in the stocks in fifteen minutes, facing the Round House. You mustn't see me. Is that clear?"

"Yes," I whispered. The clouds that had obscured the moon had moved off the island and in the moonlight I caught a glimpse of a mask. The hands that handed me a bottle and a sandwich were gloved. No way to tell if the person was a man or a woman.

I waited and then lay back, stretched my legs and arms, and then massaged my thighs and calves before struggling to my feet. My stomach still ached but the food and orange drink tasted good. I scanned the empty square, looked at my watch, and then went to the Round House. The door was open. One candle was still burning inside. Used condoms were in the trash and the center of the bed was wet. Rose and Frankie had done it. I stood, tears welling up from frustration and anger. I took one last look at the door and was about to leave when I saw the glint of something under the bed. I reached down and retrieved two dangly earrings. For a moment, I was bewildered. Then I understood. The Queen had not been Rose. She was only one of the other six women. Esther was the Queen! Patsy—and who knew who else—had made a fool of me. I wanted to find out more, but had to force myself back to the stocks.

I finished the drink and positioned myself in the bars. Shortly afterward, I heard the person return. "It was Esther with Frankie, wasn't it?" I said.

The only reply was a subdued chuckle. Although the weather was wretched, I felt better. This was not what I had feared when the masked men took me to the Round House. There would be no devastating scene with Rose and Frankie. The islanders would never have used Rose solely to get at me. The island was like a beehive. The islanders behaved like bees when it came to the queen bee—Penseythan they called her—she had to be developed, nurtured, and protected. In turn, she would ensure the proper survival of the colony. Rose was a future queen, not to follow immediately after Jane Trevenna, but after whoever followed her. I realized also that I did not know who that would be, and for once I didn't care.

The same hands started to replace the lock but stopped at the sound of a car approaching in the distance.

"Best leave," the voice said. "It's the Penseythan."

I removed the bars and stood. "Why?"

"She said putting you in the stocks would be enough. I trusted her." The tone was bitter.

"Should I go back to Mary's?"

"No. Too dangerous. Get up to the rookery. Run."

As I headed past the Round House, I glimpsed the person scurrying off toward Nancarrow's. I moved farther up the path to the auks and hid in the shadows. Soon after, the figure ran back carrying what might have been the dummy that I'd seen in the stocks a month or two after I'd arrived on the island. He or she placed the object in the stocks and left the way they'd come, just avoiding being spotlighted by the Lagonda's headlamps as it parked in the road at the entrance to the square. Jane Trevenna got out of the driver's side. Winston followed her. The Penseythan was carrying a stick...no, a gun. They approached the stocks. Winston ran ahead and sniffed at the dummy, raised his leg and peed on it, then started toward the Round House.

I heard a faint, "Heel, Winston!" He looked in my direction for a moment, before obeying her command. By this time she had reached the stocks. She raised her arm as if to hit the dummy then looked more closely. She pulled at the head in an angry gesture. The moonlight glinted off a gun barrel. *God, she'd planned to kill me.* I understood then that she would do anything to prevent me from getting in the way of a union between Rose and her precious son, John.

The Penseythan stood, head bowed, then raised her head and looked around the square before striding back to the car. Winston turned and ran to her side. I didn't wait any longer but hurried toward the rookery, listening to the sound of the Lagonda heading back to Trewince.

36.

I DIDN'T SLEEP WELL AND GOT UP AT FIRST LIGHT OF DAWN to walk off the stiffness from my time in the stocks and then lying on the hard floor of the hide. I wasn't sure what I expected to see, but I brought my binoculars as a precaution. Thirst drove me to the stream that emerged from the cloud covering the peak of Brown Willy and then tumbled down its southern flank. I lay on the ground and dipped my head briefly into the cold water. I cupped my hands and drank. Now fully awake, I stood and took my binoculars and scanned them over Veryan. The square was empty, but when I looked closer I could make out the Lagonda parked behind the Round House on the wider part of the path that led to the rookery. Then I saw Winston, nose to the ground coming up the path. Jane Trevenna followed him. Nearer Veryan, I spotted other people starting up the track. *Oh, God, a lynch mob.*

I ducked down and thought about where I could hide. The lay of the land was such that I could get back to the rookery without being seen, but then what? Winston could track me anywhere...or maybe not? The variety of scents in the rookery might confuse him. If I went over the cliff using Frankie's ropes, he wouldn't be able to follow, and the Penseythan might assume that I'd managed to sneak back to the village. It was worth a try.

I kept low and ran back to the rookery, avoiding the blind, but suffering the spite of the vicious gorse on the little used trail. When I got to the cliff, I went to the edge of the rookery and followed Frankie's route down. After a short while, I found a relatively wide ledge under an overhang and wedged myself into it.

With sun rising above the horizon, a few of the auks had started flying over me to fetch fish for the chicks. The gulls and skuas were circling. A light drizzle started and the wind picked up. After about twenty minutes, a loud bark joined the keening of the gulls and the noise of the waves slapping the rocks below me. Winston had arrived. Some of the returning auks swung back to sea. A short while later I heard Jane Trevenna say sharply, "Heel, Winston."

Silence followed. Then what I had dreaded happened.

"Mr. Ferguson, we knew you'd come here," Jane Trevenna shouted.

We? Her and Winston or…. I didn't have time to think more about it.

"I know where you are. My nephew, Frankie, showed me where he goes to collect gulls' eggs. Winston has tracked you to the edge."

I nestled closer into the cliff.

"I heard what happened last time. You'll get vertigo again. Look down at those rocks. You won't die immediately, you know. The skuas and gulls won't wait until your dead."

I tried not to look, but she was right about the rocks. I looked up and saw that the auks were back to delivering fish to the chicks.

"You are going to have to face me sometime," she said. "It might as well be now."

She was right. No way I could hang on until other villagers came looking for me—assuming anyone would come. I had no choice. I started the climb back to the edge.

Looking up, I saw Dracula circling lower. I bet he thinks I've got fish. *Maybe....* I found a lateral rope and moved around the cliff to be under the rookery, so that I would come up onto the area that harbored the lowest burrows. I hesitated a moment before grasping a tussock of grass and easing my-self up. The footing was poor and my feet slipped a few times on the wet rock as I pulled myself onto the ledge. Facing the blind, I saw Jane Trevenna with Winston on a leash standing some twenty feet away and one row of burrows up.

"Steady, Winston," the Penseythan said, restraining him as he tried to lunge toward me.

While she looked down at him, I put my right hand quickly, in turn, into the nearest burrows. In the last one I felt the chick scurrying away. Please God let there be...*yes!* I felt a mess of partially-chewed snaveling. I grasped some and knelt with my right hand on the ground. Looking up, I saw her revolver. "You won't need the gun," I said. "I'll come quietly."

"Stand up, Mr. Ferguson," she said, moving down onto my ledge to stand nearer to me. "You're not going anywhere."

"Why?" I watched Dracula circling closer.

"Let me count the reasons," she screamed. "You flouted my authority. You have tried, like Professor Jones before you, to tell us how we should manage our affairs." Veins stood out on her neck. "You have tried to seduce away the future of our community." The hand holding the gun was shaking. "Yesterday my son sent me a message that Rose had called off their engagement. I know that you are the cause."

I saw her draw a deep breath and steady the gun, which was pointed in my direction. My last chance. I threw the fish at her face. "What are—"

I saw Dracula swoop as I dropped to the ground. The sound of the gun didn't deter him. He went straight for the fish at her throat. I felt a sharp pain in my left thigh. She raised her gun hand and tried to ward off the great skua. The noise of a second shot drove the remaining auks into the air. The Penseythan, distracted by the cloud of whirring birds and Dracula clawing at her head, staggered. Winston lunged at me again, causing her to lose her balance on the slippery ground in front of the burrow.

I tried to reach out to her, but she slid away too fast and went off the edge, dragging Winston, barking frantically, with her. I heard her screams and watched as they tumbled end over end to land in a broken heap on the rocks below.

I stood with difficulty and hobbled head down to the blind. *What to do? Would anybody believe me? Did it make any difference?* I had to tell the villagers. Maybe she was still alive, and they could send a boat to rescue her.

"Andy, are you okay?" Mary shouted.

I looked up. Mary was coming down through the gorse, followed by Cap'n Billing, Arthur Nancarrow, Clara and Frankie, Charlie, and Petunia Gay. More islanders stood back, watching from the top of the rise.

I felt dizzy and held on the end post of the blind with my right hand. "How did you know to come here?" I said.

"Rose called Nancarrow's and got hold of Isaac. Thank God." She put her finger to my lips. "You didn't hear that."

I nodded, but what did it mean? Was Arthur my enemy, not Isaac? Not likely, he'd always helped me.

"Rose told Isaac that Jane had taken the Lagonda," Mary said. "She saw Jane carrying the gun and suspected what she was going to do. Isaac got hold of me, Cap'n Artley, and the others as quick as I could."

"What'll happen now?" I asked. My left leg ached, and I reached down to rub it. The cloth of my jeans was wet and my hand felt sticky.

"Seythan will have to discuss it, Andy," Captain Billing replied. "We saw her shoot as we came over the top. You're lucky we saw what happened next."

"I think...I need...help," I said as the world spun and everything became dark.

* * *

The darkness that had settled around me at the rookery cleared slowly. I looked up. Light filtered into the room through a half-closed door and a porthole. I was back in jail in the Seythan House, on the lower bunk bed. *Why?* I tried to sit, but could only raise up on my elbows. "Anybody there?" I called out. My voice sounded weak. I heard a scuffling outside.

Martha Nancarrow poked her head around the door. "Now you lie down, Master Andrew. You need to save your strength. You lost a lot of blood."

I lay back feeling the bandage that covered my thigh. "Why am I here...in jail?"

"Don't you worry yourself." Martha laughed. "We use the cell as an infirmary like. Don't often have any prisoners. Easier than taking you upstairs at Mary's."

Thank God for that. "Who fixed me up?"

"Rose did," Martha said proudly. "She'll make a fine doctor."

With Jane Trevenna gone, did this mean Rose would have to stay on the island? "But Rose'll have to finish her training. She's got a year or two to go. How will you cope?"

Martha looked thoughtful. "We had this problem before, after Agnes Nichols…. Anyway, we can handle it."

"If you can handle it, why did the Penseythan insist on Rose giving up university for a year?"

"Make sure she got broken in, likely." Martha chuckled. "Of course, Jean Nichols went and had another boy."

"Great."

"Anyway, better if Rose finishes." She looked hard at me. "And comes back. You understand?"

My problem now was to come up with a way for me to be with her. "Yes, ma'am. I do," I said. Rose needed to finish her training, and I needed to start mine. I'd take up a career I'd never thought would be mine, in agriculture. I drifted into sleep, seeing my father nodding appreciatively at the herd of cows munching hay.

I woke to the feel of a light touch on my forehead and opened my eyes.

Rose withdrew her hand. "How are you feeling, Andy?" she said. Her hair was pinned up and she wore pale blue scrubs.

"Sore, but relieved." I tried to sit up.

"Not yet," Rose said. "I need to look at your leg." She pulled the blanket and sheet down and studied the bandage. "Looks good. You were bleeding badly. Lucky Mum put a tourniquet on quick-like up at rookery"

"When can I get out of here?"

"A couple of days and then you need to rest."

I managed to get up onto my elbows.

"Let me help you," Rose said, taking my arm and placing a second pillow under my back.

Great. I'd have time to talk to Rose about the future. My elation evaporated quickly when I understood the implication of my having to rest. "I can still take the boat. January 2nd, I think." I said.

"'Fraid not." Rose face showed sympathy. "The boat's leaving tomorrow. Rough sea wouldn't be good for you. You'll have to wait for the next boat in March."

"You're leaving tomorrow!"

"Uncle Artley and the lads are doing it for me. University says I have to be there beginning of term."

"We need to talk."

Rose glanced at her watch. "Yes, but I've got to go. George is here to take me to see Ernie. He's fading fast."

"Rose, before you go I've got to say something," I pleaded. "I want to come back here to live. I never believed I'd be saying this, but I'm serious about going back to school to learn about making farms more self-sufficient. I've talked to Morley and Jacob and Edgar and I think they're interested." I looked intently at her.

Rose chuckled. "You made a big impression on Morley. He's talking about building a pit to collect manure." Rose's expression changed. "But how long would all this training take?"

"My Dad says there's a two-year course. I could start in September. In the meantime, I could help him on our farm— hands-on experience."

"And your father would like it, wouldn't he?"

I pictured Dad smiling. "Yes." Now for the difficult part—never ask a question if you think you won't like the answer. But I didn't have time. "Will you wait for me?"

"Andy, there's lots of things I have to work out. Jane Trevenna's gone. I told John I didn't want to marry him, but he still wants to see me. I must concentrate on finishing my training. It's all too…." Her face crumpled briefly and she wiped away tears.

"I love you, Rose."

A knock on the door interrupted her reply. George Anthony poked his head around. "Rose, you ready?" He held the door. "Now, you get well, Andy."

Rose shrugged and held out her hand. "You can write," she said. "Mum has my address."

I shook her hand. "I'll live in hope."

"Me, too." She squeezed my hand reassuringly, smiled, and left me alone.

37.

THAT AFTERNOON, AUNT FLO SUFFERED A RELAPSE AND I DID not see Rose again before she left for Cape Town. After a couple of days, I moved back into Mary's house. The first thing I did, when I was seated in the living room and Cap'n Billing and Martha Nancarrow had left, was ask Mary for Rose's address in England.

Mary smiled and went to the kitchen. She returned with a piece of paper, which she handed to me, saying, "Now, don't you lose this."

"So I have a chance?"

"If she replies, yes."

"You're not sure?"

Mary looked worried. "I just hope that Johnny Trevenna doesn't take after his mother." She walked to the door. "I have to go help Martha with Aunty Flo. Petunia'll come over to look after you. Will you be all right?"

"Yes."

* * *

The rest of my time on Roseland passed slowly, but there

were rewarding moments. Petunia gave birth to a baby girl and called her Martha. A thank you, I suspected, to Martha Nancarrow, recently elected the new Penseythan. I spent time with Morley, Jacob, and Edgar, taking extensive notes on their questions about producing energy from manure. With Frankie's help, I cleared out the hide and watched Nellie and the other auks head back out to sea. Frankie and I took a ceremonial pee at the skuas and gulls.

On my last day, I went to the library. I found Clara seated at a table in the back, making notes on old news sheets.

"Preparing another game, Clara?" I asked.

"Why, Mister Andrew, what do you mean?" Clara glanced away.

"Why did you set me up to believe Rose had been chosen?" I looked closely at her. "I can understand the game with Patsy was your way of having fun, but…."

"Would you have gone to Trewince to see Rose if…" Clara looked straight at me.

Was that the reason, to prod me into action? "Probably not, I guess." I said. "But look what happened."

A shadow crossed Clara's face. "I didn't expect Rose to tell Jane right then that she wasn't going to marry Johnny."

"Nor what the Penseythan would do?"

"My brother never should have married her." Clara sounded bitter. "He wouldn't listen to me."

Her comment about Jane Trevenna reminded me of something that had worried me. "When the Penseythan found I'd gone down the cliff, she said, 'We knew you'd come here.' Do you know what she meant by we?"

Clara looked hard at me.

"Was it you who let me out of the stocks?"

"You don't get to know everything," she said, turned away and started reading a newsletter. She was humming "The Floral Dance."

Back to walkabout, and I'd never know how much had been a game and how much a serious threat from Jane Trevenna and maybe somebody else. "So who's the next victim?" I asked.

Clara didn't answer until I was at the door. "Governor's got an aide. He was rude to Frankie."

God help him. I returned to the house to finish packing.

Because so many islanders wanted to say goodbye, I was the last to board the St. Just.

"We hope you'll be back, Andy," Morley Thomas said, shaking my hand.

"I plan to," I said. "In the meantime, I'll write about what I learn.

"We'll miss you on the trumpet come Guy Fawkes and Midsummer's." Charlie Gay, carrying his baby girl, patted me on the shoulder with his spare hand.

Petunia hugged me and whispered, "Don't you give up on Rose."

"You listen to her," Mary said, holding out her arms. "I'll miss you."

"I'll be back," I said, kissing her on the cheek.

"Got to board, Andy," Cap'n Billing barked. "Storms coming from the west."

I picked up my bags and boarded. As the boat headed down the channel to the open sea, I saw Clara, Frankie, and Esther waving from the end of the dock. Clara clutched a handful of paper. That aide didn't stand a chance, the poor bastard.

* * *

After landing in Richmond, I went to Elkton to pick up my car.

The professor and Mabel came out of the Manse as my taxi rolled into the driveway. I paid the driver and got out. "Good, good, good," the Prof said, shaking my hand. "All recovered from your ordeal, I hope?"

"Yes, I was lucky."

"You must tell Mabel and me all about it over dinner."

"Professor, I'd like to, but I need to get home. I called my parents from New York. My mother's been really worried."

"Of course, of course." The eyebrows expressed disappointment. "But you will return soon? We need to tie up your dissertation."

"Would two weeks time be okay?"

"Yes." He turned to Mabel. "Do you have Andrew's keys handy?"

Mabel held them out. "I heard what happened, Mr. Andrew. I never liked Jane Trevenna, but I didn't expect her to go off the deep end like that." She paused. "You watch out for that Johnny Trevenna."

After a brief discussion of the events on the cliff, I left, worrying now about whether Rose would be able to handle him.

As I drove up to my family's house, I noticed a site had been cleared near the main barn. Buildings were going up on a concrete pad, and next to them was a deep hole, maybe 100 by 50 feet in size—for the manure lagoon, I guessed.

My father met me at the door. "The professor called us at

Christmas time." He hugged me. I could feel him tremble. "Said you'd been shot. Didn't explain what happened."

"I'll tell you all about it." I wondered how much they knew. "Where's Mom?"

He let go quickly. "Your mother will be back soon…gone shopping."

We went to my room. I looked out of the window and could see the new construction. "I see you're going ahead with the hogs and everything." I said.

"The bank gave me a loan in November. The weather during the winter was bad and I couldn't do much until last month." His eyes sparkled. "It should be finished in June."

I heard the sound of a car turning into our drive. "I'll help."

"I'd like that, Andy." He smiled. "Have you thought any more about going back to school?"

"Yes. Can you and Mom help?"

"We'll find a way," he said. "Better get downstairs. Your mother's beside herself wanting to hear what happened. You can tell me about the auks later."

The minute we were seated in the living room, my mother said, "I want to hear everything from the beginning."

I started with a more revealing but still expurgated account of the events with Patsy during my first time on Roseland.

"Poor Andy, no woman to keep you happy." She teased.

"Mom! It wasn't funny. Many nights I heard a sound like a bed banging on the wall, and sex." If I had expected to shock my mother, her response was a disappointment.

"You sure you didn't have a wet dream?"

"The banging!"

"So what was the explanation?"

"The lady next door, Clara Quick, was messing with me."

"Why?"

"It's a long story. The bottom line is that she got badly treated when she was young. As far as I can tell, she gets back at the world by manipulating people, particularly foreigners."

"Is that all?"

"Clara made jigsaw puzzles for Mary and me and they always showed something that was going to happen."

My mother made a face.

"It's true. She changes the newsletter so you don't know what's real and what's not. And she puts on classic plays, but with little adjustments to amuse the islanders. *The Tempest* was set on Tristan da Cunha. Prospero became Prospera. I could go on."

"She has a sense of humor. I don't see how this got you into trouble."

"What did the professor tell you?"

"That they put you in jail and punished you. He didn't say why."

"Things got wilder the second time I was on the island. Particularly after Rose returned."

"Your landlady's daughter?"

"I've never seen anyone like Rose, Mom. She's smart, beautiful, sexy, and as they would say, bloody perfect!"

"How does she feel about you?"

"I know she likes me. We nearly…you know what."

"Is that how you judge everything?" My mother frowned.

"No, no! I was trying to show she found me attractive. We had fun when we were together. Rose is easy to talk to, educated, traveled."

"Andy, growing up is hard." My mother put her arms around me. "But how did you get shot?"

I explained how Clara's last game had propelled me into trying to see Rose. I left out the part about the Round House, and explained that I was tried for trespassing and put in the stocks. My parents were stunned when I told how Jane Trevenna had come to kill me when she found out Rose wasn't going to marry her son.

When I finished with the story of how Dracula had saved my life, my mother interrupted me. "It's like a soap opera."

"Power corrupts. Absolute power corrupts absolutely," my dad said. "The woman must have thought she could get away with it."

"Would have, too, except for Dracula, and Rose calling her mother to warn what Jane Trevenna was planning."

"What are you going to do now?" my mother asked.

"As I told Dad, I'd like to go to agricultural school. Learn new farming techniques so when I go back to the island I can be useful. I can also help here and learn from Dad."

My mother looked down at her lap. "That means you'll be leaving for good…eventually."

My father put his arm around. "Does Rose agree?"

"I'm not sure, but I hope so."

"You should follow your heart," my mother said, rising to her feet. "I need to go for a walk." She held out her hand. My father took it and they left the room.

* * *

Over the following weeks, I worked on the farm. After telephoning North Carolina State and receiving the forms, I applied for the fall semester. Professor Llewellyn Jones wrote a strong letter of recommendation, telling them that I would receive my PhD in the summer. After an agonizing wait, I received an acceptance letter from the university. Immediately, I wrote a long letter to Rose, telling her that I loved her and had started on the path to learning how to be useful on the island.

Today I received her reply. On the back of the envelope was the drawing of a heart. Around the edges were the words "Rum tum ti rum tum tum."

PENSEYTHANS

Florence Billing: 1920-1924, 1925-1929, 1930-1934.

Agnes Nichols: 1935-1939, 1940-1944, 1945-1947.

Prudence Nancarrow: 1948-1949, 1950-1954, 1955-1959.

Jane Cocking: 1960-1964, 1965-1969, 1970-1974.

Jane Trevenna: 1975-1977, Martha Nancarrow: 1978-

GENEALOGY
OF
ROSELAND

according to

ANDREW FERGUSON

ANTHONY:

George +   Ernest

John

BILLING: Florence (1882, grandmother)

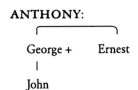

Cap'n Hartley (1930)   Albert +

Young Hartley (1957)

COCKING: Jane (1905, née Pasco)

Anne   Edgar (1932) +   Primrose

Esther (1959)

GAY: Charlie + Petunia (née Quick)

Rodney   Jennifer

JAGO: Emily

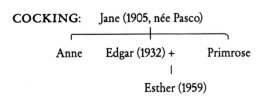

Jacob +   Miriam   Mabel

Patsy (1958)   Paul (1960)

NANCARROW: George + Prudence (née Gay)

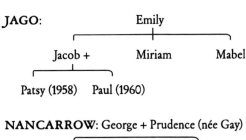

Isaac + Elizabeth   Arthur + Martha

Sandy   Samuel + Jennifer (née Gay)

NICHOLS: Agnes

├─────────────┬──────────────┐

John (dec) Jane (1927) + Susan

PASCOE

┌──────────────────────────────────────┐

David (dec) + Mary (1935, née Billing)   Albert

│

Rose (1956)

QUICK

┌──────────────────────────────────┐

Peter (dec) + Clara (née Trevenna)   Petunia

│

Frankie (1948)

THOMAS: Albert + Emily

┌──────────────────────────┐

Morley + Hilda   James + Miriam (née Jago)

┌────────┴────────┐

Nicholas   Susan

TREVENNA: John + Martha (née Cocking)

┌─────────────────────────┐

Charles (dec) + Jane (née Nichols)   Clara (1928)

│

John (1956)

About the Author

JOHN SHEFFIELD SPENT AN ENJOYABLE PART OF HIS CHILD-hood living in a fishing village in the Roseland Peninsula. Roseland is a scenic part of Cornwall in the west of England, with round houses to keep the devil out of the quaint village of Veryan. As a teenager he danced with his girlfriend, Judy, following the band in the annual Floral Dance on Midsummer's Day. He has used his experiences to set the background for Andy Ferguson's adventures on the remote island of Roseland in the southern Atlantic.

CPSIA information can be obtained
at www.ICGtesting.com
Printed in the USA
FFOW05n0731260615